TRUST ME

Bruce Forman

LOST
COAST
PRESS
Fort Bragg
California

Lost Coast Press
155 Cypress Street
Fort Bragg, CA 95437
(800) 773-7782
www.cypresshouse.com

DISCLAIMER
This novel is a work of fiction. Any references to real events, businesses, organizations and locales are intended only to give the fiction a sense of reality and authenticity. Except for well-known historical and public figures, any resemblance to actual persons, living or dead, is entirely coincidental.

Cover and book design: Michael Brechner / Cypress House
Cover image: "Head of Border Collie": ©2002 Corbis Images / PictureQuest

Library of Congress Cataloging-in-Publication Data
Forman, Bruce.
  Trust me : a novel / Bruce Forman.-- 1st ed.
    p. cm.
  ISBN 1-882897-75-7 (alk. paper)
  1. Swindlers and swindling--Fiction. 2. San Francisco
(Calif.)--Fiction. 3. Jazz musicians--Fiction. 4. Revenge--Fiction.
  I. Title.
  PS3606.O7477 T78 2003
  813'.6--dc21   2002152540

2   4   6   8   9   7   5   3   1

Printed in Canada

ACT I
SEDUCTION

"Trust me."

Sam should have known to run as soon as he heard the words. After all, the phrase was the anthem of bullshitters and scam artists, at least in the music business. He couldn't run, though; he was frozen, like a jacklighted deer, by his own ambition and desire.

Maybe this time, he prayed.

Jimm continued. "I'm saying that because I like what I see in you. You know, ever since my retirement I've been looking for a project. What the hell, if we get rich together it wouldn't be the worst thing in the world."

He shrugged his shoulders and grinned, showing the green flecks of spinach salad buried in the recesses of his teeth. *Retirement* seemed like an odd choice of words to Sam. Jimm looked ageless: a fleshy, unkempt cross between Damon Runyon and Dorian Grey; boyish, yet worn.

Jimm took another bite of spinach salad, chewing as he spoke. "Between the way you play, all you have already accomplished, and *my* expertise, we could really make everyone take notice."

Finally, he pulled the cloth napkin from his lap to wipe the fleck of green from his lower lip. Sam realized he'd been wiping his own furiously, as if the spinach were there, even though he was having soup.

"I have plenty of money," Jimm continued, shrugging, as if the mere mention of lucre were a waste of his valuable energy. "I just quit because I got fed up with all the bullshit. Here—"

He handed Sam his promo pack, a messy stack of tattered pages. They were the type you could send away for in a magazine or buy in an arcade, and might as well have said that Jimm Dibbook had killed Jesse James. Still, Sam was caught in the lure of the possibility that what Jimm was saying was workable and true.

Jimm paid the check. "Let's get out of here, all these yuppies make it hard for me to concentrate."

Sam turned to take in the surroundings. The dark wood tones and navy linens gave the almost-empty tavern a nighttime look, muted and womb-like. A few tables were still occupied by people desperately trying to make a deal or finalize a sale. It wasn't a good sign that they were still hucking; if they hadn't closed yet, they probably never would. *I'm the one he's pitching,* Sam thought, *and he's the one that's paying.* That helped drown out any cautious misgivings.

"Let's take a walk," Jimm said, pulling his green sweater down over his belly before pulling on his nylon slicker. It looked more like a bivouac tent.

The weather had turned three shades grayer while they'd been in the restaurant. Dewy moisture hung suspended in the air, appearing weightless. Jimm adjusted his wide-wale corduroy cap—reminiscent of the '60s British look—so that his black curls escaped from all sides equally. Then he headed down Lake Street in the direction of a small park.

Sam noticed that Jimm didn't really walk, he waddled. His short frame miraculously supported his weight, and he looked like an over-ripe turnip. Nonetheless, there was an agile, balletic quality to his movements, giving him the appearance of being light on his feet.

Without a word spoken, Jimm led. Sam followed, noticing the stately homes that lined the street, expansive two- and three-story dwellings with perfectly landscaped yards. *Yards! In San Francisco!* Sam's only claim to a patch of this town's precious real estate was his lease on a rent-controlled flat, now well into its fifteenth year.

Sam kept his mind fixed on the neighborhood so as not to dwell on the impending conversation. It was like an intricate and exotic dance, in which his enthusiasm would only serve to trip his partner.

Jimm turned into the park—actually more of a playground—that bordered on a small lake, and scurried to a set of swings that were buried deep in a sandbox and listing heavily to one side. He nodded, signifying that Sam should take a seat.

Sam wasn't sure if Jimm was going to sit or stand. There was an odd dramatic tension to everything; almost operatic. The play area was free of children; the swings and jungle gym looked like the bones of an ancient dinosaur. Faint distant echoes, the phantom laughter and shrieks of children who had spent countless hours playing there gave the overall impression of a ghost town. When Jimm finally sat down, his feet swung freely, hanging two inches above the ground.

"Tell me, what is it that you really want?" Jimm asked, breaking the silence.

Although Jimm had spoken in a subdued tone, Sam winced from the force of its delivery. Jimm kicked his legs out, pointing the toes of his shoes, giving the impression that he could reach the ground if he wanted to. They'd yet to make eye contact since leaving lunch.

Sam paused, thinking, as he put his hands into the pockets of his leather jacket and stared off across the glassy surface of the pond to the yellow reeds on the far shore. He took a deep breath before speaking. It had become a familiar ritual—almost like dating—where he shared with yet another prospective agent his plans and hopes, exaggerating his assets.

3

He exhaled a sigh that carried the weight of his burdensome plight, and began: "I want someone to put everything together, to help me take what I already do and make use of it. You know, all the projects I've done: the records, books, videos, and years of gigs and reviews. Someone who brings their own energy and expertise and vision to the mix to create some motion and energy. I want the freedom of creativity that comes from . . . *success*, for want of a better word."

Sam's eyes had become furtive. They were no longer fixed on Jimm; he scanned the park as if suspecting that someone was eavesdropping. "I'm not necessarily talking financial, but I wouldn't turn the bread down. I want to play with the guys I like and admire, keep writing and producing, and be recognized for it too."

"You shouldn't sound so apologetic about it. You want *fame* and you deserve it."

Sam smiled. "Well, there are a lot of people who are good and deserving, we both know there's more to it than that."

"When I was managing Billy Crystal. . ." Jimm began, puffing out his bulbous chest.

"*You* managed Billy Crystal?" Sam asked, suddenly realizing how incredulous he sounded. *Great, I'm insulting this guy right off the bat.*

"It's there in my résumé," Jimm said. "When you get a chance, look it over; it was among the papers I gave you at lunch. Anyway, I saw that he had something. What he *didn't* have was someone to fight for him. There are so many aspects to show business that you don't know about. I don't mean to be condescending, it's understandable. You have consumed yourself with playing jazz and practicing, doing what you should have been doing. You need to consider letting me do some of the rest. Otherwise, you're just spinning your wheels."

Sam smiled as he looked away. He didn't want to seem over-anxious. It was a typical midwinter day in San Francisco: the sky a light gray with darker shades hanging below in nondescript patterns, the air just barely cold enough to see his own breath.

4

Sam expelled a wisp of steam as he watched an old goose walk toward them. "I'll tell you, I'd love to have someone fight for me, someone with contacts. I hope you're aware of the jazz idiom and its small market share."

"That's part of your problem, Sam. You see jazz and this teeny part of the entertainment industry. I see Sam Mann, a *star*. You are much more than a musician, you said so yourself. We need to think of the whole picture; categories like *jazz musician* are what limit you and your potential. But you have to *trust me*. I know what I'm doing."

"I *am* a jazz musician, that's what got me here," Sam protested. He could put down the silliness of the jazz world, but he had trouble with other people doing it. Even so, he felt intoxicated; Jimm was hitting on the same points he'd hammered away on in arguments with his peers, word for word.

"I'm sorry if I offended you in any way," Jimm offered, still without looking in Sam's direction, as if he were speaking into a hidden camera. "I was merely trying to point out some marketing realities as I understand them. We can extend beyond all that old bullshit that's holding you and others like you back. The time is right, and I think you're the one who could pull it off—with *professional* direction, of course. But if you're one of those jazz guys like I knew in New York, who just want to be some obscure downtrodden artist, tell me now and save me the fucking time."

"No, no," Sam said, reaching over, grabbing Jimm by the arm. Through the thin parka he could feel his forearm, devoid of muscle like a giant marshmallow. Jimm recoiled at the touch, and Sam quickly withdrew his hand. "I think we're really on the same page. There's a lot more I'd like to do in my career. But I've got to warn you, I'm not so sure that the world is going to go gaga over a middle-aged white guitar player."

Jimm laughed a strange laugh. "Let me worry about that. You're obviously in good shape, old enough to be experienced, yet young and vital. The young lion and old veteran angles are overdone as far as I'm concerned. How old are you?"

"Thirty-nine."

Jimm laughed again. "That's not middle-aged. And you're Jewish, right?"

"What's that got to do with anything?"

"Nothing. It would just make my mother happy to know that I'm helping out a nice Jewish boy."

The goose—which was much bigger than it had originally seemed—came closer and offered a distraction. Sam snapped his fingers loudly and the bird tilted its head. He whistled a Charlie Parker lick, a bebop phrase with the typical rhythmic squiggles and characteristic interval drop at the end. The goose cocked its head to one side and flapped its beak before rushing up to him. "What do you know? The bird digs *Bird.*"

"You see?" Jimm said. "You are a man of many talents. Maybe we can work it into the act."

Sam smiled as he petted the goose on the top of its head. The bird looked at him quizzically from eye level while he continued whistling. The goose gracefully bent its neck, directing his fingers to the right spots, moving in closer as it exposed the thick tufts of its chest. Sam scratched through the downy layers as the bird lightly flapped its wings, exploring his pockets in hopes of finding food. "Well, where do we go from here?" Sam asked.

"When we go back to the office, I'll give you a contract. It's just a standard form, something to start with. We can adjust it according to whatever you want. You give me a copy of that new method book you wrote, and I promise that by the end of the week I'll have a publishing offer for it—plus I'll have some leads on a new recording contract. By the time we sign the book contract, I promise I'll have a multi-CD deal to sign with the same pen, the same day! But hey, are you sure you're still interested?" Jim's voice was suddenly cold.

Sam's attention was on the goose as they played hide-and-seek with his car keys in the pockets of his jacket. "Oh yeah, sure, sorry," Sam answered. The reprimand stung and he felt the goose stiffen, tensing. "I heard you, and you have to forgive me, I've had a lot of disappointments. So if I seem skeptical, it's not because I don't believe you. I *want* to believe in you, more than you'll probably ever know!"

"Never doubt Jimm Dibbook." It sounded more like a threat than a promise. "I *always* deliver . . . and I *always* tell the truth."

Normally, Sam hated people who said they *always* did anything; they were *always* full of shit. But in his current hopeful euphoria, he never even noticed the declaration of the gnome-like man who sat next to him, swinging his fat legs and promising the world. Sam was too busy scratching a fleck of dirt from the goose's yellow beak; the bird peering myopically as it tried to focus on his finger.

"I've got to get going, and it appears as though you are busy," Jimm said, sounding like a neglected lover.

"Sorry," Sam apologized, for what seemed like no reason. "I love animals, they seem to like me too. Actually, it helps me focus. It was easier for me to sit still and hear you out with him here. Otherwise, I'd have been so excited I wouldn't have heard shit and I'd have had to call you later to get you to repeat it. Believe me, I hope you're serious and that I don't let you down."

"Don't worry, Sam," Jimm said, patting him on the back of the shoulder. "Why don't you think it over here? You can commune with nature or that swan. . ."

"It's a goose."

"Whatever. I'll meet you back at the office and answer any other questions you come up with. You're going to be *famous*. I'll make sure of it."

Sam responded with the understatement of his life: "It sure would be nice."

Jimm stood, offering his hand. The goose was swift; it stretched out its long, supple neck and struck twice with blinding speed. The first caught Jimm on the sleeve, leaving a wet half smile on his jacket.

The second was a direct hit on the back of his hand, raising a red welt out of the pudginess.

Jimm was almost as quick, pulling a butterfly knife from his pocket and flinging it open in one smooth, well-rehearsed motion. If Sam hadn't been within inches of the blade—which gleamed wickedly in the soft light of the winter day, its white pearl handle disappearing into the fleshy folds of Jimm's palm—he would have laughed at the situation: a fat man pulling a knife on a goose, a surreal version of *West Side Story*.

"I'll kill that flying rat!" Jimm said as the goose retreated, honking and flapping its wings.

"Hold on, Jimm," Sam said, intervening, but careful not to place himself between the two.

The sound of Sam's voice stemmed the outburst. Jimm looked down at the blade as if wondering how it had gotten into his hand. The goose had backed off, but was still facing him down.

"I hate that bird. I should call the parks department," Jimm said, snapping the knife shut with a flick of his wrist. His composure was returning; his speech became slower, the syllables carefully enunciated. "It's probably sick. I'm lucky it didn't break the skin. You'd better be careful," he advised, finally looking directly at Sam.

It was hard for Sam to read Jimm. *Is he challenging me to dispute the fact? To chance a return of the switchblade? Or is he looking for some sort of approval and agreement?*

"You're right," Sam said. It seemed like the only answer. "I'll see you in a while. I've got to go to my car to get that manuscript of my method book. I'll be at your office in a half hour or so, depending on parking."

"Fine," Jimm snapped, his hand still on the knife in his jacket pocket. He extended it once more. This time they shook on their agreement without any interruptions.

Sam watched his prospective agent make his way out of the

park. Then he smiled and shook his head at the meeting's strange ending. He whistled a few bars and the goose immediately returned, waddling in much the same fashion as Jimm.

"You sure know how to make an impression," Sam said.

"Hi, I'm Patty. You must be Sam."

The woman smiled as she shook his hand. She appeared to be in her mid-twenties, a spindly blonde with a noticeable Irish brogue. She led Sam up the long stairway to the headquarters of Worldwide Artists, Inc.

The office was not what Sam had expected. Jimm had cleared out a small space for a phone and a filing cabinet in a third-floor railroad flat that functioned as some sort of warehouse. Cardboard boxes of various shapes and sizes filled every room to the ceiling.

"Interesting," Sam mused, taking in the surroundings.

"It's temporary, while I'm waiting for the decorator to finish my space on the floor below," Jimm said, not even looking up from his desk, an old interior door laid on top of two boxes. "I see you met Patty."

The box on the left was sagging under the weight of Jimm's elbow. Sam stood to the side, mindlessly scratching at some chipped paint on the door where a hinge had once been attached.

Jimm took notice and glared.

"How's your hand?" Sam asked, quickly changing the subject. He pulled his own hand away from the door and shoved it into his back pocket.

"It doesn't hurt too much," Jimm answered, holding it up. The red mark was gone.

"Some people showed up to feed that goose, and he was nipping at them, too. He must've thought you had some food."

"Nip? That fucker *struck* me." Jimm's eyes got round and angry again. "We're not here to discuss that, anyway. Patty!" he yelled out into the sea of boxes. "Can you bring me the management contract form for Sam to take a look at?"

The word *management* raised the hair on Sam's spine. "I thought we were talking about your representing me as an agent."

"Well, Sam, after our talk it seems as though you are in need of something a little more specialized than just a person who is going to get you gigs. You brought up organizing your projects and creating a unified strategy for all your talents. *That's* management. It means more work for the agency, and we have to protect our interests. If we agree to do hundreds of hours of work on your behalf, we need to be in a place where we can speak for you. Don't worry, I have no need or desire to take anything away from you. As I said, I'm already set. If I don't create anything for you, there's nothing there for me either."

As he spoke, Jimm rocked back and forth in his overstuffed office chair, the only chair in the office space. Sam felt uncomfortable having to stand as he watched the fat little man who seemed to be waiting for an answer. *Was there a question?*

"The contract actually covers both managing and booking. Like I said at the park, we'll reword it to your liking. It's just an outline we can start with."

Sam looked around. At just over six feet, he could see the tops of the stacks of boxes. They had obviously been there awhile; a herd of free-range dust bunnies ran rampant across the expanse of cardboard. He reached over to the top of one of the nearby stacks, pulled down a videotape, and dusted off the cover. It was a music instruction tape entitled "Play like the Devil," with Ozzy Osborne on the cover, dressed in satanic regalia.

"Interesting," Sam mused. "What is this, a distribution warehouse or something?"

"I'm not exactly sure," Jimm said. "The guy who owns the building is an entrepreneur who's into a lot of businesses." He snatched the cassette from Sam and tossed it back where it came from. "I don't think he wants us messing with his inventory."

"Sorry." For the second time that day, Sam felt like he was apologizing for nothing. Patty came in and handed them each a contract, then quickly scurried out of the room.

The contract had an imposing and unfriendly look. There were more than fifteen *whereases* and *heretofores* in the first paragraph. "I'll have to study this, then I may want to get a lawyer to take a look," Sam said.

Jimm's eyes grew cold and he thrust out his jaw. "If you think I'm trying to fuck you, just say so."

Sam braced himself, thinking Jimm might pull out his knife again. "I'm thinking nothing of the kind. It's just always better to have an expert look at anything like this, for your protection as well as mine."

Jimm sank back into the chair and shrugged. "I've gone through so many of these, I know where all the loopholes are. Believe me, if either of us wants to get out of it, we can. Look it over. Tell me what you need or what you want changed or reworded and it'll be done. If you want me to jumpstart your career, you're going to have to *trust me*; I know this business."

"O.K.," Sam quickly agreed. There was no way he was going to give Jimm time to take it all back. "I'll look it over this weekend. Here's the manuscript." He slid it across the makeshift desk.

Jimm quickly leafed through it and put it on the corner. "I'll call a couple of friends in New York and I promise I'll have a nice offer in hand when we meet to hash out the fine print on the contract. Any other questions?"

"Yeah, actually. How can you be so sure of an offer so quickly? When I submit this stuff it usually sits on a desk for weeks before it gets rejected."

"Before I got into managing, I was a writer and publisher. I've made millions for those people. If I say I've got something, they'll take it. Don't you worry."

"Have I heard anything you wrote?"

"Probably. I helped write and arrange most of the major Motown hits of the late '60s, but I went under the name of Reese Archer." Again, that aloof tone. "You see, Sam, I'm not a threat to you or your money. I just want to help because I believe in you."

"Why did you stop managing Billy Crystal?"

"He wanted to move on, his wife was going to take over. I didn't want to stand in the way, although if I had been handling him all along he'd be making a whole lot more than he is now. Same with Robin."

"Robin? *Williams?*"

"Yeah, back in his early days. That's why Billy came to me. It's all there in my bio, somewhere."

Sam was speechless. He wanted to sign right there, but he could tell by Jimm's demeanor that he considered the meeting already over.

The buzzer in the corner sang out, *subito* in the stillness of the room. "Patty!" Jimm yelled, "get the door." He looked at the clock mounted high on the wall and said, "If that's all, Sam, I have another appointment. Feel free to call if you have any other questions. I'll work on getting you a book and CD deal." He extended his fat paw. "I'm looking forward to accomplishing a lot together. I hope you're ready to be *famous.*"

"Thanks for your faith in me," Sam answered, shaking Jimm's hand in both of his own, nearly delirious with hope.

"Billy!" Sam said as he started down the stairs.

Billy Bronstein was an old high school friend and fellow guitarist who had turned to country-rock and had changed his last name to Barber. He looked comical in his faded jean jacket and red Stetson, long, curly blond hair pouring out from under the brim. His matching mustache obscured all of his upper lip and most of the bottom one as well.

Billy's band had met with a certain amount of success lately, mostly because of the infusion of comedy into his act. The San Francisco gay community ate up his comedic redneck style and skin-tight jeans.

If they only knew he's a nice Jewish boy from Pacific Heights. "Hey, Billy, how've you been?"

"Howdy, Sam," Billy drawled. "Good to see you."

"It's been a long time, Billy. We ought to get together and play some time. It's been about twenty years, I *reckon*."

Billy smiled, ignoring Sam's jibe. "Shee-it, I can't keep up with that far-out stuff you play. I get a headache just thinking about it."

"Come on, Billy, there's always the blues."

"That's about two more chords than I need, Sam, thanks all the same. But if you want to come sit in with *my* band, you're always welcome. Here's my card."

Billy seemed nervous, fidgeting, in a hurry to get away. Sam shrugged, chalking it all up to high school, the countless musical ass-kickings.

"Cool, man," he said, taking the card.

"Adios, pard," said Billy.

Jennifer was a liar—an unabashed, look-right-in-your-face, unrepentant, pathological liar. She didn't know why, or care. She was completely at ease with it and felt no desire or need to change on any level. The only place she never lied was in her diary.

She had come to the Krieger family in her early twenties, just out of college, in search of a profession. Instead, she had ended up with a lifestyle. The Kriegers wanted a baby sitter for their teenage son, Henry. Not that Henry needed anyone.

Henry never got into trouble, *ever*. Henry, a strange boy whose oversized head appeared to have been shortchanged of a few layers of skin, so that the veins underneath his translucent face were reminiscent of a road atlas. He had a few friends his own age but they quickly bored him. He was more interested in politics, science, and most of all, finance. By fourteen he had taken over the portfolio planning of his parents' retirement accounts and had more than doubled them in less than two years. Money was his religion; his reliance on its immutable laws was unshakable, the very cornerstone of his existence.

That Jennifer came into the Krieger family at all was only because of Henry's parents' love for travel. They couldn't leave him all alone at such a young age—even if he could take care of himself. After all, what would the neighbors think?

Jennifer had been referred by the Stanford Agency, a company that specialized in placing au pairs and domestics with the wealthy. Little did Percy Krieger know that the agency had no affiliation with his (and soon to be his son's) alma mater. He wanted a female, thinking that they were more responsible, better able to parent a child who needed no parenting.

Jennifer had had all the right answers for Mrs. Krieger, and the right legs for Percy, which she bounced playfully during the interview when she noticed him staring at them. It was a turning point; she often wondered what path her life might have taken had the Krieger family not been so taken with her that afternoon.

The phone rang. Jennifer set down her diary, picked up the wireless, and thumbed the button.

"Is my son there?" It was the old man himself, Kreiger *pere*.

"No, Mr. Krieger, Percy's still gone. He and Mrs. Kreiger won't be back until next Thursday." She sighed. "The same day as I told you before."

"What about Henry? I want to talk to my grandson."

"Not here either," Jennifer lied. She assumed Henry didn't want to be bothered, and she didn't want to have to get up and walk across the room to the intercom to find out. "Where is Pascal?" she asked. Usually the calls came when the old man's day-nurse was in the bathroom or getting something at the store.

"He's never here. He won't even—"

A voice broke in: "Mr. Krieger, who are you talking to?" Jennifer heard the Latin accent and knew that Mr. Krieger hadn't really been left alone. All the same, as a fellow liar, she appreciated his attempt at deception.

"Hello?" Pascal said after wresting the phone away.

"Hi, Pascal. It's me, Jennifer. Tell Mr. Krieger I'll tell everyone he called." Another lie—*so what?*

"I see you at the wedding, *jes?* Tell Mr. Henry that we look forward to it. It is all Mr. Krieger talks about, that is, when he is not yelling at me."

"Seeya, *jes*," Jennifer said boredly as she hung up the phone and picked up her diary. *Where was I?* she thought. *Or, more to the point, where am I?*

The old man, Frank Krieger, to whom the entire family owed their extraordinary wealth, was an Irish immigrant. He had arrived in 1928, at fifteen, with a guile and toughness perfectly suited to bootlegging. When prohibition ended, he diversified into other alcohol and food products, and invested all his leftover capital in real estate, both commercial and residential. He'd found the perfect place to stash the mountain of cash earned from the illegal dealings that had become legal overnight.

Now, some seventy years later, he lived with his round-the-clock attendants in a luxury apartment on San Francisco's Cathedral Hill. He was too lucid to go quietly into a nursing home, although he knew that if he didn't keep up a constant vigil, that was where his family would conspire to put him.

"Pascal, did you know that they sold off everything that I gave them for pieces of paper? Those goddamn papers are worthless. What can a piece of paper make, other than a fire? I'll take a brewery, a factory, a house, or a truck any day. They call that crap 'funds,' a bunch of Jews' ideas of how to make money."

"Now, Mr. Krieger, I hear Mr. Henry explain to you about the stocks."

"What do you know?" Krieger snapped.

Pascal winced, waiting for the racial epithet that never came. Krieger had dropped off into a noisy nap, his flabby jowls vibrating, his chin resting against his chest. He was doing that more and more lately, barely finishing sentences. Nonetheless, for a man of eighty-four, he was more than holding his own.

He popped out of his sleep mid-sentence. "...he's a comer, that Henry. He had more on the ball than his father did from day one. He's getting married, you know."

"*Jes*, sir. I go to the wedding with you, Saturday. Remember?"

"Pascal...fuck you!"

Jennifer wrote:

Still haven't decided whether or not I'm really going to the wed-ding this weekend—not that a weekend in Big Sur would be all that bad. It's just that I can't stand those awful gatherings, and which is worse, I wonder, that the old men all gawk and hit on me whenever their wives are gone, or that the young guys are only interested in money and kissing up to them. Not much hope for the species, I'm afraid, at least at this social stratum. I'm sure the right thing will come to me—it always does. Cheer up!

Jennifer put down her journal and picked up the remote. There was a chorus of laughs from the audience as *Oprah* batted her big eyes. "Cheer up!" she said, to no one in particular.

"Cheers," answered Jennifer.

The studio was stifling as Kelly read through the thirteenth take. She was shut in a trapezoid-shaped recording booth so small that it would be impossible to lie down. In fact, if she fainted from lack of oxygen—which seemed likely at this point—she would probably end up propped against one of the walls.

"No! No!" The voice came through her headphones so loud that she lurched forward and banged her forehead against the flat screen that shielded her from the microphone. "I want it sexier, breathier."

Kelly took a deep breath and prepared herself for more.

"So let's try again," the voice in her cans said, the tone insultingly frustrated and condescending. "Remember: sexy . . . breathy."

Kelly nodded as she picked up the pencil on the music stand and scribbled on the copy in front of her as if she were adding emphasis to the content. She began to embellish the drawing of an ogre: bulging eyes, hooked nose that hung below his chin, his long finger pushing on the button of a mixing console. The caption read: I'M AN ASSHOLE! His thirteen takes had already broken her personal record of eight.

She rolled her neck to loosen her larynx muscles. After a nod to the engineer, she heard the words: "Take fourteen." Rage came bubbling up from a place deep down. Be sexy and breathy about a disinfectant—when all she really wanted to do was go out and throttle the jerk who'd been pulling her chain all afternoon? The word would get out, whether she liked it or not: Two-Take Kelly Tuffalos had gone into double digits, and now it looked like triple was a distinct possibility.

She began slowly, seductively, breathy, like a spraypaint can pushing out its last bit of mist. Then she heard it. She'd read: "No rubbing, just one spray swallows the germs," but heard herself say, "Just one gay swallows the sperms!" She winced and braced herself.

"Cut, cut!"

"I'm sorry. I guess I need a little break. I'm suffocating in here.

Can I get a few minutes, please?"

"Just a second," the voice answered. "I'll come in there."

Panic struck. Kelly felt the footsteps nearing the door. *What am I going to do?* The ogre on her copy was too big to erase—or miss—and the caption seemed to vibrate in neon brilliance. Through her headphones she heard a laughing voice, the engineer: "One gay swallows the sperms?"

She pulled the headphones off her ears and backed into the corner. The producer pulled open the door and Kelly felt her ears pop at the pressure change. He walked in with a scowl on his face. The strength of his aftershave added the last touch to the thick air inside the booth. Kelly didn't know whether to faint or throw up.

"May I see the copy? I always felt that that line was a little awkward, anyway. Those bubbles are already eating the germs on the video, and I don't think our client will mind my changing that one word to something a little less given to double-entendre." He extended his hand, his eyes still and cold.

Kelly stood frozen, her gaze fixed on his thick mane of curly blond hair, swept to the side, yet defying gravity as if made of stone.

He self-consciously tried to straighten his do. "Please," he asked again, extending his hand after rubbing the mousse residue off on his pant leg.

"I've already marked this one up so much," Kelly stammered, crumpling it into a ball in her fist. "I think that's why I screwed up. Do you have another?"

"No, the only other copy is mine and it has a lot of direction marks and time-code references. That's the only one."

Kelly considered eating it. That would be a grand way to register her refusal. But she usually left the melodrama to her boyfriends. She knew that was exactly what Sam would have done in the same situation.

"Would you please give me that before you ruin it? It's the agency's property. Ms. Tuffalos!"

"O.K., here!" she said, throwing the crumpled ball down on the floor at his feet. "Fuck you *and* your disinfectant. I've been doing voice-over for years and have never been given such horrible direction, to say nothing of the copy. I gave you more than ten good takes and all you do is continue to fuck with me."

He stood his ground, his expression unchanged. He appeared to be silently counting, waiting for her to pick up the script before begging for another chance. The silence was louder than her outburst.

"I guess that's it, then," he said, sighing as he bent to pick up the trash.

Kelly made her move. She pressed her back against the wall and slid toward the door.

He grabbed her wrist. "Rest assured," he said, his grin exposing his too-long teeth, "I'll be talking to your agent."

"Let go of me!" she screamed, jerking her hand free. She picked up her jacket and purse and stomped out of the studio, avoiding eye contact with the engineer.

Outside, she sat on the cement stairs. Her wrist throbbed, and there was a red handprint encircling it. "What am I going to do?" She pulled a cell phone from her purse and punched in #4 on the speed dial. After two short rings there was a click. "Howdy!" Then a short drum pickup led to a pedal steel whining out a pentatonic yodel that sounded like a cat whose tail had been stepped on. "Billy here. If'n you wanna leave a message for me or my band, go right on ahead. Adios."

She flapped the mouthpiece back in with a quick flick, ending the call. Her mood darkened. "Why am I such a wimp?" She got up, slung her purse over her shoulder, and marched off down the street.

"Hello?" Billy sang out cautiously. He'd seen the lights on and Kelly's car out front. The only time she showed up unannounced like this was when she was in crisis, which mysteriously happened with monthly regularity. He knew better than to mention the coincidence should it ever come up in conversation. "Sugar?"

"In here," she intoned from the other room, an injured bird, fallen from its nest.

Billy hung his hat on the rack by the door; he ran his hands through his hair and smoothed his mustache.

"Didn't hear from you so we went out and had a few beers after rehearsal. Got this new tune called 'The Jew Buckaroo,' all about this guy who upsets his momma by wanting to be a cowboy. Can't decide whether to throw a Jewish princess into the mix, might make for a couple of good verses. Whaddaya think?" he said, making his way to the bedroom. The TV was on, the mute engaged as Kelly lay there reading a novel. "Something wrong, sugar?"

"Does there have to be something wrong for me to want to see you?" she challenged, then sobbed, "Oh, Billy, it was horrible!"

Billy pulled a bandana from his rear pocket and handed it to her, then sat down beside her on the bed. "What's the matter, baby? Why don't you tell Billy all about it?"

When she got to the end of her drawn-out version, Billy erupted: "One gay swallows the sperm?! Sugar, I wish I'd written that."

"It was humiliating! The way that producer was nit-picking over every line. I gave him at least four perfect takes before that."

Billy was still giggling. "One *gay*?"

"All right, already. It's not so funny. Jesus, Billy, everything's not a joke, you know. Some things are serious, which reminds me…"

Uh-oh, Billy thought. *Must be that time of the month. Why do women get so all-darned serious when they're about to come into season?*

"I got a brochure from Gray Elk today," Kelly said. "I told you about him, he's that shaman down south. The Spring Vision Quest is coming up pretty soon. I thought it would be a great thing to do. You and me."

"Well, I don't know," opined Billy. "I got to check out what's happening with the boys. It's not just me when I take off work, I got a band, and we work just about every weekend..." He saw her disapproving stare; combined with her present state of mind, it began to take on a scary quality. "Tell you what, we'll talk about some time off, all of us, at tomorrow's gig. O.K.?"

She leaned forward and kissed him. "I understand the nature of your work. I'm freelance too, Billy, and you're not the first musician I've ever gone out with."

"Oh, yeah! That reminds me," Billy said. "Did you ever tell Sam about us?"

"No. Why?"

"I saw him today. Went to see this new manager-agent-type dude. Sam musta been there for the same reason. This guy was kinda creepy, Kelly. This fat little New Yorker, always saying, 'Trust me, trust me.'"

"Did Sam sign with him?"

"I don't know. Anyway, it was weird running into Sam after all these years. I didn't tell him about us. It's not like we're cheatin' on him or anything. I asked him to sit in with my band. Maybe you should tell him, in case he shows up one night. I'd hate him to get embarrassed like that."

"I'll tell him, if you want me to, but believe me, Billy, you'll never see Sam Mann at one of your gigs—he's too much of a musical snob. But quit trying to change the subject. Back to Gray Elk. Vision Quest is during the week, Monday through Thursday. I've got the flyers at my house."

"I don't know about going on an Injun Vision Quest. Once they all get hungry, who do you think they're gonna wanna eat?"

"It's Native Americans or Indigenous Tribes now. Remember that and you'll be fine."

Billy picked up his acoustic guitar and began twanging away, humming an atonal melody, in search of something—anything—to change the subject.

"Sugar?" he asked as she got up to go the bathroom, "what rhymes with circumcise?"

The polite applause began to die down as Sam sat back on his stool, decompressing from his solo. The bass took over with angular thumping double-stops, before incorporating a bass line, punctuating chord tones on the off-beats. It was Wil Strunk's favorite trick, and Sam wondered what he was going to do for the rest of his solo; he still had a couple of choruses to go.

Such concerns usually wouldn't have worried Sam, but tonight he had the *feeling* that always followed one of those hopeful dances with prospective agents. In Sam's mind, he'd already moved on; it was as if the Lotto ticket in his pocket had transformed itself from that one-in-thirteen-billion chance to the sure winner. No more dealing with the gig. No more nights giving blood to an audience of tin-eared tourists, accompanying the clink of ice cubes in their glasses and their swells of chatter and laughter.

It was all perspective; it *had* to be. Just the night before, Sam had told a friend that a gig in your hometown on an off-night, playing what you want with whom you want, was as close to jazz Utopia as anyone got. Somehow, the lunch meeting with Jimm had changed that.

Wil was treading water. "Sam," he whispered, his black bald head hanging over the fingerboard, hands nearly to the bridge as the strings yelped out a *falsetto pizzicato*, "Do something, man!"

Sam turned down the guitar, opting to strum acoustically in quarter-note fashion. "Freddie Green to the rescue," he quietly announced, his head down, as if he was carefully monitoring the wrist action.

There was a long sliding cascade down the E-string as Wil bombed out his low G, his bass's best note. "Shit," he'd been know to say, "that note is so damn good, I can use it no matter what key we're in."

Somehow the tune endured. After a long tag with a drawn-out fade, the song ended with a sizzle from the lone rivet suspended from a small hole along the edge of the ride cymbal.

That *feeling* again. Sam shook his head, then took a drink. It wouldn't leave. He caught himself thinking of his next record date.

I guess I can use Wil; just better keep the bass solos to a minimum. That Basie stuff seems to work the best for him.

"What's next? Clyde is staring!" Wil whispered.

Sam began to noodle, a generic introduction to a yet unformed tune. He looked up and saw the owner shaking his head as he walked to the bar from his perch by the front door. That was usual. If the break between tunes was longer than a few seconds, Clyde Worthington would glare and, if need be, approach. He didn't have to say anything—the six-feet-seven-inch, 275-pound former All-Pro linebacker let his eyes do the talking.

The tune wouldn't come. First, Sam tried an exploration of the landscape of F major. Nothing. Then a move to A-flat. When that proved just as useless he tried the relative minor. *Great, back in F again*, he thought. That it wasn't major was of minor consequence. Then it came to him: Dut dut dat dat duh do doe dat! *"Moanin!"* But the band had gone to sleep, and their entry—the response of the opening melody, which was just as important as the theme itself—sounded like someone falling over a metal card table.

Sam tried to play the second phrase in time, as if the response had been perfect. No way, his footing was gone, and now the *feeling* mocked him: *You're going to be a big star and you can't even play a simple fucking melody!* The notes came out tentative, an impossible search for the center of the beat. The bass and drums tried to collect the song, which was on its way down the toilet, but they made it even worse. Now the metal chairs were going down, along with the card table and the poker chips.

Clyde moved from the bar, glaring. Sam saw him. *Shit!* He mustered every ounce of concentration. The third phrase rang out centered and on track. The band's reply was perfect, and they flowed smoothly into the second A-section, as if their lame opening had been a comedic arrangement designed to test Clyde.

"What's happening up there?" Clyde asked as Sam sat at down at the bar during the break.

"Sorry, Clyde," Sam said, angry that he was apologizing for a little mistake. The *feeling* was worming its way down, settling into his psyche. It seemed that every time this chronic disease came out of remission, it was more intense. "I guess my intro was a little long and I caught the cats by surprise."

"I'll say!"

Sam felt rather than saw Clyde move away as he watched the bourbon flow into his glass.

"I'll say," Ginger, the bartender, mimicked, her high voice barely managing to drop into a contralto. She had been bartending at Clyde's longer than Sam had been playing there. "Don't let him fool you with that big-and-black shit. He loves you, Sam. He just needs to play club owner every now and again."

"Thanks, Ginger." Sam wanted to laugh with her, but the *feeling* had him: *Pretty soon I won't have to deal with this bullshit anymore.* He looked around, saw everyone having fun—everyone, that is, except him—so he ordered another shot. Chemotherapy for the *feeling*.

"Hey, Sam," Wil said. "There's this cat in town, a drummer, on the road with a Broadway touring company. He's played with everybody back in New York and he's dying to sit in. Name's DG Thornton."

"If it's all right with Quentin, it's all right with me," Sam said. "They're his drums."

As Sam slid the empty glass back across the bar and started toward the bandstand, a familiar presence entered the room. Kelly walked as if she were on a mission, her lips pursed and her steps purposeful. She wore a tight sweater, and the curve of her shoulder and silhouette of a breast in the light that flooded in from the street softened her entrance somewhat; but to someone like Sam—a veteran of the wars—the energy was tangible, as if she had an accompanist.

The scenario set off a familiar reaction that Sam assumed was now firmly entrenched in his genetic code: self-righteous indignation, heightened pulse, and an odd sexual frenzy revving up his libido. He felt Clyde's impatient stare drilling holes in his back, and considering the ending of the previous set, he decided it would be better to sort out the reason for Kelly's visit later.

DG was a foot taller than the trio's diminutive drummer. His neck was as thick as a tree trunk, and the stool groaned when he sat down, as if the metal were being tested for tensile strength. DG's knees popped out of his long shorts, and Sam couldn't help noticing that, together, they looked like the biggest, blackest ass he'd ever seen.

"What do you feel like playing?" Sam asked, unable to unfix his eyes from DG's bald knees.

"Just something swingin'. I been playing this theater shit and they won't let me hit. Everything's so fuckin' po-lite."

Sam started a simple blues with a riff-type phrase that repeated three times to make a chorus—a drummer's type of tune. By the fifth bar, DG knew all he needed to know, and punctuated the melody with accents while setting up each phrase with thundering pyrotechnics. He slammed the bass drum with his right foot; instead of the usual boom or thud, it came out *whack*, with a raise in pitch as he pressed the beater into the head, punishing it.

Sam tensed, steering a course through a maze of exploding landmines that had his ears ringing. Every phrase he played set off another barrage of *whacks* and rimshots. He ended his solo with a decrescendo of long, sustained descending chords. It was a standard ending, but DG missed and rumbled on, a train without brakes, riding over the opening of Wil's bass solo for at least two choruses. Even the applause of the audience was obscured by his unrelenting assault on the crash cymbal.

When he realized his mistake, DG smiled a gap-toothed smile, shoved the sticks under his arm, and grabbed the wire brushes that sat on the windowsill behind him. People on the street had stopped to peer inside, amazed at the volume of sound from behind the glass. The windows wobbled and the candles at the farthest tables flickered with every slap on the snare—even from the brushes, which were already bent and fraying like whiskbrooms under the stress.

After the bass solo, with shards of wire amassing at DG's feet, Sam attempted to trade fours. The space for his four bars in exchange with DG's became oddly uneven and irregular. Sam resigned as diplomatically as he could and silently mouthed the words: "You got it." DG understood. He pressed his upper teeth over his bottom lip and winked at Sam as if to say, *Check this out!*

Sam rested on his stool, his back on the brass railings that separated the stage area from the floor. As he looked out he saw that most of the people seated near the band were covering their ears in a variety of ways, ranging from subtle to fingers-in. He tried feigning interest in the monstrous swoops that came crashing down on the brass, wood, and skin of Quentin's modest drum set. The barrage began to take on more of the character of an all-out assault. Sam shut his eyes as he absorbed the pounding like a fighter in the ring. Three quick hits on the tom-tom were like body shots; he felt them in his ribs. A double crash on the cymbals were a near-fatal one-two, like open palms to the ears. Sam hunched his shoulders, hoping the ref would step in and break it up before any permanent damage was done.

Not a chance. Next came a rumbling, spastic roll on the floor tom, which wobbled on thin metal legs, buckling. *This must be what a fucking volcano sounds like!*

DG looked up, smiling, his arms a flurry, working all three toms as hard as he could as he swept in for the kill, crashing down on five pounds of Turkish brass.

The concussion rocked Sam back into the brass rail, knocking the breath out of him as DG went back at the snare. There was another crash, but this time it had a faraway sound, ethereal, tinkling, like a shower of fairy dust.

"That's it! I just lost my hearing! My fucking high end!" Sam felt himself moving forward off the stool, into the salvo of rim shots. He heard someone screaming: "You fucking asshole, what the fuck do you think you're doing? I can't believe this shit. No wonder you're out on tour with a goddamn play! Ain't no motherfucker got any sense or ears left is going to give you a fucking gig."

DG looked toward Sam, confused as he decrescendoed into the hi-hat.

"What did I ever fucking do to you? What did these people ever do to you?"

DG now realized that Sam was yelling at him, but why? He continued to play as if they had found a new way to trade fours. The audience was captivated, the band having taken improvisation to the highest level.

"What the fuck did those poor drums ever do to you, you fucking *animal?!*"

Sam finally figured out that it was he who was yelling. His throat was raw, and the realization that he had just called the biggest man he'd ever played with an animal didn't ease the pain.

DG slowly put down the sticks and began to stand. Sam eyed his routes of escape as an odd silence fell over the room, an eerie quiet, even louder than the thunderous drum solo.

I've got to take my axe. He'll break it into toothpicks!

Sam pulled the cord out of his guitar; the exposed end hit the floor and began humming. DG was upright now, straightening out his pants as they fell below his knees, concealing the two skulls. He seemed to be in no hurry. Maybe he hadn't heard anything. *Hell, it must have been just as loud behind there as it was out here,* Sam thought.

Then he heard it. "Excuse me," DG said to Wil, "I got some business with Shorty over there."

It chilled Sam to the bone.

"Wait a second, man." Wil said. "Everybody just cool down. We can work this out."

"I'm totally cool, and I'm sure we'll work this out," DG said, his teeth glistening in the stage lighting.

"That's not what I mean," Wil offered, trying to impede DG's way through the bandstand. Wil gave Sam an imploring look: *What are you waiting for? Go!*

Sam stood frozen, stuck to the stage.

"What the hell is going on here?" The cavalry, saving the day, in the nick of time. "You all heard me," Clyde said. "What's going on?"

"This little white fuck insulted me in front of all these people," said DG with an alarming calmness. "I'm going to work out our little disagreement in private though. It seems more dignified."

"You ain't doing nothing of the kind, my man," said Clyde. "Sam, what has gotten into you? You get your shit and clear out. Take tomorrow night off, too."

"Excuse me," DG interrupted. "There's still a slight matter we got to resolve."

"You ain't resolvin' nothin'," Clyde said. He pushed Sam toward the bar. "You heard me, get your shit and clear out. And get some fucking rest."

"Who the fuck are you?" DG demanded, as Sam picked up his case and moved toward the front door.

"I'm Clyde Worthington. This is my club. And before we go any further, I'm *that* Clyde Worthington. The Super Bowl ring should be enough fucking proof. So unless you want to go rolling back over that drum set, I suggest you rethink your plans."

DG stood, hands clenched, staring into Clyde's eyes. The crowd sat in stunned silence, waiting.

"I don't have any problem with you," DG said, giving up on the stare-down.

Clyde saw Sam clear the door. "I'll tell you what, why don't you have a seat and I'll buy you a taste?"

"Sam!"

He looked up as he threw the guitar into the back seat. "Kelly. I thought I saw you come in."

"What the hell is wrong with you? Have you gone crazy?"

"Listen, I'd love to stand here and have another of our usual discussions, but I don't know how long Clyde is going to be able to hold that guy off."

"I need to talk to you."

"Shit." He sighed.

"Open the damn door," she said, pulling on the handle, the car rocking in place.

"You need to press the razor against the skin, you wetback. Otherwise you only pull the cream off. Don't you ever shave yourself?"

"*Jes* sir, Mr. Krieger. Where do we go this morning?"

"The usual is fine, Pascal. The parking lot at Baker Beach ought to do it. I'll pretend to sleep in the car so you can go outside and smoke those funny cigarettes. When do we leave for the wedding?"

"Tomorrow morning? Today? We take our time? I hear it is very beautiful."

"I know your scheme, Pascal. If we leave today, that's another sixteen hours' overtime for you, and a paid vacation."

"Mr. Krieger," Pascal protested, finishing the last fold of skin that hung from Krieger's neck, careful to make sure he got all of the stubble.

"What—you never seen a turkey before?"

"*Señor* Krieger!" Pascal liked Frank Krieger; he knew that the old man's constant state of irritation was well earned. If *he* had lived to be that old and rich, only to end up relegated to twenty-four-hour nursing, he'd be plenty irritated. Frank Krieger was generous, always carrying a roll of hundred-dollar bills, peeling them off liberally.

"On second thought, Pascal, let's go to Hillsborough. I had another dream; I need to talk to Henry."

"These dreams—"

"Don't you start with me! The last one came true. There I was, dancing to "9:20 Special," an old song, way before your time, with the prettiest girl I ever saw. Red hair, blue eyes, scent like heather in the morning dew. As soon as I said the words "9:20 Special," she turned cold and said she had to leave, and that I ought to leave too, if I knew what was good for me. She said she'd be right back, though. I knew what it meant, Pascal! I called Henry. Right then the stock market was on its way through the roof. I told Henry to sell those index funds he was holding."

"Mr. Krieger—"

"Shut up, Pascal, don't interrupt. Maybe you'll learn something. So I says, get out at 9200, wait for a correction and then buy short. The train will be back on line. Get it? So he says, 'I'll tell you what, I'll take half of all the funds that are left in your name and do just that.' I thought he was patronizing me, for all I knew there were none left."

"Mr. Krieger, please drink the juice."

"I said don't interrupt. I pay you to listen! All the experts—experts, hah, what do they know—they said the market was on its way straight through 10,000. Sure enough, guess what happened?"

Pascal sighed. "You right?"

"You bet your ass. Henry sold off 2 million dollars' worth, and bought short a week later. We made a killing. Now, he has that sitting aside, awaiting my instructions. That Henry, he's a comer, not a deadbeat like his father."

"Mr. Krieger, that is—"

No need to finish. Krieger was snoring, his chin resting on his chest. Pascal tried to pick him up out of the chair and put him on the couch, as he woke up, furious.

"Fuck you!"

Sam's morning began with a familiar scent, a trace of perfume and a delicate hint of musk. Pleasure gave way to panic when he heard the water running in the bathroom. He tried to sort out the events of the previous evening, but they were jumbled together. He remembered DG, his escape, the *feeling's* crushing hold on his psyche, and Kelly's admonishing tone. All through it he remembered that she had something she needed to tell him. Had she?

He coughed.

"Morning," Kelly sang out from behind the half-closed door.

As innocuous as the statement was, he was afraid to respond. Silence was his best (his only) resort once she started in; ambush lurking around every corner.

She yelled to be heard over the running water. "Sam, that was a stretch even by your standards. What the hell were you trying to prove, screaming at that guy?"

Sam clung to his silence, sure that the conversation was really headed elsewhere.

"All those explosions do is enable you to indulge in your other bullshit: booze, dramatics . . . were you doing coke, too?"

She had hit the mark; found unguarded territory. He sat up, feeling possessed. "Hey, I don't know where you get off coming to my gig, my pad, and starting up all this old shit again. Maybe we should try dating before we sleep together next time."

She stormed back into the room and stood over the bed as if transported. Her dark eyes were full of fury. She was biting her lip, hyperventilating, water dripping from her face. "We didn't *do* anything! FYI, you had a drink and passed out . . . well, I guess that probably means no coke."

Sam froze, well aware he was overmatched.

"Jeez, Sam," she said, wiping her face with a towel, "I come all the way to your fucking gig to do you a favor, to tell you something, and you pull this crap all over again?"

"So," he answered, careful not to leave any openings or set any traps he would surely end up stepping in, "what is it you wanted to tell—" The phone rang out, stopping him in mid-sentence.

"Sam, Jimm here. I didn't call too early, did I?"

"No, what's up?" Sam started to panic. *Has he already heard about the scene last night?*

"I just wanted you to know that I got you a book deal with Music Arts, the big publisher out of New York. The editor is an old buddy of mine; we used to job records on the East Side together. He took it sight unseen, and he wants an accompanying CD and video. If you're ready we can produce it next week, when you get back. When will that be?"

Sam was dumbstruck. *So much, so fast.*

He heard Kelly sigh and move away from the edge of the bed. He waited to look over until he heard her put on her coat. She looked over and he shrugged, pointing to the receiver.

"Sam?"

"Yeah, I'm here. Uh, I can get back Sunday night. I'm only going to Big Sur."

"O.K., Monday is good, let's do lunch, noon, same place. I also checked into a record deal, and I have to tell you, even though I got a couple of bites at Columbia and Blue Note . . ."

Is this for real? Sam wondered. *I must be dreaming.*

"...I think it might be best to place you at this new label I found out here. That way, I can keep my eyes on the marketing. Sometimes guys get buried at the big houses, and once you're in there, there's very little I can do. They change management every year, and the recently signed artists get swept under the rug—sort of a flavor of the month kind of thing. If we make some noise with your new project—and we will—they'll be coming to get you. That's the way we want it. *Trust me.*"

Kelly slung her purse over her shoulder. Sam held up his finger, sure the call was winding up, but not in a hurry to resume their confrontation.

Kelly sighed. "What was I thinking?" she asked the air around her. "Later, Sam." She smirked, shook her head and paced out of the room.

"Cool," Sam said, trying to focus again on his career-making phone call.

"Did you look at the contract?"

"Not yet. I'll do that this weekend. If I have any questions, I'll call. What's your home phone?"

"Call me? *No one* calls me at home! I don't give that number to *anyone!*"

"Sorry!" Sam apologized. *For what?* "I'll just leave them on the machine, I guess."

"Don't worry, Sam, those contracts are just outlines. We can change any or all of it. And remember, a contract isn't worth the paper it's printed on. It has to do with people doing what they say they will do. And *I* always do. Rest assured, I don't want anything from you, I want to do my job *for* you. Any details are minor, and I'll bring a pen to lunch. You'll sign that and a book and CD deal before dessert." Sam tensed, thinking he was going to say *trust me* again. "Have a good weekend, Sam."

Pascal took El Camino Real, the old highway. In Millbrae, the road was lined with eucalyptus trees; falling buttons pelted the top of the car. "This used to be the main road," Krieger said, popping out of his nap. "I knew every path through those hills up there. No one could catch Frank Krieger. I had this mule, and I'd take the kegs through the woods on little rickety wagons. Long before they built all those houses. Those were the days. I can still taste it. Ask anyone: no one could brew a good Irish stout like Frank Krieger."

"Was the road here?"

"Of course."

"Then why carts on the hill?"

"Never mind," Krieger said, disgusted. He didn't have the energy to explain Prohibition.

The large houses of Burlingame gave way to the expansive estates of Hillsborough. They drove past grassy lawns, verdant in the crisp winter sun, perfectly manicured hedges, and terraced flowerbeds, some blooming even at the end of January. Winding driveways made their way to the doors of the mansions; that is, the ones that were visible from the street.

"Slow down! It's this one," Krieger said. It was a huge Tudor mansion up on a rise, designed and built in 1938. The sign at the entrance to the drive said KINSALE; it was named for the town his family came from, on the Irish coast just south of Cork.

"You see that fence?" Kreiger asked. Pascal nodded. "They wanted to replace it with an iron fence. Can you believe that? I had my brother Mike bring in a crew from Ireland to build that. There aren't any stonemasons in America who can build something like *that*.

"It is beautiful, Mr. Krieger."

"Yeah, yeah. They're probably waiting for me to die to tear it up and put in some electric wire-looking monstrosity. Then they'll sell off the stones for fireplaces in a condo development. Pascal, our only hope is Henry."

Pascal swerved to avoid a white Miata that came speeding down the drive. "What was that?" Krieger asked.

"Just Miss Jennifer. She in a big hurry."

"Women drivers!" Krieger spat as they pulled up in front of the house.

"Hi, Dad," Percy Krieger said, opening the door. "You're looking great!"

"Too bad, huh?"

"I didn't know you were coming down. We just got in from the airport. Marsha forgot one of her bags, so we sent Jennifer back to get it. You just missed her."

"I think we scraped her." Kreiger hated the way his son was always so nervous around him, his nonstop chatter. "Hello, Marsha. Back in time for the wedding, I'm glad to see."

His daughter-in-law scowled. "Everything has been planned for months, and as you know, most of it is up to the bride's family. We just helped out a little, only where help was needed. The Post Ranch is a beautiful spot. I hope the weather holds."

"Are we going to stand out here or are you going to offer me a drink?" Krieger snapped.

Percy Krieger took his father's arm and helped him up the stone stairs to the front door. "Lucinda," he said to the maid, "will you serve cocktails in the living room?"

"Let's use the library," Krieger growled.

Percy smiled. "The library it is!"

Percy was more than a foot taller than his shrunken father. His thin, bald forehead was rimmed at the bottom with the characteristic Krieger eyebrows, full and bushy, still dark even though his hair had turned gray. The nervous tremor in his leg sent ripples through the loose fabric of his trousers.

"So, Dad, what brings you down today?"

"Just out for a drive. Had a dream, wanted to tell Henry about it." Kreiger walked to the corner of the library and sank into the armchair. He traced the fabric with his fingers as his eyes took in the bookshelves stuffed with unread volumes that had been collected over the years. The mahogany paneling and indirect lighting gave the library a muted, dignified ambience.

"You know," he said, "I made this room to impress all the people I had to work with over the years. I always hated it. I wanted to come in here today to see if I still do; I do. I had much more fun downstairs in the billiard room, drinking beer and smoking cigars. It wasn't until you went to college that anyone ever used this room for what it was intended."

"It was my favorite place in the house."

Krieger noticed the strange way his son had used the past tense. Percy was gazing about the room with the kind of nostalgic expression usually reserved for lost loves and missed opportunities.

"I've decided to give the house to Henry, Dad. Marsha and I want to move into the condo in Palm Springs full time. This house seems too cumbersome for us, and Marsha has been having a hard time the past few winters, all the cold and wet up here. We made the final decision last week while playing tennis. It was eighty-two degrees!"

"I see." Krieger sat back in the chair, his son's wiggling leg making him dizzy. "I ain't moving down there, I'll tell you right now. And if you think you're going to put me into a home—"

"I didn't mean that, Dad. I'm sorry, I should have phrased it differently. We'll still be coming up here a lot, and nothing will change for you. At least until you say so. It just seemed like the right place for Henry to start a family, right here, where you put down roots. I talked to Leah's mother and she's excited to help with any redecorating that needs to be done. We thought we'd announce it this weekend at the wedding."

Percy walked over to the chair, where his father seemed on the verge of sleep. "To another generation of Kriegers gracing these grounds." He tapped his drink against his father's before he gently removed the glass from his failing grip. "Sweet dreams, Dad," he said tenderly.

"Fuck you," Krieger answered, nodding off into noisy slumber.

As soon as Sam crossed the Carmel River Bridge, the gateway to Big Sur, he felt better. The weird sense of hope mixed with dissatisfaction from the *feeling* had him in a psychic tug-of-war that had turned into full-on insomnia the night before. Now, moving southward, with the sun reflecting off the azure waters of the Pacific, he felt his body easing into relaxation. A nap out on some sunny deck in Big Sur was exactly what he needed.

After the Carmel Highlands he hit the first of many slide spots, where the road was now one lane, monitored by timed stoplights. Winter landslides had stripped much of the road and a couple of bridges from their tenuous grip on the westernmost edge of the coast. As Sam waited for the light to change, he peered out to the horizon; it was so sharp that he thought he could see the curve of the earth, the ocean dropping out of sight like it had fallen off the edge of a table.

As he approached the Bixby Bridge, the light changed from yellow to red. He eased off the gas just as a white Miata passed, speeding to catch up with the last car through the light. Sam stopped and settled in for the long wait. He looked down; golden sunlight danced on the waves that circled the rocks far below—so far below that he was struck with a severe attack of dizziness.

The bridge ahead looked shaky. One lane was officially determined safe, but Sam had his doubts. When the light changed, he raced across as if the road were falling into the ocean behind him.

At the first turnout, he saw the white Miata stopped by a Highway Patrol officer. An exceptionally pretty woman wearing a pink scarf that gleamed in the sunlight seemed to be pleading her case to a captivated state trooper. Sam gave a thumb's up as he passed. She shot him a quick smile as if to say, "I've got this one in the bag."

Not five miles down the road, as Sam descended to the Little Sur River, the white two-seater flew by him again, the pink scarf flowing in the wind. The woman blew him a kiss and waved.

The entrance to the Post Ranch was barely marked, almost hidden from anyone traveling from the north. When Sam finally saw the turnoff, he'd passed it. He U-turned and waited for the oncoming cars, two limos that barely navigated the hairpin turn into the driveway. He went past the guardhouse and saw the sign: POST RANCH WILL BE CLOSED FROM 5:00 P.M. FRIDAY FOR PRIVATE PARTY.

"Wow! The whole place? I should've asked for more bread," Sam said as he drove up to reception.

He waited for the two parties in the limousines, as they transferred their luggage into little SUVs and were carted up the hill. Then Sam introduced himself.

"Oh, Mr. Mann," said the girl at the desk, "we have you in the manager's apartment. The rest of your band is staying in one of the nearby apartments."

"I don't understand."

"It's on site, not that far. It's behind the pond you went by as you came up the road." She pointed out the picture window behind him.

"Not that," Sam said. "I'm sure it's quite nice. You said my band? I'm playing solo."

"Oh! There must be another group. They haven't checked in yet. That must be why you have a private room. I just thought you might be the *star* or something."

There it was again. God, he loved that word. He sure as hell wasn't going to dispute it, the *feeling* making a cameo appearance.

"Here's a package for you. Why don't you sit down and read through it. There's also a letter for you from the bridal party, and I think your check is in there as well. When one of our vehicles comes back, they'll drive you over to your room. Have a glass of wine if you'd like."

Sam sat down on a suede couch. There was a roaring fire in the stone hearth in the corner of the lobby. He opened the envelope. Along with brochures about herbal rubs, aromatherapy and nature walks, the history of the ranch, and maps of the property, there was also a letter from Mrs. Guilford Murchison:

Dear Mr. Mann, (He'd always hated the way that sounded, so redundant.)

We are so glad that you could be a part of our daughter's wedding. If there is anything that you need, please feel free to ask the hotel staff. They are at your disposal. The schedule is quite flexible; try to feel as if you are a guest. Tonight, we would like you to play for a cocktail reception in the bar area of the restaurant at 5:30. Attire is tres *casual—we are in Big Sur!*

After depositing his luggage, Sam opted to return in the ranch vehicle to set up his amp and check out the resort. As they rode back up the hill, Sam eyed a still pond encircled by tall pink flowers; a flock of wild turkeys strolled across the grass on the far side. To the east, craggy peaks stood out against the cloudless deep blue sky. A lone hawk hung suspended in mid-air.

The restaurant, Sierra Mar, was cleverly cut into the natural terrain. It had the look of a bunker scooped out of the top of the ridge. Stepping down into it, Sam saw the ocean and the Big Sur coast through geometric picture windows. He set his guitar down near a freestanding circular fireplace and went out onto the deck.

It was still early in the afternoon. He headed for the far table, beside a wrought iron railing separating the deck from the apparently endless drop to sea level. He ordered a beer and sat in the sun, basking away the tension and seesaw emotions of the past week.

He heard a *chirp.*

Looking at the railing he saw a scrub jay, chasing the sparrows away. "That's not very nice," Sam said, then emitted a high *peep,* picking one of the peanuts out of the nut mix on the table. The jay cocked his head, curious. "Peep," Sam sang again. This time, the people at the nearby tables looked up and stared.

Sam rolled the nut in his hand until he had the bird's attention. He extended the index finger of his free hand to create a landing perch. "Come on, don't be afraid," he whispered. The jay looked around, quickly turning his head left and right before he jumped across to Sam's finger, stole the nut and flew off.

Thinking nothing of it, Sam took a sip of his beer and sank back into his reverie. *Chirp* again: this time louder, demanding. "Back so soon? Your nest must be close by." He took another peanut, rolled it in his hand, and made a perch again. The jay was quick this time; he made his move without hesitation.

"That's impressive," a female voice said, startling Sam. He looked up but the sun blinded him. Looking down he saw bright pink shoes, the same as a scarf he remembered. The woman in the white convertible.

"Hi," he said, beginning to stand.

"Don't get up." She sat down, smiling at him before gazing off at the horizon. It allowed him a chance to look her over. Pink shoes, shapely brown bare legs, a white sundress, and a wide-brimmed straw hat. The pink scarf that had been flowing in the wind the last time he'd seen her was now tied around her waist.

The bird returned, screaming for more. Sam dug out one of the remaining nuts and extended his finger. The bird eyed the new person at the table, assessed the risk, and made another raid.

"I've never seen anything like that before! Blue jays never trust people."

"I think it's a scrub."

"Same species. That's amazing."

"The birds around here are probably really tame," Sam said. "Jays are brash. If they want some food, they'll make you give it to them. I bet they have to shoo them away from the people out here."

"Let me try."

"Here," he said. "Hold it in one hand like this and use the other for a perch."

The jay returned. He squawked, upset at the change in the game. "See, I told you," she said.

"Just give him a second, he's got to make sure."

The bird looked at her, then looked back at Sam. He ruffled his feathers and cried out an ugly shriek before squirting a pasty white mess onto the railing and flying off.

"Well, there you have it," she said, surveying the puddle on the iron rail. "Name is Jennifer, Jennifer Holman." She extended her hand.

"Sam Mann." Her hand was soft, like creamy suede. He didn't want to let go.

"Sam Mann? Economical."

"Yeah, I've heard it all. Sammann filet. Sammann to watch over me. Sammannchanted evening."

"O.K., I get the picture," she said before he could go any further. "Are you here for the wedding?" She didn't recall ever having seen him, and he didn't seem like the type that either Henry or Leah would invite.

He nodded. "I'm one of the musicians. You?"

"I guess you could say I'm sort of a member of the family." She pushed her hat back and smiled.

Perfection. Just the way Sam liked it, everything too right, and then a little flaw, just the way he'd create if it were up to him. Sam loved little imperfections; it was false perfection that brought out the evil in him. Her smile: bright white teeth, one front slightly overlapping; moist lips glistening in the afternoon light. Her nose: smooth but with a slight downward curve; no chiseled rhinoplasty lines. Her eyes: blue like the ocean behind her, but one open just a bit more than the other, a tiny blue vein beneath it, barely visible.

Perfection. It was hard to assess her body, other than her incredible legs, which she bounced as she sat there, eyes closed, as if she wanted him to take inventory.

"I'd have thought you had some sort of job that had to do with animals," she said, finally opening her eyes. "Vet or pet shrink, something like that."

"I love animals, you're right. And they seem to like me too. But I could never be a vet; I'd probably crumble if I had to deal with an animal in pain. Animals are great, though; you know where you stand around them. They aren't *hypocritical* like people."

Jennifer noticed the way he spat the word. "Did you have pets growing up?"

"No, my mother wouldn't let me. She was this neat-freak, the worst kind. Whenever I asked, she always said, 'They are so dirty. Ooh, the fe-ces...the fe-ces...I can't bear it.'"

Jennifer laughed. His impersonation, yelling "fe-ces" as he waved his arms, had captured the attention of everyone sitting on the deck.

Sam continued. "She was the height of hypocrisy. It actually killed her."

Immediately, Jennifer chilled. *His mother?* She wasn't sure she was ready to go there, especially considering the coldness of his eyes as he reminisced.

"After all the neat-freaking, do you know what she did? Her hobby?"

Jennifer shook her head, afraid to ask.

"She was a mushroom lover. You know, those people that go on truffle and wild mushroom hunts? They take picnics with fine wine and stuff, collect mushrooms, and act superior. Half the time it was all the way over in France. She always called herself a 'truffiere' with a thick French accent, her nose in the air. You know what killed her?"

Sam appeared agitated; Jennifer was beginning to wish that she'd sat somewhere else. "She got some bad 'shrooms man! And you know what? They grow in fe-ces!"

Sam took a sip of chardonnay between tunes, resigned to being wallpaper music. It was all right; much better than people scowling while he tried to figure out what they wanted. Path of least resistance vs. artistic integrity. He shook his head, chugged another gulp, and began a slow *ostinato* that led to "How Deep is the Ocean."

Might as well play water tunes, see if anyone notices. Mrs. Murchison, the bride's mother, was dressed in a woolen poncho that looked like a prop from the movie *The Sandpiper, tres* Big Sur. She was snapping her fingers in time as she greeted the guests. *One convert.*

"What you're playing isn't music!"

Sam looked up, startled. A tiny old man with jowls like an unhappy basset hound stood in front of him. "I wish you had told me that twenty years ago. It would have saved me a lot of trouble."

The retort seemed to stun Krieger. Pascal rapidly approached, carrying a plate of fruit. "Mr. Krieger, the man is playing."

"Pascal, let go of me!" He turned back to Sam. "You should play songs like "I'm Looking Over a Four-leaf Clover," or anything from *Finian's Rainbow.* This crap isn't music!"

Pascal shrugged apologetically and led Frank Krieger to a nearby table. Sam avoided eye contact with the old fart, but could feel his stare. *Shit.* He tried "Devil and the Deep Blue Sea"—still staring; "Beyond the Sea"—scowling. *Shit!* The craggy old bastard was standing now, approaching. He was closing quickly. *Where the hell is his attendant?*

Krieger rested against his cane as he breathed on Sam. There was no way to ignore him. Sam looked up. "Have I told you lately that I loved you?" Krieger requested.

Now he wants Van Morrison? "No, you haven't!" Sam snapped. "And frankly, I'm getting tired of it. You never write, you never call!"

Krieger leaned back, teetering on his heels before managing to right himself with his cane. He peered, one eye almost closed, as if sizing Sam up. Finally, he shook his head and ambled back to his seat.

"Don't let him bother you. He's a bit irritable, and a lot outspoken."
It was Jennifer, bringing Sam a fresh glass of wine.

"It doesn't bother me. At least you know where he stands."

"Oh, that's right. You and hypocrites!"

Sam looked for a sign, unable to tell whether she was mocking him or not. She was impossible to read. "Thanks for the taste."

"Hey kid! C'mere!"

Sam rested his guitar against the windows in the corner, put his watch back on his wrist, and scanned the room. He saw the old man waving. "Bring me a Jameson's . . . neat!"

Sam looked around, hoping Krieger was talking to someone else.

"It's O.K. Do it!"

He walked to the bar, got a shot, and went to the table. "Here you go. Are you sure it's all right?"

"It won't kill me, don't worry. Tell me something?"

"Sure." Sam braced himself.

"If you're so fucking funny, how come you ain't famous?"

Sam winced. That word.

"What's your name?"

"Sam Mann."

"Mann . . . Irish? Short for McMahon?"

"Jewish."

"Better for you; Jews are better musicians. Can't sing for shit, though."

"Who are you?" Sam asked.

"Frank Krieger, pleased to meet you." Krieger held out his hand; it shook like a leaf in the wind. He held Sam's until their eyes finally met. "Shit, I thought I'd have to wait all day."

"Huh?"

"You kids today." He shook his head. "Never look anyone in the eye. I waited until you gave me some recognition, some respect. I like to see who I'm dealing with. Especially if I'm shaking hands with a Jew." He laughed.

"So you get off by fucking with people, and if that doesn't work you insult them."

Krieger's head snapped back and his stare hardened as the table went quiet. Pascal began to get up to interrupt.

Finally, that gurgling wet laugh again. "You're good." He slugged Sam on the jaw, as hard as his eighty-plus years would allow.

"Well, if you've had enough," Sam said, getting up, "I'll leave you to your misery."

"Wait a sec, kid. Here. I appreciated talking to you." Krieger peeled off a $100 bill and pressed it into Sam's hand. He took another and ripped it in half. "You can have the other half if you can play "When you're Smiling."

Sam smiled and grabbed the torn bill. He bent down to whisper in Krieger's ear: "If you hit me again, I'll knock those dentures back to your dentist's office . . . with your head attached."

Krieger cocked his head back, alarmed.

Sam felt Pascal's sudden anxiety, as if he were trying to figure out what to do. Sam lightly slapped Krieger's face and they both broke into laughter. Pascal sighed; Sam walked away.

"Fuck you," Krieger said.

The seven-piece band had set up at the far end of the dining room. Mrs. Murchison had given Sam the rest of the cocktail party off so the band could do a sound check before dinner. Most of the guests had moved out to the deck to watch the sunset, or had gone back to their rooms to change.

Sam went to the bar. Amidst *check one, check two* and *check-check,* he heard voices, animated yet subdued, behind him. The woman sounded like Jennifer: "You can't just give me notice!"

The man was arrogant: "Well, it appears I am."

"I won't let you."

"There's nothing you can do about it. Plus, I know you have a good nest egg saved up, and I've always looked the other way in regards to your little embezzlements, haven't I?"

"Embezzlements? Get real! I've always looked the other way from those rubs, those looks, all those suggestions. I should have let you set me up in that condo downtown, shouldn't I?"

Sam couldn't turn around without giving away that he was eavesdropping. He tried to listen, but the bartender started steaming milk for a cappuccino. As the foaming subsided, he heard the woman's voice again: "*True?* You think that matters? People believe what they want. You know that."

The male voice, a feeble attempt at contrition: "Well, what can I do, Jenn? What do you want me to do?"

"I'll let you know. I need to think about it."

"Just don't make a big deal out of it, O.K.? And don't tell Henry. He doesn't even know about it yet. I was going to announce it tomorrow."

"You'd like that, wouldn't you?"

Out of the corner of his eye, Sam saw Jennifer march out the door. Then a man sat beside him and ordered a martini.

Percy Kreiger.

Sam left a five on the bar—Percy hadn't even noticed him sitting there—and decided to walk to the point to get a better view of the sunset. At the door he saw a vase of white Ecuadorian roses, each bud almost as big as a newborn baby's head. "Take one," Mrs. Murchison suggested. "They're beautiful, aren't they?"

"Yes ma'am, they sure are."

The walkway to the point had a berm on the left side, and a sign: Please don't walk on the rooftops. They were dugouts, apartments carved into the hillside. "What a view!" Sam said, imagining himself in front of a fire, watching the orange globe descend into the sea.

To his right were tree houses—in a loose sense of the word—perched on beams anchored to tree trunks. At the end of the trail, he came to a carved bench, smooth and surreal, as if Gaudi had sculpted it especially for the setting. As the sun sank, the faraway water's edge seemed to be ablaze.

A doe and her fawn approached. Sam smiled. "Thought some of you would be around here. Noticed all the scat on the walkway earlier this afternoon."

The spotted baby investigated curiously, while the mother held back. "I know you love these," Sam said, waving the rose, sure they could smell its strong aroma. "I won't hurt you," he promised.

The doe took a step closer, sniffing intently. The fawn moved in, forcing the doe into a quick decision. She had to keep her baby safe, but the only way to do that was to walk right up to Sam. "It's O.K.," he whispered, holding the rose at arm's length.

The doe took a quick bite, then darted back, the fawn retreating with her.

"See, I won't hurt you," Sam said.

The fawn approached again. This time the mother stood her ground, watching. Sam held the rose close to his chest. "If you want it, you have to come get it."

The fawn took a few whiffs and walked up to the bench. Sam put his hand on its back as it nibbled daintily at the petals. The mother watched, concerned.

"Can I pet it?" a voice interrupted.

Both deer fled, bounding high above the thick growth down the steep hillside.

"I can't believe that," Jennifer said. "They came right up to you!"

"Roses," Sam explained. "They can't resist them."

"I wish you had held on to that baby. It was so cute. I've never touched one. What did it feel like?"

"You can't hold them back. That's why they come to me, they

know I'll let them go. They can sense it."

"I guess you're right," Jennifer said, frowning as if she'd been reprimanded. "Still, what did it feel like?"

"The baby was soft, trembling while it nibbled."

She sat down next to Sam on the bench; the sun was almost gone. The sky had turned to pink, the cliffs to the south a soft green. Jennifer had changed; she wore jeans and a denim blouse with a black suede yoke. A pair of tan hiking boots completed the change to rustic. Sam hadn't noticed before how small her feet were; the pink shoes had exaggerated their impact.

Sam wanted to ask her about the argument he'd heard, but knew he couldn't. As the light faded he felt the temperature dropping. "So, Jennifer, what is it that you do?"

"Property management," she said in a faraway tone. "Real estate."

"Are you related to the bride or the groom?"

He was fishing. But she wasn't biting.

"It's a long story and you look like you're freezing. We'd better get you back before you catch pneumonia."

They got up and went back toward the resort, each taking in the serenity of the setting. Sam wanted to hold her hand, to share it, as if he needed to have someone else acknowledge that it really existed. There was stillness, a quiet that Sam hadn't known for a long time, and with it came a peace, a sense of fulfillment that almost obscured the *feeling*.

Almost.

Near the restaurant, he flagged down one of the roving resort vehicles and got in. "I'll see you in a few minutes. Got to change," he explained. "My room is way down the hill. They keep the musicians in the projects."

He looked back as they drove off, and saw Jennifer's silky brown hair flowing gently in the breeze.

Small yellow globes designed to look like candles barely illuminated the road as Sam walked back up the hill. The night air was cool and bracing. Countless stars had created a dense canopy, their brightness in the moonless sky giving his skin an silvery hue. The scent of pine mixed with the faint sweet stink of a distant skunk wafted through the property, suspended in the motionless quiet.

Sam arrived at the Sierra Mar restaurant out of breath. The room embraced him with its competing aromas: pheasants roasting, bread baking, oak and madrone on the fire. He wanted to stop the world, to cling as long as he could to this fleeting second of perfection, but Mrs. Murchison's shrill voice shattered the moment.

"Mr. Mann," her mohair poncho swayed as she lifted her arm, "Mr. Krieger seems to have taken quite a liking to you. He requested that you be seated at the family table. I trust you'll find a way to both play and partake of dinner. I'll leave it up to you."

"Thanks." Sam walked to the bar, looking for Jennifer. A loud *pop* followed by a *bang* caused him to jump back: a champagne cork hit the copper flue of the fireplace, right next to him. A gaggle of young voices broke out in laughter. Sam eyed a table of twenty-year-olds, frat-types with dates, already drunk and boisterous.

"Children," Jennifer said as she approached Sam from the deck behind him.

Sam couldn't tell if her tone was nostalgic or disgusted. He turned, hoping her face would give it away, and was taken aback by her beauty, that imperfect perfection. All he could muster in response was, "Good shot, though."

Sam was seated at the far end of the table, next to Frank Krieger, across from Pascal, making it easier for him to get up and play between courses. Jennifer was in the center, not far from the father of the groom. Even from a distance it was obvious that there was trouble between the two of them. *She's definitely a Krieger. By insinuation, if not by blood or marriage.*

"Percy!" Frank Krieger yelled after abruptly waking from a snooze.

The elder Krieger made a few vague signals, the middle Krieger passed them on, and few minutes later the piano started up at the other end of the room.

The old man winked at Sam. "I found it pretty rude to expect you to jump up and down. Plus, it was making me dizzy. You'll have plenty of time to play. Enjoy your meal."

After the plates had been cleared for the next course, the bridal couple began working the room. "Ah, Henry and Leah," Jennifer announced. "To the happy couple!" Sam saw Percy squirm, as if he expected Jennifer to say something else. She smiled and winked, toying with him.

The table applauded and drank a toast. Henry Krieger seemed ill at ease with the attention. His pudgy cheeks made him look ten years younger than his twenty-six. He wore slacks and a Post Ranch polo shirt, probably bought that day. Leah, however, was basking in the attention. She was taller than Henry, and her lifeless blond hair hung straight down, framing washed-out blue eyes. The braces on her teeth caught the fire's glow.

Henry moved to the head of the table. "How are you, Grampa?"

"Doing fine, Henry. I came by to see you yesterday. I had another dream, but by the time I'd had a drink with your father I'd forgotten it. It was a good one. Like '9:20 Special!'"

"You sure called that one, Grampa. I'm glad you talked me into it. It was the best move of last year, you know."

"'9:20 Special?'" Sam asked.

"That's right," Henry answered, wondering who the new face at the family table was. He began to tell the story, but the old man kept interrupting. "You tell it, Grampa," Henry said as Leah pulled on his arm and led him to the next table.

The story dragged on; Sam was sorry he'd asked. Finally, after the girl, the red hair, the scent of heather, the old man got to the "9:20 Special." He started humming the tune.

"That's it!" Sam said. He began humming along with the old

man, both hopelessly out of tune.

Krieger's eyes lit up. "You know that song? It's got to be at least twenty years older than you are!"

"So are most of the songs I play," Sam explained.

"My favorite was Harry James, although Count Basie's version was pretty good. Once I heard the James band playing it at the Palace Hotel, in the grand ballroom."

"Have you heard Zoot Sims' version? It's a small band thing, really great."

"Zoot? What kind of name is Zoot?"

"It's a nickname. He's one of the greatest saxophone players of all time. Here…" Sam fished a card out of his wallet and handed it to the old man. "Give me a call. Let me know where to find you and I'll get you a copy. You'll love it."

Krieger took the card, examined it carefully, and stashed it in his jacket pocket as if it were a cherished gift. "Thanks, kid."

Sam snuck away during one of Krieger's naps to spell the piano player. He noodled for a moment before starting up the riff from "9:20 Special."

The old man raised his head, seeming disoriented, unsure if it was a dream or not. When he saw Sam playing, he smiled and started to get up. Mrs. Murchison tried to help, but stepped back when he chanted his mantra: "Fuck you."

He tottered unsteadily to the bandstand, standing so close that Sam could feel his breath. He peeled off another crisp bill and placed it in Sam's pocket. "Thanks again, kid."

Sam found it hard to figure out which family had all the bread. Since the bride's family usually got caught with most of the bill, he had assumed it was the Murchisons. But the way Mrs. Murchison was kissing ass, combined with the placement of the Kriegers' table, gave him the distinct impression they were the rich ones. *What does it matter? I'm sure the check will clear.*

One short set and it was over. The staff came and moved all the

51

tables to make space for dancing. Sam found a comfortable perch at the bar.

"Mr. Mann?"

God I hate that! "Yes sir."

"My name is Percy Krieger."

"It's my son, Henry, who's getting married tomorrow. I'm grateful that you are playing, adding so much to the atmosphere. You sure have made a big impression on my father. He wanted me to give this to you." He handed Sam yet another hundred dollars. "I'll tell you, he can be a tough old goat. I'm sure you've earned this."

"Thanks." Sam grunted. He had taken an instant dislike to Percy, and was glad to hear his departing footsteps and know he was alone again, at last.

Or so he thought.

"Are you going to sit there all night or are you going to ask me to dance?" It was Jennifer; she'd once again managed to sneak up on him.

"Do you want to dance?"

"Not especially. I was just out looking at the stars through the telescope on the deck. It's beautiful, that is, when you can see through the cigar smoke. All the kids are out there sucking away on *Cubanos*, because they think it makes them look older."

"And it's a sure bet that if they keep it up, it will," said Sam, as he got up to follow her.

The stars were ablaze, a blanket of white thrown over a sea of black. Jennifer elbowed her way in to the railing and commandeered the telescope.

"That's Mars," she said after a long search. "You can tell from the color." The smokers seemed to resent the invasion of the middle-aged astronomer; they snuffed out their turd-like cylinders and headed inside for the dance floor.

"I don't see a thing," Sam said, peering into the telescope.

"I just did that to get rid of those kids. I wouldn't know Mars from Pluto. It worked, though."

Sam hardly knew what to think of the vision that stood before him. She could appear at will, could make up lies and effortlessly manipulate situations, and she had something on Percy Krieger—so much so that the prick actually feared her.

She smiled, waiting for him to say something, in no hurry to help him. The band inside began playing: *Blap-boom-boom*, a drum intro to a 12/8 ballad, doo-wop style, the singer high, piercing: "For all we know . . . we may never meet again."

Sam heard himself saying, "How about that dance?"

Twice during the tune, people came out to smoke or get air, then turned around and went back in as soon as they realized that they had stumbled uninvited into a private party. As the song ended—an alto sax wailing a long cadenza on the final chord—Jennifer and Sam continued to dance. The rhythm had become their own, and only when the band started into a raucous rockabilly number were they even aware that they'd been unaware.

"Follow me," Jennifer said, taking Sam's hand. She led him off the deck, away from the bar and restaurant. She opened a gate Sam hadn't even known was there. "Voilà!"

It was a pool, set on the edge of the cliff overlooking the ocean. The water at the far edge spilled over the cliff. Steam rose from the surface, and the light at the bottom looked like the beacon from a faraway lighthouse. "Not bad, huh? Let's try it out."

"Now?"

"When else?"

"What about them?" Sam pointed back in the direction of the sounds of music and voices. "Won't they hear us?"

"What if they do?"

"I don't have a bathing suit." He was running out of excuses.

"You do what you want to," Jennifer said, beginning to unsnap her blouse. "What are you looking at? It's not a peepshow."

"Sorry," Sam said, turning, wishing he had a rearview mirror.

"The moon just came up," he said, stalling. He heard a whoosh of water, a torrent spilling over the far wall.

"You can turn around now."

He saw her, immersed in the steam, her silhouette rippling in the water. Her breasts floated at the surface, glistening in the pool lighting from below and the moonlight from above.

"Why don't you turn off the light. I'll bet the only reason they have it is to keep people from falling in. We can warn anyone that shows up. The switch is over there, next to the towels."

"You seem to have been here before."

"I did some reconnaissance during daylight hours, while you were cavorting with wildlife. Come on in, it's just right."

Sam took a look around to make sure they were alone, then kicked off his shoes. Jennifer watched intently. "It's not a show," he mocked.

"I'll be the judge of that," she said, smiling.

"Hey, I gave you some privacy when you asked for it."

"Yes, you did. But I still would have gotten in either way."

"*Now* you tell me."

"It was just a test."

"Did I pass or fail?"

"That's for me to know."

They quietly soaked in the tub as the party next door raged on at fever pitch. Sam sat across from Jennifer; she seemed to glow in the moonlight, holding on to the back wall while she floated. Her rounded toes wiggled as they broke the surface. *God, even her toes are cute,* Sam thought.

She flicked some water toward him with her feet. "So, Sam, you seem like a man with a lot on his mind."

She'd caught him off guard again; this time she hadn't appeared out of nowhere, but she might as well have. "What makes you say that?"

"I don't know. Like you're preoccupied, but not exactly. Like you've got a secret, but one you're not totally comfortable with. Something you don't trust, so you act like it isn't there, that way you won't screw it up."

"Wow."

"Close?"

"Yes, close." It was as good a definition of the *feeling* as he'd heard yet. "I just got tied up with this agent and he seems to be really connected, plus he really believes in me. Everything out of his mouth is what I want to hear, but it's what I've heard more than a few times. I'm so close I can taste it, but I'm scared to believe it."

Jennifer watched him flick at the water with his finger; saw his vulnerability, that he was afraid to look up. The wake sent out a perfect pattern of delicate circles, waves that appeared as fragile as the fawn she'd seen him with earlier in the day. She wanted to go to him, to hold him, to tell him that his worth was already a part of him, not something given out for a job well done; that he held the answer, that integrity and hypocrisy were only vague concepts, not things to be ruled by or to be afraid of.

She swam across, sidling up next to him to offer a hug. "I think it will all work out for you, Sam."

Then, before he could answer, she pulled herself out of the water, onto the poolside.

"Sounds like the party is getting closer." She threw him a towel. "Dry off and get dressed. Let's get out of here."

While walking down the walkway, the moon beaming down, they heard a splash and a loud scream.

"Oops," Jennifer giggled, "I forgot to turn the light back on."

She held Sam's hand and led him out to the point. "So, Sam Mann, do you have a wife or girlfriend?"

"Not right now," Sam answered. "I, uh..." He stopped and crouched down, peering into the darkness.

"What?!"

"I heard something... over there." He pointed into the bushes.

"Let's get out of here, then!" Jennifer said, taking his hand. "I don't want to see your Saint Francis act at this time of night. If anything's out there, it's probably a mountain lion."

He kissed her, to stop her from saying more. After a long embrace, she pulled away and smiled. Her eyes seemed bright in the night's darkness.

"Let's go," she said again.

"Where?"

"Well, we can't go to my place," she said. "I'm sort of bunking with the old man and Pascal. I have my own room, but it isn't private."

"My place is clear on the other end of the ranch. I guess we could try to get a ride—it's a bitch of a walk."

Jennifer stood in the clearing, sucking on her finger, thinking. Then she giggled as she led him down a gravel walkway. "The perfect place—the library! I saw it today. It's out of the way. If the Murchisons are like the Kriegers, there's nothing to worry about. The library is the last place you'll find them."

Still, Sam searched the shadows as they entered, expecting to find someone. Shelves of dusty books lined the dark wooden walls; two wing chairs, a coffee table, and a couch with wide stripes sat against the wall under the window. As Jennifer had predicted, it was deserted.

She turned off the lamp and pulled off her jeans. "Don't just stand there," she said. Sam barely had his shoes and pants off before she pushed him down onto the sofa. She sat on his lap facing him as she deftly guided him inside. She shivered, emitting a throaty wail, pulling open her blouse, the snaps ringing out a *staccato* cadence. She yanked Sam's shirt open, ripping off the buttons before pressing her bare chest against his.

"Ooh!" he sighed. Her skin was silky smooth, warm, still moist from the tub. He was drowning in her softness and scent, frustrated, unable to get his lips on all of her. Then he heard footsteps on the gravel path under the window.

"There's someone outside," he panted, not wanting her to stop—but wanting her to.

Jennifer froze in mid-thrust, trying to suppress her orgasmic spasms.

They both heard the steps as the visitor entered the room. Sam made out the outline of a man; he watched him walk to the end table by the door and reach for the lamp. He was just about to say something when the man stopped, as if sensing their presence on the couch. He pulled his hand away from the lamp and tiptoed out of the room.

"That was close," Sam said.

"I just came." Jennifer giggled. "And came and came. Must have been the hot tub, too. Anyway, I don't think he'll be back any time soon."

She pulled him over on top of her, wanting, demanding, more.

Tucked into the southeast side of San Bruno Mountain, around the corner from San Francisco's Cow Palace, the two-block stretch of downtown Brisbane was rocking. At the center of the drab little strip of mom-and-pop stores that hadn't changed for fifty years was DeMarco's 23 Club.

The marquee boasted: BILLY BARBER—PREMIER APPEARANCE. Although it was already after midnight, the second set was still underway, and there wasn't an empty parking space for two blocks.

The old-time cowboy bar was packed for the first time in months. Red lighting and dusty neon beer ads showing bucking horses, cowboy hats, and boots barely illuminated the yellowed posters on the wall. Two buffalo heads mounted above the stage had cobwebs hanging from their mouths, lichen-like threads that swayed in the barrage of decibels emanating from the bandstand below.

Aging ranchers and ranch hands, all drinking beer from the bottle, occupied every stool at the bar. The tables and booths alongside the dance floor had proprietary coats and purses flung over them—the line-dancer's version of barbed wire.

Leonard West stood at the end of the bar, smiling and pondering how soon he could book Billy Barber again.

The regulars were there, middle-aged Asian (mostly Filipino) line-dancing zealots who kept the club afloat during hard times. Even when Leonard had been unable to afford a band, they'd loyally line-danced to the jukebox. Their matching hats, boots and belts swayed in harmony as the lines twirled, sashayed, and dipped in perfect syncopation.

And tonight, adding to Leonard's bread and butter, Billy Barber had brought a pilgrimage of San Francisco's *Gay RoughRiders* to the Mecca of country music. All of them seemed flabbergasted that a place like this actually existed right under their noses, within spitting distance of the Castro.

Leonard chuckled as he watched the two groups interact on the dance floor. The *RoughRiders* were clad in black hats, leather vests, belts, and studded collars and cuffs. At least it was line-dancing. Leonard was only mildly concerned about what might happen if the cowboys at the bar got an eyeful of the gays couple-dancing. It had been so long since the club had been full; he couldn't remember the last time he'd hired a bouncer.

The leather chaps crowd had moved to the front, applauding as the tune ended, chanting for a new one. Leonard had trouble making out the title; something like "Poor Donna's Fool." It didn't really matter; if it was newer than 1959 he was sure not to know it anyway.

The chant grew into a rhythmic stomp, boots clacking on the wooden floor, resounding in a thunderous wave. The cowpokes at the bar were waving their hats. A fat little Korean squaw was jumping up and down, her lime-green dress and deerskin vest flopping, the fringe on her white boots whipping in time to the mob's imploring beat.

Billy was on the bandstand, wondering what to do. He'd made it—a shot at a real club, with history, not the usual gay bar or tourist venue that featured a different kind of music every night. DeMarco's, a place he'd always dreamed of headlining; although it had fallen from its once high standing, there was no denying history. All anyone had to do was look at the wall: 8×10s of every major star of the '50s, '60s, and '70s—Johnny Cash, Buck Owens, George Jones...Patsy Cline!

Billy had wanted to play it straight tonight, make it or break it on the merit of his music, yet, there in front of him was a wild throng, screaming for his newest gimmick tune, a *joke!*

"Well, folks," he drawled, adjusting the capo on his guitar, avoiding eye contact, "we kinda' planned a different tune for the end of this set..."

At the bar, Leonard heard the crowd groan, then chant: "Poor Donna's Fool, Poor Donna's Fool."

From the stage, Billy saw the *RoughRiders* mocking him, unbuttoning their flies.

"Might as well dance with the horse that brung ya'," Billy said, flashing his million-dollar smile. He turned to the band. "Well boys, you heard 'em."

The pedal steel whined out, *be-durp durp doowee*, and the band broke into a straight-out country groove. Leonard had trouble making out the words, but he saw that Billy had worked the crowd masterfully; they had retreated to their lines and were doing what looked like the *tush-push*, a sea of humanity moving in perfect unison. The tune was country but the words were strange, Leonard thought: no pickup, no dog, no *Donna?*

Then the lead guitar spanked out a pickup to the chorus, and the *Rough Riders* came in, on cue, in perfect sing-along harmony:

Down in Polk Gulch, they got a thing that's cool,
When the bars are crowded they can get four on a stool.
Man, these queers are the smartest in town,

They just take 'em and turn 'em upside dooownnnn.

As the crowd sang the last word, holding it as the chord rung out, the *Rough Riders* grouped in clusters of four, asses together, wriggling up and down in fake ecstasy as they held the *nnn*. The Asian contingent moved off the dance floor, looking on in horror. The cowboys all looked away and ordered another Bud.

Leonard laughed and went to his office, realizing that "Poor Donna's Fool" was "Four on a Stool," one of the dumbest gay-bar jokes he'd ever heard.

The band congregated in the dressing room behind the stage. Billy took off his hat and ran his hands through his hair. He'd seen Leonard West leave his perch at the end of the bar during the last tune, and he assumed that his premiere appearance at DeMarco's might as well have been billed as his farewell.

The door burst open. Jimm Dibbook materialized at the center of the room. Just behind him was Patty, the little blonde who'd let Billy into the office days before.

Jimm held a crumpled piece of paper. "That was great, Billy! You sure know how to work a room! I have that contract I told you about. We can record anytime you say, and I promise, it will be number one on the charts. *Trust me!*"

"Excuse me, sir!" A waitress entered the overcrowded cubicle. She pushed Jimm's arm out of the way. "This dressing room is for band members only—insurance regulations. Plus, I've been instructed by the lady at the door to collect your cover charge." She had two bottles of beer on her tray.

Jimm spun around. By the time he was facing her, his eye aflame with hate, his knife was out and opened. "Don't you ever touch me! I'm here to do business with this man. I'm *his* guest."

No one moved; no one spoke. The waitress dropped the tray and ran out. Beer gushed out of the bottles in foamy spurts onto the stained carpet as the thirsty musicians watched, afraid to rescue them.

"Uh, Jimm," Billy said, finally breaking the silence. "I told you the other day, I appreciate what you want to do for me . . . for us. But I think I'm going to decline at this time."

Jimm's eyes stayed angry. He flipped his knife closed and shoved it into the pocket of his parka. "Well, if you want to stay around here and be the darling of the faggot-bar scene, then go ahead. I'm offering you a ticket out of this filth, straight to Nashville. It's your choice," he said, thrusting the contract at him. "Come on, Patty, this place gives me the creeps."

They were both gone as suddenly as they had arrived. The band sat in an odd, collective quiet: *Did that really happen?*

"What's going on here?" Leonard asked, marching in behind two police officers.

"Nothing at all," Billy said.

"Tammy said there was somebody in here who threatened her with a knife."

"Just a booking agent," Billy answered.

"Where is he now?" one of the cops asked. "Do you know the man's name?"

"He left. I'm sorry, Mr. West. It won't happen again."

"I need to talk to you in my office, Billy." He turned to the cops. "I guess that's it. Thanks for coming so quick."

"Does Tammy want to press charges?"

"It's an isolated incident, and it's been taken care of, I promise," Leonard pleaded as the cops looked at each other, trying to decide what to do.

"O.K.," the senior of the two said. "No official call was put in. But I think we'll hang around, just to make sure he doesn't come back."

"I'd appreciate that," Leonard said, aware he had no choice in the matter. He hated cops at the bar: all of a sudden everyone would take to drinking soda water before skulking out the back.

"Sit down, Billy," Leonard said. His office was a small, poorly lit cubicle off the side of the liquor storage room. No personally inscribed pictures of stars—not what Billy had expected.

"Sorry 'bout that," Billy said. "I just met that weirdo a couple days ago."

"Don't worry about it. Those cops didn't understand, but believe me, when you said he was an agent, it made perfect sense." Leonard laughed.

Billy nervously laughed along. He started to explain about "Four on a Stool." "I have a pretty big following in the City, if you know what I mean, and..."

"Billy, you don't have to explain a damn thing, especially to me! I'm grateful to see this place full again. It's been a long time."

"I know, but hell, when I saw you walk away during that last tune—I mean, I don't want to be some novelty act."

"Don't be so hard on yourself," Leonard said. "You're a musician...an entertainer. Do you think Johnny Cash liked black shirts? He thought it was the stupidest gimmick in the world, and he hated his manager for it. He sat right in that chair and told me that if he could wish for one thing, it would be to wear something other than a black shirt."

Leonard was lying. He'd never spoken with Johnny Cash in his life.

"Really?" Billy asked, his eyes lighting up.

"Would I lie to you?" In the brighter light of the office, Leonard saw exactly how good-looking Billy was: flaxen mane and mustache, a smile that could charm the pants off anyone. "Here's the deal: you pick the nights you want, no more than two a month, don't want to burn you out. I'll call a few friends in Bakersfield, Fresno, and Turlock. And don't you worry about the clients, that's my job. Just give 'em what they want...that's your job."

"Sam, wake up, you're crushing me," Jennifer groaned.

"Oh," Sam said, disoriented. He felt her warm, soft body underneath him as he pushed himself off. His chest immediately felt chilled in the cool air of the library. "I must have passed out."

"You did, but not for long. You were so peaceful I didn't want to disturb you."

He sat up, trying to adjust his eyes to the darkness. "I can't find a damn thing in here. That guy must have turned off the lamp on the walkway."

"Either that or they're on a timer." Jennifer felt her way across the room to the lamp. She clicked it on and the room was flooded with harsh rays. Squinting, they gathered their clothes.

Sam put on his shirt. The buttons had been ripped off, leaving matching holes on both sides. He stared at it, still dazed, trying to remember what had happened.

"Sorry, I thought they were snaps, like mine." Jennifer found a kite in the corner, partially obscured by a wing chair. She unraveled some string, breaking off little pieces with her teeth. Then she sat on Sam's lap—facing him like she'd done earlier—and meticulously laced his shirt back together.

"This is the most domestic thing I've ever done," she said.

Sam doubted it; she seemed so at ease, so resourceful, so in control yet coquettish. *Who is she?*

"I wish you could sleep with me, but there are eyes everywhere. I'll leave first. You wait for a while, then head back to your place, O.K.?"

Sam wondered if she had a boyfriend after all. *Maybe he was here, or coming in tomorrow.* "O.K.," he agreed. "There are things I can occupy my time with here. Maybe I'll read the Bible."

"I think you did enough praying for one night—'Oh God . . . Oh God!'" She laughed and bent over to kiss him, her soft lips enveloping his soul. Then she was gone.

Sam trekked down the hill toward his cabin. The night air was bracing, but the faint scent of their sex seemed to hover and mix with pine. As he cut across the field in front of the pond, he heard the yipping of a coyote. It seemed close, in the trees just across the road.

He stopped, peered in the direction of the sound, and sat ... waiting.

Frogs bellowed in the nearby pond. The moon illuminated the weeds, giving them a shimmery hue. Sam caught some movement at the edge of the woods, and there it was: the coyote trotted across the road, the ticking of its nails on the asphalt an *allegro* tempo, its range high above the low rustle of the treetops in the faint breeze.

"Hey, little fella," Sam said, his voice soft.

The coyote stopped, peered in his direction and raised its nose, sniffing the air, assessing the danger.

"You're probably on a turkey hunt. I'm the only turkey here tonight."

The coyote began to move again, making a wide circle around Sam, all the while keeping its eyes fixed on him. Its coat seemed to glow in the soft moonlight. A faraway yip, a call, echoed through the bowl created by the pond. The coyote stared back into the forest, and then moved toward Sam.

As it approached, Sam saw that its eyes were silver-gray, moon-colored, the exact color of the light, as if they were free of pigment. When it got within five feet, the coyote stopped and sat, nonchalantly licking its balls, unconcerned with Sam and any danger he might present.

"You're a cocky little guy."

The coyote moved in to sniff Sam, then rolled over, scratching his back against the seam of Sam's pants.

"You are a stinky little guy, too." The stench was rancid meat, as if the coyote had been rolling in a decaying carcass. "No wonder you're alone. And hungry too. I'll bet your prey can smell you coming a mile away."

Sam petted the top of its head; suddenly the coyote snapped and twisted, then headed for the trees.

"Hey!" Sam lunged and barely managed to grab the band of his wristwatch from the coyote's mouth. "You little thief." He wrestled it free, ending up stretched out on the ground, looking up at the starry sky. The coyote growled and jumped on his chest, its blank eyes staring into his own, the foul breath nearly asphyxiating him. Sam lay frozen, terrified.

The standoff ended suddenly, the coyote plunging into his chest, near his jugular. Sam heard a rip—a tearing sound—as he managed to roll over and scramble to his feet. The coyote jumped back, a piece of kite string hanging out of his mouth, caught between his bottom teeth like dental floss. Then he cackled and retreated with his bounty.

The putrid stench clung to Sam all the way to his apartment. He took off his clothes and turned on the shower. As he waited for it to heat up, he pondered his stupidity and good fortune. "That fucking thing could have killed me!"

In the morning, Jennifer reread the entry from the night before. It was scribbled, written in the darkness of the moonlight:

I wish I could figure out a way to get him to let me help him. This thing he has with animals, I don't quite get it. They're the best judges of character, aren't they? His trouble with integrity, hypocrisy, he says it like he's spitting out a bad piece of food, and it's exactly the thing I can help him with. Let's keep our fingers crossed. Meanwhile, what to do about Percy? Where am I going to go?

The point was awash in flowers. A small trellis had been set up; ivy intertwined with white lilies encircled the bridal couple, the Pacific Ocean a spectacular backdrop. Leah was clad in white lace; her bountiful bouquet seemed to explode in her grasp. She stood barefoot, wiggling her toes as she intoned, "... for as long as we shall inhabit this worldly plane."

Henry was ill at ease, his eyes furtive as he sped through his recitation. The personalized vows, made up by Leah and her mother, were so full of post-hippie New-Age rhetoric that Sam expected a mention of granola or sprouts.

He played light *arpeggiated* chords on Mrs. Murchison's last-minute choice, the "Pachelbel Canon in D," known as the "Taco Bell" to musicians. *The world's first New-Age tune,* Sam thought. Leah's mother turned and gave him the thumbs-up as he melodically drifted through the deepest regions of the flavor vanilla.

Jennifer stood on the edge of the crowd, glaring at Percy Krieger. Sam was glad to see that she had no boyfriend in tow.

A table of gifts filled the foyer at the entrance to Sierra Mar. Champagne flowed freely as the sunrays filtered into the restaurant. Frank Krieger sat in a chair in the corner and snoozed, drooling onto his green jacket.

Sam played as a buffet lunch was served. Then a clinking quieted the room. Percy Krieger stood, his wife, Marsha, hanging on his arm. "I'd like to thank the Murchisons for putting all of this together, all of you who took the time to grace us with your presence on this special occasion, and most of all, Henry and Leah."

Thunderous applause erupted, with hoots and hollers from the younger contingent. Percy continued, tapping a butter knife against his champagne flute. "Before we cut the cake, I have an announcement to make." He waited until the room quieted. "Marsha and I have decided to move to Palm Springs. I know you're thinking 'what does this have to do with anything?' Well, it has a lot to do with this happy event, because we have decided to deed Kinsale to Henry and Leah as a wedding present."

Mrs. Murchison rushed up and put her arms around her daughter as the well-wishers heartily applauded and cheered. In the flurry, Sam caught Jennifer's cold stare, directed at Percy before she turned to stalk out of the room.

After watching her exit, Percy lifted his glass. "I trust the new landlords will give us ample time to vacate."

The tables were moved and the cake was brought in. The band started up in the back of the room; Sam packed up and waited for someone on the hotel staff to move his equipment. The gig was over.

"Mr. Mann?"

God, I wish she wouldn't do that! "Yes, Mrs. Murchison?"

"Thank you for your contribution to my daughter's wedding. Your music, especially today, was perfect. I trust that you got your check when you arrived and that it was sufficient."

"It was generous, thank you. And it's been a pleasure, I assure you. Convey my congratulations to your daughter, will you?"

"Of course. Please feel free to stay on as long as you'd like. You have your room until tomorrow afternoon." She whisked off without even a goodbye.

Sam went out on the walkway in search of Jennifer. *Where did she go?* He heard the distinct whine of a Japanese engine: a sewing machine in distress. He looked down through the trees to the road below and saw Jennifer's white Miata, top down, racing toward the gate, her pink scarf flowing in her wake.

That gig was over too.

Monday morning, the phone woke Sam at eight-thirty. "Hello, Mr. Mann?"

That was always the worst thing to hear the first thing in the day. *I hope it's not an omen.* "Yes?"

"My name is Pascal Rodriguez. I met you at the wedding. I am the nurse for Mr. Frank Krieger."

"Oh, yeah." *9:20 Special.* "Sure." He cleared his throat, hoping that Pascal would realize how early it was and offer to call back later.

No such luck. "I was wondering if you would like a job. You see . . . I am going to school for a license and I need help with Mr. Krieger. He like you very much."

"Look, Pascal—it is Pascal? I don't do that kind of work. I'm a musician."

"Pascal, *jes*, and that does not matter. When I started I was fixing this apartment. He liked me, so his son give me the job. Now, I want to get certified for eldercare; it raises my pay."

Eldercare? "Still, I don't know how I could help you." Sam sat up in the bed and took a drink of stale water from the glass by his bedside.

"All you do is stay with him. You can play your guitar. He likes to go for rides in his car. You will not have to shave him or feed him or give him bath, only take him for lunch. He pays for that, too! Fifteen dollars an hour."

"Can I think about it?" The bread was low, but the sight of those crisp Ben Franklins on his bureau piqued Sam's interest. "I'll tell you what: why don't I come by tomorrow and we'll talk about it? Where are you?"

"Cathedral Hill," he said. Sam wrote down the number. "Eleven o'clock? We take you for lunch. Thank you, Mr. Mann!"

It didn't sound any better with a Spanish accent.

Jimm was already there, waiting. Sam noticed the stack of papers perched on the edge of the table. He expected them to cascade onto the floor just before he could get them in his hand. The *feeling* was back.

"I hope you're in the mood for some good news."

What an opening! It sure beat the shit out of Mr. Mann! "What you got?"

"Here is the contract for your book—standard publishing stuff. Just to show you my heart is in the right place, I waived my claim to any of the royalties. I'll just take my commission from the advance."

"Advance?"

He handed Sam a check for $2,000 from Music Arts. Sam stared at it as if expecting it to disappear from his hand.

"They'll send the proofs in a month or so. My commission on things like that is twenty percent, also standard."

"Twenty percent?" The highest Sam had ever heard of was fifteen.

"Yeah." Challenging eyes; not quite angry, just a stare-down. "This is management stuff, Sam. You're thinking of booking. In the next contracts you'll see the things you're thinking about." Jimm shook his head and snickered as he took a sip from his glass of iced tea, as if he had just told himself a joke.

Sam felt no need to argue; he *had* the check, plus, cash in his pocket. He could outdo Jimm—show him where he was coming from. "Will you take cash?"

"Sure."

"Give me a receipt when you get around to it."

They ordered food and ate quietly. Sam was afraid to ask about the messy pile of papers, yet his eye was constantly drawn to them.

When the plates had been cleared, Jimm finally asked: "Are you ready to get down to some business."

"Sure!" Sam answered, nearly jumping out of his skin.

"These are contracts, one of which I showed you before. Did you get a chance to look at it?"

Sam nodded.

"Good. First of all, here is the record contract."

Sam's eyes lit up as he pulled it from Jimm's hand.

"I told you we're going to place you in a small, relatively new company. The owner is a friend of mine, Paul Goddard. He's a big fan of yours, and he's committed to making this work. I'll get you to the top of the charts, then we'll have the big boys coming for you—Columbia or Verve."

Sam nodded. Jimm continued: "We'll go into the studio as soon as you can and burn the discs. With the new technology we can have this released in a matter of weeks. Paul already has a high profile on the Internet, which will just be icing on the cake. *My* expertise is airplay and sales. Check out the figures. I take it that two thousand up front for you is acceptable. It just comes out of your royalties. With my production expertise and your playing we can probably produce this thing for spit. We'll be in the black by the beginning of summer."

Sam was swimming. *So much, so fast.* "We haven't even talked concept yet."

"You tell me. Remember our conversation? I'm the producer, you're the artist. You tell me what you want and I'll make sure it makes it to the CD. Which brings us to the other contract. I don't want to sign this without that. I need some protection."

"Well, Jimm, my only problem is in the wording of a few things." Sam hesitated. He didn't want to lose that record deal, just when it was almost in his grasp.

"Such as?" Jimm called for the waiter to refill his iced tea. "Do you want a drink?"

"Yeah, thanks. Chardonnay, please."

Sam waited to speak until the wine was delivered and he'd had a sip. The crispness of the taste seemed to cut through, loosening his tongue. "I have a problem with the wording of the title. It says 'exclusive' management and booking contract. I intended to keep working with a few bookers and promoters that I've worked with over the years. Besides, isn't it illegal to represent someone that way? Conflict of interest?"

"Not anymore." Jimm sighed. "Hey, I thought you wanted to be a *star.* If you're happy to just keep playing those nickel-and-dime gigs, go right ahead. I don't want any part of that shit, anyway."

Sam panicked. Jimm seemed to be shifting in his chair, ready to call for the check. "You got to understand, Jimm, I've been doing this for a long time, and until my income profile changes, I need that work." *Income profile? Did I actually say that?*

"I'll tell you what," Jimm said, as if he'd just thought of it, "I'll change it to non-exclusive booking. See?" He added the *non* and initialed it, handing over the pen for Sam to do as well. He pulled out a yellow lined pad from the bottom of the stack and began to write. "So, what I need to know is, *do* you want me to represent you and get gigs?"

"Of course," Sam pleaded.

"O.K." Jimm wrote down *O.K.* "What you have to understand is, I'm not going to call people when you are already working the area with others and undercutting my prices. Don't you see? That would be embarrassing and very bad business for both of us."

"I see your point. But I have a lot of contacts, including some that might be good for both of us."

"I don't understand where you're going with this, Sam. I'm talking big gigs, good money. You can't just take every chickenshit gig that comes along. You're going to have to decide: stay the way you are, or become something bigger."

Maybe he's right... got to shut some doors before I open new ones. Hell, I can always do that Krieger gig for bread. Sure would be nice to have someone deal with all the bullshit. "What is it exactly you want me to do?"

"For now, concentrate on your CD. Do any tune-up gigs you need to, and keep me abreast of your schedule. Write it down or email it to me. I'll put it in the contract that it's non-exclusive, but if you undermine me..."

The implied threat was frightening. "Don't worry," Sam said. "I really want this, Jimm. All we need to do is communicate."

71

"You're right. I don't want you to feel that I'm taking anything from you. I don't need your money. I just need to know that you won't screw up anything I work hard to put together."

"How about if I send any inquiries to you?"

"We could do that. But you realize, that kind of makes me your exclusive agent."

Sam thought it over. It started to have a nice ring to it. He read through the rest of the contract. "Shouldn't the percentage change if I generate the work?"

"Of course," Jimm sighed. "You've dealt with a lot of shysters, haven't you? O.K., how about this?" Jimm scribbled figures on the yellow pad, pointing as he spoke. "Fifteen percent for normal gigs, five percent for gigs that you bring to the agency, and twenty percent for feature gigs?"

"Feature gigs?"

"TV shows, concerts that we co-produce, recordings—things that generate more work for us. Hell, five percent is nothing, and the gigs you bring in are going to be as much work for us as the ones we find. But hey, I'll do this to prove to you that I'm shooting straight. Sam you're just going to have to *trust me* sometime."

Percy firmly shut the door to the library. Jennifer wondered why he'd picked this room to have it out. *I guess it's because no one ever comes in.* She remembered the last time she had been in a library, bouncing on Sam's lap.

Percy slowly moved around the desk and opened the curtain. The glare of the afternoon light was harsh. He sat and rocked back and forth, the old chair squeaking under his weight. "I don't really understand why we have to have this discussion, Jennifer. I've always treated you like family."

"So, you dump family out on the street? Just like that?"

"I'm not dumping you out on the street."

"Bullshit! You come to me and announce that you're giving the house to Henry and Leah, and Mrs. Murchison wants to start re-modeling, and she doesn't want me around. So, hit the road."

"I didn't word it exactly like that..." Percy began. But when she shot him a cold stare he chose another tack. He cleared his throat. "You have done very well here, Jennifer, but Henry is married now, he's twenty-five, he doesn't need a babysitter."

God, what an idiot! "He's twenty-six," she corrected. "I have been your caretaker, your errand girl, your gofer, your scapegoat; it's been my career, and now you want me to walk away. Fat chance of that!"

"I don't see that you have a choice, my dear."

"Oh, yeah, *dear?*" Her eyes narrowed, the blue vein under her right one darkening with each beat of her pulse. "Listen, you ar-rogant bastard, I'd reconsider your hard-line stance before that stupid mouth of yours loses everything you've got. I'll sue you for sexual harassment, for starters."

"That's silly—nothing ever happened between us."

"Depends on your definition of nothing. That time in the billiard room, where you wanted to take me on the table ... remember?"

"But you didn't let me! Where's the harassment? You still work here, live here, in fact." Percy's leg began to tremble. He pinned it against the side of the desk, hoping Jennifer hadn't noticed.

"Come on, can we cut the bullshit? I know you told George An-derson that we did it, because he requested the same treatment. That story is probably halfway through the Olympic Club, and I don't think I'll have trouble finding corroborating witnesses. Plus, whom is dear old Marsha going to believe? And how about all those times you made me lie for you, to cover for those bimbos. That secretary, the Swedish one?"

Percy winced.

"*My sister?* I can't believe Marsha actually bought that. *I* made it up to save your ass, Percy. And this is the thanks I get?"

It wasn't going as planned. Percy considered his options, his eyes darting left and right. "What do you want? You know I could coun-ter-sue for embezzlement. There's no way you could have amassed three hundred thousand in a mutual fund on your salary."

Jennifer stood, her hands on the desk, leaning over, ready to strike. She could tell he wished he hadn't said that. "I've been frugal, careful, and it's *your* son who invested the money and turned it into what it is—mine. We are talking severance, for the best years of my life, covering for you, and taking care of you. Percy, I'm not asking for a lot, just what's right."

She sounded almost reasonable. *Have I dodged a bullet here?* Percy wondered. "So, Jennifer, why don't you sit down and tell me . . . what is right?"

She sat and crossed her legs, watching his eyes as they drifted south. "Percy, basically, I need a place to live. I think I ought to go house hunting, don't you? That and a small severance stipend, a modest monthly income for the transition period. And it might be best for your marital harmony that we keep this between ourselves. Do you think you can manage this transaction without your son?"

Percy nodded, beaten.

"Well, then, that wasn't so bad, was it?" She stood, let her skirt fall, and turned to leave the library.

When she got to the door, Percy finally managed to speak. "Jen-nifer."

She turned, her eyes daring him to try to bargain.

He stared, hateful. "Fuck you."

"Careful, Percy, you're starting to sound like your father."

Sam drove up Franklin Street to Cathedral Hill. Saint Mary's Church—as white and angular as the agitator in a washing machine—was bright against the winter sky. The air was crisp, and the vivid colors of the buildings and hills to the south seemed to vibrate in the sunlight. He grabbed the CD from the seat next to him and crossed the street to the entrance of the skyscraper: Cathedral Arms.

"Kreiger?"

The doorman rang up, then pointed to the elevator. "Twenty-third floor, 2309."

Pascal was waiting in the hallway. "Mr. Mann!"

Sam winced. "It's Sam."

"I am happy that you are here! So is Mr. Krieger. Please come in."

Frank Krieger sat in an overstuffed chair facing the TV. He appeared to be in the process of being swallowed by a brocade carnivore. He turned his head and smiled when he saw Sam, his face transforming from a depressed basset hound. "Pardon me for not getting up," he said.

Sam walked across the room to shake his hand. In the apartment, Krieger seemed smaller and weaker than he had at the resort. Other than the TV and the chair, the room had an armoire, a dining area off the kitchen nook, and a large couch. Sam saw the indentation from Pascal's body—it was probably where all the nurses slept out their shifts as Krieger sat mindlessly flipping channels. The apartment had a furnished but unlived-in quality: all the amenities and niceties without any soul or history, hotel suite style. The air was musty and still. *Do the windows even open?*

The ventilation was forced air, and underpowered if working at all. Sam had the feeling that they shut everything off late at night to conserve pennies. It had been the same for his grandmother at that home in Pacifica. Sam knew the smell of old age from those weekly trips to Grandma's before she died.

He felt a chill. During the drive over, this gig had seemed to be just the thing, especially since he had to back off from his usual gigs to let Jimm work his magic. But now, faced with Krieger and his frailty, Sam was worried that the old man might croak on his shift.

"Where's your guitar?" Krieger asked. "I hope you didn't leave it in your car. They break into everyone's up here. All night long I hear the alarms going off. All the way up here, a mile from the street."

"I left it at home."

"Bring it next time. It would be nice to have some decent music in here."

Sam realized part of what had seemed so cold, so hotel-like about the condo: no stereo. They all probably ignored the old man when he said he wanted music, and turned on the boob tube.

He felt the same indignant anger that he'd felt when his parents had made up lies why Grandma couldn't come along when she pleaded to get out of that home, if only for an hour. Sam decided to take the job right then and there. *Since they had the arrogance to assume I was already working, I'll use the leverage to get more bread.* "I *did* bring you a present," he said, offering up the CD.

Krieger examined the jewel-pack intently. "These records sure seem smaller than they did when I was young."

Sam laughed. "It's a compact disc. New technology." He looked at Pascal. "Why don't we get out of here, it's a beautiful day."

Krieger had nodded off. "No problem," Pascal said, "he will wake up soon. He does that very much. I get everything ready. I show you where his clothes are kept and the important telephone numbers."

"We still need to talk," Sam said. "I haven't taken this job yet."

Pascal nodded, ignoring the comment.

They took the elevator to the garage. Pascal led them to a forest green Lincoln Town Car, holding Kreiger by the arm.

"Pascal, let me do it! Fuck you!"

Sam smiled. *At least I won't lose the gig by swearing.* Luckily, the car was near the elevator.

"Mr. Mann—"

"It's Sam, please!" The way Pascal said it was even worse than usual: "Meester Mann."

"Sam—you want to drive?"

"No, you go ahead, Pascal. Will I need a chauffeur's license?"

"Oh, no. But I need to tell the insurance company, they add your name."

They drove toward downtown. Van Ness Avenue was teeming with cars, the windows in the storefronts glaring in the brilliant daylight.

"Stop here," Sam said. Pascal pulled into the bus stop in front of an electronics store. It had twenty-five televisions stacked five by five, each one carrying its tiny portion of some daytime soap opera.

Sam saw Krieger eyeing the activity, trying to make sense out of it. "Do you want to come in?"

Kreiger nodded. Pascal fidgeted in his seat, seeming uncomfortable with the idea.

"Don't worry, we won't be long," Sam said. "You can wait here in the car in case a cop comes. Bus stops are around three hundred bucks now." Before Pascal could answer, Sam was helping Krieger out of the car.

The old man stood on the sidewalk by the door, where hidden speakers pounded out a loud beat. He looked around as if trying to get his bearings.

Sam stood waiting, smiling.

"What are you looking at?" Krieger snapped. "Fuck you!"

Sam led the old man through the maze of computers and big-screen TVs to the personal stereo section. "I thought that a boom box would be best for you. That way you can move it from room to room and keep it next to you, so you won't have to get up to change any settings or anything. They have radios and tape cassette players in them along with CD players, and the sound is really good, even in the small ones."

"Boom box? Sounds like explosives. What are you talking about?"

Sam laughed. "It's a stereo. Music, right? That TV just puts you to sleep. We're going to get you something to play '9:20 Special.'"

"Oh. Why didn't you say so? This place sure is noisy."

Sam picked out a sleek black Sony, the lightest one available. While Krieger was testing it, to see if he could lift it, Pascal showed up. "Hi Pascal. Just getting Mr. Krieger a stereo. I noticed he didn't have one."

Pascal nodded and wiped his brow with a white hanky, seemingly relieved to have found them. The salesman returned with the receipt. "Just bring this to the cashier, they'll have one in the box for you."

"Thanks," Sam said.

"We pay!" Pascal said, trying to grab the invoice from Sam's hand. "I put it on the monthly expense record."

"No, you don't!" Sam said. "This is my gift to Mr. Krieger."

"Thanks, kid," Krieger said, touched.

Sam smiled. "Fuck you."

"It's all set, Sam," Jimm said, swinging his thick legs freely under his chair. "The studio time is block-booked for next Monday and Tuesday. Figure out what part of the day or night you want and I'll fill up the rest with a few other projects I have going."

"Other projects?"

"Don't fret," Jimm said, employing the same dumb guitar pun Sam had had to endure his entire adult life. "You're my top priority."

"Billy Barber?"

"Under consideration. He's O.K. for a novelty act, the kind that gets over with one funny cover and then flares out. No staying power. I hope you're in for the long haul, Sam. Getting you up there, that'll be easy. Keeping you up there and building from there, that's where I'll show you how it's really done."

"What's your plan?" The *feeling* was screaming, *tell me more!*

Jimm leaned forward and picked up the yellow legal pad. He placed it in his lap and rocked in the chair. "You record Monday and Tuesday, and we'll mix it on Thursday or Friday."

"You mean I have two days to record?"

"Of course. Unless you feel you need more."

"No, I usually make a record in four hours. If we mix, that's another four hours or so."

"If that's all it takes, great, but I don't want you to rush. Take your time. I got the studio at a great rate. The owner is honored to have someone of your stature recording there. I can have the artwork done in a week and the first run to the radio and big city stores the week after that. I have a marketing team in LA, Mainline. You ever heard of them?"

Sam shook his head. He felt weightless, as if he were about to levitate.

"They're the best in the business. They have assured me that you'll make the top five within three or four weeks, maybe number one in airplay. Sam, I want every contact you have. I'm going to book you anywhere they'll take you on short notice, and ride this first wave where you're already strong. Can you write all the contacts down? Don't worry, they'll be five percenters, just as we agreed. Patty is rewriting the contract as per our agreement. I take it we're still *in* agreement?"

Sam nodded so heartily that he felt the muscles in his neck tighten from the force.

"Sam, I also want you to write down a few of your concepts for the next projects. Believe me, the big boys are going to be coming at you—at us—like sharks. I want to have everything in front of me. The more specific we are, the more we get. *Trust me*, I know these guys."

Sam felt out of breath, dizzy. The *feeling* had finally become a tangible physical presence, occupying precious space inside his skin. An ecstatic sense of well-being overtook him.

"Do you want something to drink?" He wanted to thank Jimm, but all he could manage was a feeble trip to the Coke machine.

Jimm set his aside for later and got on the phone. Sam sipped at his soda while Jimm made more arrangements for the recording date and alerted the CD factory that he wanted a run of 5,000 within forty-eight hours of providing the master, which he promised by a week from Friday.

"That means Monday, right? Jimm paused to listen, scribbling in the upper corner of the legal pad. "What? You don't work on weekends! What is this? I have a new company going, with a slew of new releases, and *you* won't do this over the weekend? I'm already agreeing to pay more than I would in LA! If you don't want the business, then you can fuck yourself!"

Another pause; more scribbles. "That's better. Now, I mean it, I want delivery by Monday noon, or I'll be down there with a knife to take it out of someone's ass. Good. That's more like it."

Jimm hung up and leaned back, a smug smile showing how pleased he was with himself. "They only understand threats. They're dealing with a New Yorker now. That smiley West Coast shit doesn't cut it with me."

Sam went home, euphoria clinging to him like a shroud. Finally, *it* was coming, he could feel it. He looked at his apartment with new eyes. Things felt different, looked different, smelled different. His rent-controlled two-bedroom apartment in Noe Valley—only $560 and the envy of all who knew him—seemed small all of a sudden, depressing... *beneath* him. "I'll get a sunnier place, with parking," he said; or was it the *feeling?*

He sat at the table and put his feet up as he started sorting through the week-old pile of mail. He opened the brochure from Gray Elk, announcing the upcoming Spring Vision Quest, and his mind drifted back to Kelly and their shaman-guided weekend attempt at reconciliation. "I just couldn't fake it," Sam explained to the pamphlet. "It was bullshit."

In answer, he heard her diatribe during the long car ride back to civilization, as if it were an echo: "You're too tied to the physical plane, to outer validation. I love the Sam who doesn't need to prove himself or be loved by everyone. Don't you see that *that* is what's in the way?"

"How's the boom box?" Sam asked. It was his first day on the job, and his maiden voyage behind the wheel of Krieger's massive Lincoln. He was nervous, having realized how much responsibility the job entailed, and how little training he'd had.

"I'm having trouble figuring out the buttons," Krieger answered. "The radio is easy. I like to search for stations late at night, just like when I was a kid. I got a jazz station in Salt Lake City last night; it sounded like the announcer was as old as me. He played big bands; it reminded me of Bridget, my wife. We met at a dance downtown. She was a pretty thing, fresh off the boat, from Cork, not far from Kinsale, where my family came from. Who would ever have known Bridget would turn into such a bossy broad? All the same, I miss her. Life is so quiet. What I'd give to hear her yell at me just one more time."

He fell silent as Sam drove the Town Car toward the ocean. Sam thought he had fallen asleep. But when he looked over, he saw him scratching away at the top of his wooden cane, whittling with his thumbnail.

"You know, you don't seem to fall asleep as much when you're in the car," Sam said. "I'll bet it's that stale air in your apartment. Do any of the windows open?"

"How the hell would I know? Pascal won't even let me wipe my own ass."

Sam froze in panic. *This guy can go to the bathroom by himself, can't he?*

Krieger laughed. "Don't worry, Sammy, it was just a figure of speech."

Sammy? Not another nickname! I can hear it now: Sam-my mann!

Yet it was hard to hate, Krieger had said it with such warmth. The old man seemed to be coming out of his shell.

Sam parked the car at Ocean Beach. "Do you want to get out and take a walk?"

"I'll try, but I might not get very far. I hope you're a patient man."

"As far and slow as you want."

They inched their way along the seawall, past seagulls squawking as barking dogs chased them across the sandy esplanade. Krieger pulled his hat down over his squinting eyes. "We used to walk here. We'd come up to get away from Kinsale—that's what I named the estate in Hillsborough—and to get away from Percy. He was a bit of a spoiled brat. I'm surprised he gave that house to Henry; he acted as if it was his sole property and always would be from the day he was born. I always hated that name though."

"Which name? Kinsale?" Sam asked.

"Percy. I tried to warn Bridget that all the boys would beat him up and call him *pussy*, but she'd decided, it had to be Percy. I wanted a Frank, but we never could have any kids after Percy. After two miscarriages we stopped trying. She wouldn't even let me touch her; she thought it was my fault."

Krieger was still squinting. Sam couldn't tell if it was from the sun or the tear in the corner of his right eye.

They had stopped walking. "Do you mind getting the car, Sammy? I feel like sitting down somewhere comfortable."

It was the first time he'd ended a conversation with something other than "fuck you."

"Sam, that was beautiful," Jimm said. "I've spent a lot of time in the studio, but I've never seen or heard anything flow like that before."

He clinked his wineglass against Sam's before taking a swig. They were celebrating the session, sitting in a booth that was recessed into a dark corner in a trendy North Beach *trattoria*.

"You guys went in there and took care of business. We have at least fifteen tunes we can use. I don't think there's any need to go back tomorrow, do you? I can resell the studio time or bill it back to another artist and we can take that right off the top. No studio costs, and you're a month closer to your royalties."

Sam was beaming. The trio had played their tunes like the finely tuned band they were. He had opted to go for the working band, forgoing a big name 'guest star.' "The guys really responded."

"It was more than that. It was seamless. It felt like a live date. In fact, from what I heard in the booth, the direct to two-track is the way to go. The engineer never touched the dials; you guys controlled the dynamics. That means no mix, more money saved! I was thinking, since there was no overdubbing or second takes, why don't we call it a live date? After all, it was—just no audience. I thought of a great title: *Mann Alive.*"

Not him too! Sam almost choked on his wine.

"Are you O.K.?" Jimm asked. He reached over to pat Sam on the back.

Sam raised his hand to stop him. "I'm fine. I guess I'm a little touchy about my name. Ever since I was a kid, everyone made fun of it. It's such a pun magnet."

"Well, I guess I can understand that. But Sam, it is who you are, and the more ways we put things like that together, the better it is for you . . . and the easier it is for me."

Sam felt himself trying to like the idea. "I'll think about it."

They finished and Jimm poured the last of the wine. "Sam, I've got to tell you, I'm feeling something really big, something special. This is deep down in my gut. I feel this sense of power, that with you I can pull off some things like when I was a kid, when the business was wide open and anything could happen."

Sam nodded, intoxicated by the *feeling*. He felt like screaming,

Go on!

Jimm swirled the wineglass and took a gulp. "The whole world of music and entertainment has become factionalized—little people holding on to little pieces, creating categories and sub-categories without any vision, without any sense of the big picture. No risk taking. A bunch of chickenshits, afraid to step out."

Sam found it hard to believe what he was hearing. He had said those same words countless times, to deaf ears, to the same frightened chickenshits Jimm was talking about. Jazz players who were happy to hold onto their shrinking little piece of the pie, to watch their niche fading into nothing.

"We once ran the biggest PR game in history—the biggest. We thought it up and carried the whole American market on it. It was great, like pioneering, writing new rules. Are you ready for that kind of action, Sam Mann?"

Ready and willing, sir. Sam felt like jumping up and saluting.

"Good. Here are cassettes of the date today. Pick eleven tunes and decide if any mixing is needed. Even though it's digital, there does seem to be some compression that occurs when we mix from the multi-track. Almost like a second-generation analog. Go over this and get back to me. Also, I'll take a check for the four hundred dollars."

"Four hundred?"

"Twenty percent of your front money for the date," Jimm said. "Simple arithmetic. And get ready for a story. I'll tell you the next time I see you. Maybe we can make it work for you. It was the biggest thing I've ever been involved in. We can top it! *Trust me!*"

The *feeling* had Sam in its grip. It was like spiritual walking pneumonia, a functional dementia. The string of gigs had run out, and without any of Sam's energy since the signing of the contract, the trail had gone cold. Wil and Quentin were both picking up the slack with other bands, waiting for the *triumphant* CD release tour.

Sam had hardly played for weeks, and a strange numbness had settled in. An hour or so of practice every other day in Krieger's living room was about it; but the steady stream of Ben Franklins brought more than gigging did, anyway.

How strange that the *pipeline to stardom* meant no music, no clubs, no friends. But Sam understood that he had to stay off the scene and allow Jimm to work his magic.

Sam's libido had also slowed to a crawl. Once, he'd started to mention Jennifer Holman, hoping that Krieger might know how to find her. However, moments later, he had forgotten.

The only thing Sam felt interested in were those weekly copies of the *Gavin Report* and *Radio & Records* that Jimm showed him when they came out. "A seventeen with a bullet, in its first week! Sam, those guys are incredible. They say it's a done deal: three weeks and you're number one!"

Sam remembered stumbling out of the office, almost getting hit by a car as he mindlessly jaywalked, blinded by the *feeling*.

"Something bothering you, Sammy?"

Sam heard Frank Krieger's creaking voice out on the edges of his consciousness as he guided the car toward the Golden Gate Bridge.

"Pardon me?"

"You can tell me to mind my own business, but you seem different. If you've got problems, I'd like to help."

"Thanks," Sam said. "I'm just preoccupied with my new record, you remember the one we listened to? It's doing well, and I feel like I'm in a dream, like everything is finally working out. At the same time it's surreal, like someone else is here living it."

"You lost me there. Do you need any help or don't you?"

Sam laughed. "I'm fine, thanks."

They drove on in silence, Krieger scratching away at the top of his cane. The breathtaking view of Alcatraz and Angel Island floating in the blue swells of the bay abruptly appeared before them as they reached the top of Fillmore Street.

"Beautiful day today, no fog or haze." Krieger said. "Thanks, Sammy."

"Thanks? For what?" Sam reappeared out of his personal cloud cover.

"I know you're a musician and you got a lot of important things you need to do. I knew that about you when I met you at the wedding. I want to thank you for spending time with me. Babysitting an old man is probably embarrassing, demeaning work. Still, I kind of feel like you're a friend. I pay you 'cause you deserve it. I ain't trying to buy you, I want you to know that."

"I like you too," Sam said. "And I'm grateful for the job. It's just what I need right now. I kind of wanted to get off the scene. And you are partly responsible. I sensed the need to get away from things even before my manager suggested it."

"You sure know how to talk in circles. It's good you don't play that way. I know you got better things to do than sit around with an old guy who's waiting to die."

What do you say to that? Sam waited for that last idea to clear out of the car, but it hung like thick fog, unmoving, all-encompassing. Krieger pulled off his sunglasses, rubbed his eye, and returned to scratching at his cane, *accelerando poco a poco*. The sound, like a squirrel climbing a tree, lingered like the unspoken sentiment that chilled the air.

Sam turned along Bay Street and skirted the edge of Fort Mason toward the Golden Gate Bridge.

"Don't do it, Sam," Krieger said, an Irish brogue appearing out of nowhere.

"What?"

"Get old. I can't do a damn thing anymore. I can't get a hard-on, can

86

hardly pee, can barely walk, can't even fucking drive a car!" The tears started, twin streams flowing freely down pasty, drawn cheeks.

They turned along Marina Green—a wide strip of perfectly manicured grass—and Sam entered the driveway at the far end of the St. Francis Yacht Club parking lot. Midday, it was practically deserted.

Sam stopped the car.

"What's this?" Krieger asked, wiping his wet face with a white handkerchief.

"You can too drive, you son of a bitch."

"I haven't driven in thirty years!"

"So? It's easier now. This thing practically drives itself."

"I don't know—"

"Look, if you think I'm going to listen to that 'poor old me' shit when you're perfectly capable, you've got another think coming. It's time to put up or shut up, Frankie." Sam shoved the car in PARK and got out. He walked around and opened the door. "Scoot over. I'll tell you what to do if you've forgotten."

Krieger scooted over and reached up for the wheel; he strained to see out the windshield.

"Oops, I forgot." Sam reached over and adjusted the seat as high and close as it would go. "O.K. Do you remember the pedal part?"

"There's only two," Krieger said.

"One's the gas, the other's the brake. No clutch, see how easy? It's probably best for you to two-foot it, one foot on each. Just watch the road and steer. Ready?"

"Just one thing, Sammy: Fuck you."

Sam shrugged his shoulders and put the transmission in gear. The car lurched forward then stopped dead, bouncing high on its suspension. Another jump, this time more of a two-step, rubber squealing as Krieger stomped on the brake pedal. He smiled from ear to ear, tears of glee filling his eyes. "I'm driving...I'm driving!"

"More like hopping," Sam said. "See if you can *drive.*"

Krieger let go of the brake and the car shot forward again. The speed seemed to freeze him. He swerved toward the lawn full of joggers and people throwing Frisbees to their dogs.

"The brake, step on the brake!" Sam yelled as the car jumped the curb into the grassy expanse. Sam grabbed the wheel, trying to turn the car back to the parking area. For all his frailty, Krieger's grip was bionic. The Town Car spun, throwing sod in all directions. Screaming people ran toward the main road, the parking lot—anywhere to get away from the car that was cutting a wild serpentine path across the lawn.

Sam managed to wrest the wheel from the old man and steered the car back toward the waterfront and the asphalt parking area. The car bounced onto the asphalt and picked up speed, bee-lining for the bay and the million-dollar yachts just behind a chain link fence.

"The brake, man, the brake!" Sam heard someone yelling; it sounded like his own voice. Just before the fence, the last thing between them and San Francisco Bay, Sam's foot found the brake, and he heard a crash as the car shuddered to a stop against some trashcans stacked against the fence.

They looked at each other, wide-eyed. After a long silence they both sighed and began to laugh, tears welling up in their eyes. The next sound was a loud *whoop*, a fart-like blast from the siren of a SFPD patrol car.

"Shit," Sam said. *How am I going to explain this to the family? Oh well, back to fifty-dollar gigs.*

"May I see your license and registration please," the tough-looking lady cop said to Krieger.

The old man sat stoically, eyes forward.

"License and registration," she yelled again. Her short blond hair framed a round face that was half covered by aviator sunglasses. She opened her black ticket book as she waited.

Sam reached over to lower the window. "What's the problem, officer?" he asked. He realized how stupid it sounded when he said it.

"Excuse me?"

"I'm sorry, officer, I was just giving Mr. Krieger some driving lessons."

"On Marina Green?

"That wasn't the plan. He just got his foot caught, I think."

She walked to the front and checked the plate as Sam searched the glove box for the registration. He was relieved to see her righting the garbage cans they'd knocked over. *Please, don't arrest me!*

She smacked her hands together to rub off the residue from the cans and returned to study the registration. "I take it this man doesn't have a license."

"No ma'am, I believe he doesn't."

"Can he talk?"

"Of course I can!" Krieger snapped.

Sam was glad that he hadn't said *fuck you.* "He was just reminiscing about when he could drive, and I thought I'd give him a chance here in the open spaces. It was my dumb idea." *If one of us has to go to jail, it'd better be me.*

"I'll say. It says Krieger Corporation here."

"This is Mr. Krieger; his family leases or owns this car."

"You his nurse?"

"No, ma'am, just a friend of the family."

"Well, I guess I can't take you up on charges for negligence or get *your* license revoked. And believe me, I would!" She adjusted her glasses menacingly. "Let me see your driver's license."

Sam considered debating the need for that, since he hadn't been driving. He assessed the situation and surrendered his papers.

"Mr. Mann?" He winced, then nodded. "I'm going to let Mr. Krieger *and you* off. I don't know why, maybe because I can't quite figure how I would write it up. You should end up doing community service, starting with pounding out the dents in those cans and re-sodding the grass. I'll just forget it this time. Consider yourself lucky. And I think you ought to let professionals undertake Mr.

Krieger's driving instruction."

Finally Krieger said something. "Thank you, honey."

Sam winced again. This woman was far from a honey—and armed.

"Give my regards to Sergeant Sullivan, and here's something for your trouble," Kreiger said, peeling off a couple of bills.

Sam grabbed his arm. Too late. The cop already had the money in her hand.

"I'm sorry, officer," Sam said. "He does that with everybody. It was no attempt to bribe you or influence..."

"Stop right there!" the cop ordered. She looked at the money: 200 dollars. She folded it carefully and inserted it into her black book. Sam groaned, imagining himself cuffed in the back of the squad car.

"It couldn't be a bribe," the cop said with a smile—the first crack in her armor exterior—and a wink at the old man. "I had already let you off. Have a nice day. I'll wait until you drive out. And I mean *you*, Mr. Mann."

For the first time, Sam was relieved to hear a sentence that ended that way.

"Hello?" Jennifer yelled out, walking across the heavy canvas drop cloth, trying to avoid fresh splotches of pinkish adobe-colored paint. The muted turquoise molding added a neo-Howard Johnson touch to the entryway and living room. She made her way to the far wing—the guestrooms, which included her old bedroom—to pick up the last of her things, now that her new condo/loft was finished. Her shoes scraped on the heavy plastic runner covering the carpet.

She heard a scurrying as she approached the door to her room. She turned the doorknob and heard a cry. "Just a minute! Don't come in!"

She released the handle and waited—more footsteps, the bath-room door slamming. "O.K., come on in!"

She entered and saw Mrs. Murchison sitting on the bed, barefoot, wearing tight black leggings and a mustard-colored mohair poncho, inside out. The sheets were mussed; the blankets lay in a heap on the floor at the foot of the bed.

"Oh, it's you! I thought you were Henry or Leah."

"I thought I'd come and get the rest of my stuff," said Jennifer. "Sorry to barge in on you like this." It seemed like the right thing to say, even though she realized she was apologizing to a trespasser. *It's still my room.*

"No problem. Norm, you can come out."

A beautifully chiseled specimen of a young man came out of the bathroom, buttoning the last part of his paint-splattered coveralls. He picked up his paper hat from the bed and exited the room, avoiding eye contact with either of them.

"I guess you caught us," said Mrs. Murchison. "What are you doing here anyway?"

"Just came to pick some of my stuff. I don't care what you do, don't worry." Jennifer shrugged.

"I guess I owe you an apology; you probably hate me. I can't say that I blame you."

"Why would I hate you?"

"Because I made Percy kick you out. I hope you understand it was nothing personal; I just wanted Henry and Leah to get a fresh start."

Yeah, and so you could get your rocks off with a bunch of boy-toys and foist your bad taste on this poor mansion. "Look, it was time for me to go, Mrs. Murchison."

"Carol, please."

Great, now we're buddies. "Carol." Jennifer cleared her throat. "The wedding was great, Carol. I enjoyed the whole presentation. I was wondering, do you happen to know how I might get in touch with the musicians that you hired? I was thinking of having a party myself."

"I imagine I have that in a folder, but it's in my office. Can I call you and let you know?"

"Hello?" A man's voice in the hallway.

"It's Henry!" Mrs. Murchison whispered. She guided Jennifer out of the room and pulled the door closed behind her. "We're here, Henry."

"Jennifer!" Henry lit up, his alabaster cheeks redder than usual. "How are you? How do you like the living room?"

"I love it," Jennifer answered. *Smooth as silk.* "I just came by to pick up some more of my things."

Mrs. Murchison started to fidget, realizing that her smock was on backwards and inside out. "That and to ask about the musicians," she said, as if covering for something.

Henry looked puzzled. "Which musicians?"

"The guitar player who played at your wedding. I'm throwing a party, and he seemed like the perfect thing."

"It's funny you should bring him up. I just wrote him a check."

"I paid him!" Mrs. Murchison interjected. "He didn't call you and demand more money, did he? You have to watch out for those musicians."

"No it's not that. It seems as though he's working for Pascal, taking care of my grandfather part time. They took quite a liking to each other at the wedding."

"I noticed," Mrs. Murchison said.

"Then you've got his number?" Jennifer asked.

"I'll get it for you," Henry answered. He turned and went to the glass door that led to the backyard and to his office in the converted poolside cabana.

When he was out of sight, Mrs. Murchison pulled off her top and flipped it over before pulling her head through. She sighed, straightening her hair. "That was close!"

"Here they are," Jimm said, beaming.

Sam studied Xerox copies of the recent issues of *Gaven* and *R&R*. "See that?" Jimm asked, pointing. "Number three with a bullet! My man in LA says that you'll be number one next week! That goddamn Marsalis record is holding on tough, but it's been there for a while; 'time to go', he says. Number two is already headed south, so that leaves you. *Mann Alive!*"

Jimm smacked the top of his makeshift desk. Sam winced, but only slightly; a pun tied to a number-one rating was more than tolerable.

"Sam, sit down, I've got a little story to tell you. Patty!" She appeared as if by magic. "Hold all my calls. I don't want to be disturbed for any reason." She left the room, closing the door behind her.

There it was again: the *feeling*. Sam calmed his nerves by rereading the radio reports to make sure that nothing had changed since he'd last looked at them.

"Like I told you, Sam, I've got a story," Jimm said, pacing his tiny office as Sam watched from his chair. "I know I've been mysterious about it, and I appreciate that you didn't dig or try to pry it out of me. I like that about you; you give your word and you stick to it."

Sam's hands began to sweat, smudging the toner on the Xeroxes. *Where is he going with all this?*

"I think you're the man to pull off something just like it, but with a modern twist." Jimm nodded, as if reassuring himself of something. "What would you say was the biggest marketing gambit of our lifetime?"

It was a tough question. *Is there a right or wrong answer?* Sam stared like a devoted disciple, waiting.

"I'll tell you. It was Paul McCartney, right after the White Album. *Turn me on, dead man,*" he chanted in a low monotone. "Remember the record playing backwards, on every radio station, at least every hip one in the late '60s?"

Remember?! Sam hunched forward in his chair, eyes wide, mouth open. "You? The Beatles?"

Jimm shrugged. "Actually I had a partner. It was our idea and we handled it here in the U.S. In one night the rumor spread like wildfire, and it was complete bullshit, of course. All Paul had to do was lay low. It was right at the time when the Beatles were kind of in flux stylistically, and there were lots of others looking to grab that top spot. But we smashed 'em all. Child's play."

"But... what's this got to do with me?"

"I was thinking of trying the same thing with you. That is, if you think you're up to it. I know, I know, you aren't exactly as popular as the Beatles were... that was a joke!"

Sam laughed to show that he got it—and hide his astonishment.

"Anyway, today, the Internet is made for this kind of thing. Rumor and truth smudge together like that Xerox you're holding. So we turn you into the missing *Jazz God*. Number one record, where did he go? Get it?"

"Isn't that illegal?"

"Hell, no. If I don't know where you are—and I won't!—and you just disappear, then who's to stop people from wondering and speculating? It's not against the law to drop out of sight. No one did a thing after Paul's gambit. He just showed up, as if to say: 'What is wrong with all of you?' Like he didn't know what was going on!" Jimm laughed. "Plus, *you* can say that you had a breakdown. Hell, everyone knows that you freaked out that night and called that huge black guy King Kong—or was it gorilla?"

He's heard about that? Sam's eyes dropped to the floor and he shook his head. *"Animal."*

"So, you just split town for a bit, while I do *my* thing. In the meantime, I'll try to get a hold of your old masters and buy them out from your old record companies. We'll own the rights, and when you become the lost hero, you know what'll happen to your sales figures?"

"But when I return, what do I say?"

"That you were stressed out, you needed some time to get your head together, whatever; you aren't required to give anyone a fucking explanation. You'll have had nothing to do with any of it."

"Well, actually," Sam said, "I *have* wanted to get away for awhile and straighten my head out. I was down in Big Sur, and it felt good to be off the scene and around nature."

"See? That would probably do you some good. Better than baiting behemoths with racial epithets. Do you have anywhere you can go?"

"Well, there's this guy who..."

"Whoa! I don't want to know any names or places. That way, I'm not lying. Listen," Jimm's eyes got suddenly cold, "I'm exposing myself a hundred ways here. If you aren't going to back me up, or if I can't trust you to keep up your part, say so now!"

"I've always done what I've said, haven't I?" Sam hated the word "always;" he never thought he'd hear himself use it.

"Just making sure. So, you want to do this? Or, rather, you want to let me do this for you?"

Sam nodded. *Why not?* "Yes."

"I want you to find a nice out-of-the way place to hide out, then I'll do the rest. When can you let me know?"

"Pretty soon. I don't know, tomorrow? When are we going to do this?"

"Next week! Strike while the iron's hot! I got you a CD release party at Clyde's. I hope you don't mind. Got extra money for the band. I can't believe how little he's been paying you. The gig is Monday, and you leave Tuesday. Make those calls and let me know...ASAP."

Sam steered the Town Car through the park, hardly noticing the daffodils already in bloom, silently replaying his deal with Gray Elk: a trailer at the bottom of the property, far away from the roundhouse and sweat lodge, at a hefty but affordable price (thanks to Krieger's C-notes). *I always figured he was just looking to slice a buck out of guilty whites.*

Gray Elk had seemed to understand Sam's desire to keep everything a secret. "The only person who will know is my wife Iris," he had said, before his famous incantation: "We all take different paths."

Sam shook his head at the bullshit. *That faux-shaman even acted as if he knew I would call and ask. And he graciously offered to buy supplies for me when he goes to town—at a nominal fee, of course.*

"You seem quiet again," Krieger said. "I hope you're paying attention. If you want, I'll drive."

"No way!" They both laughed. Then Sam got serious. "I'm going to give notice for a while, Mr. Krieger."

The old man turned, stunned by the formality.

"I've got a CD release party on Monday and I need to woodshed for it."

"Woodshed?"

"You know, practice. After that, I've got some plans." *Better be careful!* "I won't be around for a while. Some gigs..." Sam hated lying, but what other excuse could there be? At least it was one that wouldn't meet an argument.

"I understand, Sammy. All my life, I've been kind of alone," Kreiger said, managing a sad smile. "I struck out for this country when I was fifteen, sent for my brother after I had made it. He did the stonework at Kinsale. Bridget never wanted to be part of the Irish community here. She wanted our child to grow up American. She hated the poverty, the violence, and drinking, the way it was both here and at home for people like our families. She didn't want to call our home Kinsale, the one thing I refused to go back on. That property was Kinsale, I told her that. I said, 'Bridget you can leave or you can ignore it,' that's what I said."

The old man's shock and sadness had released a flood. His speech had changed; it sounded younger, more musical, with more than a hint of a brogue.

"So, Mike and his family moved here." He pointed to the left, out the window. "To the Sunset district, where a lot of Irish families settled. There is still a tight-knit community. They stayed in the trades, bringing over the family, one nephew or niece at a time. They all talk the Irish; I lost mine a long time ago. I would sneak out every now and then to have a pint or two. Bridget always knew; she never let on, though. She apologized for coming between Mike and me at Mike's wake. She was truly a lovely woman; I wish you could have met her, Sam. Even when she was old and dying, that awful cancer eating her up, I don't think I ever saw anyone as beautiful as she was. I still saw that same darling I saw that night at the Palace Hotel."

The nostalgia had begun to overwhelm the old man. The sun made rainbow-like prisms in the tears that perched on his eyelids, welling up, about to spill over to his cheeks.

"I think you need something to eat," Sam said. He turned out of the park and drove to a diner. They sat at the counter, because Krieger was avoiding eye contact, pulling his hat down, constantly adjusting his dark glasses.

As they sat next to each other Sam realized how small and frail the old man was. He fought the desire to embrace him, to comfort him, to tell him something that would give meaning to the predicament he was in: old and alone, the only one of his contemporaries still around.

The warm din of the diner—plates rattling, waitresses calling out orders—heightened the silence between them. Krieger slowly picked at his salad, a blotch of white on his chin. As Sam started to remove his napkin from his lap to clean the blob, he noticed the tears.

"I'll miss you, Sammy." Krieger said.

Sam's felt as if he might melt right there at the counter as he swabbed Krieger's face. It was as close as he'd ever get to a father's care for a baby. He wanted to stop the movement of time by the sheer force of his will. "I'll miss you too," he said. "It won't be that long. I'll see you again."

"A day for you ain't like a day for me. I'm not saying this to make you feel bad. I'm sorry!" Kreiger pulled out his handkerchief and wiped his face dry. "I'll tell you a story. Something I ain't never said to anyone."

The words carried the weight of a strange *deja vu*.

"You ever notice I say 'Fuck you' a lot?" Sam nodded. "I admit I like the way it shocks some people ... but do you want to know the real reason I say it?"

"If you want to tell me."

"Well, I had this friend, Ben Mulhern—he's dead too, just like everyone I know. You'd best be careful, my boy, you might be getting out in the nick of time; people seem to die around me."

If he only knew. I wonder what he'll think when Jimm's rumor hits the papers? "Jesus, Frankie, it's not your fault."

"I'm only kidding."

"So am I."

"Can I finish this story already?"

Sam nodded.

"So, Ben Mulhern, he's on his deathbed. Boy, was he rich, and everyone was doting on him. It was the longest deathwatch anyone had ever seen. I think half of them wanted to know who was in and who was out of the will. His daughter was sweet, caring, what a dear. She was there by his side for months, but it bugged him after a while; her sad face was driving him crazy.

"He talked her into hiring a nurse, said he didn't know how long he was going to take. I think he was worried it would take forever. So, anyway, she hires this mean bitch of a nurse, a real tank of a woman. Rough? Hell, she had more hair on her face than I did. So the end is finally there, he tells everyone he loves 'em dearly and not to cry for him when he's gone, that he'll finally be out of his pain.

It was sad, but beautiful.

"Then he calls the nurse over, and her eyes light up like the fourth of July, like he's going to give her a chunk of the estate. So she leans over, and he barks out his last words with his dying breath, loud enough for all of us to hear: 'Fuck you!'"

"Excited, Sam?" Sam nodded, standing amidst the dusty cardboard boxes in Jimm's makeshift office. "You ought to be. Everything is set on our end; there are just a couple of things you need to do. Pay your rent early—nothing weird about that, you just got a couple of checks and it's almost the end of the month. We'll see how things go and then I'll do what I have to on this end."

"That reminds me," Sam said. "I still haven't been paid for the session."

"I know. I just read Paul Goddard the riot act. He says those Internet companies are slow in paying, they kind of float things. He assured me he'd get right on it with his accounting department. In the mean time, I got cash for you. Here." Jimm handed Sam a fat wad of messy bills. "It's sixteen hundred. I took my cut out already, since it's my cash in the first place, to save you the trouble of writing me a check. When your check shows I'll deposit it in my account. In any case, you still ought to leave a couple of checks and deposit slips for me."

"What?"

"Someone has to take care of your business while you're gone," Jimm said. "Do you realize the small window of opportunity we have when this hits? If I don't have the leverage to speak for you and act for you, then we miss. If we wait until you get back, it's just an exercise in futility. You going to get cold feet now?"

"It's not cold feet. I guess I didn't figure on turning over my entire financial empire, be it ever so humble," Sam said.

"I'm not in the mood for any fucking jokes," Jimm said coldly.

"I've spent a hundred hours in the last week setting this up. If you're going to pull the rug out from under me, tell me now."

"Of course not," Sam assured him. "I've put a lot into this too, don't forget." He tore a couple of checks and deposit slips out of his checkbook and laid them on Jimm's desk. After all, what was there to lose? He was already looking forward to a couple of months of getting in touch with himself, and emerging a *star*—a metamorphosis of legendary proportions.

"You'll want to sign this," Jimm said, offering a sheet of paper filled with legalese.

"What is it?"

"Standard power of attorney."

"Why?"

Jimm sighed. "So I can act on your behalf while you're gone. I told you: the window of opportunity. I think I've proven myself to be worthy of it. I've delivered everything as promised, didn't I?"

Sam nodded as he picked up the document and studied it, assessing the risk of signing it against the certainty of kissing his life's dream goodbye.

"It's not such a big deal, Sam. Some of the things granted in that are already part and parcel of our management agreement. You have a number of legal recourses if I do anything wrong. You're going to have to decide whether to *trust me*. I'm the one who is going to be in violation of about a thousand ethics statutes and probably just as many legal ones."

Sam nodded and scribbled his name. *Hell, I've already told Gray Elk to expect me.*

"Patty, will you notarize this?" Once again she appeared as if out of thin air. She quietly opened her book, filled out the names and stamped everything.

"Handy, having a notary in the office," Sam said.

"Patty worked at a mortgage office before I met her; she kept the status. Saved us ten bucks," Jimm said, pleased. He quickly stashed their agreement in the stack of papers on the far side of the desk, out of Sam's reach. "Are you ready for tomorrow night?"

"Ready as I'll ever be. It'll be fun to play, it's been awhile."

"Go ahead and blow the doors down. Why save it? You'll have plenty of time to recharge your batteries. One other thing: when you're gone, pay cash for everything. That way there will be no way to trace anything to you. Do you need some help with that?"

Sam shook his head. "No, between what you just gave me and that gig with Krieger, I'm O.K. in that department." All the same, Sam was happy he'd asked. It took the sting out of that power of attorney.

"No credit cards, no checks, Sam. I mean it. Don't call, don't write. Remember, you're dead. Did you call the guy where you're staying from your house?"

"Yeah."

"Shit!"

"What?"

"Tell him to tell anyone who asks that you called for information or to chat, not to tell anyone you're there. Can you trust him to do that?"

"I imagine."

"Good," Jimm said. "I'll ride with you to somewhere near where you're going. You said it was in the country?"

Sam nodded. It seemed better not to speak, more clandestine.

"I'll bring your car back and park it near your house."

"But what about street cleaning?"

"So, you'll get a few tickets. Big deal. We're going to make a killing here. Patty will take the tickets off; it probably won't get towed. And if it does, so what? I'll make you a deal: I'll pay for any towing or storage, because you won't be gone *that* long. Travel light, Sam. It has to appear as if you dropped off the face of the earth, nothing planned. Don't take a guitar. If you want to play, get your friend to bring you one. Understood?"

Sam nodded again.

"Good, I'll be at the club tomorrow night. We'll leave from your house Tuesday morning, ten o'clock. It's going to be biggest thing to hit the music industry in the last thirty years . . . *trust me!*"

The return to Clyde's had a familiar yet distant quality, as if the ghosts of a million eighth notes hung suspended in the air, waiting for a host vehicle to come through. It was less than a month since the night Sam had flirted with death in this very same room, yet it seemed like a homecoming after a long absence. Sam had hardly stepped in a nightclub since.

The *feeling* had added a surreal extension to the passage of time. He felt out of touch, a voyeur, watching from a safe and insulated psychic distance.

"Hey Q, look," Wil shouted, "it's our *man Sam!* I'd have thought his manager would have made the rehearsal. We want our *star* to conserve his precious energy. A man like you shouldn't be carrying his own amplifier. Give it to me."

Wil wrested the amp from Sam's grip and toted it to the bandstand. Sam pulled the guitar from its case and plugged it in. He felt embarrassed; he'd made no effort to get in touch with either of them since the recording date. He'd been so consumed by the *feeling*, his inescapable road to stardom, and his new job babysitting a rich old man, that he actually feared a question as innocuous as "How you doing?"

Quentin looked up from his drum throne as he tightened the screws on his cymbal stands. "Good to see you too."

Sam looked up, stunned. The sound of Quentin's voice had that same familiar yet distant quality that everything else did. *It's a good thing I'm getting away for a while.* "Hey Q, good to see both of you."

"I was wondering if you were still allowed to talk to us," Wil said.

"Your new agent and all. He called *us* for the gig, *here at Clyde's*. That was some weird shit! Not that I mind the extra taste. By the way, I still haven't gotten my bread for the recording date. When I called your man, he got pissed off, said I was accusing him of being a cheat and a liar. I hope he don't conduct business with everyone that way."

Sam shuddered, recalling Jimm's phone conversation with the CD factory. "He told me about the checks. He says the company is one of those corporations that bills and pays in cycles, they live on the float. I'm sorry about that. You'll get your bread, I promise."

"Chill, man," Wil said. "I imagine I'll need the bread just as much when I get it as I do now. It ain't your fault. You need to play, man; your wig seems like it's a little tight. How about this?"

Wil launched into his famous intro, a thunderous low note answered by *staccato* double stops three octaves above, near the end of the fingerboard. Sam saw the wrinkles in the back of his shiny black skull as he leaned over the shoulder of his double bass. They seemed to say, "Welcome home!"

Wil was right: once the music started, Sam's world seemed to right itself, spinning perfectly on its axis. Intricate interplay, dynamic crescendos, phrases shared by the group like the unspoken understandings of a long marriage filled the empty club, a concert for a roomful of tables and chairs. Clyde had come up the rear stairs and was listening intently from behind the brass railing at the back of the stage. The tune ended with Wil sliding down his bottom string to the low G, *pizzicato profundo*.

"Bravo," Clyde said. "Good to have you guys back. Even though it's costing me more than I've ever paid for any group. And you motherfuckers are only a trio!"

Sam felt embarrassed, as if he were guilty of mugging a friend, especially after Clyde had saved his life the last time he'd played at the club.

"Tell you what," Clyde said, towering over Sam. "You can make it up to me—to us—by taking us all out to dinner. I sure am hungry, how about you guys?"

It seemed like a fine idea to Sam. He would have given the entire wad of bills in his pocket to buy himself out of his guilt. Besides having iced the band and Clyde out of his life, he had this secret he couldn't tell anyone, even them. He felt certain they'd sense something.

Got to keep the conversation going, he thought, putting down his guitar. "Have I told you all about my number-one record?"

Clyde ordered a second bottle of wine. "Thought I'd get the expensive stuff," he said, determined to recover every last penny of the group's raise. "It's good gorilla juice. What do you think, Sam?"

Sam looked up from his spaghetti. "Animal."

"Q tells me that you guys are planning a big tour for the CD now that it's doing so good," Clyde said, filling the glasses.

Sam almost dropped his fork. *Why wouldn't Jimm tell me that, even though we've got another plan? I guess it'll make for a better PR blitz*. He took a sip of wine. "Yeah, I guess he's working a few things out, but everything is swinging."

Quentin and Wil appeared concerned by Sam's tentative and secretive answer. He was relieved to see them give each other a knowing glance, as if they understood. After all, deep down, every musician has a superstitious streak as wide as any baseball player's.

"They delivered four boxes of CDs for tonight," Clyde announced. "Mann Alive!"

Sam cringed.

Clyde laughed. "That white man of yours drives a motherfucker of a bargain. He's only giving me two bucks for every one we sell. If it's crowded I may just get him to sell them himself and keep the fucking money, Ginger will have enough to do just serving drinks."

"Why don't *you* do it?" Sam asked.

"I've got a club to run. Why don't *you*? Everyone will want you to sign the goddamn thing, anyway."

Back at the club, they were shocked to find a long line of people waiting for the doors to open. "Here, Sam," Clyde said, handing over a set of keys. "You guys take the back door. I'll let these folks in. Might as well play the *star* role now that you got yo'self a manager. Hate for these folks to see you comin' in like the normal peeps."

Downstairs in the dressing room, Sam paced like a caged lion as Quentin and Wil read the magazines stacked on the makeup table. "Q, we don't got to wait down here," Wil said. "*He's* the star. Let's go to the bar and get a taste. Would you like us to bring you something, sir? Or perhaps you need your manager to make that decision."

The trio waited on the stairs while Clyde made his opening remarks to the packed house. Clyde often resorted to personal experience and metaphors, most of them dealing with the similarities between music and sports. Half the time the audience expected him to smile and hold his finger high in the air, giving the number-one sign, like he'd done on national TV when his fourth-quarter interception had clinched the Super Bowl seven years earlier.

"Ladies and gentlemen, I'm pleased to see all of you here tonight." Clyde held the microphone as close to his mouth as his bulging biceps would allow, and craned his neck to make up the rest of the distance. "I've had this trio in the club for almost as long as I've had this establishment, and I'm glad to present them in their first appearance since the release of their new CD: *Mann Alive!* I can tell you that Sam Mann is a man..."

"Please don't!" Sam quietly prayed at the top of the stairs.

"That was a joke," Clyde instructed. The crowd showed mercy.

"Anyway, Sam is a real colorful character. I can tell you from personal experience that as a man he challenges life and takes risks personally, just like his music."

Not the gorilla story, please!

"I hope all of you are ready for some tasty and exciting music tonight," Clyde said, trying to incite the audience. "Are you ready?"

No response. Sam could see that Clyde had momentarily forgotten where he was. Jazz audiences tended to differ from the coliseum crowds Clyde had performed for. It was as if the unusually large crowd in his club had unlocked some genetic sports code deep in his DNA structure.

Clyde's voice went up more than ten decibels as he yelled into the microphone: "Ladies and gentleman, Clyde's is proud to present the Sam Mann Trio, and just like their new CD, they are NUMBER ONE!" He thrust his arm high in the air, his index finger extended, as the audience gave a polite round of applause.

Sam groaned but kept a smile on his face as he followed Wil and Q onto the stage. He picked up his guitar and waited for the room to fall quiet. Then he took two deep breaths and nodded to Quentin, who answered with a slow roll on the cymbal with a pair of mallets. The sound seemed to rise from the earth, a low rumble becoming a drawn-out, perfectly uniform crescendo until the sound shimmered: a heavenly racket, like wind chimes in a gale-force breeze. As the glitter faded, the bass, which had been present in a subtle brooding *ostinato*, began building a foundation, one stone-solid note at a time.

A high trill from the guitar, two sparkling notes meshing as one, while Quentin's mallets began a muted syncopation on the tom-toms, the sock cymbal adding a faint click on the off-beats.

"Patience, patience," Sam said to himself, trying to restrain the adrenaline rush that was tempting him to let fly a blistering speedy line in a misguided and egocentric attempt to blow the crowd away.

Instead, he took a deep breath and waited for one more cycle of the bass riff to complete before repeating his opening minimalist trill, this time a third higher, faint, like fine china clinking, *pinky extended*.

The tension was mounting. Wil even seemed edgy, his eyes imploring: *come on man!* The bass was exposed, its rich woody tone melting into the pounding of the skin on the low tom.

Another long pause from the guitar, and the room was locked in a hypnotic anxiety, ready to jump.

Finally, Sam struck he first strain of the melody and answered it with a slowly strummed chord replete with tension and resolution, a mixture of what you want and what you don't. The crowd sighed, barely audible, still holding on to the echoes of the dissonance that begged for release. The rest of the song seemed to melt into itself, the ghosts of choruses past, present, and future channeling through Sam as if he were an innocent bystander.

The coda was an exposed fading soliloquy that turned transparent as the guitar and mallets became a distant echoing call. The bass, now completely exposed, dropped to its lowest register. There was a quick stutter, then low G, Wil's million-dollar note. The crowd sat transfixed by the strains that seemed to hang in the air, before offering a rousing ovation.

Sam smiled and acknowledged his sidemen. Wil leaned in close and whispered as he smiled, nodding to the room. "I thought you were going to wait forever. Don't you ever leave me hanging out there like that again, motherfucker!"

Sam began his monologue by thanking Quentin and Wil, the club, and Jimm Dibbook, who had made this all possible. "Most of all, I want to thank all of you for your support over the years." In context, the statement seemed maudlin and melodramatic.

As he launched into the sales pitch for the new CD, his eyes scanning the room, he saw unexpected but familiar faces. He felt disoriented; they were from another life. "Uh…" He caught himself:

"Available from Ginger at the bar. Only fifteen dollars—two for thirty. Remember, only around three hundred shopping days till Christmas."

Again his eyes caught the odd couple in the corner. It was Frank Krieger and Pascal. Sam smiled and waved, grateful to see them, and glad that his separate lives—previously pried apart by the *feeling*—were beginning to converge.

The third familiar face was right beside them, framed with chestnut hair and adorned with a smile of imperfect perfection. *Jennifer!*

Sam launched into the next piece, one full of swoops of high energy and rhythmic outbursts, as his spirit soared to new heights. As he charged through the song, Sam felt his libido return, the music illuminating the path to rebirth, back to his essence.

The break seemed to materialize in an instant, as if the band had been caught in a time warp. Clyde gave the hook sign: a finger slicing away at his jugular. The band navigated through the sea of fans and friends, shaking hands like politicians in search of office. Sam veered off course and steered toward the back.

"It's a surprise to see all of you. Hi Jennifer, long time." He bent over and kissed her cheek. Her hair was soft and smelled of apricots; her face was warm, radiating sensuality.

Pascal slid over to make room for Sam next to Krieger. "Hey, Frankie, good to see you."

"Fuck you," the old man answered. "I wouldn't have missed this for the world. You boys are doing pretty good up there. Though it would be nice to hear something from..."

"I know, *Finian's Rainbow!*"

Jennifer seemed intrigued by the strong rapport between the two. Sam watched her sipping her drink, smiling, flapping her shoe against the heel of her foot. The sound and sight was driving him into a sexual frenzy. *An adoring crowd, my stardom fantasy finally becoming a reality, and all I can think of is being alone with her.*

"Now that you are a big *star*, I guess we won't be seeing much of you?" Krieger said.

And Sam remembered; it hit him like a punch in the gut. He was leaving! He was dying! *What can I tell them?* His integrity was at war with his desire, his lifelong dream.

Luckily, Jimm came and interrupted. "Sam, Patty had to take over selling CDs; that woman behind the bar was useless. A lot of people would love for you to sign them." He turned to the others. "Do you think you could spare him for a little while?"

Sam got up to leave and used it as an excuse to kiss Jennifer one more time. As he bent to kiss her cheek, she turned and planted her soft lips on his as she squeezed his arm with quiet urgency. Their eyes met, an unspoken promise. When Sam nodded in recognition of it, she released her hold.

"Sammy, one thing!" Krieger said, calling him back to the table with the wag of his finger. Sam bent over as the old man's raspy whisper tickled his ear. "You can save your money, but you can't save your hard-ons. Use 'em up."

They both laughed as Sam made his way the steps.

"And another thing!" Krieger yelled.

Sam turned.

"Fuck you!" they sang in concert.

During the second set, the band forayed into new territory, embellishing on embellishment, variations that twisted and turned; exploring fragmented motifs that became contrapuntal canons, swirling seamlessly into stream of consciousness. The audience was spellbound by the three-way conversation with interludes of solo exploration; it was improvisation without structure, anarchy in its purest sense.

Sam was fixated on the image of Jennifer in orgasmic free fall that night in the library; he could still taste the sweetness of her flesh as he thrashed on the bandstand, living, dying, and being born again in contrasting flashes of bombast, subtlety, and intricacy.

Quentin and Wil were trying to keep up with Sam, who was playing hide-and-seek, ducking in and out of corners, leading them down dead-end alleys, doubling back: the edge, defined, only to be redefined with each ensuing permutation. *If I'm going to die, I don't see any reason to save this lick for later.* It gave Sam a scary freedom, like reading his own obituary. The *feeling* had reemerged and was now in complete control. *Come and get me.*

After the twenty-minute free improvisation, the band stopped short on a pet phrase—a lick specifically designed to catch the unsuspecting crowd by surprise. It worked. They sat in awe, thinking the silence was merely another section of the piece.

Sam saw then that the corner table was empty; Jennifer had left during his self-indulgent swan song. Kreiger and Pascal, too. They were gone. *So am I.* A sardonic laugh welled up inside him, filled with sorrow, hope, and fear. "After that," Sam said, "all that's left is the blues."

And the blues it was. Sam's loud triplets in a slow 12/8, accompanied by Q's heavy back-beat, got thunderous opening applause. It was both acknowledgement of the previous offering, and gratitude for the transport back to the street, a place everyone could relate to.

As he played, Sam scanned the bar and the entryway, hoping that Jennifer might have lingered, hoping to bask in her loveliness one last time before dying. Instead, he was stunned by another set of out-of-place images. He closed his eyes. *Maybe I am dying. My whole fucking life feels like it's flashing before my eyes.* He finished the theme, turned over the lead to Wil, and allowed himself another peek.

There they were . . . *they?* Billy Barber tipped his Stetson and smiled; he left his other arm wrapped around Kelly's neck.

They're together? It's no optical illusion. It's good that a motherfucker only dies once. Too many surprises . . .

Jennifer poured herself a glass of wine. She surveyed her new apartment. Her perfect loneliness matched the perfect view of the waterfront: all those cars on the street below, all those apartments on the hills across the bay, all those lives filled with love and hope. And her with nothing. In the past she'd been so good at lying that she could even lie to herself, but something was changing. "Maybe I'm just out of practice, living alone and all."

She headed for the shower, leaving a trail of shed clothing all the way to the bathroom. The hot water did little more than stir up the feelings inside her, adding depth to the previously unshaped unease.

She considered throwing on her clothes and running back to the club. *Maybe he's there hanging out with his buddies. Then again, maybe he's there with a girl; there were plenty of women who had their eyes on him.*

"What's wrong with you, Jennifer?" she admonished. "Get a grip, girl."

She got in bed, eyeing the diary on her nightstand, stalking it, predator and prey. *But which of us is which?*

She picked it up and grabbed the pen.

Saw him tonight. What is it with him and the old man? Like they have a secret handshake and everything. No wonder he's good with animals, if he can tame that irascible old fart.

"Fuck," she said, disgusted, her eyes tearing.

I promised I wouldn't bullshit here! It has nothing to do with the old man or those fucking animals. He played this song, at least I think it was a song. It was so full of . . . everything. It felt like he was undressing me, and not just my clothes—all the way down to my soul. I was sure everyone else knew it, too. It embarrassed and scared me. I had to get out of there. And yet, for what? I feel like he's still here, swirling around in my head. I'm so lonely.

The tears clouded her vision; one rolled off her cheek and landed on the page, smearing the last word of her entry so that *lonely* looked like *lovely*.

"What is happening to me?" Jennifer cried out, throwing the pen across the room and turning off the light.

"Ready, Sam?" Jimm asked as he fastened his seatbelt. Sam nodded, took a deep breath, and dropped his car into gear.

"Everything is set," Jimm said. Clasped in his pudgy paw, yet another wad of bills emerged from his drab green parka. "We sold fifty-one CDs last night. They cost seven, plus two each for Patty; your take was just over three hundred. Here."

Sam tried to figure out what to do with the wad as he drove down the freeway, finally opting to wedge it between his legs. A yellow piece of paper stuck out among the green.

He pulled it out and looked at it. It said: *Jennifer Holman,* next to a scribbled phone number. "You know her?" Sam asked.

"Who?"

"Jennifer Holman," Sam said, showing him the paper.

Jimm grabbed it. "I don't think so; let me see."

"I know her," Sam explained, wanting the scrap of yellow paper back, if only to remind himself of her during the coming lonely nights. "She must have given Patty the number as she left last night. We kind of dropped out of touch. I'll take it."

Jimm put it in his pocket, shaking his head. "Sam, this is no time to start chasing down old lovers. You're disappearing, remember?"

"I know," Sam snapped back. "I wasn't going to call her and set up a secret rendezvous."

"Good," Jimm said, ignoring Sam's defiance. "I'll hold on to it for safekeeping, and when you get back I'll give it to you."

An angry brooding silence followed which Jimm finally broke. "That was some performance last night. Boy, when this hits and you materialize, with your head together, Sam, last night will seem like a bullshit tune-up gig."

"It felt good, to be back in the saddle again." The word saddle conjured up the image of Kelly and Billy—*what a strange couple.* "I almost forgot how much I missed it."

"Sam, whatever happens, no matter how much you miss everything, you've got to follow through with this. I don't want you getting homesick for a nightclub, or some pussy, and blow all this. For the last time: Are you going to keep your word, or should we get out before we go too far?"

"I'll keep my word. I told you, I'm looking forward to getting away." *At least I was!* "A couple of months is nothing, and a layoff sure seemed to help last night. I just hope Gray Elk leaves me alone and—"

"Hey! I told you, I didn't want to know!"

South of San Jose, they entered the Coyote Valley, bordered by dry brown hills on one side and the green nose of Morgan Hill on the other. The steady stream of autos seemed to Sam like a colorful ribbon that led to tranquillity, to new connections, to rebirth. The *feeling*, which had been alienating and isolating, was being replaced by a needy humility.

Sam found it hard to sit still; he wanted to share this passage with another human—and Jimm was the only one around. *It's like when a condemned man gets visited by a priest; someone in my position can't exactly choose his partner.*

"It was weird last night," he said. "It sort of felt like I was dying. It was even different musically. Normally, when I play one of my old licks, I chastise myself for being uncreative, but last night it was like dusting off an old family photo. And I saw so many people, like the scenes of my life flashed before my eyes. I wouldn't have been all that surprised to have seen my folks, even though they're both gone."

Jimm hit SEEK on the radio, seemingly uninterested in Sam's discourse.

What the hell? I'm going to be talking to myself for a while, might as well start now. "I even saw Billy Bronstein. Of course, you know him as Billy Barber. Shit, you probably told him, didn't you?" No answer.

"Anyway, get this," Sam turned to look at Jimm. "He was there with my old girlfriend. I'll tell you, that has got to be the odd couple of the century."

Jimm put on a pair of sunglasses and leaned back into the seat. "I'm going to catch a nap, wake me up when we get close."

"We're almost there," Sam announced. To his surprise, he'd enjoyed the solitude of the ride as Jimm snored noisily in the seat next to him. The onion and garlic fields of Gilroy had given way to rolling hills dotted with cattle grazing on late winter grasses. Sam noted the sprigs of green forcing their way skyward, confident of spring's imminent arrival. A sense of hope began to envelop him. He *knew* that his dream was finally coming true, that he'd emerge from this voyage complete, happy, and successful.

As Sam turned off the highway, onto the county road that led to Gray Elk's place, his curiosity got the best of him. "How you going to do it?"

"What, Sam?" Jimm asked, suddenly wide awake.

"You know, drop the hint, get the rumor out."

"Well, these things are kind of free-flow. You've got to improvise. Be thankful for the Internet, it'll make everything fast and clean. The networks are so afraid of getting scooped these days that they run just about anything on the evening news. Have you noticed?"

"It sure seems that way. Are you going to submit some wild story to an Internet news service? Won't they be able to track it to you?"

"That would be stupid! No, I'll make it so that they come to me for help, while I pretend to be in the dark. I can drop little hints, where to look, what I suspect is happening. But they have to think it's their story. Get it?"

"How will it all start?"

"The way it always does: you don't show up somewhere when you're supposed to. It's so out of character for you; someone calls someone else, and so forth. Then the search, and then the ultimate assumption. *Humans* are so predictable. You aren't around, so you're obviously a victim of foul play and gone for good. Number-one recording artist to number-one missing person to number-one marketing ploy. Got it? Meanwhile, I'll get some reissues going, and when you come back, the world will be your oyster. And you did nothing more than check out to get in touch with your inner self."

"Sort of like drug rehab," Sam said.

"Better!" Jimm laughed. "It's going to work—*trust me.*"

"It's right up here, about another mile," Sam said, pulling into a dirt road to turn around. "I know you say you don't want to know, but we know you do anyway, so if you need to find me, continue up this road. Even then it won't be easy."

"O.K.," Jimm answered.

Sam was surprised and relieved that no reprimand followed. He stopped the car and got out. When he opened the trunk to get his duffel, and saw his amp, the gravity of what was about to happen suddenly hit him; he felt dizzy, short of breath. *I'm really doing this?*

Jimm was already in the driver's seat by the time Sam had pulled the duffel out and closed the trunk. In one smooth movement Sam slung it over his shoulder and shook hands through the open window.

"Don't worry, Sam," Jimm said. "This will work out beautifully, I can feel it. *Trust me.* I hope you're ready to be a *star.*"

Sam nodded and turned away. He heard the car pull away behind him as he took a deep breath of cool, crisp mountain air and began the trek up the steep road toward *stardom.*

ACT II
REDEMPTION

The road to stardom was a dusty, one-lane dirt road paved with alternating bouts of anxiety and excitement. Sam trekked up the hill, gasping from exertion. "What am I doing? What have I done?"

He managed to maintain his pace by promising himself that if he wasn't able to handle it—whatever *it* was—he could always return. He stopped and watched a covey of quail cross the road, the mother leading a single-file procession of bulbous early arrivals that teetered drunkenly as they hurried after her.

"Shit, Sam, what are you doing to yourself?" He put his duffel down and sat on it. "This is great. You had the best night of your career last night and you've got a number-one record. Let the man do his job. Can't live your life in a day. This is the chance of a lifetime—don't fuck it up."

A field of wild mustard radiated its brilliant yellow in the olive-toned shade of the filtered sunlight. Sam sat equalizing his breath, listening intently. There was a strange silence, a noisy *nosy* quality that drowned out the rustling of new leaves high in the trees above.

"I know you're all watching out there," he happily announced to the wildlife stealthily observing.

The gate of Gray Elk's property filled Sam with memories of his previous departure: Kelly's pursed lips and brooding silences, her accusatory half-glances and deep, disgusted sighs. He stopped and surveyed the arrival area—the parking lot, the teepees, outhouses, and makeshift office—just to make sure she wasn't there.

Now, all he had to do was lay low while Jimm made him a *star*. "I'll show her . . . I'll show them all," he said, slinging his duffel from one shoulder to the other, renewing his pace with unguarded vigor.

The roundhouse, a large dugout in the center of the meadow where meetings and sweats took place, was covered with a white plastic tarp held down by old truck tires. Soon Gray Elk would remove the plastic, allowing a return of the grass and weeds, giving it the appearance of an ancient burial mound. Sam went across the field to the far side, circling the white bump. The entrance to the subterranean room was a dormer at ground level, covered by a sheet of waterlogged plywood. A magnificent rack of elk antlers was proudly perched on the sill above the opening.

Sam continued down the flats into the lower pasture, where the road led around a stand of cottonwood, sprouting new greenish-gold leaves out of blood-red shoots, coerced by the lengthening light of the late-winter days. He felt his heart beat an almost tribal rhythm, as if he were returning home to a never-before-seen place, deep-set in his ancestral memory. His mouth was full of a strange taste: electricity, excitement?

Gray Elk's house sat on a small knoll just above the lower pasture, situated so that the entire property was visible out of the upstairs windows. The lower pasture was wired off halfway down. Against the barbed wire fence sat a small blue-and-white trailer with ornamental splotches of orange rust.

"I can see why he jumped at my proposal," Sam muttered. "Nine hundred a month for that? He probably laughed when he saw me coming in one of his premonitions."

"Sam, who are you talking to?" Gray Elk appeared from behind the open hood of the pickup parked in his driveway.

"No one," Sam offered, hoping Gray Elk hadn't heard him. "I suppose that's it?" he said, pointing at the trailer.

"Yes, it is. Good to see you!" Gray Elk wiped his hand with a dirty rag before extending it. "I'd give you a hug but I would get grease all over you."

Sam put his bag down and covered their grip with his left hand; it seemed like a blood-brotherly thing to do. "You look great, just the same as the last time I saw you."

It was true; Gray Elk's stately, ageless features might as well have been chiseled in granite. He was thin, a few inches taller than Sam—about six feet five—with sleek gray hair pulled back into a long ponytail, and a matching bushy mustache. His narrow jaw and buckteeth gave the impression that he was constantly smiling, as if tickled by a private joke or reveling in shamanistic bliss.

"I can't say that I ever expected to see you again," Gray Elk said, still working his hands with the rag. "Then again, it's often those very people who seem to return."

He grinned again. Sam wondered what the joke was. *I'm here to get off the scene for a while. I've already committed to my nine hundred bucks' worth; you don't have to fleece me with your voodoo bullshit.*

Gray Elk continued. "That trailer is a vehicle of great proportions. Many things have happened within it. Enough, though—I'll introduce you to Iris, then we'll get some of the rules straight."

Rules? I'm paying rent. What fucking rules does he mean?

Gray Elk read his expression. "Not rules in that way. We'll be living in close proximity, and *you* have requested that we do things for you. It's just a *powwow*."

Sam didn't like the sound of that any better.

The house was sparsely furnished, the bottom floor dominated by the kitchen and large pantry, the bathroom just inside the door.

In the corner, a potbelly stove stood next to a small couch; the opposite side of the room along the window was occupied by a large dining table with a mixed set of garage-sale chairs.

Gray Elk instructed Sam to sit at the table and went upstairs to get his wife. The window looked out to the upper pasture and a small, bare garden that was waiting for spring. Above him, Sam heard footsteps and muffled voices, then came a click that sounded like a big-screen TV powering down. A mild panic struck him. *What if they see my story on the news?*

"Sam, I'd like you to meet Iris," Gray Elk said. Sam had expected a soft, shy, dark-skinned woman with long braids and moccasins. The woman he met was tall, big-boned, fair-skinned, and wore country-style overalls and work boots. Her reddish-brown hair was cut square, as if she'd done it herself, all emphasis on function, none on style.

Iris' grip was strong, masculine, challenging. The steely coldness of her eyes warned that she was no one to fuck around with. Sam was relieved that she was unattractive and not glad to see him; it removed the worst type of distraction he could imagine.

Gray Elk meticulously related the ground rules. Basically, Sam was not welcome in the house or within the perimeter of the rough picket fence, except for the outdoor laundry area and the shower next to it. There was an outhouse in the trees along the fence line. "You can use the clothes washer on sunny days only, since we run all the electric on solar cells," Gray Elk said.

Iris had yet to do anything but glare.

Sam remembered the clicking sound. "Do you have TV or Internet up here?"

"No, only a TV connected to a VCR," Gray Elk said. "A man in town handles my Web site, mailings, and scheduling. I share him with a few other businesses. We're cut off from civilization, and we like it; it's why people come here." He eyed Sam sharply. "I don't know why you came. I imagine you have your reasons."

"I just came to get away for a while, like you said." A vague answer, an evasion. Sam felt anxious. *If only Iris would give up on the evil eye.*

"I'll show you around," Gray Elk offered. They got up and left the kitchen, Sam wondering if his landlord had married a mute.

"Don't let Iris bother you," Gray Elk said in hushed tones, his arm around Sam as they walked down the field toward the trailer. "The last person who lived in the trailer got out of line. It was hard to get rid of him and she's been leery of anyone else occupying it. We live in seclusion and we're used to it. I'd appreciate it if you'd make yourself as quiet and invisible as you can at first; she'll warm up to you. She is a fantastic woman, *trust me.*"

The words sent a chill down Sam's spine.

At last they reached the small sheet-metal box, jacked up on blocks, that was to be Sam's abode for the coming months.

"This is the original dwelling on the property," said Gray Elk. "I lived here while I made the house, and Iris moved up after we'd finished. I think she harbors a little jealousy toward it, since it has almost as much of a claim to be here as she does, maybe more. A lot of my spiritual awakening came in that trailer, alone, consumed with my work. I stocked it full of food and other things that I thought you'd need. Did you bring anything? Is your car in the parking area up near the gate?"

Sam shook his head.

"Oh, you really did come to get away . . . releasing all your property!"

More bullshit. Save it for the paying customers.

"There are sleeping bags for blankets, and sheets on the bed. And all the water you need, right there." Gray Elk pointed to a freestanding spigot in the yard. "It's the sweetest well water in the world. Comes from five hundred feet down. The refrigerator and stove run on propane. I filled the tank for you; it ought to last the month. When it runs out, disconnect it and put it in the pickup. I'll get it refilled when I go to town, which is twice a week on average. I'll leave a pad of paper in the cab; just write down anything you want from the store and I'll get it for you, as per our agreement."

Right. Delivery charges included.

"The property behind the fence is BLM—Bureau of Land Management—where ranchers pasture their cows and horses. I really don't think anyone will mind if you do some exploring. The property on the other side of the main road is National Forest; you can hike around there, too. I don't have anything on my schedule for about a month, so until then it's just us three. You'll be left alone, since that's what you wanted."

The door of the trailer loomed like the portal to the next phase of Sam's life. Gray Elk's voice dropped to a whisper, as if he were sharing a state secret. "I ran an electric cord out here, and there's a portable heater, more like a blow-dryer. Use it sparingly; it drains a ton of juice and we're on solar, like I told you. If the batteries start getting low, Iris will cut you off."

Sam looked back toward the house, half-expecting to see Iris peering down from the upstairs window. The house seemed haunted, its vaulted roof reaching up into the sky.

"Look, Sam, there is only one thing that *I* am adamant about."

The sudden emphasis on the word "I" sounded strange to Sam, as if he'd been dealing with an intermediary so far.

"As I told you, many things have happened on this spot. Much of it is chronicled in a journal inside the trailer. You are free to read it or write in it if you want; in fact, I encourage you to do so. But it *must not* leave the trailer. It must remain here, O.K.?"

"Sure," Sam agreed. *What's the big fucking deal?*

Gray Elk turned and retreated up the hill, to the house, as if he wanted to leave Sam alone for his first encounter. Sam took a deep breath and opened the door. The musty scent of mildew wafted out. "I guess that's to be expected," Sam said to no one—the first of a thousand conversations with himself.

He stepped up onto the metal grate that hung from the threshold and stepped in. The trailer swayed under his weight. It was an oblong box with every inch of space planned out for maximum efficiency.

"At least it looks bigger on the inside than it did from out there."

Sam shut the door behind him to get the full effect. The bed was against the back end, under a small, TV-tube shaped window with a frayed floral curtain held up by pushpins. The kitchen area was built into the wall opposite the door—a small stovetop and sink with a fridge below, reminiscent of a motel mini-bar. A kerosene lamp sat on a low ledge at the side of the bed. There was another ledge just like it on the other wall, about a foot in depth. Sam dropped to his hands and knees to investigate. The ledges connected in a U-shape along the perimeter of the trailer. The bed was hinged in a tri-fold design, which allowed it to become a dinner table with bench seating.

The cabinets were stocked with staples; Gray Elk had gone to great lengths to make him feel welcome.

"Maybe I misjudged that guy; it's his wife I'd better watch out for."

Then Sam saw it in the sink: a half-gallon jug of Jack Daniel's with a hastily scrawled card:

The sink isn't plumbed, but you can fill it full of water and wash in it. It drains on the ground outside. I hope this makes up for it.

Sam sat back on the bed. It was soft but firm, a four-inch-thick foam pad. He bounced on it, testing its strength while surveying his surroundings. Then he froze, as if grabbed from behind by a strangler, in a grip so tight that he couldn't breathe. A cold sweat broke out, yet he felt hot and began clutching at his sweater, trying to pull it off.

"Got to move," Sam said, thinking he might be able to outrun the anxiety. He found plates and glasses in a cabinet above the stove and pulled a tumbler down. Whiskey was always the best medication for the *feeling*; what else could this be?

He twisted the top off the jug and was pouring before the cap twirled to a stop on the floor. The warmth of the whiskey began to fill him with a sense of well-being and self-appreciation for having the courage to risk everything, to walk away from comfort, to follow his dreams.

He took another swig. "To indulge in bullshit," he laughed, coughing. Then he nodded knowingly. "I can do this."

"What you need ish" — slurring his words after two full glasses—"a walk up the hill to watch the first sunset." The door creaked as it opened. Sam checked the area to make sure it was clear of the enemy and skulked up toward the road. The warmth of the sunlight had faded into a sharp coolness, and everything in his visual field seemed to have a sharp black outline.

He slogged his way up the path, crossed the road, and climbed the hill that would afford an unobstructed view to the west. Halfway up he felt as though daggers were piercing his lungs. He sat to catch his breath, watching his exhalations turn to steam in the fading daylight.

"Got to see it . . . got to see it!"

He stood, and stumbled on up the hill, a man on a mission. The exertion, combined with Tennessee's finest, had him coughing by the time he reached the pinnacle and saw the last flashes of the fiery sun fade into the horizon.

Darkness seemed to crowd in instantly. Now he was atop a steep ridge (known, he learned later, as "Suicide Ridge"), learning the first lesson of the country: always carry a flashlight. He tried to retrace his steps, and managed to descend with only two falls of any consequence. The problem was, the lower he got, the darker it got. The moon had yet to rise, and the twinkling star-power was useless.

He stumbled into a ditch beside the road. It was cold; the temperature had dropped at least twenty degrees, and Sam learned the second lesson: wear a warm coat.

He righted himself, the whiskey still surging through his blood-stream, and followed what appeared to be the driveway to the house. The ground seemed lighter colored, beaten down. He stopped and listened, hoping to hear something that would assure him he was on course. When he rounded a massive pine tree and saw the glow of a TV in the upstairs window, he was relieved to know that he had returned safely from his first wilderness expedition.

The trailer was as cold as a freezer. He groped in the darkness, found the heater, and clicked it on. A small red light glowed as the high-pitched engine whirred out hot air. He reached for a light switch on the wall, as if it were his birthright to have on-demand lights, electricity, and warmth. As his hands traced the wall surfaces of the trailer, he hit the globe on top of a kerosene lamp and realized he'd found the light.

"No problem," he said, searching in the dark for matches.

It was useless. After pulling out silverware, crescent wrenches, and the journal—the *famed revered fucking journal*—he gave up.

"So much for being invisible," he said, shamed by having to bother his hosts for something as trivial as a match. "But first . . . another taste."

Taste tasted, he stumbled out the door and ambled across the clearing to the fence. The gate groaned and the spring whined as he stumbled into the yard. He knocked on the door, lightly at first, then *mezzo forte*.

The door opened and he almost fell over the threshold. Iris stood there, fresh out of the shower, the folds of her abundant skin hanging over the edge of a tightly wrapped towel, her cold eyes demanding.

"I'm shorry"—*I can't still be drunk after all that hiking!*—"I don't shmoke."

Iris shook her head, disgusted. "You don't smoke, huh? Well it's obvious you *do* drink!"

Sam recoiled. "No, I'm shorry. I mean, I don't have any matches for the kerosene lamp."

She slammed the door in his face. Sam turned to leave, not wanting to risk any further repercussions from bothering the Gray Elk family. Just then Iris opened the door and thrust a box of safety matches into his hand. Before he could thank her, the door slammed shut again.

He tipped an imaginary hat. "G'night, ma'am."

He went to the Gray Elk's truck and opened the door. He grabbed the pad of paper and scribbled in the darkness:

flashlight
batteries

Bright morning sunlight filtered through the torn sheet that covered the window above Sam's bed. A cacophony of chirping and cawing was in full fanfare outside—bird warfare, complete with scratchy feet on the metal roof. It wasn't exactly the perfect accompaniment to the fuzzy double vision and whisky-coated thick tongue of his hangover.

Although the sun was out in full force, the trailer was still cold. Sam's breath left a steamy trail as he threw off the covers and got up to make his way to the outhouse.

It was only twenty yards from the trailer. A wet splotch in the dust of the driveway attested to his failed journey sometime deep in the night.

"Iris is going to love that," he said, while returning to the trailer, squinting in the morning glare.

The next necessity was something to soak up the churning acid in his belly.

"You forgot to eat last night," he stated to the cold empty space, surprised to see that hardly a dent had been made in the jug of smoky brown liquid.

He carried a saucepan outside to the spigot in the yard. The cold, clear water had an earthy sweetness. After holding his head under it until the cold seemed to freeze his brain, he filled the pan and went back inside. Gray Elk had left a towel on the coat hook inside the door, and Sam grabbed it, grateful for his host's consideration.

"Boy, I sure came up here unprepared," he said to himself as he dried his hair. He realized that he'd embarked on the journey as if he were going to a posh resort like the Post Ranch. "That list is going to get awful full this first week."

The propane stove lit on the first match, and while the coffee water heated, Sam searched the cupboard for breakfast. After pondering his choices, cereal and oatmeal, he opted for toast. Then he remembered: "No electricity—no toaster."

In a moment of pioneering ingenuity, he removed the saucepan and singed the bread on both sides in the blue flames. The crunching sound of a peanut butter shmear on carbon-coated wheat bread had a musical quality to Sam's ears as the water on the stove began to simmer. He tossed coffee grounds into the pot and let it boil like a prehistoric tar pit. When the consistency was mud, he ran it through a strainer.

"My first country breakfast, and a wonderful one it is! I can definitely do this!"

Sustenance in his belly, fresh air, the advent of spring just around the corner: Sam felt alive, almost newborn, as he retraced his steps of the night before. It was better to get his bearings in the daylight.

"No more night excursions, Sam, you could have ended up frozen in some ditch last night. You don't want to be *that* dead!"

Dead. The word sent a chill down his spine. As if death were nothing more than a change of scenery, a move to a place out of contact with a previous existence, but not necessarily void of awareness. In the literal sense of that definition, he *was* dead. Even an *accelerando* of his pace couldn't shake the feeling that he was now treading on a parallel plane, while his friends and interests, *his world*, revolved without him. An odd sense of jealousy and loneliness fell over him, blanking out everything—even drowning out the rustling in the brush beside him.

It wasn't until the wild turkeys came rushing out of the underbrush, cackling and flapping their wings in flightless flight, that Sam returned to the plane of his new existence. Their abrupt entry into the clearing and sudden noisy departure inverted his perspective, like a familiar chord with a new and unexpected bass note. All along, that had been the most destructive part of the *feeling*: dwelling on what could be or should be, rather than reveling in what was.

"Here I am," Sam said, stopping to catch his breath. "Ready to find something new and to let Jimm create what I've always wanted." As if the *feeling* had been training and dues to pay for achieving a dream, making it reality.

A gigantic Valparaiso oak, dead for many years, lay at the top of the ridge. Its trunk undulated like a snake along the ground, with twists and turns rising up to the heavens and curving back to the earth again. The thick bark was filled with holes, stuffed with cracked acorn shells from years of woodpecker harvesting.

Sam climbed the crook in the trunk and sat appraising his surroundings: the white bump of the roundhouse in the clearing, the top of his trailer parked below the house, and the large pasture below that, dropping into what appeared to be a lush river valley. Far off to the west, through a saddle between two ridges, he saw a hazy blue expanse and the horizon beyond—the edge of the continent. "This must be about three thousand feet up! No wonder it's so fucking cold at night."

He returned to the road and heard a car coming. Ducking into a stand of high brush, he waited for it to pass, then continued down the driveway toward the trailer. It was strange to be going nowhere, with nothing to do, in stark contrast to the endless rounds of errands, business calls, and practice that had dictated his every step through adult life.

A little too strange. He felt a moment of panic and hurried to the trailer like a morning commuter goes to the office, with purposeful intent, sure that something would make itself known: a job, a task.

Getting situated in the trailer took less than ten minutes, including sweeping out the dirt he'd tracked in the night before. He opened the windows—including the vent on the top that noisily resisted every turn of the crank—and sat on the ledge next to his bed. He looked at his watch. He felt like scribbling the days on the wall, like a prisoner in solitary confinement.

"I'd better be careful," he said aloud. "Relax and enjoy the ride. Try not to think of what's happening out there."

He fought the inclination to write *newspaper* on the list in Gray Elk's truck, knowing it would only serve to heighten his boredom, and most dangerously, incite him to give up. Give up on his *word!*

"Hell, it's only a couple of months. You can do this."

This time it was more of a pitiful plea. He eyed the jug on the counter and weighed the consequences.

"I need it now more than I'll need it later. Just going through a tough adjustment period," he reasoned.

Thus began the first leg of Sam's wilderness experience, a long trek through a fiery jug, enlightenment via Tennessee. The first sips were warm, like an embrace, comforting, and served to make the stillness of his surroundings more interesting.

That's how it started. By early afternoon, he was singing, providing all the horn parts of imaginary big-band arrangements, doing Gershwin tunes before resorting to Cole Porter. His banging drum fills, open handed on the counter top, during the shout choruses (long repeated riffs laden with vibrato), set up the return to a crooning, swinging finale. The trailer jitterbugged, threatening to dance off its blocks.

"Now, ladies and gentlemen, we have to break for a small pause for the cause."

Sam downed another shot and got up to relieve himself. At the door he was knocked back by the force of the bright daylight. In his duffel he found his shades; he suavely righted them *just so* and made his way out the stage door, where his foot caught on the metallic stirrup step and he fell face-first into the dirt.

Never losing his cool, Sam got up and dusted himself off, adjusted his glasses, and checked to make sure no one had seen. To his dismay, Iris stood in the garden watering, staring, and shaking her head. The way she held the hose, along with her masculine demeanor, gave Sam the impression that she was peeing a constant, steady stream. It made his full bladder throb in empathy. He waved and waddled into the trees.

A deep bond developed between Sam and the jug. He carried it around in a lover's embrace for the next two days. Moving from clearing to clearing, following the sun, he always put it down gently, as if he were seating a date in a fancy restaurant before seating himself. Now he had something—almost a someone—to talk to. He took it to dinner; it sat on the table beside him as he wolfed down a can of chili with a side of crackers. His vision was wavy, and the boat-like swaying of the trailer was almost—

"Excuse me!" Sam said to the now less than half-full jug.

He raced to the door and scurried out. Halfway to the trees, he fell to his knees. Loud coughs, spits, and heaves echoed throughout the peaceful clearing. The bile spewed out, and in it he could taste all his past indulgences.

After a long run of cold water over his head and neck, he brushed his teeth and returned to ground zero, refreshed, beaten but not down. Not yet. He poured another taste, unable to face the headachy aftermath of vomiting in a half-sober state. There was too much going on; he couldn't be alone . . . not yet.

Sam meticulously made his bed—every blanket and sleeping bag smoothed out, hospital corners at the bottom edge, and a crisp turn-back—before he lit the lamp and took off his clothes to get in bed.

"Cheers," he said, lifting his glass to the nighttime spirits.

He drained it and set it down before blowing out the lamp, hoping to drift off into a long, dreamless sleep.

The toxic poisoning was of a type Sam had never confronted before. Two days of drunkenness without time to decompress—other than the brief respite that upchucking had afforded—left him unable to move, racked with a pain so profound that its roots were undetectable. Was it his head? His sides? He felt as though a gorilla had mugged him. His eyes were dry; they felt like sandpaper had been surgically inserted underneath the lids. His hair rustled on a pillow made of crushed glass. The sweet stench of sticky brown whisky oozed out his pores and filled the stuffy trailer, as if he were marinating in some revolting alcoholic concoction.

"I have to get up, have to get some air in here."

He tried and a wave of spins sent him crashing back into the unforgiving sharpness of his pillow.

"Shit, I'm not even hung over yet. I'm still drunk!"

The blood pounding at his temples from the exertion made the vise close, and his vision began to tighten as if he were looking through a letterbox.

When he could stand it no longer, he slid out of bed, crawled across the floor, and pushed the door open. Cool air wafted in, and he lay on the floor, panting, trying to get oxygen, too tired to move any further as he dropped off into slumber, caught in the spin cycle.

The next time he awoke it was worse. The intoxication was gone, and the hangover was now in complete command. Sam lifted his head from the cold linoleum of the floor; the spins in his head had moved to his stomach. Something was churning, forcing itself up from down below. He had to move, to clear himself from the trailer before a full-force eruption. He crawled to the doorway and thrust his body out, scraping his ribcage on the metal step as he tumbled to the ground. On his hands and knees, he began to blow loud exhalations, panting, burping, his mouth watering with acrid saliva, bile collecting while his stomach muscles began the onset of painful cramping, unrelenting involuntary contractions that seemed never-ending as he heaved and heaved.

This time it was neither cathartic nor metaphoric. It was pure self-inflicted hell.

Almost two days later, still able to stomach only water and crackers, Sam began to emerge from the grips of his colossal hangover. The sweetness of the well water was replenishing; he drank it and made cold compresses, rags soaking in a pail as he changed them with great frequency. The dusk had settled into a pinkish-gray hue over the meadow; the distant calls of calves wafted up the recesses of the canyon below. Sam sat up, half-expecting another wave of nausea, but the onslaught had receded, giving way to a hunger so complete that it seemed to envelop him.

He went outside in the last vestiges of fading sunlight and saw a yellow flashlight sitting in the muddy wet splotch by the door. Sam had been unable to make it any further than that to relieve himself during his purge. Even then he'd had to hold himself up in the jamb with both hands and spray aimlessly. Luckily, WATERPROOF was written on the side of the flashlight in large black block letters.

He took it to the spigot and rinsed it down before hanging his head under the rushing torrent. The reality of days without a shower struck him, but the cold night air encouraged him to wait it out for another day—that and the clamoring yearning deep in his gut, a far more primal need demanding attention, fuel, love: food.

Using the flashlight, Sam scoured the cabinets for bounty. The refrigerator held some wilting but edible vegetables: lettuce, broccoli, and zucchini. He took them out to the faucet and rinsed them down and filled the pail and pot.

"Now you're thinking. Conserve the trips."

Sam was becoming accustomed to the ways of the wild; the ensuing meal awaited—his first *real* meal. The attention to preparation and planning had a sensual quality that evoked a twisted sort of foreplay, where, instead of making his attempted conquest comfortable and willing, he was laying it out to devour it with cannibalistic intensity.

Spaghetti boiled in the pot as Sam ate the whole head of lettuce by hand, dipping each leaf in a crude mixture of oil, vinegar, salt, and pepper. The nutrients and vitamins seemed to rush to the aid of his depleted cells, as if he were experiencing a biological jam session, a new outlet for his creativity: gorging, thrusting himself into the self-love of nourishment. Dinner consisted of a full bag of noodles with vegetables, loaded up with hot peppers mixed with a can of tomato sauce, and half a loaf of airy wheat bread—all washed down with water of the most revered vintage, that same holy water that had saved him from dying and had pulled him out of his toxic coma.

He plugged the sink and poured half a pail of water in to soak the dishes when the idea hit him. He took the light and went to the truck and retrieved the pad of paper. The water for rinsing began to warm on the stove as Sam opened a large bag of oatmeal cookies and began to write. As if possessed, he wrote a shopping list of Biblical proportions, creating menus, designating brands and specialty items with comments as to why they were more desirable (flavor, consistency, nutrition), in case Gray Elk might wonder. All the while he shoved cookies into his mouth, each one before he'd finished chewing the previous. The milk in the fridge still had a week to go. He drank straight from the carton in an attempt to clear out the mealy clog that had developed near his esophagus.

Spent, as if in the afterglow of a two-day orgy, Sam scooted over to the bed and lay down holding his belly, imagining the entries on the pad that sat on the counter. Dreams of Cornish game hens, French fries, sautéed spinach, and peach cobbler haunted his consciousness as he descended into the bloated depths of sleep.

The scratches of a squirrel attempting a break-in on the screen covering the ceiling vent woke Sam. His belly was still so full that the only comfortable position was on his back. He awoke in the same zealous state, possessed by a craving for food so intense that he started a pot of water for oatmeal and ate a bowl of granola while it boiled, covering it with the last of his milk.

A bowl of oatmeal and eight slices of bread later, he finally went outside to greet the day. On getting up, he realized the extent of his gluttony. Even then, he snagged a fresh bag of Oreos for the trek to the outhouse. His stomach cramped as he trotted toward relief.

"I hope there's paper in there," he groaned, aware that turning back was not an option. He got to the door and swung it open and was hit by the competing stench of rotting excrement and lye. He stepped back, the knot in his intestines gripping at his midsection. He did a strange double take—the Oreos, the seat—as if something inside him wouldn't let the two share the same space on earth. He dropped the cellophane bag on the ground and jumped inside.

Exiting, he caught a bobcat digging into the bag. The plastic was ripped and the cat had managed to smash its way through most of it; only crumbly pieces covered with saliva were left strewn among the dried fallen leaves.

"Come back here, you might as well finish them off!" Sam yelled, throwing cookie bits in the direction that the cat had fled. He realized the idiocy of his actions and sat down among the leaves, the pungent odor of the outhouse pervading the gulch. *Should I cry or laugh? I carried a bag of cookies to the shithouse. What's wrong with me?*

His stomach felt distended, still cramping while he made herbal tea and lay on all fours, ass high in the air, trying to coax out any extra gas that might be the cause of the bloat that was making it difficult to breathe.

Sam spent the rest of the day visiting the outhouse and paring down his excessive shopping list. His reading of the original was embarrassing, as if he'd exposed some perverted quirk in his personality by ordering porn magazines or sex toys.

The afternoon sun beat down on the trailer. It had finally warmed up; the thermometer on the wall read 78 degrees.

"You stink, Sam. It's time you got your hygiene thing together. I know you're living up here like Grizzly Adams, but you don't have to smell like him."

He grabbed the towel from the hook by the door and went up to the house. Careful not to make a sound, he flexed the gate against the spring hinge and slid through a thin opening. He wandered around the back of the house and slipped past the sliding glass door, half-expecting Iris to be there with a shotgun.

Large square tiles marked the path around to the shady side of the house, where he found two sheds built on redwood decking. A short, wide enclosure with a hinged cover housed the washer and dryer. Next to it was a wooden booth with a corrugated plastic roof. Sam opened the door and saw the roughly plumbed shower. It looked like a half-metal, half-plastic praying mantis.

He stripped, folding his clothes, noticing they were caked with grimy dirt congealed by dried sweat.

"Not only did you forget to shower, but a change of clothes every now and then wouldn't hurt, either."

He turned the spigot and waited for the water to heat up, not sure if it even would.

"A hot shower might be too much to ask for nine hundred clams," he said, testing it with his hand.

Fortunately, the water turned scalding, sending a plume of steam that escaped from under the ridges of the makeshift roof.

Sam climbed in and shut the door behind him. The water drained through the spaces between the decking at his feet. While soaping up, he remembered Iris's disapproving stares.

"I'd better hurry, don't want to use up all the hot water."

There was a carnal quality to the scrubbing, the silkiness of the suds, the warmth of the stream rushing over, enveloping him. It awakened a hibernating libidinous desire, as if the water held some pheromonal estrous essence, teasing, taunting. Every scrub and every rub heightened a horniness so profound that his midsection ached from the weight of his suspended penis.

He shut the shower down, wrapped the towel around his midriff, gathered his clothes, and trucked back to the trailer. He passed the glass door as Iris reached the bottom of the stairs, his protruding missile lifting the towel in front.

No time to explain.

Thus began the next stage, a maniacal masturbatory smorgasbord. All of Sam's sexual experiences, both real and fantasy, flashed before his eyes as he waged an unrelenting assault on his totem. He went through the list again and again, alphabetically, chronologically, by size, by weight, by hair color.

The images began to meld into one another: Frankensteinian graftings of one woman's head onto another's body; flowing blond locks on an ebony priestess. The only mental picture left intact was

Jennifer—her bare chest against his as she straddled him, coming in stuttered *staccato* gasps. Hers was the only image that could release him from the pumping and stroking, sore chafed skin, burning urethra, throbbing balls.

As his juices began to diminish, and he resorted to changing hands and styles due to cramping, there came an urgency to his orgasms, as if they were the only thing that could release him from the grip of his manic obsession.

Finally, on what seemed like the thousandth encounter confined to the bordello of his brain, he came one last time—ejaculating a pasty, boiling-hot stain—and collapsed, every cell and muscle spent: his throat raw from groaning, his neck stiff from constant flexing, his back sore from arching and thrusting.

A profound emptiness overtook Sam as he coughed, wheezing out the last vestige of fleshly desires. An owl called in the night, mocking him, reminding that the world was going on without him, at its own pace—the opera in full procession.

A loud bang rocked Sam from his sleep. A backfire—followed by a deep diesel growl that revved before settling into an idle, like ball bearings rolling in a pan. The grinding clank of a transmission led to the sound of a truck pulling out of the drive.

Gray Elk's pickup, heading for town?

Sam sat up and a spasm seized his abdomen. Clutching it, he managed to stand and walk to the door; every step produced a stabbing pain. Breathing was laborious; each inhalation had to sneak into his lungs, careful not to disturb the angry beast that was in control of his diaphragm. The door opened to a bright blue morning, smoky remnants of spent diesel hanging in crisp, winter-tasting air.

"God, I've got to pee!"

Sam walked to the edge of the woods with small shuffling steps. The urine burned as he passed it. The day had a strange expansive feeling, as if he'd lived through a war or a Biblical trial and had emerged on the other side, the morning of the epiphany.

Clutching his stomach, he made his way back to the trailer and sat down on the bed. The open door let in the light of the day, the fresh cool air, and the sound of birds beginning their vernal awakening.

Sam surveyed his surroundings as if seeing them for both the first and millionth time—*vuja de*. His new eyes spied the journal: a faded leather book half-stuffed with dog-eared entries. The edges of the binding were frayed; the strap that held it closed was almost worn through. The book seemed to have an electric charge; the moment Sam picked it up, a ballpoint pen slid out of its spine and into his hand. He opened the snap, and the journal sprang open to the first virgin page, deep in the middle, past Gray Elk's scribbled entries. The pen took over:

> *I don't know what happened. I came up here thinking I'd get away, wait it out, get myself together—a little peace and quiet. But it's a fucking siege. Like the layers of my excess being peeled away one by one, slowly and painfully, in thick, filmy layers—like a rotting onion, poorly stored—neglected.*

It was the word "onion"—suddenly tears were flowing down his cheeks in streams, dropping to the page and smudging the ink. Sam closed the journal and snapped the strap shut. The paper looked bloated, as if it had been wet and then dried out. He wondered if his tears were mixing with those of others, creating a thread that linked him to some ancestral folklore.

The tears refused to stop. Tears of loneliness came first: tears for his missing friends, his career, his worldly world; all the things that he'd used to create and define his identity. They were followed by self-indulgent *poor-me* tears; petulant *I'll show them* tears. The word escaped his mouth before his mind had even formed the thought: "Mom."

He got up and the pain in his gut stabbed him. This time the pain was a release; he was glad to have something physical to distract him from the wound deep in his psyche. Clutching his belly, Sam stumbled out the door and made his way around the trailer. As he ducked through the barbed wire, a barb caught his shirt, slicing his back. He had to get off the property, as if it were the cause of the stripping away of all that had held him together all these years. He headed for the oak tree across the clearing, a warm place in the sun; maybe it would be a haven from the torrent of raging tears.

"Mom," Sam said again, only this time with pity, not hate; imagining her in her last days, stuck in a French hospital somewhere in the countryside, far from modern medicine, her liver giving out from the poison surging through her bloodstream.

Then came the tears of rage at the young man who blamed her for it, who hated her for it; the overgrown boy who needed her love and had still hoped to prove himself worthy of it—the boy who rated less in her life than a field fungus; the stupid youth who'd felt unloved and invalidated; who had resented her need to feel superior and recreated it within himself, as if by showing them all, he could show her. Tearful confusion, bubbling, babbling—hating himself for needing them all.

Amidst his noisy crying and sniffling, and the throbbing of the slice in his back and his tensing gut, the sun beat down on his chest as the birds sang praises of spring in the trees above. Finally, relief came. Sam lapsed into a halcyon state, beyond sleep, closer to his own supposed obituary—*the marketing ploy of the century.*

Sam awoke in stages, surfacing through psychic layers slowly, carefully, like a diver afraid of the bends. He felt wrung out, stripped, dead—yet alive in a way he had never known existed. But he had no one to share it with, making him doubt its validity.

His back burned as he lay against the rough bark of the stately oak that now shaded him from the setting sun. The cold afternoon air had chilled him through, except for his right side, which felt warm with a humid sweetness, as if the blood from the wound on his back were ebbing and flowing to the tide of his heartbeat. His eyes opened to a sandy-brown hulk lying beside him, waxing and waning half a foot with each respiration.

Shocked, he lay still, afraid to stir the monster asleep at his side.

Sam turned his head and the golden skin flinched, furry ripples stretching across a giant ribcage. It was a horse, a buckskin—black mane and tail, with deer-colored fur.

"Hey there, fella," Sam whispered.

He began to pet the horse across the shoulder and back while planning an escape route in case the animal rolled his way or got up, hooves striking out.

The horse rolled in the opposite direction, far enough to lift its head. Sam tensed, ready to bolt as he continued to pet.

"Where did you come from?" he asked. The buckskin rolled its jaw in a chewing motion. "Looks like we both got caught napping in the sun. It's getting cold now."

Sam was glad to have someone—something—to talk to. He made wider strokes, in part to comfort, but also to hold the horse, to stop it from fleeing.

Moving its weight, the horse righted its backbone as it extended its forelegs. Then a jerky motion pulled its rear legs underneath, and it rocked forward and back until it was upright. Sam rolled away and watched from a crouch, his belly cramping, his back stinging.

"How the hell did that thing lie down next to me without my even knowing?"

The two eyed each other suspiciously, like lovers who'd awakened after blackouts, wondering who their partner was and how they'd gotten there. Sam stood to stroke the horse's head; it complied by lowering its nose before turning and retreating down the ridge into the thicket of madrone trees. When the horse swished its tail as if waving goodbye, Sam saw that it was a mare.

"You tried to hold on," he told himself. "That's why she left." He didn't know if he was talking about the horse or his mother. Sam returned to the trailer feeling lighter, having shed tears and layers, having tested the limits, having learned a lesson.

He ate in silence—a *real* silence, not like the noisy, obsessive solitary confinement of the week previous. He wasn't alone; there was a forest full of creatures that might include him, teach him, show him the way. Without the gluttony of his previous meals, the food tasted fresh and nutritious, nurturing on a profoundly spiritual level.

After dinner, Sam walked the ridge, carrying the flashlight unlighted most of the way, preferring the light of the stars. He stopped to listen, to smell and taste all that surrounded him—again—for the first time.

It started as a pit-a-pat, a light tapping on a tambourine. The air had a soft, moldy smell. Then the wind came up the clearing, the trees rustling as the taps became louder, heavier, faster. Then came a crescendo, a steady drum roll of rain that reverberated inside his enclosure.

Sam thought that his tears of the day before had perhaps encouraged a sympathetic response from Mother Earth. With each gust of wind, the trailer swayed on its blocks, the sheets of water magnifying all of outdoors through the window. He raced to close the vent in the ceiling and put a pot under the steady drip in the kitchen. The wind was blowing the rain sideways now; a stream was flooding in across the threshold under the door. Sam stuffed a towel in the space and assessed his options like a submarine commander.

The air was balmy; it was a tropical storm. In less than an hour, the rain had flooded the flats and created a river across the driveway. Sometime in the night Gray Elk had returned, and his truck now sat on a small island of dirt amidst the raging rapids.

For two days the rain refused to abate. The unending, whipping winds drove the drops through newly weakened rusty holes in the trailer's hulk. They dripped down the walls, leaving soaked splotches in the thin paneling. The moldy scent was returning with a vengeance. Green splotches sprouted on the windows and walls as the bacteria moved in, multiplying.

Sam found some curly white sage leaves that Gray Elk had given him and lit them to mask the scent of the mold. While it eased the odor, it also added to the heaviness of the air. The barometric pressure was so low that the air felt like a waterbed pressing down on him.

Outdoors was encroaching. Sam's forays to the outhouse created a contamination that demanded constant vigilance. He divided the trailer into stages, like a biochemical research center. Stage One, by the door, was already past Code Red, thick with mud and sludge; he could do little more than try to contain it by making a barrier with towels and dirty clothes. Stage Two, the kitchen area, was a Stripping Zone, complete with soiled wet clothes and clumps of mud caking into the linoleum; a second set of towels hung on the cabinets, still barely usable but soon to make their way to the floor. Stage Three, Sam's bed and a two-foot square below, was top priority—Hold at All Cost. There, he was either nude or wore dry clothing from the stack on the ledge along the foot of the bed.

He tried laundry once. Fortunately, the power held out, but the enterprise only increased the mess, with all the trekking back and forth and having to re-dry the rain-soaked clothes on string clotheslines. It added to the humid ambience and fed the insatiable organisms growing inside the walls.

Through it all, Sam never considered giving up and going home. The lines had been drawn, and this war—although far more demanding on his body—had none of the deep psychic pain of the previous week. It was just a giant pain in the ass. It was Sam versus the elements, an enemy more formidable yet far less scary than himself.

"I've fought these before," he said, knowing there was no disgrace in losing, but complete failure in surrender.

And losing he was. The elements were swallowing the trailer, and him with it. During a midnight break in the rain, Sam stripped down to nothing and went out the door. The mud squished up between his toes as he fought the clay-like suction and trudged to the fence to pee. The heavens opened again; he dropped the flashlight as the wind blew his urine back onto him. He picked up the light and stood in the driving rain, showering off his tears, adding one part salt to the million parts fresh that blew in his face.

He stumbled through the mud back to his trailer; the wind had blown the door open. Stage One had burst through its levee and contaminated Stage Two. He grabbed the towels that had made up the now-collapsed dam and wiped off his feet. He laid down a pair of dirty jeans and spread the legs, trying to hold the elements back and resist their push toward Stage Three.

It was a partial success; there was still a small dry area at the foot of the bed. Sam leapt across and landed on the mattress. The trailer tilted as his weight pushed the cinder block foundation into the softening clay. Mud—gritty, grimy mud—was everywhere. It was on the bed, in the bed, between his toes, between his fingers, between his teeth, in the crack of his ass!

He got up and made dinner, giving up on keeping the various sections segregated. Mud was everywhere. As he ate, he ignored the sandpaper-like texture of his ravioli.

The next morning he awoke to nothing, absolute nothing. It wasn't only that the rain had stopped; there was a suspended stillness to everything. The light was a strange silvery gray. No birds sang, no squirrels scratched above him, even the ants that had taken refuge inside the trailer during the storm had fled.

To where? Why?

Sam pulled back the covers and the air stung his face. His breath was steam; inhaling, he felt icicles piercing his bronchia. He reached for the heater and turned it on. The red light was faint. The fan sputtered as it slowly sucked the cells of the battery dry.

"I'll just get it a little warmer and then turn it off before anyone notices."

Sam turned the fan toward him, threw off the covers and made a mad dash for clothing. He started with the cleanest, underwear and socks, before cherry picking from the mud pile for jeans and jersey. The heater clicked and went dead.

"Shit!" he said, imagining Iris standing next to the solar panels, holding the other end of the orange cord, pissed off that she might be deprived of a movie or the use of her blender.

He considered complaining and asking for a rent rebate. But no: "Fuck them, Sam, you can do this!"

Frantically, he moved about the trailer in an attempt to both shorten his exposure and generate body heat. The muddy splotches on the floor had hardened. He picked up the clothes and towels, put them by the door, and began to scrape the linoleum with the edge of a dustpan. As he thrust the door open to sweep the debris out, the cold hit him in the face with an icy slap.

"The water!" he screamed, suddenly afraid that the pipes had frozen.

He pulled on his muddy shoes and ran to the spigot. The ground was still soft underfoot. Sam turned the valve and the water rushed out. The normally frigid spring water felt almost warm in comparison with the arctic air. Sam put his muddy clothes in the plastic basin and began rinsing and wringing, rinsing and wringing—three full cycles before the water stopped turning brownish gray with each new dunking heap.

Fingers numb, Sam raced back to the trailer—carrying the bucket— and tried to reconstruct the clotheslines, which had broken days earlier. He managed to rig up a new set of double-strength twine that sagged with the weight of the moist laundry.

The trailer had turned into Siberia. His clothes and towels were sure to freeze before they had a chance to dry. Sam's terror and hopelessness gave way to a fit of urgent ingenuity. He turned on the burners of his propane stove and put a pot of water on to boil.

"Steam!" Then he imagined a sauna. "Hot rocks!" he yelled, his mind traveling to a wooden closet in a health club far back in his distant past.

Leaving the pot on the stove, Sam left the trailer with the box of safety matches. "I can light a fire; there's not much chance of the forest going up after a soaking like that. Problem is ... firewood?"

He went into the forest on the far side of the property, past the outhouse. There, the trees were thick and underbrush was plentiful. "Kindling is no problem," he happily said, gathering an armful.

He returned to the driveway in front of the trailer, dumped the pile, and went inside to get the laundry pail. Almost all the water on the stove had boiled out of the pan. The air was steamy but still frigid.

"Better save some gas for later," Sam said as he turned off the stove.

Twigs and sticks were easy; logs, however, were another matter. All he could find were waterlogged, rotten, bug-infested lumps that crumbled at his touch. Then he saw it: an eight-foot-high stack of neatly piled firewood covered with a black plastic tarp.

"I can't believe I never saw that," he said, realizing that the truck was gone too, another thing he'd missed. "They must have known the cold was coming and went to check into a hotel. Hell, they probably left during the fucking rain."

Sam approached the woodpile like he was stalking wild game. When he pulled back the tarp he gasped. "The Mother Lode! Shit, I'll pay for it. How much can I use? Spring is just around the corner."

He found a shovel beside the picket fence and began to dig a pit for his fire in case the wind returned. The labor was finally warming him, sweat dripping into his eyes. As he wiped it away with his dirty hands, mud caked into the hollows below the lids.

The labor was consuming, cathartic. After the pit was finished, he eyed the tenuous footing of the cinderblocks at the end of the trailer. He dug up some dirt and started to shore it up. Then he undertook the task of making a water bar to prevent future runoff from doing any more damage.

Finally, it was time to start the fire. In the foot-deep pit he balled a mass of lichen and paper, and built a teepee of dry oak twigs. Over that, he constructed a tripod of split logs. The fire flared up the instant he struck the match, as if it were trying to fill the vacuum created by the absence of warmth.

The bonfire raged and Sam stood back considering his next step: rocks.

"There's probably a river down in the gulch below," he said, suddenly realizing how little he'd explored his immediate surroundings in the almost two weeks he'd been living there. He stoked the fire one last time and set off with a bucket.

He ducked under the barbed wire, crossed the clearing, and made his way down into the brush. The footing was slippery; frosty wetness had collected in the dead wild oats and hibernating poison oak. Sam slid the last ten feet down to a high bank over a raging stream. He saw smooth, softball-sized river rocks on the far bank. From there it would be an easier climb back to the pasture, where horses and cows had beaten a trail up the hill.

Sam swung down on vines, Tarzan style, and filled his bucket with stones. He made three trips to the foot of the trail and stacked the rocks, opting to make the pack train in stages. He had his rocks, now to get them to the fire. The exertion was all that separated him from frostbite. Sam undertook the transfer with ardent fervor.

Spent, gasping for air as he dumped the last pail of rocks into the hot fire, Sam sat on a log and panted, the wood smoke billowing high into the colorless winter sky above him. As his hands began to thaw in the heat of the flames, they itched as if returning to life, healing from an almost-frozen state.

Now to try the first part of his experiment: with a shovel, he transferred the hot rocks from the fire into a metal bucket and into the trailer. There was nowhere to put the bucket, other than on the burners of the stove, not nearly central enough. He retreated and returned with a cinderblock he'd found along the fence line and set the pail on it.

Some heat, but not enough. Sam felt the stones' warmth only when he sat practically on top of the bucket. "Of course," he announced to the empty spaces, recalling the image of a flabby old man in the sauna pouring water on hot rocks. He spilled out a glass of water ... steam! "Now to find a balance—steam for moisture and instant heat, the bucket for radiant heat. I can always use the stove, too!"

Things were looking up; he'd found a way to deal with the most recent plague. He congratulated himself for his ingenuity while mindlessly scratching the infernal itching on his wrists and forearms.

Sam spent the rest of the day stoking the fire, transferring rocks, continually moving, scratching. As the gray light of the day began to fade, the glow of the fire took on a brightness and purpose. Sam hunkered down beside it to wait out the freeze, winter's last stand.

The experience of his staged death, his stardom, the *feeling*, had all given way to primal warfare—for his life, for his very soul. He was beginning to feel like a survivor. He warmed a can of chili in the bonfire while he exchanged some rocks that had chilled for new ultra-hot ones. Chewing on a spoonful, he sat scratching at his wrists and a new spot that had sprouted a welt on his belly.

"Must be allergic to the smoke," he said, spooning more chili out of the blackened can.

By bedtime, the trailer had achieved a modicum of warmth, at least compared to the chill that was gripping outdoors. Sam took two pairs of socks that were still damp from the morning rinse and filled each of them with two small hot rocks, fresh from the fire. He placed them under the covers of his bed and put a fresh pail on the cinderblock; he stoked the fire one last time and retreated to bed feeling successful for having survived the day, and hopeful about his chances of outlasting this new ordeal.

Crack!

Sam thought the bang was a gunshot until he heard the thunderous crash. He sprung up; the cold was more intense than ever. He went to the door and looked out. A giant piece of a tall pine lay across the driveway. The freezing temperature had split the trunk and sheared off a clean slice. A white winter light pervaded the flats; the embers in the pit were long dead. The cold bit at his skin and he felt he was being freeze-dried.

He pulled on his jacket. The scratching against his wrist as he pulled his arm through the sleeve was almost orgasmic. He felt the chills go up his spine as he continued to rub, *prestissimo, fortissimo*. He eyed the strange welts on his forearm: red around raised yellow bumps, oozing amber.

"Fuck!" His mind raced back to his wood gathering and his climb along the vines by the stream. "Poison Oak!"

There was no time to stop and ponder the situation. He had to get the fire going, then wash off, change clothes, and most of all—no scratching!

"Do your job," he commanded, dumping the pail of cold rocks into the fire pit and piling on kindling.

With the fire raging, he piled his clothes in a heap and went to wash in the spigot. The freezing air and water, the raging fire, all seemed to inflame the welts on his arms; they crawled and oozed as if a creature were trying to escape from within. A headache had accompanied his rude awakening, one that neither coffee nor aspirin had been able to conquer. Sam found some antihistamine tablets in the cupboard, and even though they were well past the expiration date, he took two in hope of stifling the raging rash that was spreading across his torso.

Time again to change rocks. Afterward, Sam boiled some water in the fire for tea, opting to save whatever propane he had left. He hadn't seen Gray Elk's truck for days. There had been no smoke from their chimney, no blue glow from the bedroom. Sam almost considered a break-in. *Would they understand?* Iris wouldn't. It was a moot point, anyway: Sam had developed a pioneer's snobbishness; this was all a test of skill, will, *integrity,* his kind of fight.

The tea was warm and soothing with a wood smoke aftertaste. Swallowing was becoming difficult; his throat was scratchy and beginning to close. A bone-tired fatigue had set in; his neck was sore from holding up the weight of his head. Sam stoked the fire, changed rocks, and went back inside. The cold of the trailer had a new strangeness to it. His body felt warm, yet with every move the cold air seemed to find an open spot to invade, to penetrate, to torture.

Sam turned on the burners of the stove, put *rock-socks* under the covers, and got into bed again, his teeth rattling as the chills took over.

A song, a far-off, indiscernible melody—a sweet siren song hanging in the open space above the cacophonous battle of percussion and harmony. Trombone glissandos, the slides wavering up and down as if played by disturbed and angry primordial beasts; glissandos that seemed to surge out of swirling eddies and get swallowed up again; an underwater bubbling tremolo descending into *basso profundo.*

The music was death—or worse, defeat—and represented all that Sam had to escape, to save himself from. He felt the cold waters envelop him. There was no choice; it was as if his psyche or his integrity had thrust him into the torrent, to live or die with dignity.

At last, the shore, the cashmere softness of the sand. "Jennifer!" Sam screamed, wailing out in relief. Her bare breasts swayed and her moist skin glistened in the sun as she moved toward him, her full hips inviting...

Splash! Back into the water. Through the swirling rapids Sam saw Jennifer standing on the dry riverbed, reaching for him, then pushing him back, dunking him as his vision darkened and he lapsed into a womb-like coma.

"Almost thought we were going to lose you there!"

A compassionate voice rang out, far off on the distant edges of consciousness, yet somehow very near.

Sam opened his eyes. His eyelids felt heavy and coarse. Everything was a fuzzy blur at first, morphing into Gray Elk, who sat smiling, his buckteeth gleaming.

Sam jolted upright, disoriented by surroundings that were completely foreign. He fell back against the pillow, poleaxed by a wave of dizziness. "Where am I?"

"In the house. When we got back, I saw the fire pit and all those rocks. The solar cells were spent; you ruined the batteries. Iris was really mad. You left your heater on, it blew a circuit when I turned on the generator."

"You have a fucking generator?!" Sam managed to say before his anger gave way to fatigue and he lay back into the pillow, defeated.

"Here," Gray Elk said, handing Sam a glass of water, holding it while he sipped. "Yeah. So I went to the cabin and you were in there. The heater was on, but no juice; the burners were on but you had run out of propane. It was as cold as a freezer even though the cold snap outside had broken.

"You were in your bed thrashing, talking about some music, asking me to make it stop. You were boiling with fever. I brought you in here; Iris probably saved your life, dipping you into those cold baths. You called her Jennifer, and started humping her leg like a horny puppy." Gray Elk laughed and shook his head. "She threw you back into the tub. I thought she was going to drown you."

Sam nodded. The dreams were beginning to merge with reality; the mere act of thinking taxed his fragile reserves.

"You need to rest," Gray Elk said, holding Sam up so he could fluff the pillow. "When you wake up you're going to have to tell me about the rocks."

Days had passed since Sam had come out of his fever; the poison oak had healed to dry scabs that didn't itch as long as he avoided contact. He had resettled in the trailer; Iris had done a masterful job of cleaning it out. The bill for the new batteries and the doctor's house call hadn't been too steep, considering how far he'd had to come: less than five hundred dollars, including antibiotics for the onset of pneumonia and the infected slash on his back, plus steroids for the poison oak.

And through it all, they had ignored the fact that they were dealing with a dead man. Or hadn't they even realized that as far as the outside world was concerned, he was at least *missing*?

Doesn't anybody around here read the paper? Although, I guess it's not Jazz Central.

Iris had softened in her feelings toward Sam; she was not friendly, but nurturing. She brought his meals and did his laundry, even after he'd regained enough strength to attempt it on his own. He was under the oak tree awakening from a nap in the sun one afternoon as she crossed the driveway to ask: "Would you like to join us for dinner?"

"Yes, thanks," he answered. He coughed a raspy, gurgling bark. The blockage in his lungs had begun to loosen and breathing was fairly free and painless now.

"I'll make you some tea for that."

"Well, Sam, you're into your fourth week. How do you like it so far?" Gray Elk asked, tongue-in-cheek. His grin was part maniac, part therapist.

"It's been weirder than I expected. I've learned a lot; I almost can't remember what everything was like before this. One thing, though: I sure miss music."

Gray Elk smiled that condescending smile that Sam remembered hating so much two years before; it didn't bother him this time.

"I was wondering how long it would take," Gray Elk said, helping himself to another serving of mashed potatoes. "I found it very strange that you arrived without an instrument or stereo, and that you didn't ask for one. Your fever dream told a lot. You have many issues surrounding music."

Many heap-big issues, Medicine Man. Sam wanted to smack him, and at the same time realized that Gray Elk was right.

Gray Elk continued: "The rest of us think of music as art and enjoyment, or even a distraction. We never imagine the gut-wrenching upheaval of the soul in regard to a man and his music. Yet, throughout history the stories are as old as the ages, even mythical, and almost cliché."

The ensuing silence was deafening. It had a symphonic texture, as if awaiting a cue from a nonexistent conductor.

It was Iris who broke it, her voice shattering the tension. Her cold blue eyes seemed to have softened; the fleshiness of her cheeks gave her face a Rubenesque yet rural beauty. "I have my father's guitar. It's very old and was his most prized possession. It hasn't been played since he died." She put her hands on the table and pushed her chair back. "Would you like to see it?"

As excited and fearful as Sam was about playing, he knew there was only one answer. "Of course." He wondered if playing would have the same existential feeling that conversation seemed to have, now that solitude had whittled his psyche down to the marrow.

Iris returned from upstairs carrying an old black case with antique brass clasps. The handle was a length of knotted rope. The case looked small in comparison to what Sam usually carried.

She laid it on the floor at his feet, as if she didn't want to open it herself, afraid something might escape. Sam slowly unlatched the clasps; the hinges groaning as he opened the case. The instrument was a beauty to behold: a small-shouldered Martin-looking thing, its nylon strings discolored with age. An exquisite black-and-white herringbone inlay circled the sound-hole; it seemed to take up more than its fair share of the spruce top, which had gone from its original virgin blond to a dark yellowed bronze. The grain was true and straight; the finish was matte, unlike the plasticky gloss of newer, factory-made instruments.

Sam looked to Iris, and she nodded, assuring him, unafraid, imploring. *Bring him back*, her eyes seemed to say.

Bring me back, Sam almost said in response. He cradled the neck under his left hand, the bottom with his right, and twisted the body of the guitar, lifting it out of the case like a nurse lifts a newborn out of an incubator. It had a feather-lightness to it.

Sam slowly spun it to examine the back, reluctant to play it just yet; it was as if he were stalking a pretty girl from across the dance floor, waiting for the perfect moment. Rhythm as life: timing—dynamics—*soul*.

The back was cigar-brown mahogany, long grained with small swirls that looked almost three-dimensional. The neck was hefty, triangular on the back and wide across the fingerboard, made to last generations. Sam held it close to his body; it was like embracing a new lover.

He lightly touched all the strings; miraculously, it had held its tune during all the years in the case. Sam wanted to ask how many, but realized it didn't matter; it was merely a stall. The silence of the room was crying out for the sound of music—*his music*.

He cradled the guitar into his lap, took a deep breath, waited, and exhaled. The first note was an E, the fifth fret on the B-string. The two open strings tuned to that pitch freely resonated in sympathy, in empathy, as the wood stretched and flexed, coming out of a long hibernation. The note was pure, clean, replenishing. Half-step below, half-step above, back to E, an elaborate slow *appoggiatura*—the E bigger than its neighbors; it had friends. He ventured into the lower regions, played a low G-sharp on the lowest string, defining the E's gender as major as the wood perked up with the wider, slower vibration. A lovely, long, somnolent cadenza followed, replete with counterpoint and chordal cascades, seamless transitions and modulations, oscillating moods that told a story: his story, Iris' father's story . . . *life's story.*

It finally petered out with E again, struck each time with a different inflection, as if to say: perspective, attitude . . . *soul.* The last note was the harmonic on the high E-string above the twelfth fret, the note ringing like a chime and hanging in the air as the guitar resonated against Sam's chest, stirring a silent human note deep within.

He looked up, almost embarrassed, feeling spiritually naked. Iris was transfixed, tears streaming freely down her alabaster cheeks. It was only then that Sam saw his own tears on the side of the guitar. He giggled, anything to break the silent connection to her, to everything. He almost played more but couldn't; it was as if the cosmos forbade it, forcing him to revel in a moment of perfection.

Speech impossible, playing impossible, tears trickling down his face, Sam finally saw a faint passing glimmer of what he was *here* for. Gray Elk's smile seemed to loudly proclaim his credo: *we all take different paths.*

Iris wiped her eyes and reached across the table to put her hand on Sam's forearm. "That was beautiful. That guitar was not always something I liked. In fact, I hated it. My father loved it more than he did me; he never let me even touch it. So many times when I wanted or needed something, he was drunk and playing and yelled at me for interrupting. I guess I was jealous."

She giggled, wiping her eyes dry. "You even look like him—I

hadn't noticed it until I saw you playing—although you play it much better than he ever did."

Sam suddenly understood the root of her mistrust and dislike for him from the beginning, all the way back to that first night when he'd shown up at the door, drunk. It was all wrapped up in the subjective, just like music. While he'd been playing, Iris was a scorned little girl and an angry yet mournful woman with complex issues, many to remain eternally unresolved, hanging in the air like that last note.

"Why don't you play it?" Sam asked, hoping to insert one distinct major chord into the progression of Iris' life.

"I can't," she answered. A little girl's voice had spoken up, not the tough matron whose intimidating presence permeated every square inch of Gray Elk's Reservation.

"Of course you can. This thing plays itself. Just stroke the strings and feel it vibrate against you. You don't even need to use your left hand." He raised it up and held it for her.

She reached out to touch it and recoiled from the contact, as if a repressed memory of a striking or beating had reemerged.

Sam saw it. "Don't be afraid," he said in the soft tone he used for a cautious yet curious fawn. "It's just a guitar: wood and strings. It neither judges nor cares. They're your memories, Iris."

Gray Elk appeared to be holding his breath, hoping. One teardrop began to form at the corner of his right eye as Iris stood to take the instrument from Sam.

She wrested the feather-light guitar from Sam's grasp and smiled. She held it and carefully ran the back of her fingernails across the open strings. The tears that ran down her cheeks formed a pool on the curved wooden side, mingling with Sam's.

Sam spent most of the next week enjoying the onset of spring. He sat in the pasture under the oak tree, playing the guitar, the wind carrying the strains across the flats, an all-points bulletin that he was back. The buckskin mare had returned and often stood nearby grazing or snoozing, reveling in the sun and sound. She jealously guarded Sam, running off two bay geldings one day, and a small herd of white-faced cows and calves the next.

As the new leaves danced in the breeze, Sam played the light *bossa nova* he'd been working on, a series of parallel triads against a pedal tone. The drone was the low A-string, now his favorite because of its pure resonance and the way its vibrations were oddly visible. The mare perked up as if she recognized it from somewhere else and moved in close—and then collapsed. Sam watched with an eerie detachment as her forelegs started to buckle. She knelt and then lay down beside him in exaggerated slow motion. Sam kept strumming but readied himself to jump out of the way.

Lightly—as lightly as a thousand-pound animal can—the mare rolled over and came to a perfect stop, delicately resting against him. Her breathing slowed to a deep steady cadence while he continued serenading. Before long, he too fell into a dreamy state, the guitar resting on him as he rested on the horse.

A loud *bang* jarred them both awake. A thick black cloud rose up from behind the trailer. This time, the backfire was not followed by the rattling sound of an idling diesel, but by Gray Elk's cursing. "Damn!" It sounded very un-shamanistic.

The mare stood up and retreated to the bottom of the pasture. Sam watched her swish her tail, as if to wave goodbye. It was matted and full of leaves. "Got to get a brush and fix that," he said, rising and carrying the guitar back to the trailer. Then he headed up the hill to lend some moral support to his landlord.

Ever since the night Iris had brought out the guitar, Sam had taken all meals with them. He was now allowed to use the indoor shower, and had actually been invited to watch a movie, though he'd declined. It had been so long that he was almost afraid of technology, like an ex-smoker who fears that first puff.

"How's it going?" Sam asked, hoping to distract Gray Elk. It was painfully obvious what the answer was.

"Not very good. I should have listened to Iris and gotten another truck this year. I thought I could milk one more out of this one," he said, sitting on the front bumper, wiping his blackened hands on the front of his dark brown coveralls.

"Let me get that," Sam offered as he saw Gray Elk begin to muss with his hair. His ponytail had begun to come loose and strands were falling into his face. The thought of greasy smears in the silver hair was much worse than even the sight of the mare's tail.

"Thanks. I've got to get this thing up and running. Vision Quest is in about a week. You never came on one; would you like to?"

"No, thanks. I'm here to lay low, not to mix with the human race—present company excepted."

Gray Elk was partly relieved, partly disappointed. The disappointment stemmed from the $800 he charged for the four days. Of all his activities, Vision Quest was by far the most lucrative; practically no overhead, almost pure profit. But he was glad he didn't need to explain that Kelly Tuffalos was coming *and* bringing a boyfriend. He had no desire to see a replay of the scene they'd made the last time the two of them had been at the roundhouse.

"Do any of them come down here?" Sam asked. "I could go into the back country for a day or two."

"No, absolutely not. It's a rule we have, ever since one client decided that he was a brave in our tribe and that he had to live here, his life transformed. We later discovered he'd taken some magic *mushrooms.*"

The word sent chills down Sam's spine, although it didn't seem to have the angry charge it once had. It was tinged with a melancholy empathy for his mother, a poor creature undone by her own folly—and for himself, a creature equally undone.

"Look, the hawk is circling," Gray Elk said.

A Red Tail was hovering above, the sun bestowing a translucent luster on the wing feathers, its tail glowing rosy pink. "Hawk Feather must be coming. I hope he's in time for the Vision Quest."

"Hawkfeathers?"

"Hawk Feather," Gray Elk corrected. "He always arrives about two days later."

"That hawk has been here all day," Sam pointed out.

"Sam, I know you think a lot of our ways are strange."

Bullshit is more like it.

Gray Elk must have heard the silent thought or seen Sam's eyes rolling. "Trust me"—another set of words that evoked chills—"there is more to all of this than any of us will ever know. When Hawk Feather comes, you will see. He is a great man, whose wisdom even the most skeptical have to acknowledge."

Gray Elk's delivery had turned Hollywood Injun. Sam saw why he was such a success; his chameleon-like personality modulated quickly and seamlessly. He would be just as natural in a suit at a Washington fundraiser as he was in his greasy coveralls.

"I didn't mean to offend."

"I know." Gray Elk smiled his Bugs Bunny smile, the one that made Sam feel like Elmer Fudd.

For the next two days Sam noticed that his contemplation had taken on a new and strange quality. His interest in the outcome of *the marketing ploy of the century* was shrinking, swallowed up in a bigger picture, however vague and unformed. He tried to talk it out; the mare was a good listener, but she offered no insight. His self-discovery had led to a fear that the destination itself was in question—like taking the wrong airplane and ending up in Oakland instead of Auckland. The bloated journal once again seemed to call, after sitting on the counter for weeks. Sam wrote:

Where am I going? Why did I do this? Who will I be when I get back? What is a fucking star? It twinkles, it's beautiful . . . and distant.

"Shit," he said, closing the book and snapping it shut.

The gnawing feeling refused to go away. Music, once again, was his refuge, as it had been throughout his life. Immersed in sound, free of intellect, he found sanctuary in the moment.

They began loading with the first light of the morning. A gooseneck trailer attached to the truck was backed up to the gate. Gray Elk and Iris were noisily loading equipment and supplies.

"Can I help?" Sam asked. It had been impossible to sleep through the racket. Each footstep on the metal trailer bed resounded through the flats like the crash of a cymbal—a Turkish onslaught.

"Sure," Iris answered. "You can grab that table and chairs."

"Isn't a Vision Quest where people go off in the woods without food and starve themselves into hallucinations?"

"That's a cynically oversimplified description," Gray Elk answered, leaning against the fence and wiping his forehead with a red bandana after having single-handedly lifted the generator. "I guide people through a ritualistic experience brought on by a variety of stimuli. You really have to experience it to understand the ramifications of the transformation that occurs spiritually."

Properly admonished, Sam continued to help, and was soon resting against the fence himself, panting. The trailer was almost full; he felt as if he were moving a family out of an apartment they'd lived in for years. *I wonder why they need so much shit for four days.*

Alone again, just him and that *feeling*—a new one; or was it the old one morphed into a fearful questioning? Wasn't the need to be recognized and feel superior based in fear anyway? All questions, no answers.

"Maybe I should have gone on that Vision Quest after all," Sam said to the buckskin mare, *arpeggiating* a simple progression, a steady stream of one repeated chord punctuated by a descending bass line. She continued to graze, offering no answers or suggestions.

Might as well try out the new act and see if this horse has perfect pitch.

The descending line crept downward, well past the consonance of the relation to the root of the chord. Sam allowed it to make its way chromatically, fret by fret, all the way to the nut at the end of the neck. He let the open A-string ring out. The mare's ears perked up.

He began the triadic shift against the drone: his new tune. Immediately, the mare stopped picking at the new grass and stepped in and crumbled at his side, delicately resting against his legs, hypnotized in a deep trance.

"I got to take this on Letterman," Sam said as he put down the guitar to pet the horse. He looked up; the hawk that had been circling was gone.

A deep rumble drifted across the pasture, followed by the crunching of rocks under the tires of an approaching vehicle, gas not diesel. What to do? After so long a solitude, interacting only with Gray Elk and Iris, Sam felt like a child looking for a mother's skirt to hide behind. *Some star you're going to make.*

An old brown Chevy pickup with a half-rusted camper pulled up and parked next to Sam's trailer. The door opened, its hinges groaning in protest. A dog jumped out—a black- and-white border collie/ Australian shepherd mix with brown legs, only much bigger—and ran to Sam's trailer. He sniffed at the corners and lifted his leg.

"Same to you, buddy," Sam said under his breath, still waiting for a person to exit the truck. *That dog couldn't have been driving.*

A pair of short legs wearing worn-out tan ropers finally emerged from under the door panel. The man who shut the truck door was short and squat, his body disfigured by age, as if time had twisted his upper torso against his pelvis. A sweat-stained yellowed straw cowboy hat rolled at the brim sat on top of a head that appeared to be fixed directly to the shoulders—neckless. He looked around, aimlessly, as if he had no idea where he was or how he'd gotten there.

Maybe the dog did drive.

The visitor pulled off his hat and scratched his head; a small red indentation from the brim circled his nearly bald bronze pate. He slowly turned, still appearing disoriented. When he saw Sam with the guitar on his lap, reclining against a thick oak, a horse asleep or dead at his side, he scratched some more and placed the hat back on his head just so.

"Pardon me." His voice was a raspy baritone, his delivery slow but deliberate, with the steadiness of a sure-footed pack mule or a top-notch bass player.

"Yes?" Sam answered.

"Is anyone home?"

"They won't be back for a few days. Can I help you?" All of a sudden Sam felt responsible for the property, and when he stood up the mare noisily followed suit. The dog, which had been busy investigating all the scents in the area around the trailer, stopped and looked up.

The old man watched the horse, which stood behind Sam as if guarding him, backing him up, much like the man's dog, which had returned to his side. He coughed a wet cough. "I'm an old friend. I guess I missed them. My name is Hawk Feather. Who are you?"

Sam looked up; the hawk was still gone. *Naw, it couldn't be.*

"Sam Mann." It sounded weird; he hadn't heard his full name spoken aloud in so long. *Too bad I'm probably already a star. It's a little late for a name change.* "They told me about you."

Carrying the guitar like a bloated baseball bat, Sam walked to the fence to complete the introduction with a shake. The dog stepped in between, while Sam felt the mare's breath on the back of his neck. He couldn't tell whether the animals were protecting their own or were in the middle of some silent communication. The dog's eyes were eerie and had a transparent quality that seemed to absorb color and light. "Wow, your dog's eyes are clear. I saw a coyote like that, not more than a month or two ago!"

"Yes they are. But I am not sure he's actually my dog. Sometimes I think I am his human. The clear eyes mean he is a very old soul."

Shaking the old man's hand, Sam felt a strange connection to campfires and peace pipes.

Hawk Feather continued. "It is his last time in an earthly body. Some of our legends disagree on what the next stage is. Some say starting over, but I think an eagle or hawk—or if it is bad medicine, an owl. Sometimes I think that he is actually in a transitional phase and can change back and forth."

Sam couldn't believe what he was hearing and was even more unnerved that it seemed true.

The old man stuck his hands in his pockets and went on. "Was the coyote a joker? Did he try to hurt you?"

"Actually, yes. He tried to steal my watch, then he pinned me to the ground. I thought he was going to kill me, but he stole a button and split." Sam realized that the word split might have a completely different meaning to an old Indian, but Hawk Feather acknowledged what he'd said without question and looked down to his dog.

"Scout?"

The dog skulked away guiltily, as if caught eating off the table or peeing in the house.

"Can I make you something or get you something?" The trailer had been stocked right before Gray Elk left.

"No, thank you. I need a nap. The drive was very long, although I don't remember the last of it," Hawk Feather said. "It is a pleasure to meet you, Sam Mann." His delivery was so deliberate that Sam's name sounded sweet to him for the first time.

A brilliant spring morning greeted Sam. Birds were chirping and the air was full of a tangible green sweetness. Nature's photosynthesis factory was churning, working overtime to restore what hadn't been killed off by the late freeze, generating newcomers to take the place of the departed. Before he'd even opened his eyes, Sam could smell, taste, even hear the brilliant symphony of colors that awaited him outside the door of his trailer.

His dreams had been strangely cinematic, as if he'd been to the movies instead of immersed in subconscious housecleaning. In one, he'd been a hawk and seen the world with an acuity of vision that shattered his concept of color and hue, as if the pigment in his eyes had been filtering and distorting everything. Movement was not just something visually perceived; it was an energy field that created waves of auras that rippled like the circles of a pebble dropped in a still pond.

"It's easy to see where that came from," Sam said as he sat up on the bed, smoothing back his hair, scratching his neck. He stopped abruptly. Ever since the episode of poison oak, itches and scratching had taken on a new gravity. But no ... *sometimes an itch is just an itch*.

As if on cue, another type of scratching began at the door. One of the squirrels who had been showing up lately, wanting to share his granola? He knew he shouldn't have indulged them, but they'd been good guests, making no mess or mischief inside the trailer and retreating as soon as the bowl was empty. But this scratching had weight, like wire brushes on a snare drum: *shu shushu shu shushu shu shushu*, each beat imploring.

Sam opened the door and Hawk Feather's dog trotted in. His clear eyes were a bluish-green, as fresh as if they'd just been topped off at some ecological filling station. He walked by and began to take inventory, sniffing at the corners.

"Make yourself at home. I hope you're housetrained." The dog was too big to challenge or chase.

Sam heard a raspy wet hacking outside, a smoker's wake-up call. He waited until it abated and went out the door. Hawk Feather was starting a fire. "Your dog is in there," Sam said, by way of starting a conversation.

Hawk Feather never looked up, his concentration unwavering as he blew on the smoky embers, encouraging them to ignite. He had apparently built a fire in the pit during the night; there was fresh ash, and the core of a thick log glowed orange under his breath. He stopped blowing to cough, then wiped his mouth on the sleeve of his brown-and-white flannel shirt. "He's not *my* dog. He adopted me a while ago. He's more in charge than we are."

Not more of that old soul shit, please!

Hawk Feather continued as if he'd read Sam's mind. "He disappears for long periods and just appears when he wants. I go weeks without feeding him, and he can stay in the truck for days without having to shit. I don't even remember leaving with him yesterday, but he arrived with me, didn't he? Scout is from another world . . . or perhaps the edge of this one."

Sam turned his rock pail upside down and sat, watching Hawk Feather's leathery arthritic hands work the fire. The flames seemed to dance with his knuckles; his hands were constantly moving. The flames were always a second late—an elegant tango, flesh and flame appearing to share the same space, as if they existed on different yet overlapping planes. The old man didn't look much like an Indian; but then again, feather headdresses were out-of-date and impractical. There was an agile elegance to his movement, a stately calm to his demeanor; he seemed to be at peace with his surroundings and himself.

"They're all out on their Vision Quest," Sam said, sipping some coffee from the tin pot on the fire. It had the taste of wood smoke.

The chief—*had Gray Elk called him a chief?*—seemed to note Sam's condescending tone, then ignored it. "It was my intention to arrive in time to go, or be part of the council, but it wasn't my time." Scout had walked over and sat at Sam's side, and was basking in his mindless strokes. "You have a friend. It is very rare; he generally has little interest or patience with humans. Be careful, he may adopt *you.*"

Sam laughed. *No reason to take the old guy seriously.* "Animals have always liked me, I don't know why."

"I think you do. But then again, maybe because you do not is why they do."

"When you finish your coffee," Sam said, "I'll show you this thing that the horse in the pasture does. It's amazing!"

Hawk Feather nodded and blew into his blue tin cup, letting the steam warm his face as he sat cross-legged by the fire. He set the cup down and pulled out a cigarette.

Now the cough makes sense. Just because he was a medicine man was no reason to think he was more than human.

Hawk Feather stood; his knee cracked with a loud snap, and he walked into the trees toward the outhouse. Scout remained at Sam's side, demanding more attention. Instead of the normal mustiness, the dog smelled of pine needles and wood smoke.

When Hawk Feather returned to the fire, Sam was strumming the guitar, with Scout at his feet. "I thought that looked familiar. That's Ray's guitar, isn't it?"

"It belongs to Iris."

"Ray was her father, a good friend. It is nice to hear it making music again."

Sam was anxious to show off his trick. The performer in him as well as the lack of human companionship had flipped the switch; he felt himself returning, but oddly different, changed.

The buckskin had heard the call of the strings and was munching the green sprigs under the giant oak. Woodpeckers were knocking holes in the trunk high above—a steady one-two-three: *Excedrin Headache #1*. Sam moved into the pasture, strumming lightly, the chords ringing out, mixing with the breeze. It turned into a chiming, blending with the birdcalls and *rat-a-tat* above. He sat and mindlessly wandered across the fingerboard as Hawk Feather sat on the running board of his pickup, watching, smoking yet another unfiltered cigarette.

A dramatic *glissando* from high up on the neck to B-flat—a half step above *the note*—landed with deadly accuracy. Sam let a B-flat7+11 ring out, awaiting its resolution. The mare's chomping slowed, her ears cocked as if she knew—*doesn't everyone*—that the chord resolved to A. Sam tickled the strings, lightly this time, flirting, teasing both the horse and the guitar. The horse moved in with a questioning look: *Do you mean it?*

Yes, I do, Sam said with a stroke of the open A-string, the vibrations warming his belly as the mahogany flexed; the nylon cord was a blur of motion, settling slowly as if double-vision were returning to normal.

And the mare began to collapse, a slow-motion boneless beast gently falling to earth. Sam glanced at Hawk Feather, who sat smoking and staring, seemingly neither amazed nor surprised. It was more as if he had a scientific interest in the whole performance.

"Interesting," Hawk Feather said, field stripping his butt and scattering it in the light breeze. "Are you going to ride?"

"Ride her?"

"Yes."

"There's no saddle or anything," Sam explained.

"So, Sam Mann, she does that for you and you don't ride her? She must wonder what is wrong with you. Or worse, what is wrong with her."

Sam felt duly reprimanded. "How?"

"Why don't you straddle her and let her get up underneath you? Like a camel."

"Good idea," Sam said, acknowledging the wisdom of centuries of tribal expertise. He put the guitar behind the tree and surveyed the golden-colored mare that lay at his feet. She was too thick in the middle; a winter of good forage showed in her belly. Toward her rear, just before her haunches, at the end of her ribcage, was where she was thinnest. Sam put his hand on her, trying to gather the courage to step over. She looked up and he stroked her some more; then she expelled a loud sigh and laid her head back down.

Sam looked over to Hawk Feather for counsel. The old chief lit another smoke and nodded. Sam stepped over the horse as quickly and calmly as he could manage. He lost his balance and dropped to the mare's flank. She stirred and he began talking, trying to calm her as she rolled, pulling her legs underneath—those big strong legs with the sharp hooves at the ends.

The movement knocked Sam further off balance. There was no way for him to vault off as she began to stand. Her front end came up, and he slid back; and just as quickly her hindquarters thrust him forward, banging his nose against the side of her neck.

In what seemed like a surreal slow-motion carnival ride, she was up and Sam was mounted, although tenuously. He was sitting way back, practically on her rump. He looked to Hawk Feather for help. The old man stared intently, a cigarette hanging from his lips, a feathery plume of smoke rising in the air above his hat.

The mare was up now; there was a moment of stillness as if time had stopped. The horse stepped away from the tree, a calm but jiggly ride. Sam had yet to find the balance point, and now that motion was in the equation it was doubly difficult. He tried to pull himself forward by gripping her mane and squeezing his legs together.

Bad idea! Her head and neck were suddenly gone as if they had dropped off her shoulders. Sam felt her spin beneath him, her midsection coiling and *crescendoing* in one violent upheaval. He was catapulted high into the air, toward the middle of the pasture.

During the flight—which seemed much longer than its actual duration—he looked over to Hawk Feather for guidance. He caught the black-and-white flash of Scout running the perimeter of the fence.

Sam hit the ground and came to a rolling stop. Lying supine, he took aural inventory first. He heard Scout running, pacing, panting. No footsteps; the old Indian wasn't coming. What drowned out almost everything was the pounding of his heart.

Next he began a physical survey, going down the checklist with deliberate care. First the extremities: he wiggled his fingers, splayed his toes. Arms bent at the elbows and legs at the knees; no pain, full freedom of movement. Sam sat up; no rib pain or dizziness. He realized the extent of his luck and breathed a sigh of relief before brushing dirt and dry grass off his shirt.

"Well?" Sam asked, turning to Hawk Feather. *See what you got me into?*

"Nice tumble." The old Indian spit a loose shred of tobacco from his mouth. "Maybe she didn't like that way; try getting on the regular way."

"What? You expect me to try that again? I'm lucky I'm not paralyzed."

"She didn't seem to be mad, just startled. Look. She's standing right there, waiting."

Sam turned and saw that it was true; the buckskin was standing right behind him. She even looked concerned as he struggled to his feet.

Hawk Feather continued: "Try getting on. If she moves away you'll never make it anyway." He turned his head and yelled, "Scout! Stop it!"

The dog was wearing down a nervous path along the fence. "If he were a person, he'd be a chain smoker," Hawk Feather said, tapping the butt end of a fresh smoke against the door panel of his truck.

How can I argue with a real shaman? He studied the mare, assessing her mood, looking for an excuse to give up on the folly. She stood quietly, relaxed, waiting. Sam walked around her, petting and stroking, giving her every chance to depart. No such luck. After two full circuits it was time to act. Sam felt Hawk Feather's eyes on his back.

"How do I get on?" he asked, stalling.

"I don't think you have much choice, Sam Mann. You need to jump on, then pull yourself over."

Sam nodded, took a breath, grabbed a big handful of her black mane and jumped up and onto her. He landed like a sack of flour—a dead man's flop. But the mare was composed, stoical, as if she had been expecting this all along. Sam felt his heart fill with gratitude and excitement. He slid his right leg over and sat up, petting the horse with loving appreciative strokes. *Time to move*, he thought, hoping for a more serene departure this time.

The mare stepped out, surefooted and slow, toward the fence. Sam had yet to find a seat; his legs began to clamp down on her ribs. It worked like a rheostat: every ounce of pressure caused an increase in speed. He pulled at her mane to direct her to the upper part of the pasture, and she broke into a trot. He clamped on tighter and she crossed into a gentle lope, reminiscent of a rocking chair. Sam's smile was so wide his cheeks began to ache. They turned along the fence, and Scout ran alongside, jumping and barking, adding energy to the pace.

The mare shifted into a gallop, her neck and head flattening out as she extended her stride. Sam remembered what had happened the last time her head had lowered—and now they were approaching the corner of the fence, a barbed-wire turnbuckle. As they sped past Hawk Feather's truck, Sam called for help. "How do I stop her?"

"Say 'whoa,'" Hawk Feather offered from his perch on the running board.

"Whoa!" Sam yelled. The buckskin slid to a stop and Sam lunged forward, bracing himself against the top of her neck. He vaulted off before she could start again, and stroked her face and neck as she panted.

"Thanks," Sam said, grinning over his shoulder at Hawk Feather. "For what?"

"Your guidance. Something happened to me when I was up there. Like I was flying, and not only physically, but spiritually." Sam no longer cared how much he'd begun to sound like the disciples of Gray Elk.

"You did it, I only watched."

"It took your knowledge of horses and nature."

Hawk Feather laughed and coughed up a wet plug. "I know nothing about horses. My people have always used pickups to get around. I've never ridden." He got up and slowly straightened his spine resting his left hand on his lower back for a brace against the pain and protest of his arthritic frame. The show was over, time to move on.

"But you told me how to stop her. Where did you learn that?"

"From TV, like everyone else."

Sam spent the rest of the day riding. He stayed in the upper pasture for a while before opening the makeshift wire gate and forging out into unexplored regions. A sense of completeness overtook him. The mechanics of riding seemed telepathic—he looked or thought, and the mare complied. The experience was cathartic, giving him the feeling that an idea was taking form deep in his soul, a connection to his center, a place where he was fulfilled, living in the moment, complete, *validated*.

Sam was grateful for the need to concentrate on the momentary requirements of riding. The nagging feeling that there was much more to his being at Gray Elk's than he'd bargained for was beginning to scare him. Being a *star* seemed so removed, so trivial—having his worth defined by others, who ultimately have their own problems and treat stars the way they do products: chew 'em up and spit 'em out.

For now, though, the mare was what defined him: she was horse, he was rider; he put his heels into her ribs, and she answered with a happy gallop.

Sam watched Hawk Feather from across the fire. The old man seemed deep in thought. The reflection of the flames danced across his well-worn face; deep crevices cast strange shadows that rolled in the heat of the air. Scout reappeared from behind the trailer and plopped down between them; his clear eyes were now a brilliant orange, reflecting the glow of the burning embers.

Sam felt a melancholy longing; his experience—more like a journey—was nearing its end. What lay before him seemed far less important than it had when he'd arrived. He longed for people he loved, although Jennifer—someone he hardly knew—was the one that most came to mind. Music was his umbilicus, the constant truth amidst all the folly and adventure, the only spiritually pure stream, the only reason to remain on his present path. Yet, home—whatever that was—called. It was still only a distant echo, a faint *pianissimo*, but the inevitable *crescendo* loomed as surely as the sunrise. Hawk Feather seemed like a good guide and a man of great wisdom, but the silence between them felt rock solid, unbreakable.

The sun had descended behind the trees; a pinkish glow hung in the western sky as the oak logs crackled in the fire pit. The only other light was the blinking end of Hawk Feather's cigarette; his puffing was a constant *moderato*, a directional beam flashing.

Someone's got to talk. "How come you didn't go on the Vision Quest?" Sam asked. His tone making it obvious he felt the whole idea stupid.

"I got here after they left." After a few quiet drags he elaborated. "I could have found them, I know where they go, but I am getting a little old for those; they are very taxing." Another long pause, then a drag. "An old man's visions are not always pleasant."

"Doesn't it bother you?'

"What?"

"The way Gray Elk is marketing and milking the whole shaman concept. Don't you feel ripped off?"

"Gray Elk is just as important a spiritual leader as anyone," Hawk Feather said, blowing a thick plume of smoke into the air. "Maybe I look the part or act the part to you, Sam Mann. You might be confusing the message with the messenger. Look around."

He waited for Sam to survey what there was to see by the glow of the fire: the silhouettes of the trees against the evening sky. "Much of this comes from a bird eating a seed and then passing it on its way to somewhere, yet, you never question the meaning or the perfection of it. Gray Elk is a great man, with the ability to guide and the power to preserve our ways. A power much greater than my own."

"How can you say that? He takes all those people out in the woods, to starve them into hallucinations. Meanwhile, he's back in his teepee in the lap of luxury. You should have seen it!" Sam protested. "I helped them pack—lawn furniture, potato chips, even a goddamn TV!"

Hawk Feather looked him over. Sam thought he'd made his point; the old man was sure to come around. A long silence ensued: one cigarette put out, a new one lit. A large *pop* from the fire sent a column of sparks dancing high into the air.

Say something, Sam thought. *Anything!*

Finally, Hawk Feather spoke. His tone was more deliberate than usual. "You are very judgmental. It must have caused much unhappiness in your life."

Sam felt clobbered. Tears began streaming down his cheeks. Another layer exposed, removed. The last part of the onion peeled away, only this one was a crystal-clear membrane, unlike the thick opaque layers that had come off slowly and painfully. Scout approached and laid his head on Sam's leg. Sam stroked the dog; its curly, smoky fur was comforting in a way that was oddly electric, as if the creature was infusing him with an energy that would enable him to face every-thing, with validation a given, not a search or demand.

Hawk Feather spoke after a long pause, his voice a distant monotone. "You are a very interesting person, Sam Mann." The two names sounded separated by an abyss. "You have many strong qualities—like a very old soul, but one that is at the same time very young. The way you talk so strongly about Gray Elk, it is as if you are a child and you are crying because people will not play fairly. My friend"—again, a long pause—"that game is destined for failure, and it is one that a person can only play by himself."

Sam felt numb, stunned, as if he were under the control of an exterior life force and incapable of his usual defense, a self-righteous rage. He had no choice but to sit there and let the knowledge wash over him and cleanse his soul.

"Yet, you are very old," Hawk Feather continued. "The way Scout and his animal people trust you—they are better judges than I."

Sam was still petting Scout, smoothing the fur on the top of his head. The dog's eyes were ablaze.

"Yes," Hawk Feather said as he slowly rose to return to his camper, "we have much to learn together."

Scout gave Sam another early morning wakeup call by scratching at his door. When Sam got up to let the dog in, he saw that Hawk Feather's truck was gone. "He must have gone into town. I wish I'd known, I'd have asked him to pick up a few things for me. I'm surprised I didn't hear it."

Sam considered going back to bed, but Scout had jumped on and taken control, his eyes reflecting the red plaid pattern of the top blanket. Sam shook his finger at the panting dog. "That's weird."

Since Hawk Feather hadn't stoked the fire, Sam opted to make coffee inside. He strummed the guitar as he drank, trying to piece together a few melodic bits that seemed to emerge every time he played. Isolated snippets, unable to stand on their own, handicapped by a lack of harmonic or thematic validity; yet they were there, every time he played.

Scout jumped off the bed, ran across to the door, and scratched. "First it's in, then it's out. Make up your mind, will you? Or maybe you don't like my new tune? Can't say that I blame you."

Sam let him out and sat back down with the guitar. He had the sneaking feeling that there was more to the melody than met the ear, more yet to discover, as was the case with most of his best offerings.

A loud, insistent barking called him back to the door. It came from the clearing by the oak tree. The yapping stopped as Sam rounded the edge of the trailer to look. The mare stood under the tree, grazing at new grass, a hawk on her back. "Where's Scout?" Sam asked the open spaces. "He was probably calling me to come and see, and now he's gone?"

The bird turned its head and offered a profile of its hooked beak and downy chest. As Sam ducked through the barbed wire to get a closer look, one strand caught on his jeans. It snapped back and twanged a perfect E-flat—a banjo-like timbre with a slow vibrato.

The buckskin looked up, as if hoping Sam had brought the guitar. The hawk stood regally on her back—an oddly placed hood ornament. Then, as Sam neared, the hawk gave what appeared to be a shrug and lit off into the sky with wide-stretched wings. The bird's eye gleamed bright gold, reflecting the morning sun as it flew off.

Once again, Sam surveyed the clearing, looking for Scout. "Naw, it can't be."

The hawk circled—low swoops and dives out of sight behind the stand of madrone at the bottom of the pasture, then soaring ascents straight up, defying gravity. It found a spot above the clearing and hung in the air atop a pillowy updraft. Its eyes were visible and had turned powder blue, the color of the morning sky. Sam watched, waiting for Scout to return. The thought that Gray Elk might have been right about the circling bird being a sign, at least partly—the hawk was the dog, not the chief—added a faint blue tinge to his mood, like the color of the sky. He would miss Hawk Feather and his dog, and he now realized that his time here was almost over also.

"It figures...just when I learn how to swing with all this, it's time to go."

The mare nudged him with her nose as he stroked lightly. "Want to go for a ride?" he asked. *Thank God she didn't do any Mr. Ed shit and nod her head.*

She did, however, present her left side for him to jump on.

Spring was out in full regalia; blossoms and golden-green sprigs on the deciduous varieties had begun to give way to more hearty, adult-like growth. Pollen floated in the air, hanging like fireflies, waiting for another soft breeze to propel it toward new life. Sam turned off the dirt road onto a trail that led into a canyon, down a steep ravine and across a brook. The trail opened into a glade with thick new grass, a gourmet offering to any equine.

"Might as well let you have a little lunch."

Sam hopped off and found a sunny spot, resting his back against a lone rock in the middle of the meadow. For the next hour, the mare's head never came up; she carefully ate a perfect circle that grew like a dilating pupil.

Between the trees—oaks stunted by tall pines that towered above—Sam saw the distant ridges radiating brilliant hues of green on their soft rolling contours. Darting among the treetops was a lone hawk, playing in the swirling breezes that came up the valley.

At the edge of the meadow, through a small shadowy opening made by two tall trees—a forest gate—the sun reappeared, seeming even brighter. The floor of the next clearing was a deep blue, almost aqua. Sam got back on the horse and trotted over to investigate. A field of dense lupine had transformed the ground to a solid swath that rippled like a mountain lake as the petals danced in the drafts.

Sam pressed his heels into the mare and she galloped across; it was like running on water. Sam felt an exhilarating sense of freedom beyond anything he'd ever known, like flying, not as a bird but as the wind. It was the freedom of existence; *validation* because of existence, not because of effort or reason. A connection with some exterior yet interior force had gripped him and had finally won the battle, taking over.

In this peace so profound, and at the gateway to his truth, Sam realized that he had to leave. At long last, he could revel in the death of the *feeling*. An exhilarating joy overcame him as he turned the horse homeward and loped up the canyon.

They returned to the pasture next to the trailer. Sam got off, thanked the mare, and retreated. He didn't know whether to pack or to write, but for some reason the guitar seemed to call. He picked it up and sat down. The melody he'd been struggling with fell out, with a natural pureness he hadn't recognized before. By repeating it, anticipating its rhythm—the first four notes off the beat—it mirrored the original theme and stood alone as well.

"Wow," Sam said, finally getting it.

He'd been trying to validate the tune by some harmonic device, or force it into some confines that were synthetic and preordained, as if the world outside were a deciding factor.

"It stands on its own," he said, as the journal on the counter began to radiate. It was calling. He felt hurled toward something, *but what?*

He placed the guitar back in its case, eyeing the journal apprehensively. He picked it up and the pen slid out from the spine as the book popped open to the first clean page, deep in the middle.

Validation, he wrote, on automatic pilot. The word seemed to unlock an inner dialogue, one that had been forming for months, maybe his whole life.

That's what this shit is about. This star shit. I want to be recognized, want to be respected, powerful. That's all outside. I need to feel it in here, not out there. Like the horse, like the melody. If I don't feel it, it's just bullshit like everything else. What do I get? What do I want?

His writing had taken on a maniacal quality, raw scribbling, his hand barely able to keep up with his thoughts, the pen speeding like a conductor's baton.

I want to play music with my friends...my music...I want to be free to create. I want to be with Jennifer, not some bimbo in a limo. I could have had that...could still have that. What was I thinking, what was wrong with me? I have practically nothing now and I'm happy...aren't I?

He slung the book across to its perch. He'd been stripped clean and finally realized that the answer was inherent in the question, like *How Long is a Chinaman's name.* The old riddle his uncle had always teased him with had become the metaphor for his whole life.

"It's a statement, not a question," he said, spent, longing for a brief respite from the psychic spin cycle. He lay on the bed as the spring breezes wafted in through the open door. Scout came in and jumped up next to him. His coat had a floral, wind-blown freshness to it.

"Welcome back," Sam said as he stroked the dog, dropping off into a stardust reverie.

The coolness of the late afternoon had permeated the trailer; only the side of Sam that was pressed against Scout was warm. Gray Elk's pickup was coming down the drive. The diesel's rattle and the clanking of the trailer reverberated through the flats. Scout sat up and stretched before taking a guard position at the door.

Sam was eager to hear about the Vision Quest, having been on one himself for the last month and a half. Gray Elk appeared harried as he maneuvered the long trailer, backing it against the fence. Iris waved.

"How was it?" Sam asked.

"Very interesting," Gray Elk said. "A most unexpected group of people and events."

Iris smiled. Her acknowledgement seemed tinged with a sarcastic glee. Gray Elk turned to her. "I'll unload later, honey. I've got to get the council going at the roundhouse."

"Hawk Feather came, like you said he would. He should be back soon." Sam thought that Gray Elk might want him involved.

"So he did come, after all. We could have used him this time. It got pretty rocky this year. How do you know he's coming back?"

"He left his dog here," Sam said. Scout skulked out of the trailer and moved close to his side.

"That doesn't mean anything. That animal is very strange; he turns up unexpected all the time, and he hates people, although he does seem to like you. You're one of the few, believe me." Gray Elk moved toward the driveway leading back to the upper part of the property. "Keep him away from the roundhouse for the rest of the night, if you can, O.K.? I don't want him terrorizing any of my clients."

"I've decided to go home," Sam said, by way of stopping him.

Gray Elk turned, a slight glint of panic on his face. "I'll take you to town after everyone leaves, if you want." He didn't want Sam mingling with his clients—especially Kelly.

Sam was hurt; he was finally ready to join in, having learned his own lessons. But it wasn't right. Whatever that group of people had shared was between them; his experiences were his own. "I hope I get to say goodbye to Hawk Feather before I leave."

"What makes you think he's coming back, besides that dog? He usually comes, then goes—at very long intervals."

"He told me 'we have a lot to learn together' before he left."

Gray Elk chuckled. "He's gone, then."

"What?"

"That's how the people of his tribe say goodbye." Gray Elk turned to leave.

"But what about the dog?"

"That's *your* problem."

Sam watched Gray Elk walk up the drive. His ponytail seemed about two shades grayer than before. He looked down to Scout at his side, happily wagging his tail. "Don't go getting any ideas. I live in a city; you wouldn't like it there."

As Sam packed his clothes into the duffel, the memories of all his trials and experiences began to replay in his mind. "I ought to write a book about this," he said. "Naw, nobody will believe it."

The attachment to being a *star*, the intrigue of *the marketing ploy of the century*, was like a faded dream that had retreated into a vague concept, its meaning and relevance bewildering. He was eager to see his friends—especially Jennifer—and reclaim his old life with a new attitude and awareness. He was only mildly curious about the outcome of whatever had happened in his absence.

A strange figure walked up the drive and entered the clearing where the truck was parked. Sam recognized it, but had difficulty placing it in context. Then the man took off his hat, and Sam saw the long blond hair, the mustache, and the face.

"Billy!" He ran out the door to greet his old acquaintance, then he slowed, remembering that he was supposedly a dead man.

"Sam?"

Good, he didn't faint. "Yeah, how are you, Billy? What are you doing up here?"

"Howdy, Sam. I'm up here with Kelly."

"Oh, that's right. I did see you together at Clyde's awhile back." Sam thought it strange that Billy hadn't mentioned a thing about his having dropped off the face of the earth.

"We came up on a Vision Quest together, although it was really her idea. Mind if I come in and sit down? Care for a little nip?"

In the doorway, Billy pulled a silver flask out of his hip pocket; it caught the glare of the afternoon sun and blinded Sam, its reflection a flash of fire in Scout's eyes.

"Wow, did you just see your dog's eyes?"

"He's not *my* dog. But they are weird, aren't they?" Sam was concerned about Gray Elk's warning ("That dog hates people") and wondered if Scout would let Billy in the trailer. But the dog tolerated Billy's presence as he watched from the bed, his eyes red plaid.

"Nice place you got here," Billy said.

Sam assumed that Billy either knew about the whole thing—*Jimm manages him, too; maybe he's even got a message for me and is just fucking around*—or was fishing for the story. *Two can play that game.* "Vision Quest, huh?"

"Yep." The word seemed to have two syllables—*yayupp.* "You know what they do? They give you a blanket and a bottle of water and tell you where there's a few springs, then everybody heads off in a different direction. For days, no food! Kelly says you start seein' things, but man, by five o'clock the first day, the only vision I had was the Golden Arches."

He began to sing: "*You deserve a break today* . . . So I hightailed it off the hill toward King City. A couple of good old boys in a truck picked me up; turns out they had a band, and I played with them for a few days. I made it back in time to meet everybody. When I showed up with clean clothes and a fresh shave, Kelly like to hit the fuckin' roof. She was screamin' and cussin', makin' apologies for me. Shit—*shee-it*—nobody cared but her, not even Gray Moose."

"Gray Elk," Sam corrected. The whiskey brought back odd, disconnected memories as it soothed his insides. Billy's shit-kicker delivery awakened none of his usual judgmental responses. *Maybe I have learned something.*

Billy took a swig from the flask and wiped his lips on his sleeve. "If you want to know the truth, I think there were a lot of folks who wished they'd done the same damn thang."

"Kelly must be pissed," Sam said, remembering his war with her, here, on the same battleground.

"Don't you know it. She told me not to even go *near* that round-house thing. I'm hitchin' a ride back to town with someone else."

"Guess it's over, huh?"

"Shit, no! She'll blow off some steam and come back. What we got is too damn good. I don't need to remind you of her good qualities, do I?" Billy's grin was impish, as if he had a secret that neither Kelly nor Sam had ever figured out.

Sam realized he really liked Billy; enjoyed his easygoing, straightforward nature. "We never got to be good friends, did we?"

"Nope, guess not. You were always such an asshole." Billy smiled. "I don't mean for you to take that personally." He laughed. "I mean, you always wanted everybody to conform to your way of doin' shit, and if we didn't, you decreed it was bullshit. There was no pleasin' you. Hell, all I wanted to do was play simple, good-soundin' music and have a good time. You tried to crucify my ass for it. I still respected you for your integrity, though. I think that's why I never tried to kick your ass. That, and the fact that you're bigger than I am."

Sam felt a surreal detachment; he was unable to argue. The similarity between what Billy was saying and what Hawk Feather had told him hadn't eluded him. Wisdom was wisdom, whether it came from the mouth of a cowboy or an Indian. *The message, not the messenger, stupid.*

Billy flashed a smile. "Kelly is a lot like you. She's a tough one. Sometimes she just needs to put all her shit on me. I decide whether I want to go for it, though. I know she loves me, but I still got to do what I got to do."

Now Billy was talking in riddles. Sam considered he might be on *Candid Camera*, with Allen Funt popping out of a dog suit on his bed.

Billy continued after another sip of whiskey. "Both of you need to feel like you're smarter than everybody else. It's really strange, 'cause most of the time you are, anyway. I'll play the dumb hick for her, but you can be damn sure I ain't gonna fight with her. She'll give up on it and we'll be better than ever. And if not, '*that's the blues*,'" Billy crooned with a sly grin. It had been Sam's sanctimonious credo throughout high school.

Sam laughed. It was a strange but nice change, enjoying someone's making fun of him. He hoped that the transformation would remain, a lifelong pattern changed.

"Have you heard anything about me ... about my being gone?" Sam asked. He had to know. "Did Jimm Dibbook tell you?" After all, it was the only plausible explanation for Billy's casual attitude. With Billy and Kelly together, one of them *had* to notice.

"Nope, not really. I ain't seen that guy since he barged in on my gig at DeMarco's and threatened that waitress with a knife."

"So he never managed you?"

"Hell, no!"

Sam thought it over carefully. Billy didn't really travel in the same circles as he did, and ever since their breakup, Kelly had avoided all of their common friends. Still, to miss *the marketing ploy of the century?* Maybe it had fizzled out and Jimm had contained it to jazz circles. It didn't really matter; Sam's experience up on the mountain had left him with a singular purpose: to be himself and enjoy his gifts, inner validation, not outer. The rest, all that *stardom* shit, was filigree, anyway.

Time to find out. "Billy, do you think I could cop a ride with you back to the city?"

"Don't see why not. There's a lady who said she had to go early; she's probably ready now. How long will it take you?"

"I'm just about ready; got to straighten out a thing or two with the landlords."

"How long you been here?"

"About a month and a half."

"Musta' been weird."

"You don't know the *hayulf* of it," Sam answered, a twang emerging from his slow delivery.

Iris came to the door, her face flushed from four days of camping out. "Hi, Sam. Come on in."

"I brought your guitar back. I've decided to leave. My friend Billy can give me a ride. It'll save Gray Elk a trip down the mountain."

"I want you to have it," Iris said. "It should be making music, not gathering dust in my closet."

"Thanks, but I think it belongs here. I'll be back; I'll play it then. Maybe you ought to get a book or take some lessons. I have a few guitars at home; I'd probably never get around to playing this one. If I record any of the tunes I wrote on it, I'll send them to you, though."

"All right," she agreed. "Come back and visit. Don't be a stranger."

Sam saw a tear forming at the corner of her eye as she advanced to give him a hug. *Who'd have thought?* "There's a matter of funds. I know I still owe some against the supplies." Sam pulled out his wad, around twelve hundred dollars. He peeled off a hundred for himself, and handed over the rest.

"That's way too much, Sam."

"It's just a token of my gratitude, for all the things that happened up here. Your hospitality, not to mention saving my life; it's the least I can do. I really want you to take it. Put it toward that new truck."

This last point turned the tide; Iris smiled and pocketed the money.

"Say goodbye to Gray Elk for me. I'll stay in touch." Sam turned and left. The sound of the screen door slamming behind him was warmly familiar music, forever imprinted.

Sam returned to the trailer to get his duffel. He surveyed the womb-like steel and plywood cavity where he'd been, in fact, reborn. The sights and smells were familiar, yet already fading into memory even as he took them in. The bulging journal sat on the countertop. It looked like it was smiling, laughing at him, saying *"I told you so ."* He slung the duffel over his shoulder, took a deep breath, and walked out.

He went to the fence hoping to say a last goodbye to the mare, but she was gone, off to other pastures. "Goodbye, girl, and thanks."

He set out down the driveway, with Scout hanging back at a careful distance. Sam turned. "Scout, you can't come with me. Hawk Feather will come back, or you can turn yourself into a hawk, or whatever." The dog dropped its head as if scolded. Sam's heart ached, deep in his chest. "Come here boy."

Scout ambled up to him, his tail wagging. "Thanks for everything," Sam said as he stroked the curly hair atop the dog's huge head. "I know it was you who guided me through a lot of all this, but now I've got to go. I know you know that. Take care of the old chief, he needs you."

The tear ducts in Sam's eyes ached as if they'd cried a lifetime of tears. "Go back to the trailer. Gray Elk doesn't want you near the roundhouse. Iris is nice, she'll take care of you."

Scout headed back with Sam watching as he made his slow retreat. The dog stopped and craned his neck for one last hopeful look before rounding the lone pine at the top of the driveway clearing.

"Sam, this is Ginny. She politely offered to take us back to the city," Billy said. "That's all you had with you for a month and a half?"

Sam nodded. "Nice to meet you, Ginny." She was a tall, boyish woman; thin-boned, dark, with jet-black hair braided into a long ponytail. Unlike Iris, she actually looked like a stereotypical Indian chief's wife.

"It's Virginia. *Clem* here just took the liberty." She smiled. It was obvious that Billy had lost little of his charm—with the slight exception of Kelly.

"Sorry," Sam said.

They stowed their bags into the trunk of her yellow Toyota and piled in. She started up and headed out to the dirt road that would lead them off the mountain. Sam felt light—as if he'd dropped a thousand pounds of psychic weight during his extended solitude.

"You didn't bring your guitar," Billy said, looking back from the front seat.

Sam saw Virginia readying herself to brake and return to get it. "It wasn't mine, it belonged to Iris, Gray Elk's wife."

"I was wondering what kind of box it was," Billy said. "It was a spiffy-looking little old case."

"It was one of those ukulele-sized Martin-looking things, with the small shoulders and a big sound-hole. It was pretty old."

Virginia adjusted her rearview mirror as they started down the hill. "There's a dog chasing us."

Sam heard the barking. He knew without looking that it was Scout.

Billy turned and peered through the dust trail following in their wake. "It's your dog, Sam."

"I told you, he's not my dog. His owner is an old Indian chief, a friend of Gray Elk. He'll come back and get him, I'm sure of it."

Sam didn't want to get into any of his suspicions about the animal or the lore attached to his spiritual status. He heard the barking; his mind's eye saw Scout in desperate chase, screaming, *"Don't leave me . . . take me!"*

The car was quiet except for the phantom reverberation of Scout's pleas. Both Billy and Virginia had turned their attention away, as one does when pretending to ignore a private family fight. Sam turned to look. Scout wasn't gaining any ground, but managing to keep an even thirty feet behind. He ran like a bear, lumbering, his tongue hanging from his open mouth.

The rocky dirt road made it impossible for Virginia to speed up and lose him—to force him to transform into a hawk, or do whatever he did. *Stop torturing me,* Sam thought.

He heard a faint answer: *"Take me . . . we have a lot to learn together."*

Am I the only one who can hear that? Sam wondered. The two in the front sat like statues, in a loud disapproving silence.

Sam had to say something. *I'm not an animal abuser!* "He'll give up eventually." *I hope he does before his heart gives out.*

Scout gave valiant chase, the full three miles to the beginning of the pavement. A thick dust clod had caked around his nostrils, his tongue was purple, the pads of his feet raw, but he refused to relent.

The car made it to the main road. The brake lights flashed and the turn signal indicated a left, forever gone, toward the highway.

"No!" Scout howled . . . a loud, defeated wail.

The yellow Toyota lurched to a stop, sliding on the last stretch of dirt and gravel, and the right rear door flew open.

Act III
Revenge

The ride back—a long decompression—was punctuated by Scout's panting, a steady *fortissimo* in the quiet of the car. Sam's pant leg was soon soaked with slobber. The first stretch was country roads, lightly traveled, winding past ranch houses dotting the rural landscape. As they neared the freeway, the overpopulation of vehicles, asphalt, and strip malls seemed to gobble up the earth.

After a month and a half of solitude, Sam assumed he had developed reclusive tendencies and sensibilities. He was relieved to find that he wasn't overwhelmed with panic while hurtling down the road surrounded by a sea of rubber and metal. After all, his return was sure to be met with a fair amount of intense publicity. He now thought of the country's quiet and solitude with the same sentimental longing that he'd carried for his old life during his walk up the hill six weeks before.

As they neared the suburbs and cities of the Greater Bay Area—San Jose and Silicon Valley—the congestion became more intense. They had caught the beginnings of rush hour, a reminder to Sam that the world had somehow managed to persist without him. He felt in his pocket for his key; it was a solid connection, a piece of the old that would unlock the portal to the new and allow him to cross the threshold with a heightened sense of self and his place in the world. Without his ever intending it to happen, the weeks in the trailer had brought him to a Buddhist-style awareness.

Maybe Gray Elk was right. True, he was returning to his material possessions, but his attachment to the outcome of this hoax that he and Jimm had played on the business and music world was at most marginal. He was more anxious to settle in and enjoy his music, to see his friends ... and find Jennifer.

An ocean of cars with flashing brake lights surrounded them. Scout slept noisily, unconcerned. Sam wondered what he was going to do with him; there was a no-pet clause in his lease, and though many of the other tenants in the building had stretched it, he wasn't bringing home a kitten or a canary.

Billy spoke, breaking the silence. "Shitfire, Sam, this must seem awful strange after so long up there in the hills. Why'd you go up there? You don't seem much like the type who goes in for that kinda' shit."

"It's a long story."

Both Billy and Virginia gave him looks that said: *"We aren't going anywhere."*

"Well, you see, I got connected with that manager, Jimm, remember? I saw you at his office?"

"You should see this guy, Ginny," Billy interjected. "He's this little fat guy who's always saying *'Trust me, trust me.'"*

"We put out this CD," Sam went on. "It got to the top of the charts, and Jimm thought it would be a good idea for me to get off the scene for a while and, uh, drive up my price." Sam didn't feel like explaining the whole marketing ploy, especially if they hadn't heard about it or might even be called as witnesses in a fraud case involving faked death, so he laid it out like a rehearsal interview for a suspicious DA: "I was getting a little stressed out, had a few run-ins; I'm lucky one of them didn't put me out of commission for good."

He told the *animal* story—omitting the subsequent encounter with Kelly—and soon had both occupants of the front seat laughing hysterically. Sam felt himself fill up with a strange electricity; even though it wasn't music, it was great to be performing again, pleasing the crowd. "So I just took awhile off to get my head together. Now I'm back." *The simpler the better.*

They turned off the freeway and made their way up the hill to Sam's apartment, located in a gentrified neighborhood called Noe Valley, the Victorians all spiffed up and painted in the latest designer colors. Rents had gone through the roof in the fifteen years since Sam had moved in. Now the housing market was undergoing yet another boom, and the rent for the unit below his—an identical two-bedroom railroad flat—was $2800; but due to the city's stringent rent-control policies, his had climbed to only $560.

Sam got out and pulled his duffel from the trunk. Scout stretched out his long body and yawned noisily before trotting off to investigate the smells at the base of a cherry tree planted in a square hole in the cement sidewalk. "Thanks for the ride, Virginia. I'll talk to you later, Billy. I hope it all works out with Kelly."

"Not a problem, Sam. Adios." Billy smiled, his white teeth gleaming, tipping an imaginary Stetson as they drove off into the sunset.

"Scout, be quiet," Sam said as they climbed the steps to the front entrance. "This is just temporary. I hope you're friendlier than Gray Elk said you were. I don't feel like turning around to drive you back, or looking for Hawk Feather. Be cool, O.K.?"

The dog wagged his tail and sat obediently as Sam pulled out his key. It felt ceremonial, a return from the dead. He took a long look around, seeing his surroundings again but as if for the first time—*vuja de* again—and took a deep breath. He raised the key. It entered halfway and resisted. He pulled it out and tried again; no luck. He spat on it. *Maybe the tumblers are corroded from lack of use.* Nothing changed. The key refused to work the lock.

"Damn!" he said to Scout, remembering that he'd left Jimm his usual house key on the key ring with the car key, and grabbed the spare. "It looks right, but I should have tested it before I left."

There was no option but to ring his landlord, a middle-aged gay bachelor who lived upstairs. "Well Scout, looks like you're going to be meeting him a little sooner than we thought. I'm going to tell him that you belong to a friend and he's coming to get you. Don't get me into any trouble—and none of those weird eye things either." The dog dropped his head, sulking. "Stay away from lights and shit. This is important."

Sam rang the bell and the light in the long stairway came on. A clean-shaven head bent over the railing at the top landing. "Hello? Who is it?"

"Larry, it's Sam. I don't have my key."

"Sam? Did you forget something?" Larry asked as he made his way down the stairs.

He opened the door and saw Scout. "Oh, you have a dog now. He's beautiful." He bent down to pet him, and Sam cringed, praying that Scout wouldn't bite. "What a cute cuddly teddy bear," Larry said, rubbing the dog on his belly. Scout had rolled over, his eyes closed.

This dog may be hipper than I thought. "My key doesn't work," Sam said, anxious to go inside.

"Of course it doesn't," Larry said, every "s" sounding like a steam kettle at full boil.

"What?"

"The new tenants changed it. It's standard procedure."

"What do you mean *new tenants*?"

"Sam, where have you been?"

Sam didn't like Larry's expression any more than he liked what he was saying. Larry was backing away as if Sam might be dangerous.

"I've been out of town."

"I know that. Your manager told me. He sent you the money, right?"

"The money?"

"Of course. I bought out your lease. The son of a bitch held me up for an extra five grand. I figure I'll make the thirty thousand back in one year though, the way the market has taken off. This dog is so cute!" Scout was in the midst of sympathy scratching, his back leg waving wildly in the air.

"You bought out my lease? From Jimm Dibbook?"

"Yes. He showed me the power of attorney and he gave me your letter O.K.'ing it, saying you had moved away. I do have a bunch of your mail; wait here, I'll get it."

Larry ran back up the stairs. Sam was stunned; numb. *I didn't O.K. anything* was running through his mind, but his mouth wouldn't say it.

"Here you are." Larry handed him a large brown sack with rope handles. "I checked your flat after he came to get your stuff; it was clean. If anything turns up, I'll hold on to it or send it to you. What's your address?"

Sam was stupefied, unable to even move his eyelids. Larry looked back up the stairs and raised his nose, sniffing. "I have to go! I have a beef Wellington in the oven and guests due any minute. Come by and visit if you're ever back in town, and you really should put in a change of address with the post office. Ta-ta, Sam."

Before Sam could say anything that might call an end to this cruel *scherzo*, the door slammed in his face. He rang the bell for his flat, his old flat. No answer. Sam stood frozen with Scout scratching at his leg and his mind screaming out a million questions, demanding explanations, while his world crumbled.

He didn't even realize he'd collapsed until Scout's cold nose against his cheek pulled him out of shock. "A phone, I've got to find a phone!"

Sam ran down the stairs to the sidewalk. He'd lived there for over fifteen years and had no idea where the nearest pay phone was. "He probably moved me out because I was dead or something, although Larry said he told him I'd moved away. Thirty grand is pretty good, almost as much as I made last year. I'm sure there's a logical explanation for all this. I'll bet my car is parked around here somewhere."

He made a slow, widening circle, block by block, his car nowhere in sight. Finally, he found a phone in front of a dilapidated grocery store. He pulled out his wallet and found the card for Worldwide Artists, Inc. He dialed the number; it was after five, but there was probably someone still there at the office. The phone never rang. It went directly to an electronic chime, *buhbee-beep*. "The number you have called has been disconnected and there is no new number."

"What?" Sam cried out. Panic seized him; his heart was racing and his throat closing down. He gasped, trying to force air down his windpipe. "This can't be. I don't fucking believe it." His hand shook as he frantically tried his own number—and got the same sickening voice with the same awful message. "Oh no. Where's my shit? That motherfucker!"

Sam raced back to his flat in the hope that he'd eventually wake up in a sweat, finding that it was only a bad dream, with another lesson about life and enlightenment. *I guess this Buddha stuff is only cool as long as I got my shit.*

He went up the stairs and tried his key again, forcing it deep into the opening. Once again, it refused. "What am I going to do?" He sat on the porch with his duffel and paper sack—afraid to look inside, afraid of what new nightmares lurked within—crying as Scout sat at his side, waiting out the storm.

A well-dressed woman approached, carrying a white plastic grocery sack, the spikes of a pineapple extending out the top. She eyed Sam warily, as if he were a homeless bum parked on her stoop. She assessed the risk and moved around him to the middle door, with a disapproving *"What is this neighborhood coming to?"* look.

Sam wanted to scream at her, to tell her that she had stolen his pad, that he wasn't a bum, that it was all a misunderstanding, a cruel joke. Then it hit him with full force: she was right. *I am a homeless bum.*

Unbeknownst to Sam, a strange transformation was happening: his cellular structure was realigning, undergoing a psychic metamorphosis from the self-validated, redeemed spirit to an animal—a primal creature concerned only with searching out the culprit, retrieving his stuff, getting to the bottom of this cavernous mess. Only one thing would sate the savage beast: revenge.

The darkening sky did nothing to lift Sam's mood as he made his way down the street. Scout hung back, watching and following. The transformation in Sam had changed the dynamics between them, awakening Scout's basic herding instinct.

They turned the corner on Noe Street and Sam saw a flashing blue neon sign: BAR, with an oscillating cocktail glass. It was a beacon in a murky night, promising release, if not salvation. He made his way to the door and looked in. "Scout, stay," he commanded.

"There's no need for that," an old voice with a wisp of an Irish brogue called out. "He's welcome in here, provided he's house-trained."

Sam didn't know if he was—*but any dog that can drive and fly probably is.* They went in and sat at the end of the deserted bar. Sam stashed his bags under the overlap.

"Here's a bowl of water for the dog," the bartender said, handing over a deep dish with FIDO printed in Gaelic script.

"Thanks," Sam answered, setting the bowl at his feet. Scout was noisily lapping at it before it hit the floor.

"What'll it be?"

"A shot and a beer."

"Any particular brand?"

"Anything that'll work," Sam answered.

"I see. Having a rough day, are ye?"

"You wouldn't believe it if I told you."

"Well, sonny, I've got nothing but time. The name's Seamus," the old man said, offering his wrinkled hand for a shake. The width of the bar was such that he had to stand on his tiptoes to reach across. His eyes were a faded blue that reflected the neon sign outside the smoked window. His wavy, slicked-back hair was mostly gray with just a hint of its original bright orange hue. He set the bottle of beer and an empty shot glass in front of Sam before retreating to the shelf below the back-bar, retrieving a bottle of Jameson.

"Can I buy you one?" Sam asked—*misery loves company*.

"That's a lovely offer, but I'm afraid I have to make it all the way to last call. Don't want to start too early."

"One for later, then."

"Thanks, sonny."

"Sam." He watched the bartender place an upside-down shot glass in the recess at the far side of the bar. Sam pulled out the crisp hundred-dollar bill from his wallet; the only one he had. "Is there an ATM nearby?"

"Sure thing, just about fifty feet, on the corner. Make a right out the door."

"Great." Sam knew he'd feel a whole lot better with a little more money in his pocket. Plus, after all that had happened so far, he had to wonder.

"Can you watch my dog?"

"Sure thing, Sam."

At the corner, Sam inserted his card and punched in his PIN. The machine thought about it for only a moment before answering:

Account closed. Card no longer valid.

"Shit, I knew it!" Without waiting to see what would happen next—whether the card came back, or an alarm sounded—Bank fraud in progress! —Sam hastened back to the safety of the bar.

"Bad news, huh?"

"I guess it shows."

"In all my years, I've never seen a man leave a full drink and a hundred dollars on the bar to go to the bank."

"I think I've been cleaned out," Sam said, the words somehow validating the truth of it.

"A woman; wife maybe?"

Sam shook his head. He downed the shot, then a healthy slug of beer to put out the fire. "No, my manager. At least I think so. Maybe I've got this all wrong. I'll take another, please." He pushed his glass toward the bottle that still sat on the bar.

"On the house. So why don't ye run it by an old man like me."

Might as well, I'm going to have to take this to the police. It can't hurt to have a dress rehearsal. "Well, to start off, I'm a musician, and I have this manager." Sam noticed he was still using the present tense. "We had this record, it was really doing well, so I decided...uh...we decided..." —*How am I going to say this?*— "...that it might be best for me to get off the scene for a while. Let him do his work, and I could come back and play for better bread, and in better clubs."

The bartender nodded as he dried wineglasses and loaded them stem-up into a wooden rack that hung from the ceiling.

Sam continued: "So I went to stay with a friend for a month or so, and I just got back." He downed the shot, this time without a chaser. It was quickly refilled. "Thanks. When I got back, I went home and found he'd sold the lease to my flat. Plus, I can't find my car, and my bank account is closed."

"Did ye call the man?"

"Phone's disconnected." Then, the disturbing revelation hit him. "What about my guitar? That motherfucker! Ah, he probably just stashed most of it somewhere. I bet I'm just overreacting."

"Sam, sounds to me as if ye been screwed." The "r" rolled off his tongue like a cascading brook. "My advice is to talk to the cops. They're a good bunch of boys; they come in after work. The station moved over to 17th and Valencia."

Sam nodded. "Thanks, Seamus," he said, popping the shot and killing off the rest of his beer. He stuffed the contents of the paper bag into the duffel. It barely zipped shut, but now he had only one bag to tote around. "Come on, Scout, I'll take you for a little walk."

"Good luck, Sam. I hope it all turns out all right," Seamus said as they sped out the door. "Poor sap."

Even though there was a cool spring chill in the air, the indignant fury and the alcohol raging through Sam's bloodstream combined to fuel him to a boiling-hot temperature. He muttered angrily while making his way toward the Mission district, intending to swear out a warrant for that lying, cheating, good-for-nothing little fat fuck of a manager named Jimm Dibbook. Instead of the sidewalk before him, he saw Jimm, handcuffed, thrown into the back of a black-and-white cruiser, on his way to a lengthy prison term.

Lost in this vengeful fantasy, Sam stepped off the curb and found himself hurled back, teetering on his heels as a car screeched to a halt in the crosswalk. Scout had jumped in front and pushed him back from the space now occupied by an SUV with a white-shirted business type yelling: "Watch where you're going, asshole! I almost killed you!"

"Thanks, Scout," Sam said. "Where did you learn about traffic?" The dog's eyes radiated bright red from the stoplight. Then they turned to green, and Sam carefully looked both ways before setting out again.

The four drinks on an empty stomach had done their job. Now Scout was doing his, trotting at Sam's side, showing little interest in any of the smells along the way.

Sam's angry rambling monologue sent the last of the strollers scurrying as he rounded the edge of Dolores Park, with a massive dog whose eyes radiated a purplish white, reflecting the brash new street lamps that had been installed to discourage drug dealing.

The station was a new building made to look old, with faux-adobe bricks, cement rounded mission style arches, and bullet-proof doors. Sam had expected a TV-show precinct house with a bustle of activity and a pudgy Irish desk sergeant. Instead, the lobby was austere: harsh lights illuminated the otherwise empty space, creating a blinding glare off the bright white walls. Mirrors and video cameras were installed in the upper corners, allowing someone to keep a constant surveillance on the area. *But who?* "Where the fuck is everybody?"

He spotted a tinted window with a phone next to it. He cautiously made his way to the window and picked up the receiver.

"How may I help you?" It was a male voice, a deep baritone.

Sam peered into the glass, shading his eyes with one hand. He could see vague forms, but that was all. It was like talking to a wall.

"The motherfucker stole everything!" Sam had rehearsed his speech, but in his fantasy it had been made to a person, at a desk, with coffee, maybe, a sympathetic environment. Here, his volcanic rage erupted, demanding justice.

"Who?" the faceless voice asked.

"Jimm Dibbook. That's Jimm with two m's."

"You say he stole something from you. What do you want to report stolen?"

"Everything! That motherfucker took everything: my house, my car, even my clothes and guitars! I'll kill him, that lousy no good—"

"Sir, please try to calm down and tell me what you're talking about."

"Calm down? It's easy for you to say! I'm completely cleaned out by that fucking prick and talking to a wall and you want me to calm down? If I knew where he was I'd—"

"Please, sir. I must warn you that everything you say is being taped. I understand you're upset."

"O.K., O.K." Sam tried to stem the tide of rage that surged, supercharged by three shots and a beer. "It's my manager—my *former* manager. I went out of town and he took everything. He sold my apartment, stole my car, and took my things."

"You have a working relationship with this man; a contract?"

"Had," Sam corrected.

"Did he have access to your property?"

"I guess it was on the key ring," Sam said. *Got to get this guy on my side, get him to let me in. Once we meet face to face he'll come around.*

"He had the keys? Sir, I'm sorry to inform you, but in that case, he is not technically guilty of theft."

Sam felt sledgehammered. He began rocking heel to toe, wavering into the glass while trying to force himself to wake up from a surreal nightmare. "What do you mean, not guilty of theft?!"

Scout began to bark.

"Sir, please calm down."

"Fuck! What do you guys do all day? Tell everyone that shit isn't a crime from behind a window? How about you let me come in and we can talk about it?"

The voice was cold. "You had a business relationship with this man, yes?"

Sam nodded, unsure whether the voice could see him, but unable to speak. He felt his life force draining at a dangerous clip.

"And he took advantage of that trust?"

Again a nod. Sam fought back the hysterical wave that was on the verge of overtaking him. He bit his lip as Scout moved close to his side.

"That might be fraud, but it is not theft."

"Fuck," Sam said, in a whisper now, leaning against the window, defeated.

"The only thing I can do for you," the voice said, now almost conciliatory, "is to put out an embezzled vehicle report on your car."

"Embezzled vehicle report? What's that?" It sure as hell didn't seem as good as having a couple of cops cuff Jimm and rough him up on his way to jail.

"It will remove your liability for any damage he does."

"That's it? You think I give a fuck about liability?!"

"Sir—"

"Don't 'sir' me! That fucker stole everything I've got and you tell me about liability? I'll tell you who the fuck is going to need liability! It's *that* asshole. If you won't help, I can see who's going to have to do your fucking dirty work. Jimm Dibbook is a dead man!"

Scout began barking, adding to the manic commotion.

"Sir, you're being taped. Calm down. Go to the fraud division tomorrow, at the Hall of Justice; maybe they can help. Right now, I suggest you sleep it off. Do *not* try to take this into your own hands. It's the worst thing you could do."

"Now you're fucking giving me advice? You won't help me but you'll sit there and tell me to calm down and sleep it off?"

"That's exactly what I'm saying, and if you don't take that damn dog and leave peacefully now, you *will* be able to explain it to an officer face to face, through a set of bars, *capisce?*"

"Fuck you!" Sam screamed, dropping the phone to the floor and making a hasty retreat in case the threat was real. "Come on Scout. Fuck these assholes."

Feeling faint, Sam sat on the curb. He eyed a brightly lit taqueria across the street, radiant colors practically vibrating off the walls. "Food, that's the ticket." Something to absorb the whiskey, so he could plan his next move. He crossed the street. "Scout, stay out here, I'll get it to go."

He emerged with a white bag, still dazed from his confrontation at the station house. "Can you believe that? The motherfucker cleans me out, steals everything, and they act like I'm the fucking criminal. Don't worry boy, we'll find him—and when we do, I wouldn't want to be Jimm Dibbook."

Scout listened to Sam's quasi-demented monologue patiently and with unconditional understanding. Humans tended to be very strange. For him, every moment was complete and happy, a rich journey through existence, no claims or expectations. He'd chosen Sam, plain and simple. *What is it with their constant territorial harping? And they think we're weird because we like to mark things with our scent. It's simple: protect, love . . . live.*

The sat on a grassy rise and ate their dinner in the harsh glow of the streetlights. Sam had gotten a super burrito for himself and a quadruple serving of *carne asada* for Scout—a pile of steak chunks that was devoured instantaneously. "I kind of figured you wouldn't mind a little human *comida*."

Sam pondered his options as he watched Scout gulp the last of his dinner, lick his chops, and emit a healthy belch. "A-flat—nice tone, too."

There were precious few options; none, to be exact. He felt like a puppet in a macabre play, a calamitous tragicomedy.

It was probably around eight or eight-thirty. *What would I normally be doing around this time?* His old life was a vague remembrance. Then he heard the distant call of a corps of drums, far off at the top of the park. "A gig! That's where I'd be going. Let's see if we can get a cab. I don't feel like walking all the way downtown. It may be tough with you, though."

Scout barked. Sam turned and saw a bright yellow cab discharging a passenger at the curb. As miracles would have it—*or had Scout planned it?*—the woman was in the company of a dog; a small cocker spaniel, but a dog nonetheless.

Sam and Scout made their way across the curb before the woman was finished paying. She gave the driver—a dark-skinned man with a white silk turban—a healthy tip and retreated, her dog equally fearful, Sam's appearance and Scout's size intimidating.

"Is this cab free?" Sam asked, trying to sound as mild-mannered as possible.

"Where do you go, sir?"

"To Clyde's, it's a nightclub downtown."

"I know precisely where it is. Please get in."

Scout jumped in and the cab listed to the side. Sam pushed him across the seat and got in.

While Sam paid the driver at the club, Scout trotted over to the front door to investigate. Sam realized that his cash reserves had now dwindled to around sixty-five bucks—not even enough for a hotel.

Assimilating the orange neon sign, Scout's eyes looked on fire, two flames in quarter-sized holes in his forehead.

"Cut that out!" Sam ordered. He looked inside. It was still early; the musicians had yet to arrive and only a few tables near the bandstand had patrons. The bar area was deserted; Ginger was deep in prep work. He turned to Scout. "You got to be cool in here. We'll sneak in along the back wall and sit at the end of the bar."

Stealthily, they made their way in, and Sam was seated on the last stool against the wall, with Scout under his feet before Ginger even noticed.

She looked up from the well, her cleavage squeezing out of her striped tight leotard top. "Hey, stranger," she said. "What happened to you?"

"What do you mean?"

Sam's response was more of an attack than a question. Ginger backtracked; confronting crazies was Clyde's job. "I mean, where have you been? Haven't seen you around for a while."

"That's right. And you have some fucking nerve showing up here now!"

Sam recognized that deep tone, always blitzing. "Clyde!"

"What's this Clyde shit? You're not welcome here, mother-fucker."

Scout stood and began to growl.

"You got a fucking dog in here? What the fuck is wrong with you?"

Scout's growl became more insistent, a slow *crescendo* toward attack.

"Scout, cool it! Clyde, look, I don't know what you're talking about."

"Get that motherfucking dog out of here, and take your conniving rip-off ass with it. You are not welcome here!"

Sam stood, Scout moving in front of him. It was strange to see Clyde backing off. *He must be afraid of dogs.* "Scout, you stay out there," Sam ordered. He pointed to the door. The dog obediently went out and looked in, sitting on his haunches.

Clyde had one eye on Sam, one on Scout. "I told you—get your fucking ass out of here or I'll kick it out!"

"Just tell me, what did I do?"

"That's funny. You rip off your friends and show up a month later like, 'What did I do?'" The singsong end to Clyde's reproach did nothing to diminish its seriousness. "Sam, you can do better than that. Just take the money and split, you fucked us, all right. I hope you feel good about it."

"What the fuck are you talking about?"

"Don't you play dumb with me. I'll kick your ass even if I have to get bitten by your little security guard. I get one good shot in, it'll be worth it."

"Clyde, cool down, please. What did I do? Exactly what did I do?"

"You *know*. Your white man comes in and books the big return of the CD party, from the triumphant tour. Gets me to put up half the bread in front, which was just as much as I paid for the first one, and you don't even show. The first time since I had this club that a motherfucker didn't even show up. You can't embarrass me like that! What's worse, you left your buddies hanging on a tour that never happened. You get them to commit to two months' work and you flake—you fucking flake on 'em! They got kids, man. What the fuck are they supposed to eat on?"

"Holy Shit!" Sam exclaimed. He felt like he was going to be sick. Instead of fighting back, trying to explain, he found himself using his precious reserves to stave off the burrito that was working its way north of the border. Sam tried to speak, but the waves of nausea kept coming. *What could I say anyway?* Tossing dinner on a pro-bowl linebacker surely wasn't the answer. He bolted out the door and ran up the street.

He heard Clyde yelling, "That's right, you stay the fuck out of here, and take that motherfucking dog with you."

Had Sam turned right at the corner instead of continuing up the hill, he would have run past Jennifer Holman, who was sitting at a sidewalk cafe with a newspaper and her diary. Her dark glasses, reflecting the colored flashing lights on Broadway, seemed to say, *Off limits, don't bother approaching.* Her brown hair fell in a straight line along her shoulders, adding to her standoffish posture. It was all for protection. Her reentry into society after almost fifteen years at Kinsale had been sudden and disorienting. Her condo/loft near the waterfront had been grabbed on the run, before Percy'd had time to change his mind about their agreement.

Her life at the estate now seemed like a long hibernation; while it had been rife with power plays and intrigues, it had all been in an enclosed, easy-to-control environment. Thrust into the free flow of human and mechanical overload, she had yet to learn new ways to define herself. Living by herself had stripped her of her identity, her purpose, her calling—there was no more reason to lie and manipulate, even for the fun of it. Now she felt as if that vital, playful part of herself had atrophied, and she had faded into a flabby, formless organism that needed focus and definition.

The obsession with Sam Mann was over, at least. After that night at his CD release party, when he'd practically raped her with his playing, right there in front of all those people ... and after she'd left a note ... and after he'd snubbed her! She'd held out for as long as she could before reality had finally sunk in: he wasn't going to call. For all she knew, he had a lover he'd been cheating on that weekend down in Big Sur.

Since giving up on him, dating had come easy. She was invisible to the kids with pierced body parts and tattoos and dyed-black hair, but the yuppies had flocked to her. How many dinners had she spent listening to the modern gladiators deliver their monologues about retiring early, making their first million by forty-five, then tripling it in five years, plus stock options, with retirement looming as some golden ribbon at the end of a four-minute mile?

She was disgusted by it all; having been retired her whole life, she wanted *un-retirement*. She wanted to be active and vital, absorbed instead of self-absorbed. She had the money, she had the condo, and she was *miserable*.

The sex had been equally disappointing. One guy was always showing off his health club physique, stealing glances at himself in the mirror, in a hurry to get away as soon as the act was done. Then there was the clingy control freak, openly proprietary with her free and uninhibited orgasms, as if he had found a special button and was the only one who knew where and how to push. Warm bodies were nice, but she longed for something deeper; it had to be out there. Yet she also knew she wasn't bringing all that much to the table.

Did Sam really have it?

She wrote it in her diary, oblivious to the hustle-bustle of the street. It was the first personal entry in over a month. The diary, which had long been her confidant, had transformed into a boring personal assistant, limited to career options, schedules, and shopping lists. She took a sip of merlot and savored the crisp dryness of the taste, which lingered on her tongue long after she'd swallowed, almost obscuring the exhaust from passing cars.

When she saw the question at the top of a fresh page, it surprised her, as if someone else had written it. Its legibility, even in the dim light, possessed an emotional clarity that suggested far more than she was ready to exhume from what she'd thought was her buried past. *Sam? I thought I had gotten over him.*

Sam stumbled up the street, each step widening the distance between them. Scout followed, on the alert to stave off any dangers that might confront his master who, in his present mindset, was vulnerable to any kind of predator. Sam attacked the hill on Vallejo Street, pounding out each step, exacting his revenge on the concrete sidewalk. Then he turned back down toward the lights, toward Jennifer, who sat staring at his name as if he'd written it telepathically—as if she knew he was there. He took the steep steps down Stockton Street three at a time, before a quick left, turning away from her.

Jennifer looked up from her journal to sip at her wine, and noticed the hairy ass of a big dog, giving chase to something down the street.

Sam sped past the sex shops, working his way beyond the busy end of Broadway, beginning the dark descent to the waterfront, to find quiet, peace. It was all so alien. He longed to be somewhere he belonged—*but where was that?* He was not only stripped of his things, but was an enemy to all he longed to be with.

He neared the Embarcadero. Its newly refurbished state—with palm trees, wrought iron lamp posts and railings, and a streetcar running down a raised cobblestone meridian—made him feel even more disassociated: there was a fakeness to it, as if he'd accidentally time-warped to a strange parallel plane. The dark brick buildings along the last two blocks were newly constructed, but made to look old, with masonry arches and paved corridors leading inward to a small park with benches and a fountain, faux Barbary Coast.

Sam's pace had been steady. He'd made it down the hill and almost all the way to the piers at the end of Broadway when he realized how light he was. "Shit, I left my fucking bag at Clyde's."

He considered returning; it was all he had left, and maybe Clyde would have calmed down by now. But no, it was futile; it was something that would need to be dealt with in a careful way, with some preparation, at least some fucking answers. *Maybe with Jimm's scalp hanging from my belt.*

It was amazing how much fuel revenge could provide for the weary and beaten. His fatigue had once again metamorphosed into rage and focus, a wired kind of energy.

"Might as well leave it behind. I've lost everything else, it'd just load me down."

"In that case—" A shadowy figure stepped out of the rounded doorway in front of him.

Sam knew the voice, or at least the tone; the setting was also painfully obvious. He was a mugger's dream come true, foolishly walking headlong into a dark place with plenty of blind alcoves. He glanced over his shoulder. *Of course, the motherfucker has an accomplice.*

Sam considered running out into the street, but the other side was fenced off for a construction site. Plus, the guy to his rear had the angle and they both were younger, more than likely armed. The man in front was almost as tall as he was, wearing a puffy parka and a woolen ski cap, his hand in his pockets: a gun . . . a knife?

"Let's see what you got."

Not exactly a question—but Sam hesitated, acting as if he didn't really understand.

"Motherfucker!" A raised voice now, pissed off. "You hard of hearing or something?"

Sam stood to confront them both head-on, his back to the street. He was hoping for a car—preferably black and white—to come rolling down the street so he could make a quick move. *Why the fuck is it so dark and deserted? It's not that late.*

The two moved out of the darkened shadows; any chance of running was now gone. Sam felt his heart pounding, dot-dot-dot— dash-dash-dash — dot-dot-dot, a cardiac SOS. *Why didn't I just stay in the country?*

"Now, look, guys, I don't have anything. I've already been cleaned out," he explained. It was the truth; maybe they'd show some mercy.

"You think we give a fuck?" The first guy swung and caught Sam's shoulder—a glancing blow, instilling terror, creating control; the brutal beating for the fun of it would come after they'd gotten everything. Sam stepped back, trying to get out of reach, teetering on the curb. "You got the balls to come down here without nothing? Where the fuck were you born? We get something or we take it off your ass. Now what the fuck you got?"

"All I've got is some cash, not very much, and it's all I've got," Sam pleaded. *Please go find someone else.*

"Well?" The taller of the two—the one who'd already hit him—waited. "Do I have to fuck you up or are you going to give it?"

Out of the corner of his eye, Sam saw the second man—the one who'd boxed him in from the rear—lunge at him, his arm coming up. *A knife?*

Sam jumped back and slipped off the curb, falling into the street. The mugger's inertia seemed to propel him as he crashed into the other, sending them both sprawling onto the sidewalk. A thunderous growl filled the air—more than a dog, or a hundred dogs—a grizzly bear.

"What the fuck!" Sam heard one of the muggers scream as the two scrambled on all fours, Scout herding them into the wall. He saw that they had been reduced to cowering wimps by a savage, rabid-looking attack dog whose clear eyes were black voids in the hollows of his forehead.

Sam approached. He wanted them to turn into Jimm Dibbook so he could pronounce sentence and exact justice.

"Good boy, Scout."

"Get your fucking dog off me."

"I don't think you're in any position to tell me what to do."

Now that Sam was in power—thanks to Scout—he had no idea what to do. He had none of the tools of violence, and although he was developing a monstrous craving for revenge, his repertoire was totally void of any usable material.

"What is it you want?" the accomplice asked, the one who'd yet to utter a word. His pants were torn at the knees from his fall to the sidewalk. He was very young and seemed almost contrite.

"I want all my shit back. I want my fucking life back!"

"But we didn't take anything," the boy explained. "We just needed some money. If you let me go I promise I won't do this anymore ... to anyone."

It actually sounded like he meant it, although so far, everyone and everything Sam had come across had been bullshit. "What about your friend?" Sam asked, hoping to exact the same kind of promise.

"Look man," the tall one said, "if that dog is going to eat me, then go the fuck ahead. I'll be glad to be out of your fucking sight. Reggie, you'd better hope I never see you again after this. Why didn't you see that fucking dog?"

"You can go, Reggie," Sam said to the younger one. "I'll keep your boss here while I'm deciding how hungry my dog is. Now!"

The kid bolted. Scout ignored him and pinned the taller mugger's arm to the wall. "Aaah," he screamed as a metal object dropped to the ground. The man crumbled to his knees and offered no attempt to fight off Scout, who had just enough of a grip to let him know that any resistance might cost an arm.

Sam picked up the dropped knife. It was a switchblade. He remembered the last time he'd seen one, in Jimm's hand. "You're lucky I don't let my dog tear off your hand or do it myself." It was starting to sound good. *Should I do it, or let the dog?*

No, no, said a distant voice. *We're not here for this. I won't indulge you.*

"Scout? Is that you, talking to me?" Sam asked. He'd been shut down and lit up at the same time, as if called by something from another world.

The look in Sam's eyes, and his discussion with a dog, had finally rattled the mugger's bravado. Something had changed and Sam now appeared eminently capable of delivering on his threat. "Look man, I'm sorry," the mugger said. "What the fuck do you want?" The voice wavered, its delivery *acciaccato*, broken separated pieces.

Sam was getting a feel for the knife, tossing it into the air, testing its balance. He liked the way it felt, the empowerment; for the first time since his return, *he* was on the good end.

No, no. Scout released his grip on the man's arm and barked, imploring. *You heard me, I will not be a part of this.*

Sam looked down and saw the knife as if for the first time. It was oddly embarrassing. "Go on, get out of here."

The mugger slid out toward the Embarcadero and vanished around the corner. "You're welcome, motherfucker," Sam muttered. He turned to the dog. "You're right Scout ... save it for Jimm." He closed the knife and put it in his pocket. "Come on, boy."

Scout stood over the storm drain and barked, refusing to move. Again, he seemed to be talking. Sam pulled the knife from his pocket; although it was the first asset he'd procured since his return, it was bad medicine. What use for it could he possibly have? If he pulled it on someone, they were liable to have one *and* know how to use it.

"You're right, Scout," he said, dropping the knife through the metal grate. "Thanks for saving my ass."

They made their way around the waterfront to the north and turned down Van Ness. Sam had nowhere to go; he felt beaten, as if he had lost rather than won the encounter with the muggers.

Almost every doorway seemed to be a homeless encampment: bodies in sleeping bags, makeshift tents of cardboard and newspaper, each with its own unique architectural presentation. "It doesn't look too bad, huh, Scout? At least we've got each other."

Sam's eyelids were leaden, descending into a sleepy blackness as he somehow managed to retain his balance and proceed at the dog's urging. The neon lights were blurred, offering a hallucinatory light show.

At Geary Street they turned up the hill, away from the movie marquees and electronic stores whose displays were showering the deserted street with cathode rays. Sam's step had become a shuffle, the sliding of his shoe soles like brushes on a snare, with just a trace of a backbeat. He was looking for a place to lie down; he needed to sleep before he could sort out what to do. Only his anger kept him from collapsing into defeat and despair. "I'll get that motherfucker, Scout," he promised as the dog led him up the block.

As they passed the old church on Franklin, Sam saw a little deserted alcove protected by a rosebush in full bloom. Maybe when they were found in the morning the priest would be understanding and charitable enough to give him coffee or let him sleep. But as he tried the gate, Scout nuzzled him forward, further up the hill. *We're almost there*, he seemed to say.

"Where are we going? I can't make it much farther." Sam felt as if he hadn't slept in days. Then, at the top of the hill, he saw Krieger's building. "Is this where we're going?"

No shit, Scout seemed to say.

"This is weird. All this shit has got me hearing things."

Sam rapped on the glass; the sentry looked up, startled. He adjusted his cap and came to the door. "Oh, it's you," the man said, letting him in. "It's almost midnight, a strange time to start a shift."

"Yeah, well, you know the old man." Sam headed for the elevator, bracing for the inevitable "You can't bring that dog in here!" But nothing was said; it was as if Scout were invisible in the dimmed lighting of the lobby.

The silver-tone elevator door closed and Sam sighed in relief. He had barely pushed the number for Krieger's floor before the darkness from which he had been running all evening overtook and overpowered him.

The first thing Sam saw was Krieger, leaning over him with a look of grave concern, his basset jowls hanging low from the sides of his face. "Pascal, he woke up. Get him some coffee."

Sam blinked twice and realized it was day. "How did I get here?"

"Late last night there was a scratching at the door. Pascal found you lying in the elevator with a dog hovering over you. He said you kept talking about a man named Jimm, how you were going to kill him. I figured maybe you were drunk and just needed to sleep it off. Then I realized you were delirious; I almost called a doctor. Here, drink this, it will make you feel better."

Sam felt Krieger's eyes on him, ready to intercede if necessary, as he negotiated the difficult task of raising the cup to his lips from a reclined position. The change in the dynamics, with Krieger now the caretaker, seemed to have given the old man an exuberant focus.

"How was your tour?"

Sam couldn't quite remember what he'd told Krieger when he'd quit. "A disaster."

"To be honest, you don't look so good."

"When I get my hands on that fat fuck of a piece of shit, I'll look just fine."

"Must be the man you were ranting about."

"Yeah. Where's the dog?" Sam asked. Scout stood up and approached from the corner of the room, where he'd been sleeping in a little wedge of sunlight that streamed through a narrow opening in the curtains. "I hope it's O.K. that I brought him. I didn't know what to do or where to go."

"Why don't you tell me about it? Pascal, make some more coffee, and bring some toast, too."

It was time to tell the whole story, no matter how embarrassing, degrading, or mortifying it might be; it was time to unravel the whole mess and come to terms with it. Sam started with his own insecurities and ambitions; how he'd been marinating in the *feeling* for years; how it would go into remission, only to rear its head again and again. He then worked his way through his various attempts at *stardom,* up to and including the day he met the devil—Jimm Dibbook.

To Krieger's credit, he listened compassionately and without a trace of judgment, not even a nod of his head, just those sympathetic dark eyes urging Sam on, to descend to the depths of his humiliation, to purge himself of the burden he seemed to be carrying.

When Sam finally got to *the marketing ploy of the century,* he had already drunk two cups of coffee and eaten four slices of cinnamon toast. Recounting the month and a half on the mountain seemed to bring him back, as if his two lives were now finally merging into one thread. He had been shown an alternative path, a way of wisdom that had always been there. It was just as true now as it had been when he'd finally accepted it on the mountain.

Yet, it became more and more obvious to Sam as he related the harsh homecoming that his life path had taken a new turn. Jimm Dibbook must pay: it was a duty beyond his selfish spiritual needs and obligations; Sam had to rid the earth of him. Only *that* would bring back a sense of completion and validation that he had mistakenly thought was totally inside himself. It had to do with balance and harmony. His voice became animated as he described in detail the many ways of dismembering his foe.

Krieger's face finally showed some emotion.

Was it concern? Fear? Sam tried to read it through the red rage that colored everything. He doubled back and retold how his apartment was gone, his stuff sold or tossed out, the cops indifferent—even his *guitars* gone! *This will get Krieger back on the sympathetic track.*

But to his dismay, it began to appear as though he was losing the old man's interest; even Scout had retreated to the corner.

"I've got to go downtown and talk to the Fraud Division at the Hall of Justice," Sam finished lamely.

Krieger nodded. "It sounds to me like you need a job and a place to stay." His tone was respectful, no hint of charity in it. "Will you come back here? Your dog can stay too. It's against the rules, but I own this fucking building."

Sam wanted to say no. How could he take advantage of this kindness, and at the same time plot his revenge? Would there be time for both?

Krieger continued: "It's a job, not a handout. Here's the key." He dropped it on the marble tabletop as he got up to leave the room. "Pascal! I need a shave!"

The Hall of Justice was an intimidating gray cement building with glass windows reflecting the harsh midday sun. Sam entered through the metal detectors and went to the directory to find the Fraud Division.

Second Floor. At least there was no line. The woman behind the counter was on the phone; when she saw Sam, she put one finger up in the air and turned her back. "I don't care," she said in a fierce whisper, "you get your things out or I'll throw them out! I'm having the locks changed tonight!" She slammed down the phone and turned to face Sam. "I'm sorry, how may I help you?"

"I'm here to report someone stealing everything I've got. He was a business associate. I talked to a policeman last night and he said

I had to come here."

"Whoa." The receptionist raised one hand. "Save it! Inspector Faulk is on office detail. Have a seat over there and I'll let him know you're here."

The inspector, a short, gray-haired man in a tan suede blazer, ushered Sam into a room split into three cubicles. They sat at the desk, both facing the gray fabric movable wall, which was plastered with pictures of young children.

"Grandchildren," the cop explained when he caught Sam's gaze. "The lights of my life. When I was young and working robbery I used to put the perps up, but things change. What can I do for you?"

It seemed odd to Sam that the man had yet to ask for his name. He acted as if this were just an informal interview. "I've been totally cleaned out," Sam explained. "I have—had—this manager, and the motherfucker, excuse me, well, he cleaned me out."

"Manager?"

"Yeah, I'm a musician." Still no writing; the inspector hadn't even reached for the yellow pad that lay on his desk. "I left town for a while, and when I came home, he'd sold the lease to my flat, my car, and even my things: clothes, guitars!"

"Shit."

"I'll say!" Things were looking up; Inspector Faulk appeared to be sympathetic. *Time to complain about the treatment at Mission Station last night.* "I went to report it last night, and the officer told me that it wasn't technically theft. I mean, he had power of attorney and the keys to my house and car, but that doesn't give him the right to fuck me like that."

The inspector gave Sam a bone-chilling look. "Doesn't it?"

Sam tried to control his outrage. "You mean it's O.K. for someone to take all my shit and sell it, because I gave him the key?!"

"You did more than give him a key; you signed over power of attorney."

"But that was so he could do business for me when I was gone."

"And so he did. You see, you entered into a fiduciary relationship with this man and he took advantage of it. There is no clear victim here."

"What!"

"Hear me out, O.K.?"

Sam stood and paced as the investigator continued. "You gave him the O.K. to do all that. The DA would laugh in my face if I brought this to him. Sounds to me like you might have a good case for civil trial."

"You're just going to pass the buck like that? You aren't even going to investigate?"

"Look," Inspector Faulk said, his temper giving color to his pasty cheeks, "I can send you to the Lawyer Referral Service; maybe they can help you out, but we can't just investigate because you say there was a crime. There is not technically a victim here, like a stolen credit card or bank fraud."

The inspector swiveled in his chair to follow Sam across the room as he paced. "I'm really sorry you got involved with the wrong guy, but that isn't a crime. We are not here to help some civil attorney litigating a business deal gone south, where one person screws another."

"Yeah, you just sit on your asses while everyone gets fucked!"

"Oh, yeah? What the fuck do you know? You just sign away your fucking life and expect us to come along and wipe your ass when it doesn't work out! We're not private investigators!"

Sam's rage spilled over: "I'll just have to do some investigating on my own, and believe me, when I find that motherfucker, you guys will have plenty to do, if you can muster the fucking interest. I'm going to kill him! Jimm Dibbook is a dead man!" Sam turned and started out the door.

A voice called to him from behind. "You'd better not. And you'd better hope nothing happens to him, either."

Sam stopped and turned. "What are you talking about?"

"You have just threatened a man's murder to a police officer, you *dumb fuck!*"

Sam fled, slamming the door behind him.

Out on the street, with the blazing spring sky in full attack, Sam paced back and forth in front of the building, plotting his next move. A shadow passed over him, and he looked up, the sun blinding him temporarily—but not before he caught a glimpse of a hawk.

"It can't be," Sam said, rubbing his eyes. He made his way down the sidewalk to get a view of the open sky: no hawk, not even a gull or a pigeon.

He turned the corner and started back toward downtown, wandering aimlessly, waiting for an idea. It came just as he was passing a phone booth; he stepped in and called Clyde's bar, hoping the machine would give him time to tell his story before cutting him off.

"Hello."

Sam hadn't expected a human voice.

"Hello? This is Clyde, who is it?"

"Clyde, this is Sam. Please don't hang up. Hear me out. O.K.?"

"Go ahead."

"Look, I understand you're upset, I don't blame you, but I had no idea of any of it, and that motherfucker did ten times more shit to me than he did to you, I promise. I left my bag there at the club last night; is it all right if I come and get it? We can talk it over then. I promise I'll make it all up to you."

There was a long silence on the line—had he hung up? Then: "We found it kind of strange, Sam, the way you were acting, and that dog. Ginger said you smelled like a forest, and had sort of a Unabomber vibe. When I looked through that bag and saw all that unopened mail, I figured something weird was up. Your helmet seemed kind of tight when you split, if I remember correctly."

"So, I can come by?"

Another long pause. "I s'pose."

Things were looking up, Sam thought. He could explain himself and start reclaiming some of his life, while he planned out how to find and execute Jimm.

He was walking through Skid Row, a smelly, beaten down section of 6th Street, with wall-to-wall pawnshops, liquor stores, and dilapidated hotels. The stench of urine mixed with the sewer gas that rose from the vents in the sidewalks, adding to his disgust. It was a far cry from the trailer.

Maybe I'll go back to the country after I settle with Jimm. This city shit doesn't have the luster it once had.

Then the reality hit. "Shit, what am I thinking? I don't belong there any more than I do here. It's money that rented that place, and more than three months would cost here." He realized that Gray Elk had no interest in his being there without paying rent.

And so what if I do find Jimm? Even if he has some of my bread left, I still got to get back to my shit . . . don't I?

Meanwhile, going to Clyde's was the perfect thing—book a few gigs and bide his time while they searched for Jimm. Clyde would be a great partner; after all, he'd been fucked too, and Clyde loved a fight. Sam resolved to take the gig with Krieger as well; he needed time to get on his feet and find Jimm, which was probably more of a daytime activity, anyway. Driving around was the best way to do that.

Sam began to feel focused and full of purpose for the first time since his return to the city. He crossed Market Street, and even the surroundings upgraded in proportion to his overall mood. The unbathed, hopeless homeless gave way to tunnel-visioned execs in finely tailored suits. It was strange that they didn't seem to look where they were going, yet there were no collisions, as if they had all developed bat-like radar. Sam tested it by weaving his way down the wide sidewalk toward the club: not even a near miss.

The smell and bustle of Chinatown was altogether another world. Sam had always loved the intensity of energy, the pulsating throngs of humanity, the overwhelming scent of food in all of its stages, from fresh and raw to total decay. Next to a dumpster that smelled as if it held a decomposing yak carcass, a street vendor's array of vegetables and herbs promised health and long life. Sam watched as an aging white man with a long steel-gray ponytail argued with an old Chinese merchant, a universe away from the suits a block south.

"It no work lie dat. Dee tail no work lie dat!" the Chinaman sang at the top of his lungs.

"I don't give a fuck—deer tail, deer dick, whatever; it don't work. I want my money back!" He held up a plastic bag full of a soggy, moldy substance that looked like rotten banana.

Sam was transfixed, feeling that he was about to watch a murder. *Maybe I'll learn something.* He felt as though he were meant to see this. He looked up in the sky, half-expecting to see a large bird of prey circling.

"I no give money back. It old now, no good. I tole you dat two day ago!" The Chinese merchant was waving his arms, his delivery a rapid *staccato*. The tension was almost visible, as the rest of the people on the street circled around the disturbance like a river around a boulder, effortlessly and without concern.

His customer's reply was a grim monotone. "That ain't the fuck what you told me. I'm going to give you ten seconds to give me my money back. Ten . . . nine . . ."

"You no tell me you have diebeeds!"

"Eight . . . seven . . . six . . ."

"Nothing make deek hawd with diebeeds!"

"Five . . . four . . ."

Sam wondered what was going to happen when the count ran out, now that the Chinaman had announced the nature of the man's problem to the world.

"Three ... two ..."

"O.K., O.K., I give money back. But you no come here again! If you want to fuck, tly Viagla!"

The old guy smirked, shook his head, and threw the plastic bag on the ground before he carefully counted the crumpled wad of bills that had been handed over. "What are you looking at?" he asked Sam.

"Nothing," Sam answered. He darted across Columbus Street, wondering why he'd been drawn to the exchange. Something in all that had screamed at him—but what was it?

Sam started laughing as he saw the club come into view. "*Viagla!*" It all became crystal clear. *Sex!. I should try to call Jennifer, like I planned, offer her my unwavering—albeit bankrupt—love.*

Clyde's seemed foreign in the light of day. The carpets were threadbare, and cigarette burns—from when it was still possible to smoke in California—looked like bugs in the harsh light that filtered through the dusty windows.

I guess clubs are like a lot of the women who hang out in them: they look better in the dark and after a couple of cocktails.

"Clyde?" Sam called out.

"Down here," Clyde yelled from the basement. "Will you shut the door and throw the bolt?"

Clyde was sitting in a tiny cubicle at the bottom of the stairs, hunched over a desk covered with papers. The glow of the video monitor that showed the entryway upstairs cast a grayish pallor on his ebony skin. "Have a seat," he said, motioning to the empty chair that sat outside the door.

Sam pulled it around and sat across the threshold to the office.

Clyde folded the paper he'd been writing on and put it in an envelope. After he licked it, he finally looked up. "You don't look so good."

"It's been rough," Sam admitted.

"What the fuck happened to you, Sam?"

As Sam recounted the story he realized he'd developed variations. He gave Clyde *Opus 3*, the one where he omitted the embarrassing *marketing ploy of the century*. He blamed his being duped into getting away on stress, directly traceable to the night Clyde had saved him on the bandstand.

Clyde pulled out a calculator. As he punched in numbers, he barked, "You know how much you're in the hole because of all this?"

"In the hole?" *What the hell is he talking about?*

"Is there a fucking echo in here? I paid a grand in front for you guys. So I lost that and any profit—let's say from a normal night, another grand. Then there's your band."

"Let me work it off, Clyde. I need a gig."

"You think I'd hire you again? You think they'd work with you? Quentin was going to go out and kill you when he found out you'd been by last night. You might be able to settle things with Wil, provided you pay, but I ain't never even seen Quentin raise his voice. Them little quiet guys are the scariest ones of all."

"But I'm telling you, that motherfucker stole everything I had. They can't blame me for that," Sam pleaded.

"It seems they do, and I don't blame them."

"They'll understand when I tell them the truth."

"You can try, but I'd start with Wil if I was you. Something about the steady temperament of a bass player."

"Can I get a gig?"

"You got a lot of nerve," Clyde said, taking off his glasses, engaging in the old stare-down.

For the first time Sam held his glare, challenging. *I've already lost everything, I don't think there's much more that you can do to me.*

Clyde blinked. "Talk to the band and we'll see. Let me think it over. What are you going to do?"

"I'm going to work for this old man. I just drive him around and keep him company. He's a nice cat, treats me like family."

"Sounds like what you need."

"Yeah, that and some bread. Do you know how much Jimm promised them for the tour?"

"They said three grand a month."

"Shit, that's twelve grand! I'll figure out a way to get most of it back, Clyde, I promise."

"I believe you, Sam. Sorry if I came down on you a little hard last night. You got any accounts receivable, you know, people that owe you?"

"Maybe that guy Paul from the CD Company. Hell it was number one! Can I use the phone?"

Sam made the call and waited as the receptionist went to see if he was in. A loud voice came on the line. "Sam Mann? I can't talk to you, you'll have to speak to my lawyer."

"Your lawyer? I was just inquiring into an advance on my royalties."

"What? Now I've heard everything! First of all, you rip me off for more than fifty-thousand dollars, and then you ask for an advance?"

"I didn't rip off anything. All I did was make a CD, and it *was* number one on the charts. I never saw anything but a two-thousand-dollar check for the session, of which I gave Jimm four hundred as a commission."

"Are you serious?"

"As a heart attack. Can we get together and talk this out?"

"O.K.," Paul agreed, "I'll meet you at Trader Sam's, on Geary, in an hour. Can you make it?"

"I'll find it. Thanks," Sam said.

Clyde watched Sam slam the phone down, looking more confused than ever. "Your bag is upstairs underneath the coat rack," he said. "How much do you figure this guy got you for?"

"I haven't figured it out yet. A lot," Sam said.

Clyde slid the calculator across the desk. It surfed on a wave of paper.

"Let's see, the house was thirty grand—"

"Ooo-weee," Clyde sang.

"My car was an easy ten, my axes—"

"Oh shit, that's right, he got your guitar." Clyde said, retrieving the calculator before Sam could hit TOTAL. "That's all I want to hear. I imagine you'll be busy carving him a new asshole for the next five years or so. If you want any help let me know."

"Thanks, Clyde. About that gig?"

"You talk to the guys. If they'll play, you can have steady Tuesdays and Wednesdays. Call me."

Sam was relieved that he'd been able to make some headway with Clyde, although he wasn't quite ready to call the guys in his band. The numbers on the readout of the calculator were spinning in his mind's eye. "I'll kill that motherfucker," he said as he hailed a cab.

They passed Krieger's building on Geary Street and Sam thought he saw a hawk sitting atop the flagpole. He turned in his seat to look, and the bird—if it had been there—was gone. "Phew," he said, wiping his brow.

"Pardon? You want the zoo?" the driver asked.

"No, just thought I saw something. Turn right here and go down Lake Street. I want to check out a few things before we get to the bar. Go kind of slow. If you see a short fat guy with black curly hair, point him out to me."

"White or black?"

"Good question." Sam laughed. "Jewish."

When they got to 11th Street, Sam asked the driver to pull over by the park and wait.

"Hold on buddy, that'll be $11.45."

"Keep the meter running," Sam said.

"Right, and you just waltz on out the other side. How long should I wait, until it hits a hundred?"

Sam shook his head. *I don't screw people. You have me mixed up with the short fat guy.* "Here's a deuce," he said, handing the man a twenty. "Keep it running."

Sam entered the park and searched the benches, hoping to see Jimm, his pudgy legs swinging freely as he lured another fool into his trap. "Shit, he's probably way the fuck out of town by now. He must have known I'd come looking." Sam saw the goose nibbling at a torn paper sack. He clapped his hands and whistled the first strain of "Salt Peanuts."

The bird responded with a loud honk.

"That's not Diz's part," Sam reproached, watching it waddle over like it was greeting a long lost flock mate. "You haven't seen the fat man, have you? Remember? The guy you pecked?" As the goose searched his pockets, Sam ran his hands down the long thin neck and ruffled the feathers. "I wish I'd listened to you." Sam laughed and started back to the cab. "If I find him, he's the goose who's going to get cooked."

They cab wove a circuitous path through the Richmond district without a sight of Jimm, further convincing Sam that he had left town.

"Maybe there's a clue in all this mail," Sam mused as he tested the weight of his bag. The piney smell of it gave him a nostalgic yearning for the mountain and simpler days.

Trader Sam's was a funky old bar stuffed with faux-Polynesian kitsch. Palm fronds hung on the wall over woven bamboo booths, while professional daytime drinkers sat at the horseshoe bar, knocking back beers and an occasional shot; not a Mai Tai in sight. Sam decided on a beer as he eyed the cobwebs floating in the breeze created by a small ceiling fan. A firm hand landed on his shoulder.

"Sam?"

"Paul, how are you?" He didn't need to ask. Paul's hair seemed several shades grayer, and bags under his eyes told a tale of sleepless nights.

"I've had a difficult go of it, Sam." He turned to the bartender. "Usual, Rick."

The bartender pulled out a bottle of Tanqueray and poured freely over a few small ice cubes that had melted by the time the clear liquid reached the top of the glass; after that, the merest spritz of tonic, and a lime for food value. Paul was starting early, and with a vengeance.

"Sam, I'm in one hell of a mess because of all this," Paul said, surveying the glass, gauging how long it would be before the inevitable reorder.

Sam heard the implicit blame. "Paul, like I told you on the phone, I don't know what you're talking about. I left town, was out in the woods for a month and a half!" It finally sunk in: Jimm hadn't even told anyone that he had disappeared—nor had anyone cared or noticed. "Then I come home and I'm completely cleaned out: homeless, car-less, guitar-less!"

"Hmm." His plight had registered, but seemed caught in the miasma of toxins marinating Paul's brain. "Your story makes sense, I've got to admit. Nevertheless, that doesn't help me much."

"What did he do to you?"

"He got me for all the money for the CDs, production and pressing, more than fifty grand."

"Fifty grand?"

Paul nodded and took another gulp.

"Where did he come up with those figures?"

"The production cost almost twenty."

"Twenty?" Sam yelled.

Everyone at the bar looked over. Rick made a move to intervene if necessary. Paul stopped him with a wave and ordered another round by holding his glass in the air.

"That record didn't cost five," Sam explained. "We did it direct to two-track, only one day in the studio. Shit, six or seven grand, max. That motherfucker."

"Then this marketing group he got me to pay for, that was another fifteen."

"Fifteen?" Again Sam could hardly believe his ears. *And here I thought I was the gullible fool; he had no chance to make any money back, this is jazz.* "But you got to face it, Paul, they did a good job. It was number one."

Paul scowled at Sam and then shook his head; he chugged the last of his drink and Rick appeared with another round. "You saw those tear-outs from the magazines, right? Did you see originals?"

Sam thought it over; it was buried in the chaos of a distant lifetime. "No, now that you mention it."

"Well, we were both taken in by some cut-and-paste and a Xerox machine. There *is* no marketing group."

"Holy shit."

"Then there's the pressing."

"That's right! At least you have product to sell. I'll help, I promise."

"That was all bullshit, Sam, fifteen grand worth. He faked a phony receipt; I think he had a friend burn a few and make covers on a PC. There's no inventory; I'm completely screwed. Then there's the IRS—"

"The what?!"

"He'd been going through things in my warehouse, where his office space was. He found some irregularities, nothing much, but you know how it is. I paid him an advance on the profits to get rid of him. He took a shitload of my inventory when he left, I'm sure of it, but because of paperwork discrepancies, I don't even know how much. Then the asshole turns me in anyway, so on top of my bankruptcy problems, I've got some fucking IRS auditor breathing down my neck. And I've had four bookkeepers in the last year, none of whom knew what the fuck they were doing."

I thought I had problems. "So he got you, too," Sam said, peeling the label off his beer.

"Yep. I went to the police, but they aren't really interested. In their minds, with all the contracts and stuff, it's low-level embezzlement at best. They suggested I file a complaint, but they want *me* to serve him. I went ahead and filed a civil case with my lawyer, but I don't know how I'm going to pay him."

"Shit. I'll tell you one thing, I'm going to find that motherfucker, and when I do, I won't wait for the police to do their fucking job."

"Wait until I collect first." Paul said, waving Rick over.

"That'll be twelve-fifty," Rick said. It was obvious which of them he was talking to.

Sam pulled out his wallet and paid up, realizing he scarcely had cab fare back to Krieger's condo.

"Thank you, Sam. Oh yeah, one more thing. Rick, I want you to witness this: Sam, I'm serving you with a summons; I'm suing *you* in this matter, too."

He pulled an envelope from his jacket and laid it on top of Sam's hand, making contact.

Sam entered the apartment to a hearty greeting from Scout. Krieger came scuttling into the room. From the back bedroom, Sam could have sworn he heard two tenor saxophones doing battle on some up-tempo "Rhythm Changes."

"There you are," the old man said as he petted Scout on his floppy ears. It was hard for Sam to tell which of the two he was talking to. Krieger looked up, "I guess you took him with you."

Sam started to answer in the negative when Scout shot him a

shocking, clear-eyed stare. He saw the open window and sat down on the couch. It was too much to even ponder, especially now, in his bankrupt state. *A summons, on top of everything else; now I've got to go to court and defend myself!*

In the next room, a tenor climbed two and a half octaves, from the depths of the horn to the top, and ended sitting on a clear high note, its tone searching, imploring. "Sounds good," Sam said.

"I went to Tower Records over on Broadway," Krieger said. "They have a whole room devoted to jazz."

Sam nodded. *Had Krieger become a jazz fan?*

"I wanted to get some more Zoot Sims CDs, and there were a whole bunch that he recorded with another guy named Al Cohn. Jewish, right?"

Sam shot him a sideways glance. He was in no mood for the old man's racist baiting.

"Not because of the obvious, the name," Krieger explained, seeming perturbed that Sam wasn't taking him seriously. "But because when you listen to the two of them side by side, it's obvious. Zoot is so lyrical and sounds resigned, just like we Irish are by nature. Is he?"

Sam shrugged.

Krieger continued, more animated than before. "But Al Cohn, wow! He's smart, I mean really smart. You can tell he's practically rewriting or rearranging as he blows..." —*blows?*— "...and his tone is so strong, it's as if it's almost demanding to be recognized. I don't even know how they could record a sound like that."

Who the fuck is this? Has he turned into Ralph Gleason? Sam sat on the couch and rubbed his temples.

"Come here, I want to show you something!" Krieger grabbed him by the arm and pulled him into the bedroom, where a new bookshelf had been placed against the wall that faced the bed. On the middle shelf was the boom box on which the two tenors were laying back for the relative calm of a piano solo. The top shelf was filled with CDs, many still unopened.

"You've been busy," Sam said.

Krieger beamed with pride. The bottom shelf held various anthologies, biographies, and an already dog-eared copy of the *Encyclopedia of Jazz*. It had happened; Krieger had gone *jazz*.

"I'm glad you're back; now we can go get a sound system for the living room, and you can take me to some clubs. Look here," Krieger said as the horns reentered, another round of trading fours. He had the complete Sam Mann discography, three of which were not even available in CD format. "I had to order the vinyl direct from the company," he proudly announced. Krieger turned and saw Sam teetering on the balls of his feet, his face ashen. "You don't look so good."

Sam felt faint.

"Why don't you take a little nap and we can talk during dinner," Krieger said as he led Sam to the couch, Scout underfoot, herding them both.

As Sam settled into the thick padding of the sofa, already half asleep, he said, "Thanks."

The last thing Sam saw before his eyes closed was Kreiger's pug nose and folded jowls undulating as he whispered with a hint of a smile, "Fuck you."

It was Sam's first restaurant meal in months. The salad and pasta were elegantly displayed—even in the moderately fashionable place Krieger had picked—and the flavors of the white wine danced on the tip of his tongue. Pascal seemed a bit gruff, but was definitely on a tight lead. *Can't say that I blame him; I come back and the old man treats me like the returning prodigal son. He's probably offering me his gig.*

Sam resolved to smooth out any misconceptions and head off any confrontations down the road. He didn't need more trouble;

after all, his main plan was to track down and exact justice on Jimm Dibbook.

"So, you *are* coming back?" Krieger asked, excited.

Until then, Sam had carefully danced around the subject. "What about Pascal?"

"It's all worked out," Krieger answered.

Sam turned to the stoic Latino, his eyes asking for a confirmation. Even though they were both employees, Pascal could speak for himself.

"If it is what Mr. Krieger wants, then it is fine with me. I prefer nights, and we have had trouble keeping any of the others for more than one week."

Krieger beamed. "I talked to Henry, my grandson—the one with the big head, who got married?" Sam nodded. "You can stay at Kinsale, in Hillsborough. There's an extra guest house, a converted gardening shed, where you'll have complete privacy. You can use my car at night. Pascal has his own, or we could take a taxi if I need to go anywhere."

Sam was dumbstruck. After his disastrous return, the turnaround was unexpected and overwhelming. He was moved beyond his own capacity to comprehend. "I can't take advantage of you like this," he said.

"You must accept," Pascal said. "Please. If you do not, he will take it out on the rest of us. I help to make sure that you can have all the time off you need."

"That might be quite a bit, there are a lot of things that I need to straighten out. It seems as though everyone I ever knew is either suing me or wants to kill me. And then there's this little unfinished matter I have to clear up."

His enthusiasm seemed to chill Krieger. "Sam, don't do anything stupid. But if you want some help, I have a lot of friends."

"I have a great one, too," Sam said, clinking his crystal goblet against the other two.

When they arrived back at the condo, Krieger—who seemed so much more vital and energetic than before—sorted out the sleeping arrangements. "Pascal, why don't you go home so Sam can sleep on the couch. Don't worry, you're still on the clock. Be back in time for breakfast."

"*Jes* sir, Mr. Krieger."

Sam noted how much better Pascal's English had gotten since he'd left, but he still had that Puerto Rican *"jes"* fixed deep in his language synapses.

"I didn't get any dog food," Krieger said. "I don't know what you feed him. Why don't we walk to the corner and get some?"

"Are you up to it?" Sam asked.

"It's only a block. But I think we should go out through the garage. Let's let the tenants get used to him before we take him through the lobby."

Scout took the cue and perfectly mimicked a real dog, running excitedly to the door, wagging his tail, his red tongue hanging from his mouth. *Damn, I'm good.*

As soon as they had settled back in from their walk, Krieger started in. "Tell me Sam, what was your favorite tenor team? Do you like Lockjaw and Johnny Griffin, or Al and Zoot?"

This might be tough. I don't know if I can baby-sit Leonard Feather, here. "Well, they're completely different, but Trane—John Coltrane—and Sonny Rollins on "Tenor Madness" is about as good as it gets, in my opinion; that and the Wardell Grey / Dexter Gordon, or the Gene Ammons/Sonny Stitt sessions."

"Make up your mind, kid!" said Kreiger, eagerly taking notes. "I can't wait to go to Tower Records with you."

"There are a few other out-of-the-way stores, run by real fans. Shit, they know as much about it as I do, if not more."

"Great," Krieger said, anxious to get to sleep so the morning would arrive sooner—the way a small child almost wills the speedy arrival of Christmas morning.

"I can't thank you enough for all you're doing for me—for us," Sam said as he watched Scout stand and stretch, as if unsure whether to remain with him or retire with the old man. It was at that moment when he recognized a strange similarity between Krieger and Hawk Feather. He dismissed it, chalking it up to the shrunken stature of anyone who had waged war with the forces of gravity for so many years.

"Sam, I'm sorry for what has happened to you, and I really want to help. But you don't need to thank me. You're working for me . . . and one more thing: fuck you."

The trees were a blur of green as Sam raced past them at full gallop. Descending into a deep valley of wildflowers and knee-high reedy grass, the rhythmic pounding of hooves heralded an overture to a symphony. Sam looked to his side and saw Jennifer high on the ridge top, waving. He turned to the other side and saw Jimm Dibbook aiming a rifle across the expanse, sighting her through the scope. Sam felt out of control; the buckskin mare was galloping straight toward a sheer cliff. He tried to scream, but was drowned out by the rushing wind and pounding of the mare's hooves.

As they neared the craggy edge, he tried to stop, but the noise obscured his "whoa!" and he had no reins. The mare pulled up just before the sheer drop, and the momentum thrust him over her head, past land's end, over the ocean.

An updraft caught him, and he found himself awed by the rush of flying. He swooped up and down, testing his newfound powers, delighting in the freedom and acuity of vision. The slightest movement—a blade of grass bending in the wind, a fish below the white-capped swells—had become as stark and present as an out-of-place billboard. And it wasn't only visual: smells and sounds were exaggerated, as vivid as touch or taste, a visceral smorgasbord.

He floated, watching the display below, his body no longer his own but a shared co-op. *What is this telling me?* A strange question to ask oneself in the midst of REM sleep; even stranger to ponder while flying above the earth as a hawk. As soon as he asked the question, the air went cold, his wings no longer giving lift, causing a tumbling free fall toward the sharp, jutting rocks at the bottom of the cliff.

Sam quickly surfaced into daytime consciousness as Scout barked, his thick paw scratching at his arm. "Thanks, boy. That was a close one. Is that really what you see?"

"Is *what* what you see?" Krieger asked. Already dressed and shaven, he sat staring from the facing wing chair.

"Were you watching me?"

"Only for a little while. You were having a whopper of a dream. I didn't want to wake you. Your dog was guarding you, anyway; I don't think he would have let me. Have you noticed his eyes? They were changing color as he watched you sleep. How do you feel?"

"O.K., I guess." Sam sat up, running his hands through the hair above his ears.

"Good. Have some coffee, we have a lot to do today."

"Where's Pascal?"

"I sent him home twenty minutes ago, when *your* shift started. I'll bring you a cup. You take it black, right?"

Sam nodded, and watched the old man make his way to the electric coffeepot on the counter that separated the living room from the kitchen. It was strange how much energy he now had. Was it the role of caretaker, or was it jazz?

"Are you ready?" Krieger asked as he watched Sam button the same shirt he'd worn the day before. "You probably need to buy some new clothes, since all your stuff is gone."

Thanks for reminding me. "I guess it'll wait until payday."

"I'll give you some loot now; you can pay me back. You jazz guys call it a draw, right?" Krieger said, proudly quoting one of his new books as he peeled off a couple of hundreds from a gold clip. Sam had almost forgotten the steady stream of Ben Franklins, many of which he'd left with Iris and Gray Elk.

He looked into Scout's eager, expectant eyes. "I really ought to call my friend down in the country and let him know I have the dog, in case the real owner comes looking for him. I just sort of adopted him temporarily. He doesn't have a phone, so I've got to leave a message with his secretary. Can I leave this number for him to call back?"

"Of course, but you may want to wait until we get to Kinsale, so you can give him that number, too. There's a phone in the guest-house. I must warn you, I'm using that term very loosely; it's only a shed. Henry's mother-in-law has taken over the estate, and even though she could accommodate the entire Basie band, the shed was all she'd agree to."

"If you saw where I've been the last month or two you'd know I'm not worried."

It felt a bit strange to Sam, finding himself at the wheel of the behemoth Town Car. Scout took up a post in the backseat, his snout stuck out the window into the wind.

"Before we head south, there's one stop I want to make," Krieger said. "It's a little alley in the Mission district. I'll tell you where to go."

"What's the secret?"

They shot across Market and fought one-way traffic, tacking their way into a maze of alleys.

"Park right there," Krieger ordered.

Sam squeezed the Lincoln between an old VW bus—orange with paisley curtains—and a Dumpster.

Krieger was out of the car and on his way around the corner

before Sam had lowered the windows properly to keep Scout from baking in the bright morning sun.

"Wait a second," he yelled, running to catch up. When he saw the old man turn into a store, he realized where they were. It was the Vintage Guitar Shop, the best place to find or sell an axe in the Bay Area. *He's not playing now, too, is he?*

Guitars covered the walls, stacked two-high on clamps secured into reinforced pegboard. Every style, from acoustic to electric solidbody and everything in between, all in a variety of natural wood tones, sunburst lacquer patterns, and glow-in-the-dark rocker colors. The floor was a hard-to-navigate labyrinth of aisles made by stacked amplifiers, many of them nearly as old as Sam himself.

Krieger walked to the back corner and pointed. "These are the ones like you used to have."

It hurt to look, to imagine Jimm selling his guitar to someone, and someone else playing it. In his rage at the evil, the injustice of it, Sam almost pushed over a wall of amps stacked three high. He was glad that no one in the store had recognized him; the humiliation of not even owning an instrument, of being outdone by his own demons, was overwhelming. He felt his breath shortening as his vision started to fade. He found an Ampeg B-15, needing a wide place to park his butt before he fell over and took about four thousand dollars' worth of inventory with him.

"Sam, are you O.K.?"

He heard it from a distance, summoning him. *Hell, I'm supposed to be taking care of him.* "It's just upsetting: all these axes... and mine gone."

"That's why we're here. You need another. They're just guitars; they don't do a damn thing until you play them."

Sam knew he'd heard those words spoken recently, in approximately the same tone.

"Play one," Kreiger commanded.

"May I help you?" asked a skinny kid with a ring in his nose and tattoos running the length of his spindly arms.

Krieger piped up. "We would like to see one of these jazz guitars. Sam, which one? That red and gold one looks like yours."

"The L5?" the kid asked.

"That'll be fine," Sam whispered, partly afraid to speak up, lest someone recognize him as the biggest fool to ever make an ascent on a fret board.

He sat on the amp and waited as the kid mounted a stepladder and handed it down. Sam took it by the belly and carefully lowered it into his lap, like a nervous father handling his firstborn. He tested it for weight, holding it at eye level, the F holes, pickups, knobs, and straight-grained spruce so close he could kiss them. Sam spun it around and cradled it in his lap, a slow-motion take of a pair of reunited lovers.

The salesman sighed, relieved to see it safely in Sam's arms. "That's a mid-'60's, really a great specimen, hardly any checking on the finish, except right there." He pointed to the dark area around the toggle switch that controlled the pickups. "It's not exactly vintage," he said, "but Shaller tuning heads are much better than the originals."

His chirping was a far-off cry; Sam was engaged, back to something that he'd been cut off from for too long. His only experiences with music in the country had been pastoral and therapeutic. Now that he held an instrument capable of reproducing his real musical voice, there was a power and connection to the world, as if a thousand renegade volts had finally been grounded.

He took a deep breath and pulled out a pick, the two looking on. He started with a lightning *appoggiatura* in the middle of the neck, the guitar's midrange liquid and velvety, then skipped into the upper reaches. The tone was crystal clear, bell-like, with plenty of body to bolster the taut strings at the end of the fingerboard. Then, just as quickly, came a descending flourish, its harmonic intent lucid as it made the briefest of pit stops cascading to the bottom of the neck. At the end of an elongated *glissando*, Sam struck a Low E;

the fundamental tone was a deep bellow, with just the right amount of overtones to perk up any listener's ears. He answered the burst of sound with an E7+11 chord, suggesting resolution to E-flat; it almost sounded as if the guitar could somehow make it that one step lower without detuning.

It might have taken two seconds, tops, but as the chord faded there was a collective sigh: the salesman satisfied that he wasn't dealing with yet another amateur player and could trust Sam with such an expensive instrument; the old man just glad Sam was back.

"Would you like to plug it in?" the kid asked as he went to get a cable from the counter.

"Sure," Sam answered, turning over the yellow tag that hung from one of the tuning pegs and catching the price. He gasped when he saw it: $8,750.

"Which amp?"

Doesn't matter, can't afford it, anyway. He felt his blood surge, imagining how much Jimm must have gotten for his—a similar model, though not as cosmetically perfect. It had lived its years on the road, not in some closet or living room. "The Fender Pro Reverb over there, I guess," he answered. Another thing Jimm had liquidated, probably for pennies on the dollar. Sam was scared to ask the kid if he'd seen a fat guy selling these things recently.

He'd scoured the room when they'd entered; but if his equipment had come through, it was long gone, and he had no way of buying it back at the current prices, anyway.

He plugged the guitar in and waited for the tubes to warm up before launching into a long piece that told the story of time lost, time to make up, time wasted. At the end—a sweet chiming harmonic that held in the air for a long time before dissipating into a wisp of memory—the salesman applauded. "You're a professional player, aren't you?"

"Sort of." *Well, it was fun while it lasted, but it's time to get back to reality.* Sam looked up at the long rack of hollow-bodies and saw a scraggly blond at the end—a Korean knockoff, placed away from the others so as not to contaminate them with its inferior status. "Let me play that one," he said to the kid, who had already chalked up the sale and was planning how to spend his commission.

The guitar was appreciably lighter and smaller, the wood grain on the fingerboard dirty and wide, not tight black ebony like the old Gibson. He connected the jack and began to play. While there was a noticeable loss in playability, the sound was mellow and would probably age, and with some work on the setup it would be an adequate gig axe. It would serve well until he got some bread together or found his old one. He made his peace with the bow at the end of the neck where it met the body, and played around that area as best he could.

He tried some samba-style, the fingers of his right hand willing the sound out of the strings, flexing the wood as it fought the resonation. Sam did his best to encourage it to wake up and begin barking.

"This will do," he said, checking the price on the tag. $650. "I could maybe go to five if you throw in an amp."

The salesman seemed disappointed. Sam didn't blame him.

Krieger interrupted. "May I see the owner or manager? Don't worry, I won't cut you out of your commission, I just wanted to talk about a cash discount."

Sam turned to Kreiger as the scraggly youngster receded toward the back of the store. He was surprised to see the old man looking stern and displeased. "Sam, we have to talk."

"Is it too much? The thing is, I need to borrow enough to buy this and an amp, too. I'll pay you right back."

"For that? Positively not!"

Sam nodded, trying not to show his disappointment. He'd be able to save enough after a few weeks, anyway; he could wait that long. Plus, the old man had done more than enough. Sam felt guilty for having even asked.

"Sam, I want you to listen to me."

Great, the old speech about how, if you wait for it, it will mean more. Spare me.

Krieger continued: "I don't tell you about music, do I?" Sam shook his head. "Then you'll let me tell you something about business?" Sam nodded, resigned. "The way I see it, if I buy you a guitar, it's my guitar, at least until you pay me back, and permanently if you don't, or if something happens to you."

"Fair enough." *Where is all this going?*

"If I buy that thing," he said, pointing to the Korean blond, "it will only be worth what I pay for it, probably less. But if I buy that Gibson, it increases in value every day. From an investment standpoint, it's the only smart decision. Especially since it's my money. The other thing is, I have to listen to you play the goddamn thing. That one sounded fine, but there was a difference in the way the Gibson responded to you, and the way you responded to it. And don't worry..." He winked. "I'll get a good deal."

Sam was trying, unsuccessfully, to think of an answer, when the salesman returned with the owner—a thick, aging hippie who waddled like a penguin, a torn Grateful Dead T-shirt exposing parts of his ape-like hairy chest. "Sam, how are you? You looking for a new axe?"

Krieger took charge; this was his realm. "No, it's for me. Sam is just offering his expertise."

Sam shot him a glance. *Thanks.*

"What can I do for you, then?" The owner seemed impatient, ready to get down to business and return to whatever he'd been pried away from.

"I plan to buy a few things and I'll pay cash. I just want to make sure we don't take all day. I want the kid here, though; I'm not doing this to cut him out of a commission. I want that guitar and an amplifier, and I want a fair price, that's all." He turned to Sam. "That amp's just like yours, right?"

Sam nodded as he went to turn over the price tag on the amplifier. "$1,450!" he gasped, realizing how much Jimm had gotten for his, which Sam had bought at the advent of the solid-state craze, when everyone had opted for the lighter amps and sold off the heavy and cumbersome tube models.

Krieger saw the near panic on Sam's face. "Why don't you two figure out the best you can do for the two of these, and I'll talk it over with Sam."

They scurried off to the counter to work it out on a calculator.

"I don't need the big amp," Sam whispered. "I only used that one on important gigs and record dates, because it was so heavy. I kept a smaller, lighter one in the trunk for most gigs. That was the one you heard me play down in Big Sur."

"Yeah, but I just heard what that one sounds like, and I heard you play one like it that night at Clyde's. There was a difference."

God, this guy has got it bad. Next thing I know, he'll be quoting Down Beat *or* Guitar Player.

"I don't see any reason to haggle, since you're with Sam," the owner said as the two returned. "How about nine thousand for both out the door?"

Krieger scratched his chin, thinking it over. "Well . . . I think I'll need a small amp, too. Sam, which one is best?"

The owner seemed to deflate on the spot. Sam found a Fender, high in power but light and small.

"How much for this one?" Sam asked; there was no tag on it.

The owner scowled. "I haven't decided," he said. "I ended up with it by mistake. I don't carry any new solid-state models; I deal in vintage. Are you sure you really want it?"

"I'll make it easy," Krieger said. "Nine grand for all three, out the door."

"Sold," the owner said before Sam could stop the madness. "I've got some important business in the back, so I'll let Ned here write it up. Nice to see you, Sam."

They loaded everything into the trunk of the car. "I think you could have done better, you know," Sam said. "You really didn't give me much chance to be of expert help."

"All you would have done was try to talk me out of it. In two years that guitar will increase in value and recover every cent we paid. I read a story about it in one of those magazines. I noticed it because it had a guitar just like yours on the cover. The way I see it, we got those two amplifiers for free."

Sam felt consumed with gratitude. "You know, you turned out to be a pretty far out half-a-motherfucker."

Krieger laughed. "Fuck you."

Sam had difficulty concentrating during the drive down to Hillsborough, managing three near misses, one with a massive beer delivery truck.

"Hey, kid!" Krieger screamed, his face only inches from the lug nuts of a four-foot-high tire, "I don't remember you being such a lousy driver. No wonder I rammed those cans at the Marina—considering the teacher."

"Sorry. It's *your* fault. Now that I have a guitar, all I can think of is how I'm going to get some gigs, and wondering how the hell I'm going to get my band back."

"Maybe I can help."

"Oh, no. You've done enough for one day. Hell, you've done enough for a lifetime."

"All the same, maybe I can give you some advice. After all this screeching, I'm thirsty. There's a bar down the next street. Make a left."

They turned down a street of old, neighborhood style shops—not the typical suburban sprawl of the Peninsula near the freeway.

"It's nice over here near El Camino," Sam said as he pulled into the angled parking space.

"You should have seen it sixty years ago. I used to run beer wagons in the hills over there."

"Nice place," Sam said, surveying the bar, hoisting his pint and tapping it lightly against the side of Krieger's. "Cheers."

"How come you never call me by my name?"

"I don't know, it never comes up in conversation, I guess."

"Do you remember what it is?"

"Of course."

"O.K. Well, even though you work for me, I want you to call me by it."

"Fair enough," Sam said.

"So?"

"*So What?*" Sam began humming the opening phrase of the classic tune from the Miles Davis album, "Kind of Blue." Call and response. He waited.

Krieger stared. He knew there was something he was supposed to do. Frustrated, he snapped. "Well? What is it?"

Sam smiled and sang the answer: "Dah duht."

"Not that!"

Sam took a swig of beer and said, "Krieger."

"My first name? For one hundred dollars?"

"I got to get you "Kind of Blue"—everyone knows "So What," Frank."

The beer began to take effect, adding to the warm and enveloping darkness of the little tavern. They were the only patrons seated at the bar; all the others had gravitated to the lunchroom upstairs and the relative brightness of its open window.

"Can I buy you some lunch, Frank?" Sam was dying to break the bill he'd won in the bet. He'd tried to give it back, first as a gesture of thanks, then as the first installment on the instrument loan, but the old man would have none of it. Every sentence out of Sam's mouth ended with Frank, and Krieger soon offered another hundred to get him to stop.

Krieger took a sip and licked the foam off his upper lip. "So what's the problem with your band? I thought you guys hooked up real well."

"Hooked up?"

"Wynton Marsalis—*Down Beat*."

"Frank, I think I'll be able to find you a gig before I can get one. It's just another by-product of my little escapade with Jimm Dibbook. He had Wil and Quentin—my bass player and drummer—block out two months for a tour, promised them three grand a month, and of course it never materialized. Meanwhile, I just dropped off the face of the earth. They figure I still owe them the bread. Especially Quentin; from what I hear, he wants to do to me what I plan to do to you-know-who. I guess I could get some other cats, but after all the work we've put in, it just wouldn't be right. In fact, it would be really chickenshit."

Krieger nodded, ordering another round.

Sam pushed his money across the bar, making sure the bartender knew who was paying. "So that leaves me in a bind. Once I get some bread together I can pay them some of it, and then when we gig I can give them most of the bread. If it's meant to be..." Sam mused as he finished off the first pint.

"I think you're taking all this a little too seriously."

"Oh, that's what you think, huh?" Sam felt the anger swell, powerless to stop it. "Here you are, sitting on a pile of bread, able to buy anything you want, and you have the fucking balls to say something like that?"

Krieger recoiled from the outburst.

"Shit, Frank, I'm really sorry. Please, forgive me."

"Look, kid, I know you got it bad right now, but can you just listen to an old man who may know a thing or two?"

"Gladly," Sam said as the next beer was set on the bar in front of him.

"Right now, everybody is mad. It was an unfortunate set of events, but your friends won't stay mad when they see that you got screwed worse than they did. They'll come around. It's the way it works, I seen it my whole life. Get some concerts, offer to pay what you can, and let them decide. How they want to go from there is their decision. For you to stop playing because of this is the worst thing you could do."

Sam felt as if he were once again listening to Hawk Feather. The old man made sense.

"It'll be all right. Trust me."

I wish he hadn't said that.

"Wow," Sam said as he turned down the drive. "That stone fence is incredible. I haven't seen anything like that since I was in England."

"England?" Krieger sounded insulted. "I brought a crew over from *Ireland* to build it."

Scout jumped up on the seat and started scratching on the window, barking.

"Let him out before we go deaf," Krieger yelled.

Sam stopped the car and reached back to open the door. Scout leaped out in full stride and gleefully ran across the green sloping lawn. His long legs stretched out, and the muscles on his side rippled across his rib cage as he turned and raced alongside the car.

"The shed is down there." Krieger pointed to the corner of the property, near the road, where the cabin was tucked into a tall hedge. "There's a path behind the tennis court, or you can drive right up to it."

"Cool," Sam said. It looked a lot more luxurious than Gray Elk's trailer, and a hell of lot cheaper. "Thanks again, Frank."

A middle-aged woman in a red mohair pullover and tightly filled leggings came out to meet them. "What's this dog?" she asked.

Sam decided to let Krieger do the talking, as he racked his brain trying to remember where he'd seen her before.

"Sam, this is Henry's mother-in-law, Mrs. Murchison. This is Sam—he'll be staying in the shed for a while."

"What about the dog?"

"It's his dog, Scout. There's plenty of room," Krieger stated.

Sam could tell she was weighing whether to fight about it. Regardless, it was painfully obvious that she didn't want either of them there.

"Pleasure to see you again, Mrs. Murchison," Sam said, walking up the brick steps to greet her. He saw her trying to place him as well. "The wedding? I played guitar."

Sam read her mind: *Oh, great, a musician.*

"Is Henry here?" Krieger asked.

"In his office by the pool."

"I'll take Sam in and reintroduce them. It's very nice that you are offering him your hospitality." Krieger looked to Sam and snickered.

The mansion's main entranceway opened into a huge hall, one side leading into a formal living room, with the bedroom wing beyond that, the other toward the library, dining room, and kitchen. Sliding glass doors in the back led out to a formal garden in full bloom. A set of redwood stairs that were shaded by a trellis overgrown with jasmine went up to a terraced pool and cabana, Henry's office.

Henry sat in a darkened room, his round face aglow from a computer monitor. Kreiger entered and pulled back the curtains. Henry looked up, startled. "Oh, it's you, Grandpa."

"I thought I'd introduce you to Sam Mann. He'll be living in the gardener's cottage."

"I remember you," Henry said, his handshake limp. "You played at our wedding. So, you're taking care of Grandpa during the day now?"

Sam nodded, eyeing the gallery of pictures on the wall behind Henry. One in particular caught his attention.

"Family pictures," Henry explained. "During the remodeling I put them all up here, out of danger. I haven't gotten around to putting them back, now that the remodeling is finished."

Sam was hardly listening. He saw a beautiful young woman in a pink bikini, her dark skin and brown hair vibrant in the summer sun as she sat with a teenage replica of Henry—shy, puffy, and pubescent. It was Jennifer, about ten years younger, but not all that much had changed. "This is Jennifer Holman?"

Henry looked up and nodded before turning his attention back to the computer screen.

"I met her at the wedding. You were with her at my CD release party. Do you know how to get in touch with her? She gave me her number and I lost it."

"I've got it. I'll give it to you when we get back to the city," the old man answered. He turned to Henry, who was clicking away on the keyboard. "I'll show him around, I can see you're busy. By the way, Sam has a dog who eats testicles, so watch out."

Henry nodded and muttered, "O.K., Grandpa."

"Testicles?" Sam asked as they left the office.

"He wouldn't understand balls, not having any. Plus, he never listens to me; probably thought I said 'fuck you.' He's got a one-track mind when it comes to money: he loves the stuff, and I thank my lucky stars he does. If it was up to his father, we'd probably be in the poor house by now. Henry has the touch, always has. He's handled the family money since he was fourteen."

They returned to the car and followed the drive around the tennis courts to the guesthouse. "There's a small bathroom, but no kitchen," Kreiger said. "I had them bring down a coffeemaker and a microwave. I hope that's enough. Do you cook?"

"Only when I'm forced to."

It was one room, eight by fourteen feet, with a loft bed and a crudely carved-out closet containing a sink, stall shower, and toilet. Between the two skylights and the glass door—a thick floral patterned curtain pulled to the side—it was full of afternoon sunlight. "It can get cold in here, but there are plenty of covers and a portable heater," Kreiger said.

The similarities between the cottage and the trailer at Gray Elk's seemed surreal. Coupled with Mrs. Murchison's cold reception, Sam felt himself tumbling into a deep well of *deja vu*.

"They'll leave you alone, don't worry. I still have a little influence down here."

"I'm not worried in the least, Frank. This is really too much. When I can, I promise I'll pay you back for all this."

"Yeah, yeah, glad to help. I think you ought to get some new clothes for yourself; you look like a mountain man, and you smell like one, too. We'll stop along the way back."

When Scout saw them start to get in the car, he came bounding across the lawn. Krieger opened the back door to let him in. "We ought to take him with us until that lady gets used to him."

"I don't like these singers!" Krieger complained. "They all try to doobie-doo all the time, and it sounds like none of them knows the real song. Why do they pick old songs like this and fuck them up?"

He turned down the radio; now the woman sounded like a mouse behind a thick wall.

"I don't think they'd agree with your characterization, Frank. I'm sure they feel that they're being creative."

"But I heard Ella Fitzgerald on that CD with Oscar Peterson," Krieger said as if he were pleading a case in court. "She *knew* the tune."

"Frank, there's a lot of shit you aren't going to like, and some you may *think* you don't, and then one day realize that you do. Your ears are still young."

"Did that happen to you?"

"Yeah. I'm embarrassed to admit it, but when I heard Trane the first time, John Coltrane?"—Krieger nodded—"I thought he was bullshit. I even said it aloud. I'm horrified by the thought of it. I guess I just needed to *hear* it. And then there's some shit that I still can't stand. Jazz is a pretty wide category, now more than ever, though I can't imagine why a lot of the more commercial forms even want to associate with the word, given its marketing stigma."

Krieger turned the radio up again as the last chord of the song rang out and the chanteuse chirped out a skittering *arpeggio* that died on a wobbly low note, hopelessly flat, the vibrato as broad as a house. "I'll never like *that*."

"Opinions are like assholes, Frank. Everybody's got one."

"What's wrong?" Krieger asked as the car sped up the Peninsula, darting in and out of lanes of thick traffic. "You haven't said a thing since we left the clothing store."

"I'm too mad."

"Don't worry, you'll pay me back. The money is no big deal."

"It's not only that. It really hit me when I saw all those things inside that department store. All the shit that that motherfucker took and either sold or trashed. He just tossed it, I'll bet. I know it's only stuff, but it was mine! I took a long time getting all that together, and now I don't even have a suit or a fucking tux if I get a formal gig. Think about all the shit he just cleaned out, and now I've got to replace it while he's busy spending the bread. I've got to get him, Frank. You want to help?"

"Me?"

"In a way. You can come along with me while I look for him. Do you mind if we do that?"

"He took you, he screwed you, but technically he wasn't even breaking the law, so even if you found him and sued him, would you win? Would you recover anything, or would it just be a waste of time?"

"I figured you'd bail out."

"Wait a minute—'bail out?' Does that mean what I think it does? You're talking to *me*, you little ingrate!" Krieger's jowls flapped, his face reddening. Scout started barking, joining in the fray. "If that's what you think of me after all this, then take me home and walk away. I don't need any of this! Bail out?" White bubbles of spittle formed on his lower lip. "Fuck you!"

Shit, I hope I don't give him a heart attack. "Frank, listen, that's not what I meant. I'm sorry. You know how grateful I am." *How could he know? All I've done is be a fucking asshole about it.* "You're the only one in this whole world who has been a help, and I appreciate it. But I *do* have to do this. All I'm asking is that you indulge me here, O.K.?"

"Do you see how useless it is?" Krieger asked in a low voice.

Lie for once in your life; placate him. "I guess," Sam answered. Krieger never heard him; he was fast asleep against the far window. Sam was relieved to hear him snoring; otherwise he would have thought the old man had died.

Got to keep this shit to myself. The old man thinks I'm a lunatic. What the fuck does he know? He has *all his shit.*

They ate in quiet in a small café on Van Ness Avenue, at a counter that faced the traffic. Colored lights sped by as the day receded into dusk. Sam felt as if he'd drained the old man of all his newfound enthusiasm and energy. Half a dozen times he opened his mouth, only to find himself unable to find a word that would undo the damage he'd done.

Face it, Mann, you're a complete fuck-up. In a pinch, self-pity and self-hatred were always readily accessible, waiting for the cue from its maestro.

As Krieger wrestled with the flaccid piece of pizza, trying to direct the sharp point into his mouth, Sam was overcome with emotion.

He put his hand across the back of the old man's stool and sighed. His anger seemed to bring everybody down, not just himself.

Krieger chewed on the rubbery mouthful and painstakingly swallowed before washing it down with a sip from his glass of ice water. "Don't take it so hard, kid. Look, I know you're going to do this, so you might as well let me help. It looks like you need someone to make sure you don't fuck up your life any worse than it is."

Sam heard the strain in his voice, as if he were trying to rally his spirits. "I'm sorry about what I've done to you, Frank. You seemed so full of life before this."

"It's not your fault, kid. You got to learn to take responsibility for your own problems. What happens to me is my business. Oh, that's right, " he grinned and forced in another wedge of pizza, "you're Jewish—you *like* to feel guilty."

"Listen, it was a joke," Krieger instructed. "Sam, I understand. I've been screwed—and royally—by a lot of people, including politicians and cops. I could have wasted my time trying to get back at them, but what for? I decided to spend my energy flying higher, and lo and behold, I just soared right over them. Now they come to me for favors. But you, Sam—you want to exact revenge, even though you think it's justice."

Sam looked around, confused, as if his surroundings had been transformed into a campfire high in the hills. All he saw was Hawk Feather in Irish drag, eating a greasy piece of pepperoni pizza.

"So how are you going to find this guy? Do you want to get a private investigator?"

The question brought Sam back to reality. A private investigator meant more money, and he didn't want to put further strain on his relationship with Kreiger. *I can't walk away from all this owing any more than I do already.*

"No. I just want to do some of that myself. I think he probably left town, but until I'm sure of it, I don't want to waste any resources just yet."

"You have a funny idea of what resources are. When you're my age, a day is about as precious as they get." Kreiger raised one finger for the check. "Now take me home. I'm an old man and I need my beauty sleep."

To avoid introducing Scout to the rest of the tenants in the high rise, they went up in the freight elevator. "Have you noticed that thing with his eyes?" Kreiger asked, scratching the dog's head, which was almost chest high to the shrunken Irishman.

"They're clear. His owner said that meant he was a very old soul on his last go-round and in a transitional stage between mammals and hawks—if you believe that kind of shit." Sam didn't feel like revealing his own suspicions.

"'That kind of shit,' as you put it, becomes more and more important the older you get. I wish I had a dime for every one of my atheist friends who turned religious when they were old or dying."

In the apartment, Scout retreated to the corner. Sam went to the couch to wait for Pascal to show up for his shift. Kreiger went into the bedroom and put on a CD—Sam's, the one that had climbed to the top of Jimm's Xerox paste-ups. The old man came back in the room and saw Sam listening intently, a pained look on his face. "Does it bother you?"

"Yes and no," Sam admitted.

"I really like it—the way everything seems to flow, like you had thought about it for a long time, yet like you were making it up on the spot, too. Which was it?"

"It depends; a lot of it just happened because we know each other—knew each other, that is—so well; some of it was prearranged, and some of it, like that, for instance—" He stopped to take in the resolution of a long polyrhythmic sequence, "—was luck. I was worried we weren't going to come out of that one together."

"Thanks, that was a lot of help. Could you be a little *less* clear?"

"Well, it's like we listen, study, and play, and then we forget everything so we can make it up again. Shelly Manne always said that—"

"Shelly Manne? Male or female? Any relation?"

"I wish we were related." Krieger had perked up, as if he were taking notes. "*He* always said, 'Jazz means never playing the same thing once.'"

A long *ostinato* began brewing on the CD—slippery slides along the fingerboard of the bass, dropping into the depths of Wil's deep tone, a cannon-like G, full of juicy vibrato as the drums complemented with muted mallet work.

"You played this song that night when I heard you," Krieger said.

"I thought old people had shitty short-term memory."

"Who are *you?*" Krieger asked, feigning a toothless chewing of his cud. "Oh that's right—aren't you looking for a certain woman's number? Or have *you* forgotten?"

"Can I get it? She left it for me that night, but Jimm took it—another thing he stole from me, fucking asshole. I can't wait to get my hands around his fat neck."

"I remember," Krieger said as he went to the counter to look in his phone book. "She gave it to Patty when we left."

"Patty?"

"Patty O'Boyle."

"You know her?" Sam perked up. Scout looked up, on alert.

"Of course, she's Brian's goddaughter."

"Brian?"

"One of the crew my brother brought over to build the fence and fireplace at Kinsale. He's brought over quite a few of his family over the years."

"Then you would know how to find Patty?"

"I could try. I haven't seen Brian for a few years, but I'll bet I'd know where to find him. Why? What's so important about this?"

"Because she is Jimm Dibbook's secretary, probably his girlfriend too. If we find her, then we'll find him. I love you and that memory of yours!" Sam kissed Krieger on the forehead and squeezed him in a hard embrace.

"Stop it, will you? Save it for Jennifer."

After a leisurely dinner outside on the sidewalk, Jennifer paid the bill and picked up her books, planning a short stroll around North Beach before—what, a movie, her lonely apartment? The City had lost its luster; there was something else she was supposed to be doing—*but what?* Her previous skills—prevarication, deception, and manipulation—had little use for her away from Kinsale. She felt like a ball player gone to seed, or a rudderless boat, floating on a tide of blood-red merlot.

Her journal slipped from her grasp and fell open to a familiar page—that night, that maniacally obsessed lonely night, finishing off a bottle as she waited for Sam to call after he'd *had his way with her* in front of all those people. She picked up the book and crossed the street, determined not to go down that road again. One thing was a given—to hope was to court loneliness. Lying and control were better. Careers were the safe haven—overworked, dedicated to projects, no time to think.

Sam quickly acclimated himself to the tiny cabin. Not having any possessions made moving in a snap. A few things hung on a pole; the rest were stashed in a drawer. Sam paced around the phone as if he were stalking wild game, afraid and excited. The piece of paper with Jennifer's number (in Kreiger's scrawl) lay on the table next to it. He rehearsed the conversation as he walked a tight circle on the braided rug that covered the painted plywood floor. There were scratches on the roof—bird claws, heavy ones—echoing his own neurotic cadence. Scout had gone out; he was probably on the roof. It gave Sam confidence, knowing he was there. "I hope he doesn't stay a hawk forever, so I can thank him," Sam said, startled by the craziness of his own words.

No matter; the phone was the thing. He picked it up and punched in the number, hoping a machine would answer so he could ease into it: *Hey, guess who, back in town, will call later, would like to get together—*

But no such luck.

"Hello?" That voice. That same mellifluous voice that had whispered in his ear and was attached to that near perfect body, those glistening teeth and that warm, inviting smile. It sounded strained, as if she'd gone through some sort of trial, but he couldn't be sure; it had been such a long time.

"Hello? Who is it?"

Sam was so overwhelmed hearing her voice that he found himself afraid to make a sound and risk awakening from a dream. *Maybe I should just leave well enough alone.* He wanted to scream, *"I love you! Take me, I'm yours!"*

"Jennifer? Is that you?" *Of course it is, you schmuck.*

"Who is this?" she asked, though she'd recognized his voice. She wanted him to say it. *Where the hell have you been? Why did you do that to me?*

"It's Sam . . . Sam Mann."

"Hi Sam. What can I do for you?"

He felt the receiver turn to ice, frostbite moving its way up his arm . . . toward his heart. "Uh—how are you?" A futile attempt. *Why do I fuck everything up?*

"I'm fine, I guess. Long time no see." She hoped he felt it—an arrow pointed directly at his chest.

Maybe if I just told her, laid it all out—naw, she'd just think I'm crazy. Sam heard the scratching on the roof, the slow flapping of long thick wings taking off for points unknown. *Take me with you!*

"You still there?" she asked, waiting.

"I've really missed you," he blurted out. *Hell, it's true.*

"I see," she said, then coldly reloaded, aimed and fired. "You'll understand if I tell you that it comes as a surprise. I don't see how I could have possibly known that."

She's mad. I can understand that. But she still cares; she hasn't hung up yet. "I've had an incredible month or two. I got your message that night but I couldn't call you back."

"I see, you were abducted by aliens—or maybe just on a mountain somewhere, no phone or anything." *God I can't believe I said that. So fucking petty and prissy.*

"Actually, yeah."

I've got to hand it to him; no one else has ever used the alien excuse. "Look Sam, I don't know why, but I really felt a connection to you. And when you did that to me at the club, just undressed me and raped me, right there in front of everyone, it was tough, scary in fact. Then you didn't call. Now I just don't have the heart to open that can of worms again. So I'm really sorry about your misfortune, if that's what it was, but I'd rather read about it in the *Enquirer.* So, I've got to go, really busy. Ta-ta."

She hung up.

What? "What the fuck is she talking about?" Sam yelled as he threw the phone onto the floor. "I didn't rape her that night or any night. That bitch has gone *Froot Loops!* Is it possible I completely misread all that? How can she just shut me down like that?"

Scout was scratching at the door and Sam let him in. The big dog went straight to the phone, took it in his mouth and brought it to him, stretching the cord, offering it as if it were a ball in a game of fetch.

"You're right, boy, I should call her back."

He hit the redial button. *It's not fair, I had to listen to her, the least she can do is hear me the fuck out.* The phone rang, finally interrupted by a message: "You have reached, etc., please leave, etc." *With any luck, she's screening.* As he waited for the beep, Sam gathered his courage. *Who knows how long the thing will go before it cuts me off.*

Beep! Off to the races. "Look Jennifer, I'm not quite sure what you're talking about that night at the club. All I know is, I was glad to see you and was even more glad that you'd left me your number. But I couldn't call! I was in the middle of this stupid publicity scam, and my agent took your number—" *Stay on point, Sam!* "—because I was supposed to disappear for a month or so, and I couldn't tell anyone. Believe it or not, we were going to fake my death." *God, I don't believe I ever fell for this!* "I went up to stay with this shaman, because I was kind of stressed out and needed a break anyway."

Sam continued, pacing tight circles on the rug. "It was an incredible experience, and there were no phones, and I just sort of went nuts and came out on the other end. I returned, and the motherfucker—my agent—had stolen everything I had. If it wasn't for your grandfather I would be out on the street right now."

My grandfather?

Sam fought on. "Up in the hills I learned a lot about myself. I shed all these weird things that I'd hung on to my whole life. I realized that my idea of happiness and fulfillment were all bullshit. I can't wait to tell you."

Still no pickup. Was the machine still recording? He hadn't heard the fatal click, like the hammer of a gun pointed directly at his temple.

"It started with all this gorging. First it was juicing, I mean a rip-roaring drunk fest, so toxic I almost died, then food, it was disgusting and embarrassing. Then sex. I couldn't keep my hands off my dick." *Might as well go all the way.* "It wasn't pleasurable. Well, maybe it was at first." It would have devastated him to hear her laughing on the other end. Sometimes screening is very humane.

Sam continued, assuming he only had precious seconds left. "Then it became this obsession, I couldn't stop, all these images, my body tired and aching. The only thing that saved me was you. The only image that brought orgasm and relief, if only for a little while, was you sitting on my lap and gasping in my ear."

"Enough already!" she barked, picking up the phone. "I recorded all that, you know."

Her voice brought him out of a nightmare. He'd almost forgotten he was telling his story while making a plea, rather than reliving it.

"That was most interesting," she said. "You have a wonderful imagination and a unique way of flirting. I guess I do find it cutely erotic that I'm your favorite masturbatory image."

He wanted to apologize but he didn't know where to start. *Don't fuck it up, Sam.* "So, you'll see me?"

"After all that, it's the least I can do. But I'm warning you, it will be in a public place. Hands above the table at all times . . . agreed?"

Sam crawled into his loft and drifted off to sleep. For the first time since his return, there was a quality of optimism that accompanied his descent. Jennifer would see him, and he had a chance of finding Patty O'Boyle. Pretty soon, he could begin to live again, put everything behind him.

His dream—another soaring dream, grounded by a relentless foghorn—evaded his grasp as he surfed through the stages just below consciousness. From soaring free and unencumbered over an ocean cliff, he found himself inside a car, hurtling through the night, a police siren wailing behind, calling him to stop and return to a more quotidian realm.

He woke up suddenly and realized that the siren was Scout howling. The dog's neck was outstretched as he unfurled an atavistic call that sliced through Sam's skin, chilling him.

"What is it boy?" Sam asked. It was almost midnight. He jumped down to the floor and went to his friend and held him as he bayed deep into the night.

It went on for hours. Images of fires seemed to flash in Scout's eyes, brilliant orange flames dancing high into a black void, as if he were somewhere else, seeing something in violent progress far away.

In the morning, Sam woke up on the small circular rug on the floor, curled up beside Scout for warmth in the misty coolness of the dawn. The dog showed no sign of the turmoil that had gripped him through the night; whatever it was, it had released him into a bear-like slumber. Sam got up and started coffee, grateful that Krieger had made arrangements to insure that the cabin was well stocked.

After coffee, there was plenty of time before his shift started, so Sam roused Scout for a long walk in the forest. It was both a remembrance of things past, passed through, and a favor to Scout after having forced him into urban blight.

The scent of the pine as the morning fog evaporated conjured up a retrospective longing, more sense memory than intellectual picture—feelings of quietude, redemption, and validation that had now been brushed aside by chaos and a new purpose—*justice.*

"When all this is over, boy," Sam promised as he watched Scout happily frolic through the bushy undergrowth, "I'll take you back to the country, to Hawk Feather, where you belong."

As if he understood the words, Scout came running to his side, panting, leaning in against his leg. *You fool, it's you that I belong with!*

Sam arrived at Cathedral Hill and went up early to relieve Pascal. "Where's the dog?" Krieger asked.

"Left him in the car. The building seems sort of busy this time of the morning. He had a rough night last night, and..."

Krieger was smiling, but when Sam noticed he quickly looked away.

"What?" Sam asked. "What have you got up your sleeve? Come on Frank, spit it out!"

"I have some surprises for you, but I ain't going to tell you, even if you torture me. I did hear from Jennifer last night; seems you two have a date. She asked me if you'd told me that space aliens had abducted you. I thought it made a lot of sense. Are there things you ain't telling me?"

"I need another cup of coffee."

"After that, I want to go and get a good stereo for the living room. The people downstairs keep complaining because the box in the bedroom's too loud. I tried to explain that I need to hear it in the rest of the house. I didn't have the heart to tell them to complain to the landlord. They'd just bring me up on charges anyway. I may own the joint, but I ain't got shit compared to the tenants' association . . . People's Republic of San Francisco."

"You're talkative this morning." Sam was heartened by his energetic mood.

"It's a lovely morning," Krieger sang in an Irish brogue, the word "morning" cracking into pieces between his normal voice and *falsetto*.

I wonder what he's up to?

As they started out the door, with Krieger bundled in his green blazer and houndstooth checked hat, the phone rang. "Just a second, Sam, be right with you."

He shuffled his way across the room to the extension and answered. "Yes. Just a second." He looked up holding the receiver as if he'd caught his first fish, "It's for you."

"Who is it? No one knows I'm here. Except Jennifer." His heart raced as he made the full distance in four steps. "Hello?"

"Sam?"

Sam's heart sank; the voice was male, a deep baritone, scratchy from fatigue. "Yes. Who is this?"

"Gray Elk. I got your number from my secretary."

"Oh yeah, I forgot. How are you?" He was glad to hear a voice from a time that he now associated with being at peace.

"I'm fine Sam. It's Hawk Feather."

"Does he want his dog back?" Sam asked, filled with a strange dread.

"No, Sam. Hawk Feather died last night."

"Oh, shit." Sam fell into a seat at the table, his mind numb. The sound of Scout's wailing the night before permeated his frozen shock.

"Sam?"

"I'm here," Sam managed to say, tears streaming down his cheeks, cheeks that felt numbed.

"I was with him; he mentioned you, was glad that the dog was with you."

"How did it happen?"

"What do you think? Emphysema, all those cigarettes. He was in and out of respiratory shock most of the night. Died just before dawn."

Sam listened and nodded. "That's when Scout finally stopped howling and went to sleep. I guess he's my dog then. Unless there's family who want him."

"No, but I think it's more like you're *his* human. At least that was what Hawk Feather said. He managed to say 'We have much to learn together' before he died. He was a great man and teacher; I'm happy you two had time together. When we decide when the spirit conference will be, I'll let you know. Are you going to be all right, Sam?"

"Yes, I will. Thanks for calling." Sam fumbled the phone back on the hook as if he were feeling his way in the dark.

"Sam?" Krieger asked. "Bad news?"

Sam nodded. "Hawk Feather, you know the Indian chief, Scout's owner? He died last night. All night long Scout was howling like he was in pain. I feel so sad," Sam said as he laid his head down on the table. "He helped me so much." His crossed arms supported him as he convulsed in silent tears.

The old man responded by leaving the apartment.

"Play a song for him," he requested as he returned from the car, carrying Sam's new guitar with Scout in tow. "I couldn't lift the amplifier."

Sam looked up at the old Irishman, the case almost as big as he was. He looked ready for business. "I don't know what I'd play—"

"Make something up. Improvise. It's what you do."

Sam took the guitar out of the case. The Gibson's golden sunburst finish was reflecting in the eyes of *his* faithful dog. Sam fingered the strings lightly, checking to make sure they had held tune. They sounded like faint wind chimes, miles or worlds away. A deep breath took him to the clearing, where he'd sat that day, awakening to the arrival of Hawk Feather's rumbling old pickup; the horse at his side, in deep trance; the tune he'd forgotten, until now, the tune almost erased by loss, chaos, fury, anger, and revenge . . . Jimm Dibbook. *This is one thing he didn't get.*

Sam began the long drone of the open A-string—only this time, in his mind's ear, the major chord that usually followed had a dirge-like, melancholy minor quality. Could it have changed overnight? Afraid to play the chord and find it altered, and affirm the loss of the entire foundation on which his world had been built, the one trustworthy unchanging element of his life, the only entity that had held its *integrity*—he continued the monochromatic drone.

Krieger sat on the arm of his chair, watching and listening as Sam played from his seat at the table. He wondered if the long, one-note introduction was Sam's idea of a Native-American chant. It resembled a tom-tom, its rhythm steady, accented strongly on the first beat of each four strikes: BOOM-boom-boom-boom, BOOM-boom-boom-boom.

The sound of the lone note as it hung in the air of the high-rise apartment seemed to change in quality as it answered itself, every cadence colored by myriad emotions and experiences. The somber low tone rose up from charcoal gray muted deadness; the harmonics forcing their way to the surface added a brilliant shimmer to the fundamental, like the sun making an appearance through thick fog. A major chord forcing its will on a mournful event, a Herculean effort, raising the third degree that half-step by the sheer will of nature, as if life's ultimate unrelenting momentum was imposing itself on the end of a cycle, transforming it into a beginning.

Scout moved to Sam's side and placed his weighty head on his leg as Sam heard the sweet hopefulness of the major triad emerge on its own. It—or Scout—seemed to say, *It's O.K. to be happy while being sad. Don't mourn his passing, mourn your own. He has gone to a better place; you have to live on.*

The next five minutes of Sam Mann's life were an experience that he'd never relate to anyone, even himself. Worlds converged. His dream life, his solitude, his experiences with animals, and his access to emotional depths through music—depths so profound that the ideas or concepts themselves were too powerful and frightening to consider—all overtook him as he played the song of the mountains, the spirits. All the things he never allowed himself to acknowledge were pouring out of him—as though he were an innocent bystander—through the guitar.

The piece ended with a short *ostinato* of the low A that faded out into a distant feral call, with an ancestral connection that dissipated into the air of the real world, Sam's *here and now.*

Krieger wiped a tear with a monogrammed handkerchief. "I want you to play something like that for me when I die."

After they had purchased an elaborate stereo system—a multi-changer for the CD, a two-deck cassette player, and a subwoofer for the floor, with a set of four smaller speakers (the salesman promised it was just like surround sound at the movies)—they loaded the car and drove off.

"That guy must have seen you coming," Sam said. "You should have let me help."

"I know what I heard," Krieger insisted. "The unit you wanted me to buy was not near as good as the one I got. I saw no reason to go cheap, considering how much enjoyment I get out of it."

"Yeah, but his idea of jazz was Kenny G. I bet you won't be able to tell the difference with the kind of jazz we're into. It's produced differently."

"I can always return it."

Sam knew it was impossible to argue with the old man, especially now, since he was right. *Why does it feel like he's spending my money? He can make his own choices.*

"Let's take a drive through the park, Sam. I haven't been there in a while."

Sam remembered their last drive through. Krieger had told him about his wife and friends, and his reason for saying, "fuck you" all the time, which he seemed to have been cured of. *Maybe he realizes he'll be around longer than he thought.*

They entered the park from the panhandle, three lanes of traffic sifting into one. The bright, all-glass Conservatory of Flowers stood out starkly against the deep-green lawn embracing the sunlit warmth of spring.

"I want to go over to Lincoln, O.K.?"

Lincoln Way, which ran alongside Golden Gate Park on the south side, was the boundary of the Sunset district, a nondescript residential area of stucco one-family dwellings, almost always shrouded in fog.

"I thought you wanted to go through the park?"

"Just do it, O.K.?"

Sam sped out of the park, toward the beach. After a few blocks, Kreiger spoke up again. "Up ahead—there. Let's stop for a beer."

It was a small bar, more like a converted storefront with no sign, only painted writing on the window. Entering it was like being thrust across the Atlantic to a tavern in the Irish countryside. There were construction workers and painters on lunch break at the bar, their brogues as thick and the paneling as dark as the beer they were drinking.

"Well, I'll be!" the bartender sang. It sounded like a Gaelic call—an upturn in pitch with a squiggle that dropped to the bottom of his register, reminiscent of a horse's neigh. "How are ye, Frankie?"

Sam thought he'd seen the man before, and he knew he'd heard his voice. *But where?*

"Hello, Seamus," Krieger answered. "Me and my friend Sam would like a pint, please."

Seamus, even the name sounds familiar.

The bartender brought two glasses, thick heads spilling over the sides onto the napkins, creating a soggy mess on the bar top.

Sam studied the man's reddened face and wavy gray hair. "I know I've seen you before," he said, expecting him to have worked at a jazz club in town.

"I also work at a bar over in Noe Valley."

"That's it! Just the other night!" *Was it really less than a week?* "I showed up there when I got home. I had just found out that I was ripped off."

"Oh yeah," Seamus sang. "Ye was the guy with the dog. I remember, I sent ye down to the Mission Station. How did the boys treat ye?"

"It seems as though the bastards only—" Sam saw Seamus' eyes tighten. "It didn't work out. I kind of have special circumstances," he said, hoisting his glass. "I'll take care of it myself, and then they'll probably be interested."

Seamus looked to Krieger for an explanation. The old man shrugged his shoulders and shook his head. "Seamus, have you seen Brian O'Hearn lately?" he asked.

Sam lit up. *So that's why he's been smiling all day.*

"Can't say that I have. I'm sure he's still around, but I think he comes in at night. I get off at two, so I can work across town. Are ye needing him for something?"

"No, I just wanted to talk to him, nothing urgent."

"Saw him last night." A man at the end of the bar looked up from his beer. His face was splotched with paint, except for the raccoon-like outline of a pair of goggles. "He's here almost every weeknight around happy hour."

"That Brian O'Hearn, he's Patty's godfather, right?" Sam asked as they drove off. The beer had created a haze in the front of his forehead that was compounded by the bright sunlight reflecting off the other cars on the road. Krieger nodded. "So why don't we just call him?"

"We might, but even if we do, we'll meet him for a pint and we'll ask about her then. It's the way we do this. You don't start calling around and asking about the family unless you've got a job or something. If she is involved with that guy that screwed you, she's probably on the outs with Brian; it could be a sore spot for the family. It's hard enough to get someone over here, and when they drift off into bad company it can be plenty embarrassing. You have to let me do this my way, Sam."

Sam walked down Broadway, so full of trepidation that he was unaware of the flashing lights, the mass of bodies, the barkers calling out from entranceways, attempting to lure him in with their promises of live sex (was there any other kind?), no cover, no minimum. Krieger had convinced him to leave his trusty sidekick at home, and Sam felt oddly vulnerable without Scout—guideless as he cautiously made his way toward the precipice of the *next* installment. He'd learned—albeit very slowly and at great cost—not to take anything for granted.

He had intended to arrive from across the street, to see if she was really there, as she'd promised she would be; but his fearful uncertainty tricked him, and he found himself standing directly in front of the sidewalk cafe, confronted by diners and drinkers under heat lamps. Jennifer was there, waving from her seat at the glass window that separated the patio from the bandstand. The backs of a piano trio playing softly for the early diners inside seemed to be a jazz pantomime, in arm's reach.

Sam's heart nearly leapt out of his chest. Jennifer's beauty radiated a vibrating aura in the turbulent ripples of heated air on the patio. Her hair had been cut shorter, making a severe line just above her shoulders, but its severity only exaggerated her soft, inviting features. Her wide smile was like the beacon of a lighthouse to a lost sailor, further reinforcing Sam's resolve ... *she's the one.*

He approached and she stood, wearing a long denim dress, a slit on one side revealing her bare knee, the curves of her supple body a perfectly contoured landscape. He went to shake hands and she moved in and kissed him on the cheek. Her warm lips were light against the side of his face, her breath a faint warm stream making its way into his ear. He sat speechless, staring, afraid his life would return to normal; surely someone or something would come along and roll up this façade, exposing the harsh reality he'd come to expect for himself.

"So, from what I hear, Grandpa thinks you're the Second Coming," Jennifer finally said, shattering the silence.

Luckily, nothing changed: she was still there; so was he, so was the trio. So far, so good. "Grandpa?"

"The old man, Frank Krieger."

"Yeah, he saved my ass."

"From what I hear, it's the other way around."

Small talk: good, Sam thought. "When I got home, he was the only one who was there for me, and boy did I need him."

"I must admit, your story, at least what you so frantically divulged on my machine last night, seems quite interesting. I think it goes with a good red, something substantial but not too pretentious."

She was putting him on, but he didn't mind. At least she was there. He remembered her playful streak from Big Sur—her ease with everything, as if nothing in life was so important that it justified any of his unease or uptightness. *It was just one day... not even. How could I have decided she was the one?*

He watched her pore over the wine list, drawn to her so intensely that he felt swallowed up, and at the same time reconnected.

She ordered a bottle of something French and smiled. "I must admit, I replayed your message several times last night after we talked. I even called Grandpa and asked him if it was safe for me to actually follow through and meet with you."

"Can't say that I blame you."

"It's a great thing, what you've done for him, Sam. I hope he's paying you well. Do you have any idea how loaded he is?"

"Believe me, he's more than generous. He saved my life."

"That's what *you* did for him. Before you, he was just a sleepy, shriveled-up old thing. Everyone was waiting for him to die. That he didn't end up in a home is a marvel to me. They just hired round-the-clock nurses to drive the old man around, and waited for him to get out of their hair. Then you come along and he perks up all of a sudden, starts bossing everyone around. I'll tell you, Percy—his son—isn't too happy. I'll guarantee Grandpa's burning up the phone lines, ragging him about something or other."

Sam thought it over and shook his head; Krieger had hardly used the phone when he was there. "All I did was get him away from the TV, open some windows so he could get some fresh air, and turn him on to jazz."

"All you did? All you did was give him a reason to keep living. I hope someone does that for us."

Even though he found her assessment over the top, Sam reveled in her esteem. "So he's really your grandfather? Are you related?"

After all, her name was Holman; maybe she'd been married...
or adopted.

"I was originally hired as Henry's au pair," she said, smelling the
cork as the waiter poured a small amount into her goblet. "I guess
I hung around so long, I bonded—at least with the old guy."

She lifted the glass, the stem in her fingers, and swirled it, sniffing and observing the clear residue as it settled toward the bottom.
All Sam could think of was his stem in her fingers, and he was glad
he was seated with his lap out of view. She nodded and the waiter
filled their glasses.

They toasted and ordered. It quickly became obvious to Sam that
Jennifer was a regular; she had practically memorized the menu, and
the waiters all came over to say hello.

When she asked, "So, Sam Mann, what are your plans?" he was
startled. It was the first time in a long while that he'd heard his full
name spoken—other than Hawk Feather's elegant delivery.

He took a sip of the wine. *Stay light*, he reminded himself. "Well,
while you've been dining with the elite, I was up in the hills, getting
in touch with my spiritual side."

Her face was almost serious before she smiled. "It sounded to me
like you had more on your hands than your spiritual side."

"I don't know why I told you all that. You'll probably have me
living it down for the rest of my life." *Did I just hear that? Did I
just imply that we would be together forever?* His rustiness in dealing with humans, especially the opposite sex, had him in a state of
post-proposal panic.

Jennifer drank a sip, enjoying the little mind-fuck he was putting
himself through, in no hurry to ease it or help him out. It reminded
her of when they'd first met—his indignant rampage about his mother
and his name, then the petulant diatribe in the hot tub, about the
music business and its lack of integrity. He was so full of spirit, so
alive, so accomplished—yet so naïve.

She saw then what she had failed to see before, had been trying to sort out through the lines of her diary, as if her own desire had obscured the obvious. He was the other half, the one that would make a perfect whole, the *yin* to her *yang*. It was the reason her heart had refused to let him go long after her brain had ordained it, the reason she was sitting across from him right now, the reason she knew they would end up in bed.

An orange glow from the waterfront lighting illuminated Jennifer's loft. Tall windows looked out over the dry docks and dilapidated piers and across the bay to the Oakland hills. In the eerie glow, Sam saw a spiral staircase that ascended to a platform suspended above the middle half of the large open room. Jennifer kicked off her shoes by the door and let him take it all in.

"I like it best without the lights; it has a strange, post-industrial feeling, don't you think? Very artsy-fartsy." She hit the rheostat and dialed in the little high-intensity track lights hung from two tightly strung cables that crossed the room at odd angles. In the light Sam saw a hardly used living room set; an office cubicle with only a few envelopes, probably bills, and a brand-new kitchen with a showroom gleam. It looked like she'd moved in the day before.

Sam was nervous. *She* had suggested they go to her loft, to show off her new place. Now, here he was, where he wanted to be—*but what to do?* She smiled in the dim light, mocking his uncertainty before finally taking his hand. As if in a dream state, he followed her bare feet up the metal stairs to her bedroom.

The bedroom was a stark contrast to downstairs. Sam could see that she spent most, if not all, of her time there. Stacks of books, clothing, and papers were strewn haphazardly on the floor beside the bed. Sam sat on the bed and watched as she began to take off her clothes. The shadows of the crosspieces in the windows traversed her body, adding to its luster and definition as she approached.

"I hope I'm as enjoyable as your fantasies of me. In a way, I feel like I'm competing with myself."

"Believe me, if that's the case, you've already won."

She stood before Sam and unbuttoned his shirt; he watched her full breasts sway freely. His eyes dropped to the curve of her hips; the dark furry mound below her navel seemed to radiate, generating its own force field. As she moved in and kissed him on the cheek, he sighed, placing his hands on her waist. The softness of her skin was so startling that he felt he might explode.

After she removed his shirt, he stood and wrestled off his pants, then watched her lie back in the orange glow from outside, like a thousand bonfires. He crouched at the end of the bed and stared.

"What?"

"I'm just looking. God, you're even more beautiful than I remembered." Then the words popped out of his mouth, those awful wonderful words that always got him into trouble: "I love you."

This time, however, he wasn't consumed with panic, worried about the ramifications or tacit promises made by the three small syllables. Instead, they fueled a desire and a need so profound that he surrendered to her, totally consumed in the moment.

The long journey up her body was one of exploration and discovery, replete with a sense of declaration, an offering. When he finally arrived at her mouth and their lips met, he was lost, falling deeper and deeper into a state of consciousness where she and only she existed.

A duet in symphonic form, with the ebb and flow of real life; lovers pledging themselves to each other in cascades and swells, *rallentando* and *accelerando*; every dynamic carrying with it the intent of a far more profound meaning; *legato* phrases accented with *staccato* bursts of fire and urgency. There was a moment in which Sam felt he'd entered her psychically, where he *was* her; he was safe in her and could never be pried out, no matter what. They were one as they *crescendoed* into each other, melting and fusing spirits that soared deep into the night, a hawk's essence of flight.

Sam awoke to clanging sounds emanating from below the loft platform and realized he was alone in the bed. The glow of dawn radiated from behind the Oakland Hills through the uncovered windows to the east. The streets were still quiet, the city having yet to cross over into its daytime cycle of traffic and noise.

Sam pounded his way down the metal staircase.

Jennifer looked up, grinned, and banged a coffee mug against the side of the stainless steel sink. "Did I wake you? I'm sorry."

She put the cup down, left the water running, and met him at the bottom of the stairs. She put her arms around his shoulders, careful not to touch him with her wet hands, and gave him a warm kiss. "I don't sleep that much," she confessed. "I guess you wouldn't know that. You may want to put some clothes on—I don't have any curtains."

Sam realized he was stark naked in front of the window that looked directly out on Third Street, across to facing windows in a new condo/loft development with corrugated aluminum siding.

They sat in quiet, reading and drinking coffee; the only noises were slurping and the roar of the buses outside, the harbingers of morning rush hour. They had discussed so much the night before, yet it seemed obscured by the passion of their lovemaking, as if they now needed to get to know each other again after bumping into one another late the previous night, drunk at a bar.

Sam watched Jennifer as she pored over the paper, her eyes clear, that little blue vein barely visible. "I wish I could take you back to bed," he said. "I hope sometime you'll linger with me in the morning. Usually, I get off the gig pretty late, and the morning is my free time. Although not now . . . now that I'm a *nurse*."

The word hurled out of his mouth like a jettisoned projectile. Jennifer calmly took a drink. "It would be nice," she agreed, ignoring the last part of his remark. "When is your next gig?" It seemed that *that* was the only thing he hadn't talked about the night before at dinner.

"I have to take care of a few things first," he said.

"Such as?"

"I can't really get down to the business of creating until I finish up with Jim Dibbook."

"What does that have to do with creating?"

Sam took a deep breath. "That motherfucker stole everything I had, and I have to get even. Don't you understand?"

Not her, too! He was getting the same condescending look he got every time he broached the subject with Kreiger. *What's wrong with them?* "He took a part of me, and until I get it back I can't move."

Jennifer felt trapped. Usually she told people whatever they wanted to hear. Now, her commitment to a new way of life, with Sam, stood in the way of it. She had to be honest and fight, if it was *really* what she wanted. Yet she had no idea how to operate in this new arena. She felt her cheeks redden, and an unstable temper rise up and demand recognition.

"How do you propose to try, Sam? Are you going to continue to thrust those who love you into a spiral of revenge, just so you can satisfy some sense of justice or appease the horror of your embarrassment?"

"What? Let someone take all your shit, and see what you think! Let someone mock everything you stand for. How can I create when I'm living under that?"

"That's exactly how most real artists do create. You're so fuck- ing egocentric! You and your artist's temperament, your precious *creations!* Where the hell do you think they come from? We're your creations! You're playing that guitar and we're supposed to sit there and take it as you rape and pillage your way through our emotions!"

"What are you talking about, raping?"

"What would you call it? I sat there that night and you stared at me in front of the crowd of people and ravaged that guitar like it was me. It was cannibalistic. Like you pulled out my heart and licked the blood off and then fucked it for good measure. Creation? Those other musicians wondering what the hell you were doing? Right after that beautiful song before it."

"Look, that wasn't what I was doing," he explained. A nervous chuckle; he couldn't admit to himself that she might be right.

"It was, Sam. And still, I'm here. What does that tell you?"

"What *does* it tell me?"

"I see something there for us, something I'm willing to fight for. I'm not going to sugarcoat or misrepresent any of it, like I've done my whole life, but I won't be sucked into this stupid revenge crusade. It scares me. Last night, when we were making love, it felt as though you were going to consume me. Not at first, but then it became like a violent intrusion; that inside of me you might be free of what you perceive as this awful thing that has happened to you."

"It *is* an awful thing!" he protested.

"I'm not so sure. You're healthy, with people who love you and are willing to support you. You're in full power of all of your natural gifts. By screwing you, that man gave you the opportunity of a lifetime."

"So now I'm supposed to thank him?"

"He sent you out to get in touch with yourself, and you did, with awarenesses and experiences that were mystical and spiritual, and here you are interested in some sickening, ass-kicking revenge. I loved making love to you."

"It sure seemed like it!"

"What is it with you men and orgasms? Sam, I'll let you in on a little secret: I come if I sneeze when I'm wearing a tight pair of jeans."

She laughed and put her hand on his arm, waiting until he looked up and made eye contact. "I love all the conflict within you, Sam, but I want you to stay you and not consume me in the process. It can't work any other way."

"But don't you see—how can it work without some resolution

for me? He trashed everything that I stand for!"

"That's why I'm here; why we're together. Look at me, Sam," she pleaded, her eyes full of tears. "I have a lot of what you wanted when you began that crazy scheme, and I've been miserable. I am or have been everything you hate and revile, and yet you love me. There are no absolutes *except* us. I needed to learn that, and how to commit to life. Until I met you I was just spinning my wheels. I never even asked myself what was missing. Now let me do the same for you."

Sam took her hands in his. "I do love you. I mean it, Jennifer. But I have to do this. What you say makes sense, and I wish I could just flip a switch and feel that way, but it would be a lie. I have to do this, and I'm sorry that it upsets you so much."

She looked up; the tears left a wet trail down her cheeks. "I took a big risk seeing you again. It was over a month before I finally got over whatever it was in that brief interlude that connected us, and from what you say it was the same for you. But I can't be connected to this useless, self-destructive, quixotic quest. The violence is too much for me. If you get through this, or get revisited by some of that wisdom of your dead friend—maybe you should go to his memorial service, whatever you called it—"

"Spirit conference."

"Whatever. Come back to me, but not until then. And please don't call and try to talk me out of this; you might be able to, but I don't want you to."

She stood and kissed him, a long slow meeting of their lips that parted with the bitter-sweetness of finality. She put her fingers to his mouth to stop him from speaking. Then, without looking at him, she turned and went to the door. She slipped on a pair of shoes and twisted the knob. "Make sure it's locked when you go."

"How did it go?" Krieger asked. "I see you didn't go home last night."

"Interesting, but I'd rather not talk about it," Sam said, scratching the top of Scout's head.

"Jennifer is a nice girl. I approve."

"I wouldn't send out any invitations just yet. Did you call your friend Brian O'Hearn?"

"Yes, I did. We are meeting him for an early lunch."

"Great. Thanks."

"Now Sam, I want you to think this all through. Even if we find this man, do you know what your next move will be?"

"I just want to confront him for now, and get a bead on him, so I can proceed in whatever way I need to. It'll be nice to turn the tables on that motherfucker. I sure hope he's still in town."

The whole thing unsettled Krieger. The undercurrent of rage percolating beneath Sam's calm was a disaster waiting to happen. Krieger decided to change the subject as he watched Sam pace, rehearsing the hoped-for meeting. "I took the dog for a walk late last night. His eyes were orange. I thought it was strange, considering the lights around here aren't that color."

Sam's mind shifted to the night before: making love to Jennifer, their bodies bathing in the orange light of the waterfront. He stopped and eyed the guilty-looking dog. "He's weird, I told you that."

"It's very comforting to have him around. I was thinking of changing the rules about pets. I can see why they say that dogs can make old people live longer."

Sam laughed. "Unlike me, who just makes it seem longer?"

As he drove the big Lincoln toward Sunset, Sam had to fight to keep his speed under the limit. There was a strange energy to the day; Scout was pacing back and forth on the backseat of the car, as if a cosmic force were propelling them toward resolution.

They parked in front of the little tavern on Lincoln Way. As they entered, Krieger tapped Sam on the arm and nodded toward the end of the bar, where a squat, silver-haired man sat staring into a pint of stout.

"Brian!" Krieger said as they approached.

The man looked up, and a warm smile replaced the tense lines across his forehead. His eyes were a deep sky blue and his skin was weathered like a sailor's. The veins in his face told of countless hours at the bar.

"Hello, Frank," he said, sliding off his stool to offer his hand.

"This is Sam Mann, he's a friend of mine."

"Nice to meet you," Brian said. His voice sounded tired, strained. "What can I do for you, Frank? I'm kind of stretched for time. I had a crew quit on me; they just went with another outfit without notice. I'll tell you, it's getting harder and harder these days. Not like when we was kids."

From the sound of his voice and his resigned demeanor, Sam placed him at over sixty; but his physique was ageless, as solid and muscular as that of any health club fanatic.

"I'll get right to the point," Krieger said. "Sam is looking for your goddaughter, Patty. Do you know where to find her?"

O'Hearn shook his head and sighed. He ran his fingers through his hair and took a long draw from his glass. "She's a real disappointment, that one. I brought her over to please Kate, my wife. Patty's grandmother was Kate's best friend, and Kate felt it was only right that we bring over a girl for a change. You know, I usually get someone who can work on a crew for me."

A long silence ensued. Krieger sensed Sam's impatience and put a hand on his leg to stop him from interrupting.

O'Hearn took another gulp of the thick black liquid and licked the foam off of his upper lip. "When Patty got here, she immediately moved out and dropped out of touch. It was the first time anyone had done that, after all we go through with Immigration, the papers and all. I did see her over Easter."

Sam ignored Kreiger's hand on his leg and broke in, sensing a window of opportunity. "When you saw her, did she mention a man named Jimm Dibbook? Her employer? Might even be her boyfriend?"

The mention of Jimm's name seemed to cause O'Hearn a thirst that consumed more than half a pint.

"I didn't see him, but she mentioned him when Kate asked why she was alone. You should have seen it: Kate was so polite to Patty, after all the grief and worry she's caused, and that little bitch didn't even have the courtesy to bring a gift or thank us for having her over."

Krieger saw that Sam was about to bound off his stool and strangle Brian because of his rambling answers. He pinched his leg to hold him back.

O'Hearn continued: "You know what she said? Right to my wife, and you know what a good Catholic she is?"

Sam gripped his glass, his knuckles white. *Will you get to the point?!*

"She says, 'Even though Jimm's Jewish, he doesn't do bullshit religious holidays. He's allergic to them.' That's what she said, Frank, I ain't lying. Kate turned white when she said it. First, he's a fucking Jew, then the word 'bullshit.' I was worried Kate was going to have a stroke. I wanted to slap the girl for the crack about allergies. Who the fuck does she think she is?"

"That asshole ripped me off for everything I had," Sam said, trying to win a friend. Then he caught O'Hearn's stare and realized his error. "Not Patty; Jimm Dibbook," he said. "Do you know where they live?"

Instead of answering, O'Hearn finished his stout and stood, reaching for his wallet.

"I've got it, my pleasure," Krieger said.

"Thanks, Frank."

For a second Sam thought O'Hearn was going to leave without

answering. He passed them at the bar on the way to the door. The quiet was deafening; then O'Hearn stopped face to face with Sam. "Nice to meet you, Sam. I wish I could help you, but I don't know where they live. I wish I'd never seen or heard about her in the first place, if you want to know the truth. And here I thought nothing could make my day any worse."

He started toward the door, then called back over his shoulder, "My son gave her a ride after Easter dinner, dropped her off at the Cliff House. I'd look around Sea Cliff if I was you. Good luck."

They watched quietly as O'Hearn headed out into the bright noontime daylight. Sam gulped down his beer and threw a twenty on the bar.

"Don't imagine you want to wait for change," Krieger said dryly. "Sea Cliff's only about five minutes from here."

"I don't know what the hurry is," Kreiger said as Sam sped toward the ocean's edge. "It's just a neighborhood. She might have had something else to do that day."

"I've just got this feeling. Had it all day," Sam explained. "I can't describe what it is or why, but we're on to something. Even Scout is acting weird, and *he* knows everything!"

The dog was pacing back and forth in the expanse of the back-seat, panting.

Sam now felt he understood the flashes of green in Scout's eyes earlier in the day. The dark tint of the cypress trees that lined the cliffs overlooking land's end were the exact hue. It was a brilliant blue day—the perfect kind of day for new beginnings. A light breeze coaxed playful whitecaps up from the small swells in the ocean hundreds of feet below.

"So, what do you plan to do?" Kreiger asked.

"What do you mean? I'm going to find that motherfucker and try to get my shit back!"

"Not that," Krieger answered. "Are you going to stake out the Cliff House or are you just going to scour all of Sea Cliff?"

"Oh," Sam said, realizing he hadn't thought about it. He was on a mission—*a crusade,* Jennifer had called it—and he now felt an inner compass guiding him toward resolution.

"I think I'll just cruise the area. He's around, I can feel it." Sam's hands had begun to sweat, leaving oily prints on the black steering wheel as he waited for the light to change.

The road skirted the cliffs that led toward the Golden Gate. Sam ascended a long grade and the panorama opened up. "This is it!" he exclaimed.

"What?" Krieger asked, sounding frightened.

"I've had this recurring dream of flying, and it's always off a cliff overlooking the ocean. I've never seen it before, except when I was sleeping."

Krieger sighed. "Now I've heard everything."

Scout began to bark, feeding into the frenzy of energy that radiated inside the car. His outbursts were deafening, as if he knew more than Sam, and was trying to communicate a greater notion, the meeting or ending of converging worlds.

"I don't believe it!" Sam yelled, with Scout howling in response.

"What?!"

He'd seen a gnome-like figure—turnip shaped, with an airy lightness to its step—enter a glade of trees off a small parking turnoff. "I think it's him! We're in luck."

"In luck? I'm not so sure."

Scout barked frantically as Sam swerved into the gravel area. The turn hurled the dog across the back seat, slamming him into the door. Sam parked at an angle, ten feet from the metal guardrail; he thrust the transmission into PARK and jumped out, slamming the door behind him, the car still idling.

He stopped abruptly just inside the trees. His quest was over. Jimm was there, standing calmly, looking off toward the point. Sam had a sudden urge to run up behind him and push him off the cliff. But his body seemed frozen; he was unable to move.

His body immobile, Sam spoke up, afraid that Jimm might walk off. "There you are, you motherfucker."

Jimm turned and smiled, as if he had known Sam was there.

"Didn't think I'd find you, did you?" Sam challenged, filled with the triumphant spirit of a long and difficult journey, completed.

"To be honest, I never gave it a moment's thought."

The smug assurance of Jimm's delivery angered Sam—and at the same time, chilled him to the bone. He heard Scout's muffled barks from inside the car, a feral soundtrack to the confrontation. "I want my shit back!"

"Your shit? What are you talking about?"

"Come on, you stole everything. It was all your idea. Are you going to make me do this, or are you going to do the right thing?"

"'The right thing?' That is so like you, Sam Mann." Jimm's smile was as cold and uncaring as a whitecap on the waves far below. "The right thing. If that isn't a Sam Mann concept."

"You duped me and then fucked me while I was going along with your stupid scheme. Your lies and deceptions. Your bullshit."

The vitriol in Sam's words was doing nothing to unstick his muscles; he felt as if he were wrapped in a tight cocoon, like a caterpillar unable to emerge and come to life.

"It was all your doing, Sam. I gave you what you wanted, you'll see. One day you'll thank me." He laughed.

The sound seemed to spew forth from below the ground, and Sam felt a rumbling tremor at his feet.

"What I wanted? I trusted you and brought you my life's ambition, and you just lied and fucked me out of everything."

Finally, Sam managed to move, making a loud *crack* as his bones and joints snapped out of their locked tension.

Jimm laughed, this time more of a roar. Scout bellowed in the distance, a faint echo of a warning call. "You really are funny. I think

that of all of my handiwork, you're the best. You should be proud;
I know I am."

Sam stopped, stunned. *This isn't going the way I planned.*

"You are so self-centered and self-righteous that you don't even
see the art in what I do. I've got to remember to work with musicians more often; they're so thick."

Jimm's laugh this time was a faint chuckle, almost human.

"Here you are, on your god-like path to creation, but when creation happens right before you, you don't even see it."

Sam's brow furrowed as he tried to comprehend the meaning of
the surreal joke. *Maybe this is another dream.* He looked around and
it was the same dream place—the same waves, the same rocks at the
bottom of the cliff.

"You call yourself an artist? Isn't there a prerequisite that you appreciate art in the first place, or at least recognize it? Think about
it, you pitiful excuse for a human being. You are so concerned with
your own playing, with communicating your shallow emotions to
an eager audience, that you don't even have the slightest respect or
admiration for *my* masterpiece. I played you better than Paganini
ever played his violin. Think about it, Sam; *you* are my art. That is
what *I* do."

"Who the fuck are you?"

"That's the funniest thing of all. You call yourself a Jew, yet you
don't know. I tried to warn you. If you ever get the chance, look up
my name in a Yiddish dictionary."

Sam felt his anger finally ignite, fueled by embarrassment and
humiliation. He leapt forward and unleashed an open-handed blow
that caught the side of Jimm's face, sending him backwards, trip-
ping on a rock.

A shrill voice—one that Sam had never heard before—came out
of Jimm's mouth: "You shouldn't have done that!"

Jimm was back on his feet without rising, as if his fury alone had
catapulted him skyward. After a quick move of his right hand from

inside his windbreaker, the glint of sunlight on metal filled the wide void between them.

Krieger watched, terrified, releasing his seat belt and scooting over behind the wheel. Surely Sam would retreat now. He unlocked the doors of the Lincoln, ready to relock if the man with the knife followed.

Jimm made a wide swipe, more for effect than damage.

Sam jumped back. "You can't do this!" he yelled, half-pleading. "On top of fraud and theft, they'll get you for murder!"

Jimm laughed. "You dumb little fuck, they can't do anything to me. That's what's so funny—that you think *you* can. I am impervious to *normal* people. I take what I want and leave the rest of you to sort it out later. It takes *something* very special to do anything to me. I wish I could get you to understand that. If I could, I wouldn't have to kill you. If I let you go, will you leave me alone?"

Did I hear that? Is this asshole actually trying to make a fucking deal?

The wind picked up, a cleansing breeze, offering him the chance to stand or run. Sam looked at Jimm, whose anger had caused strange protrusions at the side of his forehead near his hairline, and given his eyes a strange yellow glow. With words that carried the weight of his life, his perception of integrity, his calling and nature, his connection to the spirits, he said: "Never."

"I didn't think so. There is a certain *human* charm to your futile stupidity."

Barking furiously, Scout attacked the car window, trying to break out and intercede, as if it were *his* fight.

Jimm lunged again. This time it was a more directed and efficient swipe that caught the front of Sam's shirt and ripped it open, leaving the fabric flapping like a banner in the wind.

Sam was backed against the edge of the world, with nowhere to go but straight down—down to the rocks hundreds of feet below, where the waves were crashing in. Jimm raised the knife again, offering no more words. His intent was obvious: to finish this off, once and for all.

Krieger had seen enough; he grabbed the gearshift, shoved the Lincoln into DRIVE, and floored the gas pedal. The car lurched forward into the guardrail, scraping metal and toppling a sixty-gallon metal trash bin.

The car stopped and Krieger's world went black as his head hit the steering wheel. The rear door flew open on impact. The crash diverted Jimm's attention, but Sam was frozen with fear, unable to take advantage of the momentary opening for escape. In his peripheral vision he caught an onrushing blur of black and white as he saw Jimm's blade approach, its trajectory fixed, his body locked in place.

Though he knew his approaching death was the result of his own folly, Sam felt an unexpected completeness and appreciation. A resolute calm overtook him, and he looked forward to the next phase; to seeing Hawk Feather perhaps, and having a good laugh about the whole business, with a lightheartedness that had been missing on this go-round.

Caught in the still-frame motion of the approaching steel, Sam waited, watchful. As the blade neared entry, and Jimm's ugly, angry face advanced, Sam felt a rush of pity, and realized that his last sentiment was to be sympathy for a tortured creature. "I forgive you—"

And as the words left his mouth, a convergence happened in the space directly in front of him. The knife approached, sure of its ultimate resting place in his heart. As Sam braced for its piercing release, a body, with all the weight of existence, appeared in the form of a giant dog and grabbed Jimm by the wrist. Scout took the pudgy arm in his mouth, his lips rolled back, exposing bright, sharp teeth—and the two tumbled over the edge.

Sam was surprised to find himself still alive, alone in a cavernous silence. There were no screams, no barks, no wails, just a windless hush—and Sam, silent himself, beginning to realize that he was not the point of all this, not even the point of his own life. There were exterior forces acting all along that he'd mistakenly imagined were somehow controllable and, in essence, mutable.

In the rush of an oncoming wind, a giant updraft, a hawk flew up from the water's edge far below and soared in ecstatic release, playing in the wind, dreamlike, finally free. Sam watched tearfully as it circled, soaring higher and higher, until it was all but invisible.

Then the silence was shattered by a bloodcurdling scream. Sam looked up and saw a boyish-looking blonde woman standing on the edge of the cliff. It was Patty; her cry was full of terror and anger. "No!"

Sam raced to the car, where Krieger had resurfaced into consciousness. He opened the door, pushed the old man back across the seat, and restarted the engine.

"We've got to get out of here!" he cried as he threw the car into REVERSE and backed off the fence. The rear door slammed shut and the tires sprayed gravel as the car peeled onto the road and sped off, a primal declaration of escape, back to living.

As they raced down the winding road toward the bottom of the cliff, Sam saw a pair of lovers walking along the seawall. Billy's red cowboy hat was perched atop his shimmering golden hair, which fluttered in the light salt breezes. Kelly had both her arms around him, encircling his waist.

They had found their way together, just as Billy had predicted, as if the laws of nature had conspired to thrust the inevitability of destiny upon them.

At that moment—as Sam saw their faces in the rearview mirror—he heard Hawk Feather and Scout calling to him in one voice. Even Krieger seemed to hear it—*pianissimo* at first before it *crescendoed* like the swells crashing over the seawall: *"Trust me."*

ACT IV
RESOLUTION

Ironically, Sam Mann finally *did* get the fame he so dearly coveted. His highly publicized conviction for the murder of Jimm Dibbook, and his subsequent acquittal on appeal, tested the limits of media involvement in the judicial system, as well as the reliability of DNA evidence. The genetic strain on the dog bite, Sam's major line of defense, was avian—specifically, hawk—not mammalian in structure.

Sam's fame reached its crescendo when he was gunned down on the courthouse steps the day of his release. Patty O'Boyle is serving five to ten years. Sam's leg has healed well, though he walks with a slight limp. He lives with Jennifer Holman, and plays music with his friends to a small but loyal following.

He has no pets.

Once a year, when the golden hills turn green at the emergence of spring, Sam makes a pilgrimage to a heavily forested section of the Peninsula. There he sits on a masterfully constructed low stone wall that surrounds the Krieger family plot and plays a very private, very solo concert.

The Author

Bruce Forman is a jazz guitarist and founder/director of JazzMasters Workshop, a nonprofit music mentoring program. He lives in Carmel Valley, California. Bruce can be contacted at **www.bruceforman.com**.